THE TEXTURE OF SHADOWS

THE TEXTURE OF SHADOWS

A NOVEL

Mandla Langa

PICADOR AFRICA

First published in 2014 by Picador Africa
an imprint of Pan Macmillan South Africa
Private Bag X19, Northlands Johannesburg, 2116
www.panmacmillan.co.za

ISBN 978-1-77010-386-3
eBook ISBN 978-1-77010-387-0

Editing by Sharon Dell
Proofreading by Kelly Norwood-Young
Design and typesetting by Triple M Design
Cover design by K4
Printed and bound by Creda Communications

ALSO BY MANDLA LANGA

The Lost Colours of the Chameleon (2008)

'Using the universal language of allegory, Mandla Langa portrays with a paradoxical combination of sensitivity and brutal honesty how power transforms the most benign and mild-mannered of us into despots. Here is a writer who re-imagines Africa, and indeed the world, in a refreshing and timeless mode of storytelling.' – ZAKES MDA

The Memory of Stones (2000)

The Naked Song and Other Stories (1997)

A Rainbow on a Paper Sky (1989)

Tenderness of Blood (1987)

In loving memory of my late parents,
Revd Simon-Petrus Mbekwa Langa and Josephine Busisiwe Langa,
who struggled to usher in but didn't live long enough to see
the Promised Land

I came upon an owl
at the crossroads

— AMA ATA AIDOO

In the silences of the night
often past the midnight hour
when my voice dries up behind my tongue
behind corpses that rattle in my mind
I wonder where the wind is

— 'When Things Fall Apart' BY KEORAPETSE KGOSITSILE

Dear Mr President

It's taken me a long time to write this report, which was meant to cover two areas: one, the possibility that we, as a Movement, might have been remiss in our treatment of people incarcerated in our camps – especially in Sector 37; and two, the idea of starting a process to locate the graves where our young men and women might be buried on foreign soil.

A number of the events canvassed in the report have been overtaken by processes such as the succession of commissions, the most important of them being the Truth and Reconciliation Commission, which came long after the period under review.

It is not easy to deviate from the inner workings of the minds of the major actors in this drama; I have taken the liberty of reconstructing events, even the possible motives informing the actions of the major players. Needless to say, I will get it wrong here and there. In given instances, I might give people attributes they do not deserve and similarly diminish the virtues of people who need plaudits. That is regrettable.

I have to make a plea for understanding. We have all been thrust into a world of violence, a maelstrom that is very difficult to make sense of, particularly for people who were not born into it. Here, then – and my own religious background dictates it – I have had to reach deep to understand the dialectic of good and evil in the context of our struggle. I have grappled with the concept of The Individual – what forces one to become a star that is unable to extinguish its own fire, or bestows the kind of beauty that leaves destruction in its wake?

I am unswerving in my less than complimentary characterisation of those players who sacrificed others – in the cut and thrust of the struggle – while portraying themselves as heroes. Similarly, I give place of pride to the young men and women who left home to fight the regime. Some of them never returned. A few came back, having been given the names of trees, having seen revolutions in other lands, hoping to change the nature of our country and ensure that pain and suffering are a thing of the past. I have been able to connect a number of them with their families. Some have lost that important connection with their own souls and are wandering, bewildered, prey to disease, both mental and physical, especially alcoholism and AIDS.

I hope you'll enjoy the story, for I have tried to write it as a narrative of transition, which might read as a picaresque adventure story to some, with obligatory heroes and villains.

I am indebted, Mr President, to Georgina Smith, my life partner, who opened my eyes to much that is hidden in plain sight and thereby attuned my ears to the silent screams of a people writhing under the yoke of poverty.

One day, I hope, we shall truly overcome.

With comradely regards
Nerissa Rodrigues

PROLOGUE

It had taken almost two weeks for Nerissa Rodrigues to travel to Fordsburg. Now, here she was on Thursday, 21 December 1989, in Dr Yusuf Variava's waiting room among seven or eight patients. She hadn't realised that maxillofacial specialists were doing such a booming trade. Comprising mainly of women, who averted their gaze from a reedy individual of indeterminate age whose goitrous neck swelled out of his shirt collar, the patients leafed through outdated lifestyle and glamour magazines. The more daring ones cowed their more timid fellow sufferers into divulging the reasons they were in the doctor's rooms.

Nerissa kept her eyes on a spot above a travel agency calendar depicting pyramids and palm trees; she knew that the prying eyes could see nothing wrong with her. Yes, she told herself, there's nothing that needs fixing from the neck up. It was a different story when it came to the torso, which was mercifully encased in a beige knitwear blouse under a khaki denim jacket that matched her chinos. She wondered the extent to which her costly pair of suede Hush Puppies served to sustain or sabotage the persona of a scatty Indian auntie she had cultivated. In her quest for invisibility, Chaplain Nerissa had even considered a burka, but had quickly dropped the idea. Something about that voluminous garment was likely to trip her up. Besides, it was hard to smoke in a burka.

She kept a straight face, aware of some of the patients shooting furtive if hostile glances while a teenager accompanying an older woman whose face was covered in a scarf stared openly at her. It didn't take Nerissa long to work out from the intensity of the gaze that the young woman was blind. Even though she was not given to superstition and had in her earlier years been a volunteer at the Durban Service for the Blind on Stanger Street, Nerissa felt ill at ease as if the blindness were an omen. In addition, she felt on the verge of succumbing to a strange impulse. Embarrassed by her reaction and accepting it was unbecoming for a political activist, she shot to her feet and headed for the door.

'Please hold on, my dear.' The receptionist was a big-boned woman with mobile eyes and the fixed smile of someone fated to calm nervous patients. Sunnily traipsing between the waiting area and the corridor along which were ranged a bank of doors leading to consulting rooms, she beckoned Nerissa to the one that stood ajar. 'The doctor will see you now.'

Nerissa Rodrigues always found consulting rooms disappointing. Although dingy and stuffy, reception lounges like the one she had just left, had a semblance of life. Old furniture spoke to her, evoking, maybe, the souls of the hundreds of sufferers who had sat on the clunky chairs and leafed through magazines whose pages had degenerated into parchment paper. The consulting room, on the other hand, was clinical and sparse, as soulless as a prison cell. The effect of bareness was confirmed by two chairs facing each other across a table that was nothing more than a board on trestles. An adjustable stretcher doubled as a bed. Sundry equipment including a blood-pressure machine stood alongside a box container for disposal of medical waste below a lockable glass cabinet with bottled medicines and phials on shelves.

'You could at least decorate this place, Yusuf,' Nerissa said, sniffing. 'Give it some life.'

'Ah, the chaplain herself,' Dr Yusuf Variava said, smiling and motioning Nerissa to take a seat. 'Were you really going to leave before our appointment?'

'I wasn't feeling so great,' Nerissa said. She wanted to tell him that she hated to be kept waiting, even if she was the one being done a favour. 'You've put on weight.'

'No hug?'

'Perhaps after the inspection of the dressing.'

He was in his fifties, a well-built man sporting a little paunch, his hairless pate extending the face area, full lips accentuating a strong jaw. He was already sporting a five o'clock shadow at noon. He locked the door, careful to muffle the click. Wordlessly, he helped Nerissa undress and inspected her, clucking his tongue at the angry weals across the back.

She turned to face the bare wall, hands gripping the frame of the stretcher and let him work on her ruined flesh. Gritting her teeth against the pain, Nerissa half heard him murmuring approval that the burns were healing. Now and then, when his tugging elicited an involuntary twitch, Dr Yusuf Variava became concern personified, stroking the stricken skin and offering assurances that meant little to Nerissa. 'Constant cleaning of the wounds,' he said as if reading from some medical tract, 'with mild antibacterial wash such as chlorohexidine will guarantee recovery.'

'Shut up, Yusuf.'

'It won't be speedy,' he continued. 'Normally, victims of bomb blasts don't enjoy the luxury of having their wounds dressed.'

Later, he poured her a cup of sweetened mint tea from a flask kept in his bag. She drank gratefully, warming her hands around the cup, looking at the plastic container with the soiled bandages. 'Can we still talk here?' she asked.

'I've taken precautions.'

'The men have arrived.'

'All of them?'

'I'm still gathering more information.' Nerissa took another sip of her tea. 'Muzi Thabethe has sent out a reception team, but we gather the men encountered some problems.'

'What kind of problems?'

'They were intercepted.'

Yusuf Variava waited for Nerissa to marshal her thoughts into a coherent narrative. 'No doubt,' she said, 'the people who sent us the birthday parcel are also involved in this one.'

'Colonel Stander?'

'Stander.'

'But he couldn't have done it alone.'

'I'm sure our people are involved.'

Variava mulled this over. 'You and Georgina … are you going to be okay?'

'Georgina is an oak tree.'

'Ja,' he said, 'but trees do get cut down.'

'Don't worry about us,' Nerissa said. 'She might be your sister, Yusuf, but I'm the one taking care of her … of us.'

'Wearing the pants, you mean.' He swallowed something that must have tasted of bile, the Adam's apple bobbing up and down.

'You get ugly when you are spiteful,' Nerissa said, taking hold of his two hands in hers. 'You're a beautiful man. Don't let ugliness creep in.'

'My patients are waiting,' Yusuf Variava said. 'You'll have to be careful opening the merchandise. Depending on the size, you might also need storage space.'

'Do you know of a suitable candidate?'

'You might have to speak to someone in Yeoville,' Variava said, his tone telling Nerissa he wanted his name kept out of the matter. 'I'll give you a name.'

'Let's talk about it.'

1

DJANGO

Back in the time that's lost in noise and silence, a group of twelve men crosses the border from Botswana into South Africa at the shallowest point of the Pitsane Molopo. They march through the sleepy village, named after the river, at midnight on 17 December 1989.

The other side is quiet. The men cast a last look at the fence and note its spikes and coils that gleam in the moonlight. The thorn trees cultivated to discourage intrusion cast proportioned shadows that confirm the unnatural nature of borders. This one separates people who speak the same tongue. It stands between families, relatives or friends who risk arrest daily for indulging the need for human contact across a dividing line.

From the commander to the last man in the section, no one is unaware of the danger of the mission, which becomes real with the crossing. The terrain is favourable for the first two hundred metres towards the southeast, up to the pile of stones that marks the meeting spot with the contact. Further up, however, the landscape changes and for a good stretch it consists of savannah scrubland overrun by stunted trees, mostly mimosas that couldn't offer any shelter in case of a firefight. Moreover, gravel that has the texture of brittle shale forms an uneven cover on the ground and crunches under the tread of boots, sounding to the men as loud as a series of crackers going off in the quiet of the night. The moonlight, although offering them a clear view of the terrain and its lineaments, makes the men feel exposed. What your eye can see can equally put you in the other's gunsight. Bated breath, wincing, and tightened sphincter muscles punctuate the advance of the unit.

Even though they know that risking exposure is a breach of security – and that they should steer as far away from the road as possible, if this stony track could be called a road – they march along, six men on each side, hunched as they take turns lugging two heavy trunks. The commander, making sure his men don't exert themselves into uselessness, calls for periodic halts, when the men then disappear into the bush. He verifies the existence of the weapons: two light machine guns, a bazooka, some AK-47 assault rifles and, snuggling in the belt webbing of each man, offensive and defensive grenades, egg- and pineapple-like respectively. He knows that the weapons are for morale, the way you reassure yourself in the dark by holding a knife. For, without some real artillery, an anti-aircraft gun or B-10 recoilless rifle, for instance, they'd have a hard time holding out against the South African Defence Force (SADF) garrisoned in various military posts dotting the Western Transvaal. The SADF is around the Pitsane Molopo border area, all the way to Mafikeng. The guerrillas' survival depends on keeping out of harm's way. Any engagement would be fatal.

They are guerrillas, after all, used to the unexpected, but the commander feels the weight of responsibility on his shoulders. There have been far too many incidences of death or interception along border areas for anyone to take unnecessary risks. And so, on this mission,

Mahogany the commander does a regular head count to check if all the men are accounted for and that there are no stragglers. Many a mission by the People's Army has foundered with the disappearance of the last man in the unit and his subsequent reappearance as Mister X, a star prosecution witness giving evidence against former comrades.

It falls on Commander Mahogany to conduct a mental roll call. There is his commissar, Baobab, also known as Imbondeiro, the Portuguese name for the baobab. Then there are Ebony, Hickory, Linden, Pomegranate and Stinkwood, who seems to live up to his name with his cavalier attitude towards personal hygiene. There are also Avocado, Walnut, Tamarind, Pistachio and Sassafras.

The names do not make known any of the fighters' specialities or even the extent of their training. Among them are tacticians who have broken out of ambushes of the joint SADF-National Union for the Total Independence of Angola (UNITA) forces in Angola on the Eastern Front. Others are engineers, explosives experts. There is a photographer who, while shaky in combat, becomes a different person behind the lens of a camera, letting the instrument do all the fighting. Hickory is strange in that he blanches at the sight of blood but was unflinching when recording the scenes of a battle in which limbs were severed, and human tissue bespattered a church wall. In the group there are two intelligence officers trained in Cuba and the German Democratic Republic, a sniper and three or four men who possess a combination of skills, a category that includes both commander and commissar.

But no matter how effectively the fighters can cover one another's backs and provide communal support in case of an enemy strike, they are all vulnerable to the insane novelty of being back on native soil. No amount of training, no title such as commissar or psychiatrist or political philosopher – even one conversant with the complete works of Marx, Engels, Lenin *and* Jesus – can prepare anyone who's lived in exile for the exact moment of return. That moment is a condition best described by Angolans as *confusão* – an epicentre of chaos that gives rise to a widening spiral of even more confusion, which cannot be easily appreciated by anyone who has not spent a considerable period across the border. This kernel holds the birth of a perplexed turmoil. It collapses years of experiencing the unimaginable; the joys, hurts, insults and exaltation of witnessing deaths and births and marriages in strange chapels and divorces occasioned by the impossibility of maintaining a semblance of reality in unreal worlds. Simply, it's watching babies born without a unifying language under skies that forbid the unfurling of one's national flag. It is disease, malaria, suicide or a breakdown that leads a man to turn his weapon against a comrade in the camp. It is laughter and embracing strangers and accepting the generosity of people you'll never see again. It is a collapsing of all these emotions and experiences into a single node, a beat, a moment in music.

In fact, a month earlier, on 19 November 1989, music *was* playing in a safe house in Mochudi, some thirty-five kilometres to the north of Gaborone, where about twenty men were holding a meeting. Hickory, although he wasn't known as Hickory then, sat at the back of the spacious lounge, listening to 'Mamani'. Hugh Masekela, Jonas Gwangwa and Caiphus 'Katse' Semenya were belting their hearts out in unison. There was something sad and wistful about the rendition of the Xitsonga tune. The three musicians shared more than ninety years of exile. Perhaps the song conveyed their longing, and the anxiety that they might not make it back home. The song had, after all, been recorded in the United States in the early 1970s, long before the three musicians relocated to southern Africa.

To Hickory, the music was a fitting accompaniment to the drama of life being played out in the reunion of exiles, comrades and combatants who hadn't seen one another in years. There were hugs and handshakes of joy and disbelief – *'Hey, cousin, this really you?'* – those impassioned welcomes lasting an instant or spanning a long minute of a stammering silence. Here and there, people were huddled in corners like lovers working to beat a parental curfew. It was a Sunday afternoon and from somewhere in the village a church service was furiously in progress, the divine song of the congregation weaving into the more worldly instrumentation by Hugh Masekela and the Union of South Africa. Hotep Galeta's piano solo trembled, pealing and leaping and seeming to sustain the melody until it all proved nearly unbearable for the hearer. The cadence of the secular tunes provided a fitting accompaniment to the frolics of the handful of hens fleeing a randy rooster across the yard.

The atmosphere inside the house was at first carnival-like, the lounge-cum-dining room airy and sun-drenched, providing space for the ex-combatants to break into song and toyi-toyi. Everything was spontaneous; the inspired jigs brought about gales of laughter. Bra Bobby, the oldest and probably the fittest member in Hickory's platoon in Angola, chuckled as he pointed to someone he knew and had trained with a long time ago. Bra Bobby's beard, once black and thinly peppered with grey, was now totally white so that he resembled an avant-garde oracle. 'Hey, Mchinda,' he called and assumed the pose of the street hustler he had been before his conversion. 'You've put on too much weight for that routine, man.' And Mchinda, willing to take a ribbing from a friend, carried on dancing with a whisky glass held aloft as if he was toasting some moment that made sense only to him and a select few.

The jollification came to an end with entry into the house of Absalom Palweni, the legendary commander who had been in many conflicts in Africa. He was a huge man, his shoulders barely scraping past the door frames, dressed as always in an olive safari suit that enhanced the image of a soldier. He walked with a slight limp from an old wound sustained in one of the many encounters with the enemy.

Flanked by two serious-looking men at the table that was bare save for a jug of water and three glasses, Palweni flashed a genial smile and waved at some of the faces he recognised. One member of his entourage was a gaunt man with a pockmarked face. Hickory knew him to be a higher-up in Security. The man got to his feet, ensuring he'd got everyone's attention. 'General Palweni,' he said in a surprisingly reedy voice, 'needs no introduction to you, since you're all cadres familiar with the workings of the Movement and its People's Army. There might be one or two of you who have just finished a crash course. Be that as it may, it's my duty to tell you that you're all here because you possess special skills that are of utmost importance to the emergent South African dispensation.'

'Emergent what?' Hickory whispered to Mchinda seated next to him.

'Dispensation,' Mchinda said. 'Emergent dispensation.'

'What is that?'

'I don't know. Pay attention.'

The speaker rattled on about the dangerousness of the period and gave a short history lesson on the year 1989. 'When some of our stalwarts imprisoned on Robben Island were released in October, we did an analysis. We came to the conclusion that Nelson Mandela's release is imminent. That and the unbanning of our Movement.' He paused and poured himself a glass of water, which he didn't drink. 'The implications of all this, when we're so ill-prepared, will be dealt with by the general.' He sat down, abruptly, a man alert to the dangers of talking too much.

Hickory listened to the afternoon droning on. The temperature in Mochudi verged on the unbearable. In his reckoning, it was harsher than the sweltering heat of Angola. Luanda might be hot and humid but there was always something moderating about the water, the knowledge that the Atlantic Ocean, which connected to trade winds, was within walking distance. Mochudi was in a landlocked country that shared borders with hostile neighbours.

As General Palweni started his briefing, pulling himself up to his full height, prompting those seated to stand to attention, the clatter descended into the stillness of the grave. In this lull, Hickory noticed that although General Palweni's carriage was soldierly and his face unlined, his eyes were clouded with cataract. The signs of age called into question the genuineness of the full head of pitch-black hair. Somewhat dismayed, Hickory saw the touch of vanity as an indication of an infirmity, a flaw at odds with leadership.

'How old would you say the general is?' Hickory asked Mchinda.

'Shhh,' Mchinda said, pressing his finger against his lips, making a face at Hickory.

'Shush,' someone behind them hissed, much like a moviegoer reprimanding a noisy couple. 'Show some respect, comrades.'

Oblivious to the little dispute among assembled cadres, the general raised a hand in greeting. 'Comrades, good afternoon.' He then gestured for those standing to take their seats.

'First of all I bring you the revolutionary good wishes of our leadership.' He went on, 'What's happening today is both encouraging and daunting. It means that we must be vigilant and never take freedom for granted. When you look at the African continent, all that liberated space, you find that freedom there simply meant removing political chains and substituting them with economic ones. What did Nkrumah say? "Seek ye first political freedom and all else will follow." That's good to know, but it doesn't always turn out that way. People are free, there are no lords and masters, but they are victims of poverty, unemployment and disease. There is nothing different about us; we are those Africans in the north, whatever the peddlers of skin-lightening creams might say.' There was a ripple of amusement at this, which the general quietened down with the wave of a hand. 'The Movement will be required to set up a government in an economy that has been looted by the racists. We inherit a bone that's been picked clean.'

Visibly put out by the envisaged exploitation, General Palweni took a pull on his glass of water. 'The reason we're all here,' he said, 'is that we've been singled out to ensure that the Movement becomes more self-sufficient.'

Hickory rolled the words around in his head to untangle their meanings.

At the same time a thought nagged at him, something he'd heard, which came in snatches like an elusive melody. Then it hit him and before he could stop himself, his hand shot up. The general glanced at his two aides as if seeking guidance. The man with the pockmarked face got to his feet and stretched his neck as if relieving an ancient strain. The general sat down. There was a general murmur of unhappiness in the room.

'Yes, Comrade?' It was a as if Pockmarks meant to intimidate, but his thin voice, which matched his physique, couldn't quite sustain the menace. 'What is your question?'

Hickory said: 'I seem to remember hearing that the general has been suspended from the Movement. Would that be true?'

'What do you mean?' An audible rustle of a tongue moistening dry lips.

His stomach tightening, Hickory didn't budge. Cold sweat trickled down his back into the groove of his butt. 'Word from Lusaka is the general and five senior comrades are being investigated for sowing seeds of disunity.'

'What are you?' asked Pockmarks. 'Some kind of enemy agent?' His agitation rose. 'Did someone send you? *Uthunyiwe*?'

'Comrade Sizwe?' said the general urgently. 'Comrade Sizwe?'

'Yes, General?' Comrade Sizwe, the pockmarked man, responded.

'*Calma, camarada*, let me handle this,' General Palweni said. Turning to the assembled men, he smiled. 'Comrades? This is my right-hand man, Comrade Sizwe Ndawo. Without him lots of things couldn't have been achieved. He reacts this way because it often happens that provocateurs are sent to sow confusion in our ranks. But here, I know you're all patriots, combatants. And I'm happy that the comrade has brought up this matter. It's a matter that should have been clarified from the get-go.' He got to his feet.

'Some time back,' he started explaining, 'a number of us, certainly a few more than the now-celebrated Group of Six, got a mandate from Movement branches to raise two issues with the leadership. One,' he continued, slapping right index finger against left thumb, 'the question of black African leadership in all structures, and two,' the left index finger pointing upwards, 'mobilising of resources for the fighting men. And women.'

He took another sip of water, now clearly a prop. 'The leadership simply responded that we were guilty of insubordination and six of us, the so-called ringleaders, were suspended.'

'So,' Hickory pressed on, 'this … meeting in Mochudi. What's its status?'

'It has the status we grant it,' General Palweni said, his face hardening. 'In the same way that in the ANC, Anton Lembede's Youth League harnessed the brainpower and activism of Oliver Tambo and Nelson Mandela to energise the mother body, we're also giving muscle to the Movement so that it's adequate to the challenges of the new era.'

He paused, thinking.

'The new era simply means we've been thrown into history,' he continued. 'The Angolan government has agreed to shut down any bases and camps of the People's Army, in accordance with the terms that ended the war in Angola. Already early this year, the Soviets have airlifted thousands of our combatants to camps in Uganda.'

'Uganda? That's half a continent away from the action in the frontline. Does this mean a negotiated settlement?' Hickory asked.

'What would you have preferred?' This was Comrade Sizwe. 'Would it have been better for the comrades to be dumped in the Soviet Union?'

'From what I gather,' Hickory put in stubbornly, 'we might not have a Soviet Union for long.'

'You have a big mouth, Comrade,' said Comrade Sizwe. He seemed about to have a seizure.

Linden, who'd been sitting quietly in the row behind, tapped Hickory on the shoulder. 'Bro,' he said softly, 'let this thing go. You know how these people are.'

Instead of answering, Hickory turned his body slightly to cover the young man's hand with his own. It was a fleeting exchange that the rest of the people in the lounge failed to notice.

The general brushed imaginary lint from his shirtfront and moved into lecture mode. 'The comrade has a point,' he said. 'Right now, it's touch and go in the countries of the Warsaw Pact. There's turmoil. The fall of the Berlin Wall might lead to a lot of changes – and they might mean we have to rejig our own approach to the future. Ultimately, we might have to reach a settlement with the regime. In fact, there's no doubt about that; the leadership recognises how we're slowly being squeezed. Our President is unwell and the only hope now is consolidating our presence inside the country. You therefore have to carry material, equipment, resources and documents to be delivered to our internal structures in the underground. That should ensure that the liberation struggle flourishes within the borders of our country.'

He stopped and took another sip of water and then fanned his face with a sheaf of papers on the table. He seemed suddenly sapped of energy as if the heat of Mochudi was getting to him. Hickory suspected he might be unwell. 'Are there any more questions?' he asked in a tone meant to discourage questions.

Still glowering at Hickory, Comrade Sizwe sucked in his teeth. 'You've heard the general,' he said. 'Any more questions?'

'I do have questions,' Hickory persisted. 'Are we the expendable ones? Are we on a mission of no return? You'll remember that some of the comrades here have had problems with the security structures of the Movement. They were not trusted; some were accused of being enemy agents, some were persecuted for drinking caproto or smoking maconha. A few of them have seen the inside of Camp 46, where they were treated badly, and were later transported to Mogadishu in Somalia. Mchinda and I were the lucky ones because we were able to attend the Nouakchott Conference in June 1985.'

'Even then,' Mchinda now joined in, 'there were people who tried to gag us from participating in the conference.'

'So,' Sizwe asked, attempting a sarcastic smile, 'what's the point of this history lesson? The Sermon in the Bush?'

'We'd just like to know,' Hickory asked, 'if this is another pep talk or if we are finally going home? You remember this was our original demand.' He let it linger in everyone's mind that it was exactly the insistence to go and fight inside South Africa that had led to the conflict with security structures.

'To fight!' Mchinda said this with fervour.

'You are going home, comrades,' General Palweni said. 'This time you'll be the vanguard to offset the pernicious and exploitative policies of the World Bank and the IMF.'

Sizwe, enjoying the effect of the general's words on the assembled guerrillas, asked: 'Are there any questions?'

You're going home, comrades. There was a random murmuring. Then people were talking all at once, some having got to their feet in breach of the instruction to allow for an orderly meeting. Palweni watched, slightly amused.

'What is it, comrades?' he asked. 'It seems you are surprised by this development. Did you expect a telex, perhaps, giving you notice that zero hour is approaching?'

The men didn't answer; those who'd been engaged in argument suddenly became quiet. To Hickory it was not clear what the beef was all about. These people were reluctant to take centre stage and express what they feared could possibly get them singled out for some future torment. Hiding in a bush of sound. Hickory wondered about the wisdom of voicing his own thoughts. Finally, Hickory shrugged and put up his hand. Rather be hanged for a sheep as a lamb.

'One last question,' he said. 'How many such groups are there? Bringing in material assets and everything?'

'Many more than you might imagine,' said the general with a chuckle, shaking his head at the question. 'Material assets,' he muttered. 'The lad's got a way with words.'

'Thank you, Comrade General,' Hickory said and sat down. He was overwhelmed by an indescribable emotion, something that filled him with anger and sadness – and confusion. He was happy that they'd be going home, but something told him that the strategy to return hadn't been thought through.

'I'm glad,' the general said, 'that we have a youth with an enquiring mind. The future will be hard and we will need men and women with spunk. Those of you who chose to do military training instead of going to school will return home and be part of the reconstruction, of building a new society. The values of that society will be different. Book knowledge will be more important than knowing how to assemble and disassemble an anti-aircraft gun. Some of your counterparts will despise you. They will ask: what did your training, your exile, your years of deprivation gain you? When that happens, white people will slink off into the shadows and you will have to go cap in hand to seek support from the newfound friends of white people who will speak English through their nostrils and who'll forever remind you that the days of apartheid were a lot better than the days wrought by freedom fighters. The youth, then, will have to be stronger and more forceful than we are. They will have to balance the scales because, since the world is not fair or moral, we'll need a new strength, a different type of muscle, to reclaim what we have lost.'

To Hickory, the speech was like a valediction by a father giving away a bride who had been a source of great parental anxiety. It was not a rallying speech like the ones the President used to make on days of trouble. It seemed to Hickory that the erosion of the calibre of leadership was directly proportional to the ticking of the clock, the countdown to going back home. God alone knew the kind of riff-raff that would masquerade as leaders in a liberated South Africa. Despairingly, he wondered if the President – a latter-day Moses – would ever see the Promised Land. It was like a recording. The master tape in Lusaka was strong in giving the Movement its direction at home or in exile, from

Kilimanjaro to Kuala Lumpur; the grooves on the succession of copies got smoothed out with each generation. At home they'd have to start all over again. A new recording of things.

In the late afternoon, as the sun set on the horizon and streaked the clouds with red, two columns of twelve men were given new names, uniforms and weapons. The two groups waved each other goodbye. Some of the former guerrillas hugged each other. Hickory and Linden spoke to each other in low tones.

'I'm glad you'll be part of the unit,' Hickory said.

'Likewise,' Linden responded. 'And what's even better news is that we are going home.'

'Have you thought what we'll tell Dad?' This was the first time in almost a decade that either one of them had initiated a discussion that involved family.

'Well,' Linden said in his slow and careful manner. 'Maybe we should find a more suitable time and place to talk about it.'

'I hear you.' Linden had always shown wisdom beyond his young age. Hickory sensed that Linden was struggling with something. 'What is it?'

'Did you have to show them that you're such a wise guy?' Linden asked. 'People hate to be shown up. Especially leadership types.'

'You don't have to worry,' Hickory said. 'It's going to be all right.'

'I hope so.'

'Trust me.'

'That,' Linden said, 'is exactly what scares me.'

Hickory laughed, but it was forced laughter, what his father used to call whistling past the graveyard, because he knew that Linden's warning was not without basis. Linden had been part of the Movement's security structures. One time he did a stint at Camp 46, the prison for enemy agents, habitual offenders and mutineers. Hickory knew that

Linden had seen his fair share of corpses.

'Is there a chance to pull out of this thing?' Hickory asked.

'Why would you want to do that?'

'I don't know. It's just a feeling.' He paused, scratching his head. 'I do want to go home, like everyone. But the whole operation doesn't seem to have been properly planned. Somewhere, I believe, secrecy has been compromised. And we're likely to have a very unwelcome welcoming committee on arrival.'

'Suspend your distrust, brother,' Linden said. 'It's going to be fine.'

'I'll take your word for it,' Hickory said. It was his turn to sound unconvinced.

'The level of secrecy is high,' Linden said, an evangelist intent on converting at least one member of a cynical congregation. 'The preparations are far advanced.'

Linden didn't have to spell it out that if Hickory ever tried to pull out of the mission, someone would put a bullet in his head. It was not so much what the general had said as the looks Hickory, the designated smart aleck with a fatally enquiring mind, was getting from a few of his compatriots; looks of a wondering pity, as if some were already seeing him in the past tense, a dead man walking.

In addition to the weapons, each group had to carry material in sealed, waterproofed and vinyl-covered footlockers. The pressboard was reinforced with brass rivets and the corners protected with brass plating. Secured with hasps and padlocks, the trunks reminded Hickory of the time he took some provisions to Eustace, his elder brother, at boarding school, the heft of those galvanised iron trunks.

Someone whispered that the two units would be immediately assigned to different locations skirting the border and from there into South Africa. It might take a week or two before they were on home soil. The men had waited a lifetime to get back home; a few more weeks wouldn't make a difference. At the same time, Hickory felt impatience coursing through him like a fever, something alive and threatening to burst forth.

The sun had set although it was not yet dark. The day's heat had abated.

Four Toyota HiAce minibuses stood with their engines idling on the driveway; the twelve-man team loaded the weapons and the trunks, and the men crammed inside. As the vehicles moved away, leaving dust swirling behind, the passengers broke out into a song. Hickory wanted to ask about the contents of the dorm lockers, which the men carried with the solemnity of pallbearers, but decided he had used up almost all of his lives. Time to keep that old trap shut. Without asking the commander, a short and lean fellow named Mahogany, if it was all right to check his weapon, he went right ahead and field-stripped his AK-47. Deciding that this was a soldierly thing to do, most of the men followed suit, even the guy lugging the PKM, checking that their weapons actually worked. For a long minute there was the rattle and snap of metal as magazines were ejected and chambers emptied. While no one thanked Hickory for belling this particular cat, a few of his colleagues from Angola or Lusaka flashed him a smile. It was enough for him. Many a guerrilla had rued not checking his gun at the start of a mission. That the commander overlooked conducting a weapons inspection filled Hickory with anxiety. I need to survive this, he thought.

On the evening of 18 December 1989, a date etched in his memory, he almost didn't survive.

The heat was unbearable up in the cave where the men were bivouacked, and it took them a while to discover that one of the walls formed the back part of a kiln where the villagers fired their clay. Someone said that there was a manganese seam in this part of Western Transvaal, which stretched all the way to Botswana. Villagers had their own side-line in manganese mining, processing the ore in these rude furnaces.

The guerrillas – Hickory jokingly referred to the group as the advance detachment of economic freedom fighters – had made contact with their guide. Mahogany, reticent and somewhat surly, even managed a grim smile when he introduced Rre Malatsi, a slight man with the features of a gemsbok, whose dark pumpkin complexion made him indistinguishable from the tawny termite mounds that abounded all over the plain. Even some of the more impatient members of the platoon were mollified. Hickory indulged an uncharitable thought that a family of mongooses must have reared the wiry and quick-witted Malatsi. Not waiting for Mahogany to take charge, Malatsi impressed on the unit the need to move once the sun had set. 'The troopers,' he said, 'patrol the road and they shoot to kill.' The area was also teeming with wild animals. It was decided that the unit would move at 9:00 p.m. Each day spent in this godforsaken stretch of the Western Transvaal increased the chances of detection. They had taken all the necessary precautions to cover their tracks, but were still at risk, given their numbers and resources. It was Malatsi's guidance that led them into the cave, one of the topographical surprises recessed into the hillside, a hole in the mountain. There were a few of these shelters spread across the region, traditional hiding places for lovers or audacious children, with entrances sometimes covered by screens of tangled bush and thorn trees.

From the vantage point of a few hundred feet above the scrubby plain, Hickory was suddenly struck by the rhythmical nature of the rolling hills, some so low that he could see their tree-covered tops, the early evening turning the brown-green vegetation into the denser colour of battledress, the dark-green camouflage cloth shot through with ochre. In there, he knew – in that great silence – lurked all kinds of dangerous animals. Wild dogs, leopards, even lions had been known to roam this stretch of Highveld. At that moment, however, they did not pose any danger, remote as they were, outside of his most immediate preoccupation. There was something addictive about nightfall, its tenderness, the sounds, far off, of a silence coming from the villages signified only by smoke. Together with Sassafras, he stepped out of the cave to assume sentry duty for two hours and relieve the earlier detail. It was 7:00 p.m. The rest of the men were already eating, scoffing their rations hurriedly because the march would start again in another two hours.

As they were leaving the camp, Hickory asked Sassafras: 'What do you think is in the trunks?'

'Django?' Sassafras said, admonishing his old comrade, unconscious of the lapse in security in not calling him by his *nom de guerre*. 'What's with you and all the questions? Are you becoming a lawyer on us?'

'Come on, Mchinda,' Hickory said, also breaching security. 'Here we are, hundreds of clicks from Gabs with boxes that might be full of propaganda stuff, journals like *El Guerrero* or leaflets with instructions on how to make a pamphlet bomb. How'd you feel getting caught carrying useless stuff like that?'

'Look, Django,' Sassafras said. 'Let's go do our bit tonight and stop worrying about what's inside the trunks. We're breaking up camp in two hours. Leave it alone. Don't you know, curiosity killed the cat?'

'What do you think is in the trunks?' This time he asked softly, comrade to comrade. He had an idea Mchinda must have been party to the packing, since he'd worked in Ordnance with some legendary comrades. 'Come on, do tell.'

'Money. Dollars, pounds, Deutschmarks, what do I know?'

'Ja,' Hickory said, unconvinced. 'Is money that heavy?' He wanted Mchinda to say if there were gold bars.

'When we get back,' Sassafras said, heading off to his post, 'why don't you ask Mahogany.'

'Mahogany?' Hickory said. 'Mahogany knows fuck-all.'

'No, really, he knows. He's the general's blue-eyed boy.'

'I'll ask him, but I know it's just going to be bullshit.'

'You're the lawyer with all the questions. If you feel so hot about the truth, you've got to follow your nose.' Sassafras paused, slung the rifle over his shoulder. 'Django?'

'Yes?'

'Be careful,' Sassafras said. 'We are hard men coming from a hard place where we dealt with violence. But we're a little rusty now and we're in the land of people who really thrive on violence and cruelty.'

'They might think it's their land, Mchinda,' Hickory said. 'But it's our land. That's why we went out to get military training. So that we can reclaim it.'

'Just be careful.' Sassafras repeated, disappearing into the bush. 'Okay?'

'Okay.'

He said 'Okay' but still felt ill at ease. The muffled chirring of busy insects deepened the silence. Something Sassafras had said recently gnawed at him, but he couldn't put a finger on it. He just hoped his friend didn't get into trouble with Stinkwood, who'd ended his five-to-seven shift; his and Sassafras's, seven-to-nine, was a killer. Time seemed to drag on forever the later it became. He probed the dark, looking for the outlines of trees or contours of the hills that dotted the landscape by day and got swallowed up in the foggy dark by night. Only the sky was constant, black and liquid like a sombre shroud that allowed tiny pinpoints of light to filter through. At its edge, the drape disappeared into tendrils of mist and fused with the edges of the world.

It was here, hearing a long squawk of a bird or a monkey, that he thought of home and imagined what everything would look like if he were to show up suddenly at the doorstep. He knew that he was dreaming because it would now be a different doorstep; people had moved from KwaMashu, forty clicks to the north of Durban, all the way to the Transvaal, Johannesburg. The doorway of his youth had disappeared; the house in G Section was no longer his father's house. His brother Eustace, who was always a pain in the neck, was now a married man with children, Django's nephews and nieces. They didn't know their uncle who'd left the country to become a terrorist, in the parlance of the rulers of the land. His father, a believer in law and order, who had stayed faithful to the military of the regime, albeit in the Transkei Army of Brigadier Bantu Holomisa, maintained he was also fighting the struggle. Django wondered what his rank was now and whether he had ever forgiven him, Django or Hickory or Ezekiel Zimu, for his wife's death. 'You kill everything that loves you,' his father once said.

Your mother gave up her will to live after your departure,' someone told him in the camp, echoing the old man's grievance.

I love you, he thought, listening to the night. He willed the time to speed up so that his two hours of sentry duty could come to pass, but he knew that that was not going to happen. Time would take its own sweet time. He thought of Mchinda, Sassafras, also out there on his post. He thought of the young man he had just relieved, Pomegranate, who was almost asleep on his feet when Hickory arrived. He had to say the password twice after he heard Pomegranate cocking his gun; that's how you got shot in these situations and friendly fire was one of the stupidest ways of dying. I'm slipping, he thought, when I call Pomegranate a youngster. Anyone who'd ever served in the People's Army tended to think of people in terms of the time they entered the military. Pomegranate was sixteen when inducted into the PA and given his first *nom de guerre*. And today, in 1989, he must be over twenty-five and still I see him as a boy; got to get my bearings right.

On the spot under a nameless tree, his nostrils assailed by nature's fecund discharges, Hickory lapsed into that state of blankness common among people on guard duty, where the mind loops around itself and creates meaningless patterns. When he tired of doing nothing and thinking empty thoughts, he busied himself with counting like a boxing referee counting down a fallen fighter, from one to sixty, stretching the intervals between the numbers and hoping to be still on his feet when he reached the seconds that made up two hours. He was perhaps near the number representing the first hour when he heard the screech of a bird or a hyena or some other wild animal, a scream that was near-human in its fluent expression of pain and longing.

I owe Linden an explanation, he thought. The young man's father was still on Robben Island and his mother, after years of struggling alone, had simply collapsed from exhaustion and despair – and having to feed so many mouths – and died. Linden and his sisters – two of them, much older and more capable of taking care of themselves – parted ways. Alone, bewildered, he found himself in a succession of homes before, as he put it, breaking out of juvie. Then, one day, he showed up at the house in G Section, where he'd heard that Brigadier Zimu's son, Django – not Eustace – ran a small network of people who wanted to change things. And he, Linden, who was not known as Linden in those days, could certainly do with some change. He had followed Django like a faithful dog, all the way to the camps in Angola.

Something whizzed past his head and smacked into the stem of the tree, the tree he'd christened the Watching Tree on account of its importance to guard duty. At first Hickory thought it was one of the night-time bugs, a big one by the sound of it, but then he hit the ground as everything he'd learnt about survival became a single instinct. Something with the heft of a kick struck him in the ribs and immediately he felt a warm wetness glue his shirt to his side. Even as he waited for the crack of the gun, which didn't come – telling him he'd been shot by someone using a gun fitted with a silencer – he wondered why a South African Defence Force's operational unit would employ the tactics of assassins. Soldiers, especially when they had the upper hand, loved the loud bang, which had the added benefit of confusing the enemy. He tensed, ready to make a run for it and then hesitated as the cough-spit sound followed slugs that chewed up the stony ground just a few feet ahead of him. The shooters weren't sure of the target's location. This was reconnaissance by fire.

Strangely, even though he'd been here before, in the line of fire, he'd never been as scared. His mouth was dry and he could feel his whole body shaking. Trembling, he couldn't trust himself to engage the enemy even if he were to be in his gun sights. In the past, the battles were heated moments, full of sound and noise and confusion, but there'd been something logical about them, even where he'd witnessed people dying randomly about him. This … this was different. It was also layered with an enduring irony: to come home was to die.

He smelled the earth. It had a metallic tang that now matched the taste in his mouth. He swirled the salty mixture of blood and saliva in his mouth, wondering if some vital organ had been punctured. Even his ears felt funny, burning, and he imagined bleeding through these orifices. He spat and crawled slowly, the rifle held some six inches off the ground, aware of his elbows operating like independent units of his body, levering him up and forward. Distantly, as if all this were happening to someone else, he noted that he was actually crawling over his own blood and spit and thinking; We are the sum total of tissues and shameful fluids. And it all emanates from the blasphemed earth, anyway. He didn't know why the thought occurred to him in the way it did, but it seemed to make sense. The fear, a ball in a region of his stomach, which, he suspected, was his centre, tasted like stale breath. If it had a colour, it would be grey-green with a dark centre. That centre would be crimson. It would be the colour of his blood. He saw himself squashed, like a bug, grey-green slime oozing out of him.

Somewhere in the sphere of silence and fear, Hickory felt the ground shuddering and a blast of dust raged over him with the force of a sandblasting machine. Then he heard the rotor blades of a helicopter whirling above him. It's all over, he thought, imagining that he made a perfect target, as he lay prone on the ground. The blades slap-slapping against the air were like the loose sandals of a fast walker. The sound spurred the shooter who must have been lurking in the bush to crash through the thicket in flight. The helicopter circled above for a second or two, seconds that felt like hours, before droning off, leaving an aural after-image of itself. Then he heard the muted call: 'Django? Django?'

Only one person called him by that name. 'Mchinda?' he responded.

'Django? You okay?'

'I think I've been shot,' Hickory said. He was still lying face down on the ground. He felt more wetness leaking out of him.

'When you've been shot,' Mchinda said, approaching, 'you don't think. You know for sure.'

'Well,' Hickory said. 'I think I know.'

He *had* been shot but it was a ricochet bullet that was lodged somewhere in his side. Hickory couldn't stop thinking it must have hit his lung or somewhere vital because of the taste of blood in his mouth. We'll see, he thought. Then there was more thrashing in the bush and Stinkwood and Pomegranate, eyes the size of moons, appeared, waving their guns in a manner that Hickory, even in his disoriented state, thought was far from soldierly. In a haze, he became aware of Sassafras calming them.

'What's happening?' he asked.

'The camp's been taken,' Stinkwood said. 'They came.'

'Who came?'

'I don't know, ten, twelve. It's dark and they just shot everyone in the cave.' Stinkwood's fear was palpable and seemed to have opened up his sweat glands. His body odour wafted over the area like gas and Hickory thought the SADF with dogs would have a field day here.

'They shot everyone,' Stinkwood said.

'Stinkwood, for fuck's sake,' Sassafras said. 'Get hold of yourself.' Then he turned to the other man. 'Did you see what happened, Pomegranate?' The assumed names were uncomfortable to the tongue.

'He's right,' Pomegranate replied. 'It's a swarm of people, maybe a platoon. Twaa! Twaaa!' He enacted the shooting, or, more accurately, the reaction of the men caught up in ambush. It pointed to a lightning raid where small arms possibly fitted with silencers and night scopes were used in the slaughter. The coups de grâce were accomplished with bayonets.

'Night scopes and silencers,' Sassafras said. 'The People's Army doesn't have that type of weaponry.'

Hickory wasn't interested in the sophisticated weapons of the enemy. 'Did they get the trunks?'

'They took one box,' Pomegranate said.

'Just the one box?'

'Yes. I think the other one must have been cached away already. They must have ransacked the cave but couldn't find the second one. By then, I suppose everyone was dead.'

'Mahogany?'

'Dead. He was the first to go, I suppose.'

'You suppose a lot for someone who was watching from the outside.' Sassafras thought for a minute. 'Why didn't you shoot?'

'I don't know. I froze,' Pomegranate said. Even in the dark, he looked very young. 'I didn't expect anything like that.'

'Was it the Boers?' Sassafras asked.

'I had a feeling it was our people, even if the weapons were different.' There was sadness in Pomegranate's tone. 'The way they walked, their style. Those are ours.'

'Jesus.'

'They dashed away. They were fast.' Pomegranate added. 'They were fast.'

'Think you'd know them again, if you saw them?' It was clear Sassafras was not satisfied with the answers. 'You think the helicopter is theirs?'

'I don't know. It was dark, which is why I think they could see us clearly and pick us off easily. They were quick.' There was a lilt of excitement in his tone as if he'd just witnessed a virtuoso performance. 'The People's Army sure knows how to train them.'

'That,' Sassafras said, 'isn't the People's Army. Those are enemy agents that have infiltrated us. Anyway, let's carry this corpse back to camp,' he said, pointing at Hickory who was lolling about as if ready to faint. See what's going on. What we can save.'

There was nothing to save.

At about 9:00 p.m., the killers' achievement resounded in the happy buzzing of insects, the sated green flies making repeated stabs at the skewered flesh. Even in the half-light of shielded torches, the complete carnage was evident and took its witnesses into the minds of men ordered to dismember, slice and hack and glory in the sight of sausage coils of intestines. The smell was of something that had once been human, which had been bled to emptiness. Pomegranate and Stinkwood doubled up and vomited against the stunted trees, adding their own elemental fluids to the blasphemed ground. Even though he didn't want to look, Hickory studied the faces until he found the one he was looking for. Linden's face was unmarked save for a misleadingly small entry wound in his forehead, whose exit left a gaping hole at the back of the skull. Sassafras entered and closed the eyes of the dead men. Then he went behind the wall and knocked on the ground until there was a resonance that gave him a clue to the whereabouts of what he was looking for. With a massive heave, he pulled out the leather straps that acted as handles for the trunk. 'Here,' he said to no one in particular. 'Help me.'

Four men left the cave, the trunk a dead weight, and stopped just outside its entrance. The unburied bodies inside lay in a dozen unflattering poses of death. They had tried their best, in the short time they had, to seal the cave against wild animals, but they knew that the gestures were as ceremonial as salutes. They conveyed nothing to the dead and they granted nothing to the living.

They had no reference point, nothing to help them make sense of their fear, the horror of seeing the insides of people with whom they'd been swapping stories less than three hours before. The deaths were all the more outrageous because almost everyone had survived the various ambushes in the Eastern Front, and some of the men, like Django and Mchinda, had paid a price for rebelling and standing up to the powers-that-be and raising their voices in their campaign to go home and fight the enemy, the SADF. Here they discovered how easy it was to become an enemy among their own forces, and that erstwhile compatriots could be harsher by far than anything the Pretoria regime could muster.

As they fought the flies in Zeerust, in the hour of murder, they recalled how they had challenged their own leadership in the camp and were readied for harsh punishment before the chaplain interceded on their behalf. It was fortunate that she had come to Angola that time. In the privacy of their tents, they had told one another that the chaplain had saved their lives. Otherwise they were dead meat.

And yet, here they were – alive – leaving behind corpses, shredded and dismembered, and there was no longer a need for pretence. The next of kin would have to discover their *nom de guerres* and reclaim their dead, even if it took a lifetime.

'Perhaps one of you should lead us in prayer,' Pomegranate said. A hand, which, hardly a minute earlier, had embraced a dead comrade, now gestured towards both Django and Mchinda, his seniors. They in turn looked at one another and shrugged, stunned by the request and its implications. The closest they had come to engaging with religion was in the camp, a long time ago, when the chaplain passed through and requested the whole assembly – a battalion of troops – to observe a minute of silence on an anniversary of one more massacre across the border, by the South African Defence Force.

This evening, however, Mchinda shook his head. No. He might have wished for the chaplain to be there, to administer something, perhaps the last rites for the believers and grant the dead some measure of dignity in their passage. However, Django, who came from a religious family, was adamant in his grief. To say any prayer in his view would have been an indirect way of paying homage to the same god that might have sanctioned the slaughter.

The men saw Django crying for the first time. They left after doing what was necessary and possible.

The men cast long morning shadows. From their gait, there was no doubt it was going to be a long walk home.

2

BRUISED SILHOUETTES

They lay on the mattress on the floor, looking up at the wardrobe and dressing table, the mirror shimmering and increasing in the mind the size of the small bedroom. The iron bedstead stood leaning against the wall, hiding part of the window area, which was covered with a blanket instead of the usual curtain. This made the room darker and increased the sense of intimacy and isolation for the couple.

Ngobese got to his feet, padding to the dressing table. He was aware of Laura's gaze on his back, seeing himself through her eyes, the big almost unmanly buttocks of which he was conscious, the thick thighs that tapered to more muscular legs with calves used to walking in rugged terrain. As always, when he looked at his reflection, he found it hard to shake off the impression that he was made up of body parts and features that belonged to other people, like an assemblage by a mischievous collagist. Short-cropped hair on a head that was too small for the neck and shoulders, a brow that was permanently furrowed – something that puzzled him as he was, in his own eyes at least, an easy-going type, not given to worrying unduly. The eyes were his father's bequest, black and heavy-lidded, beneath eyebrows that looked like a moustache turned upside down, the nose broad, claiming a lot of the area normally reserved for the cheeks. Having stopped shaving, Ngobese sported a scraggly beard, which he hoped served more to intimidate Mvumbi, his wayward son, than act as an adornment. It was actually in Mvumbi's sketchbook that Ngobese had come across collages that made him think that the little bastard had promise, a long time ago when Mvumbi still attended school.

'Are you worried about your son?' Laura, balanced on one elbow, asked.

'Yes, and the fact that I can't keep my eye on him.' Ngobese felt that his son's rebelliousness was a form of punishment for what he, the father, was doing. But still, he wouldn't trade his life for anything. It was dangerous, but forbidden fruit was as heady as a narcotic.

He looked at her on the bed and realised she had wrapped herself up in the sheet, back into a zone where wakefulness was unwanted.

He had warned other men – and not a few women, too – about the dangers of making cuckolds of powerful men. As an inyanga, a healer, he had a ringside seat at battles between husbands and wives. One thing he knew, also, was that forbidden fruit had put many a good man into the ground.

He was therefore conflicted, his whole body exulting in insane joy, all his extremities tingling at the end of the first bout. He thought of them as bouts, these sessions with her mainly because even though they were an expression of great tenderness, their peaks were often preceded by a violent struggle. Looking at her, her chest lifting and falling beneath the tangled sheets, he wondered how such a small and compact body could possess her kind of strength. How did she manage to conceal the bruises and weals of his passion from Muzi Thabethe, her husband?

'Laura?'

Laura Thabethe stirred like someone disturbed from a pleasurable dream. 'What?' There was a touch of hostility in her tone. She knew what he was going to say. Their encounters always followed the same pattern, like clockwork. 'Le'me sleep, Thula.'

Thula was her name for him, which also meant 'keep quiet', in isi-Zulu. He wished for nothing more than to keep quiet and let her sleep. Forever eager to please her and even a little afraid he'd lose her if she ever put her mind to it, he would have liked to snuggle and spend the rest of the afternoon in bed, in their borrowed space. But he knew that she had to go back home. His sister, Nomusa, who regularly allowed him – them – to use this room in KwaDambuza, expected him to be gone by the time the kids came back from school. He and Laura could easily have conducted their trysts at his base in Ben Bella, but that was fraught with danger as his patients tended to drop in unannounced. And someone might have recognised Laura as Muzi Thabethe's wife. Thabethe had returned eighteen months ago from a lengthy stretch inside for political offences. In these days of summary executions, anyone sleeping with a wife of a political prisoner was simply asking for trouble.

'Hey?'

This time Laura sat up, the sheet pulled up to her neck, a demonstration of modesty that caused Ngobese to laugh. What was she hiding? 'I know,' she said, 'that I have to go.'

'Actually,' he said, 'it's your husband who's sent me on an errand.'

'Let's not talk about him,' Laura said. Then: 'What's it about?'

'I've got to collect some people from Zeerust.'

'Where's that?'

'It's in the western Transvaal. Near the border with Botswana.'

'Why you, Thula?'

'Because I can pretend I'm looking for herbs,' he said. 'I'm not being sent to my death, don't worry.'

'Were you always an inyanga?' she asked, smiling. 'Or was it just a ploy to get close to other men's wives?'

'I'm my father's son,' Ngobese said. 'It's a calling, something I couldn't refuse.'

'You could have turned down my overtures to you,' Laura said. 'Knowing it's wrong.'

'We're fated to do wrong things,' Ngobese said, 'the flesh being so weak and being overpowered by desire.' A wave of tenderness washed over him. 'Come here,' he said.

Later, she got busy, restoring the room to its original state before freshening up. Looking at herself in the mirror, she was mystified by people who called her beautiful. She saw her eyes as too wide apart, eyebrows too bushy for a woman, nose flattish and lips too thick. To compound the perceived imperfection was a protruding upper left incisor, which caused her to cover the corner of her mouth whenever she smiled. The strangest thing was that these flaws, which she elevated to the status of disfigurement in dark moments, were what seemed to draw men to her. Strangers would steal looks at her, as admiring as they were lustful.

In her reckoning almost all men were nothing but randy goats. That said she was concerned about the two men in her life. She wasn't a praying person but sometimes she would steal a moment in her house, in the loneliness of her quiet bedroom, and question the meaning of her life with either one of them. Muzi Thabethe was a loving man, providing, unstinting; and he wasn't what the girls called a dud in the sack either. Even stranger was the fact that Thulasizwe Ngobese, her Thula, exciting and adventurous, almost always left her high and dry. It was his company, however, that she enjoyed more – that, and, perhaps, the illicit nature of it all.

Sitting inside the minibus taxi, looking at the back of the braided head of a woman, about forty years old, Laura Mdunge wondered if she, too, was cheating on her husband. Most of the passengers, it being midweek, 20 December 1989, were women, possibly en route to the big shops in the city. Or running errands to ease the lives of their children, husbands and unsatisfying lovers.

Laura knew she wasn't cut out for marriage. At heart she was a rebel. She remembered an incident, or a series of events, in early July 1971, a simultaneous beginning and ending of what had shaped her apprehension of life. There had been police raids, netting people she had known. For some reason she hadn't really thought of herself as a target. Her naïve invincibility came from an understanding that to be politically involved was as logical for the people of KwaMashu as was being born black.

This notion made her increasingly rebellious, moody and somewhat dismissive of the older generation, which, she felt, was not pulling its weight on important issues. Her father was a lay preacher. Always sombre in a dark suit and hat, which he tilted towards anyone greeting him, Reverend Mdunge had become a regular, if ridiculed, absence in the household. This left Laura's mother, Selina – and her maternal uncle, Mziwonke Maseko – to man the fort.

Laura held the older generation responsible for a country of huge inequalities. Fighting the system had fallen on the shoulders of the youth, her boyfriend, Muzi Thabethe, included. They had been going out with an intention to get married when the time came, and had ramped up the relationship from holding hands to actual kissing and cuddling. Who knew what the future held? And now, this: a visit from the police.

An elderly, bony and wheezy officer, who introduced himself as Jackson Lerule, believed in wheedling the information he needed out of a sympathetic subject. Despite his unhealthy appearance, he was chain-smoking from a packet of Lexington's, flipping ash into a saucer he had requested in lieu of an ashtray. It was this habit – regarded by Laura's mother as the height of disrespect – that fanned everyone's hostility towards him. A church-going, God-fearing woman, Mrs Selina Mdunge heard him out politely as he introduced the matter that brought him to the household. Then he asked for privacy while he interviewed the young woman. Complying, Selina Mdunge withdrew into the bedroom, leaving the door open a crack. She heard him mumbling what he must have thought were reassuring words to put the young Laura at ease. He doesn't know Laura, she thought; I also don't know my Laura.

'Look at me,' he was saying. 'I became a policeman out of need, because I have young children to feed.'

Laura said, 'That's nice.'

Then he said, 'You're fourteen years old and from what I hear you're pretty smart at school. Why are you mixing yourself up with bad elements?'

'I don't know what you're talking about.'

'I'm sure you do, young lady. The communists and the terrorists ...'

'I don't know any communists or terrorists.'

'That Thabethe boy ... you know he's in deep trouble?'

'Is that the communist you're talking about?'

'Look ...' Selina Mdunge's ears pricked up as she heard the edgy note in his voice, he was losing it. 'You're in deep trouble ...'

'If I'm in trouble and you have something to charge me with, go ahead. If you don't, then you'd better leave.'

'You stupid little ...'

Selina Mdunge appeared in the doorway, standing with arms akimbo. 'Mr Lerule, I gave you permission to talk to my daughter,' she said. 'I think we're done here.'

'Mrs Mdunge,' Jackson Lerule said, showing small, nicotine-stained teeth, 'you don't know the kind of trouble we can cause you ...'

'*We*?' Laura Mdunge cried. 'What *stupid* "we" are you talking about?'

Officer Lerule opened his mouth to speak, and stopped, showing the brown teeth. Laura, her chest heaving, stepped forward, picked up the improvised ashtray off the table and flung the contents in Lerule's direction. Standing up, he tried to back away as if the cigarette ash and dead stubs were aflame. Tripping over his chair, he fell backwards to the floor as if felled by the force of a massive blow.

Standing above him as he lay with his legs in the air, the two women broke out laughing. The crashing chair and the thud on the floor had attracted some of the neighbours. They had also noticed the unfamiliar car parked on the road in front of the Mdunge home. In a moment onlookers were crowding the door. They joined in the laughter, watching Lerule getting up and dusting himself, patting the jacket to feel if his weapon was still snug in its holster. Snarling at the curious, he turned to scowl at Laura, his eyes promising, *you haven't heard the last of me.* Emboldened by the sight of an agent of the mighty in adverse circumstances, the small crowd of neighbours shouted, *Voetsek, bloody sell-out*! The unmarked police car was already idling by the time Lerule reached it. He had run as fast as his legs could carry him while dodging stones and various missiles. His partner had been waiting in the car, probably radioing the police HQ all along.

After the incident, the cops were regular visitors, on a campaign of harassment. They turned the house upside down, threatening Selina her mother and actually pistol-whipping her uncle. This had instilled a cold anger in her. 'I'll fight these people,' she told Selina.

'You're just a young woman,' Selina said. 'They will crush you.'

And so, to prove her own mother wrong – and to prove the enemy wrong – she became an organiser, a courier, and a recruiter for the Movement. She remembered some particularly hairy moments in KwaMashu, driving with crazy comrades in the middle of the night, to meet activists in Newlands East, at a time, in the early 1980s, when the name of the Movement wasn't as fashionable as it was now. On the road, they skirted roadblocks, getting out of the car, running into the bush and risking their lives – for what? To distribute pamphlets about the Movement and to set up underground branches and cells, working hand in hand with the emergent trade union movement. In a way,

Laura Mdunge had never felt as alive as she felt then. There were outings into far-flung parts of the country, where young people got crash courses in the history of South Africa, history that wasn't part of the school curricula. Here, too, the Lauras of the world were forced out of their shells in sessions where they shared their knowledge with other young people. It was during these activities that she met Ngobese, who was nothing, really, until much later. Seeing her at work, he had said: 'You're actually a leader in your own right.'

'A leader in my own right,' she said in the moving taxi, causing the well-groomed woman in front to turn and gaze at the madwoman behind her. 'It's all right,' Laura Mdunge said.

It wasn't all right. Muzi Thabethe returned from prison a hero – and Laura Mdunge became a housewife. She participated, in her own way, in the political activities, which had become even more dangerous with the proclamation of a succession of states of emergency. But she was aware that Muzi Thabethe had relegated her from the status of comrade and colleague to one of helpmate.

They were no longer equal before the eyes of the struggle.

Other women who came on board tacitly endorsed this demotion. Nomasonto Sokhela, for one, treated her with condescension. The men were useless, fawning around the top dog, her husband. They all urged her to bask in his reflected glory. How scandalised they'd all be if they knew what she sometimes got up to. What was more scandalous, however, is that her infidelity would consign her to Hell if it ever came out. If it were Muzi Thabethe two-timing her, his hero status would shoot to stellar heights for, apart from being a hero of the revolution, he would have also proven himself to be a real man. Ngobese had regaled her with stories of some of the top-ranking members of the leadership whose promiscuity was the stuff of legend. Some of those who flaunted their runaway libidos now and then contracted some unnameable diseases, a punishment, Ngobese would say, 'for that runaway snake in their trousers'. Notwithstanding all these failings, these men were taken seriously. They were taken more seriously than all the women activists who managed to keep their legs locked tighter than those of live chickens being readied for road transportation.

Flying solo, thinking of Laura, Thulasizwe Ngobese had no illusions that he was in for a hard time. After being with her, he felt guilty, wondering if he hadn't breached security. He shouldn't, for instance, have told her about the indiscretions of certain political players.

He inhaled deeply, smelling the dry Highveld air.

It was the late afternoon of 20 December, which he knew was Nomusa's birthday. His only sibling, she still managed to intimidate him, seeing him as a somewhat inefficient copy of their father. Storm clouds swirled against the sky, far out in the west, but he knew it wouldn't rain, not just yet.

It took a while for the guerrillas to accept that he had come to pick them up, men naturally taught to smell a rat. They had watched from behind a clump of trees as the vehicle approached, their guns cocked. When Ngobese got out, he went around the double-cab, opening all the doors to show the hidden eyes that there was no enemy waiting to ambush them. Then he called out, his voice scattering in the windless field of wild grass, scrub and thorn trees, asking the men waiting in the shadows if they wanted to see him naked to have proof that he was Muzi Thabethe's emissary. Those were the magic words, the phrase Mahogany had advised on before the fateful assigning of sentry duties in the caves. Slowly, one by one, the combatants came out of hiding.

There were four of them, bad-tempered people with strange names, all starving, trying to mask their shock. Ngobese waited while they dug up a large military trunk and stored it in the back of his double-cab VW bakkie. He took pride in his car, which he bought brand-new when it came onto the market in 1983 and thus hated the critical eye the men cast over it, much as he would were someone passing snide comments about his wife, he supposed. When he made a move to help them, they calmly but firmly informed him that the trunk was out of bounds. When Stinkwood, who drove getaway cars in a previous life, offered to drive, Ngobese said no. He stood his ground to their sullen bullying. It was his bakkie. They relented.

Later, listening to their stories as he drove, Ngobese identified Mchinda as their leader. Sixteen in 1976 when he joined the Movement, he was almost thirty years old now, a senior member of the unit. Seated next to Mchinda in the front with a hand pressed against the wad of bloody dressing over the bullet wound in his side, was Django, twenty-nine. He didn't share much, gritting his teeth each time the bakkie hit a bump. Ngobese had a sense that his quietness had less to do with pain than with natural reticence. He became more intrigued when he heard of Django's exploits from Stinkwood and Pomegranate, who were talking from the back. Their chattiness was likely an expression of relief. They might have been young but they had all clocked up miles of experience in the bush, thought Ngobese.

'I thought we were going to die back there,' Stinkwood said.

'We're not out of the woods yet,' Ngobese warned. 'There might be roadblocks ahead.'

'I have my gun,' Pomegranate said. 'No one's taking me alive.'

'You two cowboys,' Mchinda said. 'Let's have less talk and more vigilance.'

'Yebo, Komandir,' Pomegranate said.

'This "Komandir" …' Ngobese asked, 'is it Russian?'

'No. It's Telegu.'

Both Pomegranate and Stinkwood broke out laughing. Django shot Mchinda a sharp glance and shook his head. Ngobese drove on.

They think I'm a fool. He was Mchinda's age-mate but he felt old, someone with one foot in the grave when he compared himself to the guerrillas. It was a paradox of sorts; these men had just come out of a truly horrific experience, yet they evinced a zest for life that left him, someone who had never really faced danger, feeling like a freshly embalmed corpse. His self-consciousness derived not so much from being inexperienced in things military as from a generalised feeling of inadequacy, uselessness. The nearest he had come to a similar situation was when he was treating ex-prisoners returning from long-term sentences. Their privation seemed to have strengthened them and made them more capable of facing day-to-day challenges. Even Django, who slid in and out of sleep, would be a much better man, if it ever came to a fight. But then – and the tingling sensation returned – they didn't have what he had. It was childish, he knew – something more suited to Mvumbi's temperament than to a full-grown man. But still, the memory of Laura thrashing and flailing brought a smile to his face.

'Happy memories, Mr Ngobese?' Mchinda asked.

'Just thinking of my sister and my son,' Ngobese lied. But he still harboured a feeling that he might not be able to dissemble for long among men who had spent their adult lives perfecting the art. In the company of guerrillas he was like a man who hadn't been to initiation school.

'What do they do, your relatives?' asked Django. For a while, he had been quietly watching the landscape flit past and shooing off a fly buzzing around.

'My sister is twenty-eight,' Ngobese said. 'She teaches in a school for the deaf in KwaMashu.' He thought of the times Nomusa had tried to take him through the sign-language alphabet and how he always fluffed it.

'You sound proud of her,' Django said. 'And your son?'

'He's a seventeen-year-old bundle of trouble,' Ngobese said, a proud father conflicted because his son's wilfulness might have meant he was a chip off the old block. 'When I see what he gets up to, though, I sympathise with those parents who encouraged their sons to jump the fence into exile.'

'What's he do – chase girls?'

'That would be okay,' Ngobese said. 'But most boys his age have taken to the weed like there's no tomorrow.'

There was silence in the car for a while. Everyone knew that when a father spoke of being troubled by his child's fondness for the weed he might be talking about drugs that were harder and more difficult to manage.

'It's the merchants,' Ngobese said. 'They've sprung up like mushrooms.'

'But the merchants are merely servicing a need,' Pomegranate said from the back. 'There must be a market.'

'I feel,' Ngobese said with spirit, 'that the merchants make it possible for our children to crave stuff that kills them.'

'And there's no muthi to fight that problem?' Mchinda said. It was as if he wanted to lighten the increasingly tense atmosphere.

'No. People go mad,' Ngobese said with a heavy tone. 'Rehabilitation is costly. People die. Drugs are everywhere.'

'What's your son's name?' Mchinda asked.

'Mvumbi. I named him after Chief Albert Luthuli, whose other name was Mvumbi,' Ngobese said. 'But you know what they call my son on the street?'

'No,' Mchinda said. 'What?'

'Mvee or V-man.' Ngobese gave a small laugh. 'Imagine that. A name of honour turned into a joke.'

'It's not funny,' Mchinda said. 'We might have to talk to him?'

'I'd appreciate that.'

It was late at night, around 9:30 p.m., when five silhouettes walking in Indian file opened the squeaky gate and proceeded down a few stony steps to the door of one of the sturdier houses standing amid shacks and tumbledown dwellings. The man leading them was heavyset and walked with unencumbered ease. His slenderer followers lugged a box that seemed as heavy and as awkward as a coffin down the narrow path, the unevenness of the ground adding to their difficulty. The second man with free hands walked with a limp. Now and then he slowed down almost to a stop during the short journey from where the pickup dropped them off on the roadside to the threshold of the stone house. Like team members who had participated in too many tournaments, the other men instinctively knew when to pick up speed or slow the game down, an ensemble trained to march at the speed of the slowest. The others, then, halted and waited for Django.

One of them called out, 'You okay there, Django?'

'I'm fine, Mchinda,' Django said. 'You guys go in.'

'Yes,' said the shadow in front, fumbling for keys. 'We've got to make it fast.'

'Ja,' Mchinda said, at once agreeable and annoyed. While the two men struggled with the trunk, he was weighed down with knapsacks that contained weapons, rockets and grenades. 'We know the people here have big mouths. But we can't leave him outside.'

'I'm just saying he must snap it up.' The older man sounded a bit put out. 'You're all safer if no one sees you coming in.'

'Ja, Ngobese, give him a chance,' Mchinda said. 'He will come in. His wound must have opened up.'

'We'll get someone to check him out tomorrow,' Ngobese said. 'A couple of stitches will do the job.' He fiddled with keys and opened the door and ushered the men inside. 'Here we are, *madoda*.'

Inside, the gloomy lounge was eerily quiet. The power was out and the darkness almost complete. Gradually the men got used to it. They were comforted by the fact that the other houses in the neighbourhood were also in darkness. If I can't see you, the logic went, then you cannot see me. Even though there was a general blackout, Django suspected that Ben Bella was awake.

On their journey here, there hadn't been a soul on the road. The passages between shacks were empty except for two or three stray dogs on the prowl. He was surprised that there weren't any teenage lovers – a breed that normally took to these hidden places for that last, illicit squeeze.

But still – with all these absences – there was a brooding presence, a watchful eye, perhaps, peering from behind darkened curtains. Even the shebeens – for there must have been shebeens around, which were vital to the social life of any community – were quiet. Tonight they seemed incapable of luring the thirsty traveller with their sounds of loud music and the raised voices of impassioned, homegrown intellectuals holding forth about the state of the nation. Django imagined that everyone knew the state of the nation.

He found it remarkable that Ngobese remained pleasant and obliging although it was clear he was very tired. He set about collecting candles and paraffin lamps. The light from the yellowish flames bounced off the men's faces and the shadows emphasised just how drained they all were.

'Everything's going to be all right,' Ngobese kept on saying as he directed the men to their sleeping places, now and then sounding slightly apologetic about the state of the place. 'It's stuffy in here,' he said. But he warned against the opening of the windows. Then he headed to the toilet.

'Ngobese,' Mchinda said. 'You should get someone in here, to clean up and cosy the place up.'

'I have a niece who comes to tidy up here once in a while,' Ngobese said from the toilet. His stream made a long splashing sound as it hit the bowl. 'Problem is she's started having an interest in boys.'

'When's she coming again?' Stinkwood asked, speaking for the first time since their arrival. 'To do some cleaning?'

'Not while you guys are here,' Ngobese said above the sound of a flushing toilet. 'I'm not crazy.' He came out hitching up his trousers. 'You're the sort of outlaws few would accept as their in-laws.'

'*Hawu*, Ngobese,' Stinkwood said with a sly grin. 'How can you say that? We're not that bad.'

'Yes, why treat us like lepers?' Mchinda asked. 'I thought women liked guerrillas?'

The guerrillas were a new element in Ngobese's life and he had not yet worked out how he would interact with them. The banter, much as it lightened the atmosphere, also heightened his insecurity. 'Jokes aside,' he said, deciding to pull rank, 'there are other groups like yours that I have seen. And some of the men there are sick and we have to provide treatment.'

'Sick? What's the matter with them?'

'AIDS. HIV. *Ingculazi*. More people have died from it than from the violence.'

The silence that followed was uncomfortable. Django felt a cold shudder starting from his navel to the tip of his penis, which he suspected would one day simply wither from lack of use. He remembered a few of the comrades in safe houses in the Lusaka suburbs of Mtendere, Chilenje or Kabwata, who were being readied for infiltration inside the country. Among them were one-time daredevils who had shrivelled up into stick figures as seen in a children's storybook, unspeaking and their eyes as eloquent as the ages. The local clinics had used up all forms of prophylactics. It was getting desperate. Calls had to be made to the Movement leaders in various capitals of the world to acquire condoms in bulk. One such leader was Robert Sitho, a conservative trade unionist based in Crewe in the United Kingdom. When told to buy about fifteen thousand condoms, Sitho blew his top. 'Could you imagine me entering a pharmacy and making such a big order of condoms?' he asked. 'They'd all look at me and ask: "Mr Robert Sitho, when are you ever going to get a rest?'" He did comply with the request, though.

Even though it was late in the night, the summer flies and mosquitoes were alive in the land. They buzzed and whined and generally made their presence felt in harassing the new arrivals.

Ngobese gave Django a long look. 'Django?' he called. 'Maybe you should take a seat while we see if we can rustle up something to eat.' Then he reached into his knapsack and took out a small plastic container and extracted two fat capsules. 'Here,' he said, 'swallow this.'

'What is it?' Django asked. 'I thought you only specialise in herbs.'

'All the material that enriches these drug companies comes out of the African soil. It's Pregabalin.'

'It's not going to make me pregnant?' Django asked, taking the capsules, popping them in his mouth. He washed them down with water.

Ngobese administered to the men, handing them tablets or potions with healing qualities, which would make them fitter for the tasks ahead.

'Go and rest,' Ngobese said. 'The painkiller will make you drowsy in a short while.'

Django hobbled over to the sofa. He was in pain although he tried to hide it, praying for the drug to take effect. 'You said something about a doctor … is there one on call?' he asked. 'If there's one, then I must take my hat off to you and your organisation.'

'Medical people have always formed the backbone of the struggle in Natal,' Ngobese said matter-of-factly. 'From way back we had Steve Biko, Aubrey Mokoape, Diliza Mji …'

'… Nkosazana Dlamini …' added the other young man. In his earlier years, Stinkwood had wanted to study to become a doctor. That was before the reality of his circumstances dictated otherwise. 'One of my brothers studied at the medical school but dropped out,' he said. 'I remember there used to be a lot of parties, gumbas, they called them. And a gumba was not complete without these gorgeous women; nurses from King Edward hospital or McCord's, real beauties, imports from the Eastern Cape.'

'Ah,' Pomegranate said, 'admit it: you just like Xhosa women.'

'Oh, ja,' Stinkwood said, 'they were fine looking. Not like some of *amagwivi* from the Western Cape, those nurses without front teeth who looked like patients.'

Ngobese looked on as the young men laughed, Mchinda, Pomegranate and Stinkwood; Django was sprawled untidily across the sofa, his one leg stretched out. He seemed to be looking for a more comfortable position.

'Let me see about the food,' said Ngobese almost to himself, a host anxious about the welfare of his guests.

Django watched him proceed to the small kitchen. In the weak light he could see the walls that were bedecked with cut-out pictures of faded pin-up girls, possibly Mvumbi's contribution to the décor, soccer clubs posing with footballs in their hands, a series featuring men receiving awards from officials garlanded with mayoral chains. Perhaps Ngobese was not who he'd wanted them to believe he was. Django heard a jangle of saucepans and a primus stove roaring into life. The smell of fuel wafted into the lounge and became part of the sizzle of meat frying. Instead of deepening his hunger, the smell of food filled him with nausea.

Having eaten their fill, pap, meat and gravy washed down with orange squash, the men prepared for bed. They would doss in the main house and relocate to the cottage in the back tomorrow morning. His otherwise robust appetite having deserted him, Django gave up after a nibble and his share was gobbled up by the ever-hungry Pomegranate. He was listless, sweaty and cold at the same time. Glancing at his host, Django wondered if his eyes were playing tricks on him. Ngobese's face registered a series of changes, or was it emotions? He was at once old and shrewd and far from avuncular and – in an instant – as convivial as an innkeeper. Which was the real Ngobese? Django wanted to ask.

He'd seen these changes on someone's face before, but couldn't quite remember whom and where. Everything was fluid. He also wished to alert Mchinda to a certain irregularity but was distracted by the fact that the latter was busy organising security arrangements for the night. Mchinda and Stinkwood drew the short straws. They had to take turns guarding the house. Although no one voiced it, there was unease about the safety of the trunk and its contents. There was anxiety about security. Anything that might happen would involve Ngobese, a civilian. In the case of an attack, even his juju wouldn't save him. The image of the bloodbath in Zeerust still loomed large in everybody's mind.

Ngobese for his part appeared untouched by the tension. Danger didn't seem to bother him at all. He said he would sleep over in the cottage, one of the backrooms on the other side of the fowl-run.

The men bade him goodnight. They waited until the door was closed and Ngobese had finally left before they took their weapons from the knapsacks: AK-47s, F-1 grenades and 9 mm Makarov pistols. It was not as if they thought Ngobese didn't know they were armed; hell, he saw them with serious ordnance in the Western Transvaal. It was just out of observance of both the code of conduct regarding the handling of weapons in civilian conditions and respect for the man, his house and generosity. Now that he was out of sight, however, they could revert to being their bastard selves.

Spaced out as he was, Django derived some comfort out of hearing the clink and snap of the weapons. Mchinda led the weapons drill. Click! The firing pin struck a void instead of the primer of a 7.62 mm projectile. Django recalled the accidents in Angola, someone removing a magazine from the stock without ejecting the last round from the chamber. 'The last round, comrades,' the firearms instructor would say. 'The last round. Even in bed, you might have performed like a sex-god, but if your last round was *ploha,* comrades, forget it.'

In that region between sleep and wakefulness, Django remembered the instructor, short and squat with a complexion so light the men had nicknamed him Camarada Mulatto. He recalled him writing the word плоха in the original Cyrillic script, and then informing the class that it stood for anything negative that a human being could achieve. If you fucked up in any way, he'd say, it was *ploha.* It was a catchall term that could get you embraced or shot, depending on the occasion. When excited, Camarada Mulatto would swear in tongues of a succession of countries where he had received training. His favourites were *filho da puta* or *ploha*, delivered with such passion that no kursant would dare ask for a translation.

Django slapped off an insistent mosquito. He thought about the trunk and wondered if there was more to it than the money. It was heretical for any guerrilla sent on such a mission to think about opening the merchandise under his care. Their case was different, he said to himself. The people who sent us on this mission are the selfsame betrayers who killed some of our compatriots. Should the code of honour hold here? Or is this a special case? He trusted his comrades wouldn't open the trunk until the time came. He also didn't know when that would be. The idea of someone else outside the unit opening it, a robber perhaps, whirled inside his head.

For some time that night he struggled to fall asleep. He was conscious of a sense of incompletion. Out of the blue, a voice told him he was acting like a perfect idiot. Being stronger than imaginings, however, the drug stilled all voices and Django fell into a deep and dreamless sleep.

Watching from his favourite spot on the street corner, under a street light that had fused so long ago its absence was taken for granted, Tikka Joe warned the two snotnoses with him to keep it down. Although not trained in any aspect of underground work or combat tactics, he knew that voices tended to carry in the night, as did smells. So he was pleased that his little trio, passing the pipe of weed around, was upwind of the group alighting from the bakkie in front of Ngobese's house.

As he'd never seen anyone visiting the inyanga that late at night, it pricked Tikka Joe's interest. The men seemed to be struggling with carrying a heavy box while helping one of theirs out of the car and down the steps into the front door. Despite their encumbrance, the men still exhibited the practical litheness common among athletes or soldiers. In fact Tikka Joe could have sworn that he saw a glint of a barrel of a rifle; being realistic about his status of a habitual smoker, however, he was more likely to keep that last titbit to himself. Many a time he'd been accused of seeing things.

Now he wished his friends, hangers-on, really, always cadging a smoke, would clear off as he needed to tell the man called Bra Gab about this latest development. It was his responsibility as a lookout to pass on information about anything out of the ordinary. And this was as out of the ordinary as they come.

But he was also thinking, calculating.

Bra Gab gave him a few rands and kept him supplied with the weed. But what was the real value of the information that he collected for the big man? And what was in that box that the men carried? They were as careful as the guards who accompanied payroll vans, the armoured trucks that came to the township on Friday afternoons, with armed guards in dark glasses, big guns that would kill you even if the bullet missed you. What's in that box?

'*Ek sê, majieta*?' he told the two smokers, 'I think it's time we called it a day.' He liked using the street language of Johannesburg gangsters.

'Awu, Tikka,' grumbled Boy-Boy, the youngest. 'Since when do you want to go to bed at the same time with the chickens?'

'Boy-Boy?' Tikka Joe said. 'You're so short and stunted, you smoke too much weed, you'll never grow any bigger.'

In a minute the boys made their way to their respective homes, the shacks where parents, if any, didn't ever question the whereabouts of their charges. Tikka Joe hotfooted it off to KwaDambuza to see his benefactor. Bra Gab had a new woman and should be in a good mood.

Although split right down the middle, with Django and Mchinda adamant that Ngobese should seek his own solution to his son's drug problem while Pomegranate and Stinkwood proposed direct action, the matter was taken out of everyone's hands barely three days after the guerrillas' arrival at Ngobese's. An overweight, acne-ridden and abbreviated version of Thulasizwe Ngobese, Mvumbi, had been mooching around his father's house. Like a few of the inhabitants of the Ben Bella section of KwaMashu, a township located some twenty miles north of Durban, Mvumbi acted as if he had no idea that his father was hosting a group of men. This was not odd. An inyanga, Ngobese from time to time played host to delegations, for instance, novices from Northern Transvaal or initiates fresh from the ceremonies of manhood in the hidden hills of the Transkei. In fact, Django's injury added credibility to the men's cover story that they were seeking treatment for one of their men who had been struck by lightning. It was also a time when it was not very healthy for someone to be sniffing about into the provenance of strangers. Many households headed by powerful people were protected by groups of men, some of whom did not even bother to conceal their firearms in a country that was beginning to be awash with weapons of all calibre. Here and there were rumours that armed men had been trained by either the state's security apparatus or by the liberation movement. There were formations that protected communities from marauding gangs, some called self-defence units. The police were conspicuous by their absence. It was said that it was unsafe then to be a policeman in uniform. Your gun and your life were up for grabs. It was a period of strife in the whole country.

Violence had already claimed thousands of lives. The rule of thumb was that people had a right to be suspicious. But they should always keep their noses clean and definitely out of the affairs of others.

Everything Mvumbi did, however, was informed by addiction, which made him an opportunist. Strangers were seen as fresh meat, a source of income. They would be new to a place and therefore a soft touch. At least that was what Mvumbi believed. Moreover, it was around Christmas-time, summertime when the living was easy, even though some people killed one another with gay abandon. It was a period for relaxation, when even strict parents tended to be a little more lenient towards their charges' transgressions.

In the few days he had been around, showing himself a lot more eager to help with household chores, Mvumbi had been monitoring the daily routine of his father's visitors in the cottage. After waking every morning they did limbering up exercises, had breakfast and went about their tasks and responsibilities. When done with washing the group's laundry, for instance, Pomegranate and Stinkwood enjoyed taking the air outside. They mostly kept within the perimeter, checking the yard for telltale footprints and catching a smoke while swapping stories at the enclosure where coal and firewood were stored. Sometimes, early in the morning, you'd hear the thwack-thwack of the axe splitting wood. Mchinda occasionally joined them, standing in his T-shirt and jeans, regaling them with stories.

Sometimes, they would catch sight of Mvumbi and beckon him over. '*Zwakala la, ntwana*,' Mchinda would say. 'Come over here, kid.'

Then either Pomegranate or Stinkwood would chide him: 'We hear you're now a big man, smoking pot.' And Mvumbi would squirm, drawing patterns with his big toe on the dust of powdered coal and sawdust. 'It's not me,' he'd say. 'It's those other kids who sit at the corner, Tikka Joe and them.'

'Tikka Joe?' someone would ask, disbelievingly. 'What kind of name is that?'

And Mvumbi with downcast eyes would say, 'It's his name,' like that explained everything. But being guerrillas, they knew that his hangdog routine was an act.

'Now,' Mchinda would say, 'don't go disappointing your father, smoking like a chimney. Your father is a very good man who's doing important stuff.'

'Yes.'

Three of the men, Mchinda, Stinkwood and Pomegranate, usually joined Ngobese on his errands and did some shopping. For them there was newness in everything, the shops stocked merchandise they'd never imagined existed. More interesting, the people looked different. The women were more alluring, the skirts shorter and the legs longer. They were like children when it came to a simple thing like eating fruit yoghurt out of tubs. Some of the ice cream flavours were simply out of this world. Ngobese watched them with a smile, happy that he had been instrumental in bringing about such joy.

The men enjoyed the visit to the market on Victoria Street or the hostel on Dalton Road where Ngobese's counterparts showed off their herbs and potions. As it was nearing Christmas Day, the hostel dwellers were preparing to visit their loved ones, way back home in the sticks. One of the men was Bhekisisa Luthuli, a six-foot tall giant weighing over 150 kilograms. He was a businessman, specialising in low-cost accommodation, who made no bones about his cash cow: a chop shop that he ran from the safety of the men's hostel in KwaMashu. Towering over Ngobese, whom he called Mzala or cousin, he extended an open invitation for the men to visit him, with or without pieces of red-hot coal, the township slang for a stolen car.

'Give you a good *plice*.' It was not uncommon for some homeboys from certain parts of Natal to confuse their R's with their L's. Then there were those men fashioning uniforms for the male combo song-and-dance competitions at the YMCA, where the winning group was rewarded with a cash prize and a white billy goat. Mchinda, who was fluent in almost all of the country's languages, was at home with them all, addressing them by their ancestral names and participating in the drinking of sorghum beer and dancing the indlamu like a true warrior. To crown it all, he joined in the stick fighting, which ranked high in the expression of camaraderie by men flung far from their homesteads, who entertained themselves with games in the city.

Although Mvumbi didn't know the extent of Django's injuries, he assumed these to be the reason Django remained behind in the cottage. He espied Django taking the walk past the chicken run to the main house where he spent the whole day cooking, while balanced on a makeshift crutch, and reading. Returning in the late afternoon or early evening, Ngobese and his group would join Django for supper. Then they left Ngobese alone and retired for the night in the cottage.

Departing from practice on the Saturday morning of 23 December, Django joined the rest in Ngobese's van. Mvumbi watched as the vehicle disappeared around the corner. He waited for what he thought was a decent moment before jumping over the neighbour's fence into his father's yard. He had no problem with opening the padlock securing the door to the cottage, having seen where the key was kept hidden. For a while he got lost examining the men's clothes, arranged on a rack in the bedroom, the shoes that always corroborated the fact of existence of people, the slender beds, each one with a sheet and blanket tucked in tightly as in a hospital ward, the extra blankets rolled up neatly and placed against the headboards. It was this sense of order that made Mvumbi uneasy, as if the orderliness hinted at minds that could move heaven and earth to shape things their way. He noticed the locked wooden trunk, which had been shoved into the corner and was covered with a Swazi cloth on which rested books and old magazines. He examined the lock and realised that it would be hard to pick. If he took a crowbar to it …

For a moment he imagined that he might have willed his thoughts into reality when something cold and hard pressed against the back of his neck. It was steel, no doubt about it, a knife or perhaps the crowbar he'd been dreaming about.

'What are you doing?' It was a voice filled with indignation.

He turned to face the threat, experiencing pressure on his bladder that had suddenly filled up and threatened to overflow. The man behind him shoved him head first onto the bed. He took in the smell of the blanket. Facing the clothes rack, Mvumbi saw what he had missed all along. Hidden behind an array of greatcoats on hangers were rifles whose wooden stocks were visible below the hemlines. I'm going to die here.

'What do you think we should do, Komandir?' asked someone behind him, telling Mvumbi that there was more than one person in the room. 'Shoot him? Please give me the order to shoot this nosey little shit.'

'Stand him up against the wall,' said a voice he recognised as Pomegranate's.

Yanked up by the fabric of his sweatshirt, Mvumbi looked into the muzzle of a pistol in Pomegranate's fist. He'd seen guns before and was quite familiar with their destructive power. He'd also seen that it took less than a wink of an eye to reduce a man from something live and vibrant to a corpse. And suddenly he wanted to live. He looked from Pomegranate to Stinkwood with pleading eyes.

'Please don't shoot me,' he said, blubbing.

'What were you doing?' Stinkwood asked. 'Going through our things. For what?'

'Answer truthfully, kid,' Pomegranate said, the gun unwavering. 'This man only has to give the word and you're dead.'

'To sell and buy stuff,' Mvumbi said.

'Speak up,' Stinkwood said. 'What?'

'To sell your things and buy stuff to smoke.'

'Who gives you the stuff?' Pomegranate asked. 'To smoke.'

'Spider.'

'You give Spider our things and in turn he provides you with stuff?'

'Yes, sir.'

Pomegranate tried to keep a straight face although it was quite clear he wanted to crack up at being called 'sir'. 'Where's this Spider?'

'He hangs out at the shopping centre,' Mvumbi said. 'With a couple of other guys.'

'Are they armed?' Stinkwood asked. 'Does he pack a gun?'

'I think so.'

They were armed, four tough youngsters used to sauntering around the small shopping centre, their uniforms consisting of T-shirts, windbreakers, Converse or Pro-Ked sneakers, denim jeans or corduroys slung low so that the underwear peeped above the belt. This was a style called *langgat* or long arse, the highest form of cool, which complemented the rolling swagger as the quartet established its presence in the area. Fans and hangers-on were always at hand to egg Spider's gang on in its exploits. This might be the administering of a beating to some poor country yokel who crossed their path or the groping of a schoolgirl who happened to be in their orbit. Physically they were not much, just scrawny, pimply specimens who bore such a close resemblance to one another they might have been two sets of identical twins. This puniness was deceptive for beneath it lay a deadly expertise in knives that was recognised in other townships. Latterly, Spider's gang had come into some guns, which were stuck into the waistband and could be shown, fleetingly, to intimidate the enemy. Some of the cops who patrolled the area were aware of Spider and his cronies; they had received countless complaints. They turned a blind eye because Spider doubled up as a trusted informer. He was also a profit centre. The cops took a cut in the sale of drugs. Those in the know had long stopped reporting Spider to the police.

Frogmarching Mvumbi to the shopping centre on this pre-Christmas Saturday afternoon, Pomegranate and Stinkwood were regaled by Mvumbi with stories of Spider's escapades. On Sundays, some congregations would say a special prayer in which they beseeched the Almighty to refrain from wasting His valuable time trying to save Spider's soul. He should simply take it and consign the little bastard to Hell.

There was a light drizzle and a number of shoppers were huddling under awnings and unfurled umbrellas. Others ranged themselves along the veranda, watching the feared foursome strut towards Mvumbi, Pomegranate and Stinkwood, who came up from the parking lot, walking resolutely, the guerrillas' faces and heads partly covered by hoods attached to their dark sweatshirts. Spider had seconds earlier got off from his perch on the low wall and beckoned his henchmen to follow him. They complied, matching his heel-to-toe rolling gait while one shoulder hung lower than the other like the gunslingers weighed down by their holstered artillery in cowboy movies.

There were many versions of what happened next. Some testified that it was Spider who slapped Mvumbi across the face, calling him a 'fokken spy', and that an emboldened Mvumbi in turn punched one of Spider's men. Others swore that Spider's striking hand was blocked before it could find a target. There was consensus, though, that Spider called Mvumbi by a bad name. And then there was a flurry of hands and, when the dust cleared, a disarmed Spider and his men were lying face down on the concrete floor with their pants off and trussed up with their own belts like Christmas turkeys. The crowd of Christmas shoppers cheered and pointed at Spider's polka-dot shorts and a T-shirt bearing the likeness of a grinning Goofy. The guerrillas disappeared as soon as their work was done. As evening fell, Spider's gang was set free by a nightwatchman. Humiliated, the young men slunk off into the dark.

The men at Ngobese's house knew this was an unwinnable war. Spider and his men would come back, possibly in an infinitely deadlier guise. The drugs would continue flowing, money exchanging hands, and cops turning a blind eye.

Even though there'd been no loss of blood, and the men took great care to protect their identities, Django felt that the whole episode should have been avoided. 'We have sent word out there,' he said during supper, 'that Ngobese's son knows people who have combat skills.'

'Doesn't that protect us, though?' Pomegranate argued. 'The fact that we can fight will mean no one will want to tangle with us?'

'When a dog bites you,' Django said, 'oftentimes it's because it thinks you're about to attack it. People under threat can be dangerous.'

'But we've not threatened anyone,' Stinkwood said, rallying behind his fellow combatant. 'We just had to show a bunch of thugs that they can't force drugs on people.'

'Okay,' Pomegranate said, a hard glint in his eye. 'For me, this whole thing was personal.'

'How so?' Django asked.

'It's wrong, I know,' Pomegranate said, 'but I had a younger sister, my sister, who got messed up by drugs. At that time, we didn't know until it was too late, believing that she'd been bewitched.'

'What happened? To her?'

'She's got a nice little plot, unmarked, at the Avalon Cemetery,' Pomegranate said. 'So,' he went on, 'of course, we fucked up with Spider and them, but were it by me, we should have killed that bastard.'

'We got them running scared,' Stinkwood said, recalling the afternoon's events. 'They won't harass people again.'

'Well, what's done is done,' Django said. 'And if scaring off some elements of the lumpen is one of our greatest achievements, then we're in big trouble.'

'Django is right,' Ngobese said. He'd been listening in with one ear to the debate. He felt somewhat to blame because of his boy, Mvumbi. 'My responsibility as it is, is to make sure you're not compromised.'

'We are compromised, Ngobese,' Django said. 'There's Mchinda out there in the Zulu hostels doing indlamu. Then Pomegranate and Stinkwood have to act like Rambo at the shopping centre. What next? Perhaps we need T-shirts printed with the sign: the guerrillas have arrived.'

'I'll find us a new place tomorrow,' Ngobese said, somewhat upset that his son's addiction had led to the need for such drastic steps. But since it was human to shift the blame or, more pertinently, to ensure that everyone was culpable, he faulted the guerrillas for having been lax in applying the laws of security. Not all of them, of course. Django had been unwavering in his adherence to the principles of MCW, military-combat work. Even though he was a civilian, Ngobese could intuit that breaking cover could constitute the guerrillas' first – and some would say fatal – breach of the code of conduct for clandestine activity. In truth, no matter how beholden the men might have been to him, going out to the shopping centre was tactless. There were other methods, which could have been used to deal with Spider and his gang. No wonder Django was angry.

Much as he tried to convince himself otherwise, Spider couldn't discard the cloak of humiliation that covered him, from the top of his head down to the shoulders. This is not me, he told himself. This is not the Spider who became famous when he faced Gindy the bully who was the terror of F Section, and stabbed him once with an Okapi. That was the time when knives were in vogue, and Spider was only fourteen, already a boy with a reputation. From then on, he knew he'd survive on his wits and street reputation. This made a few people nervous; now and then someone – one of his relatives – suggested that he find a job, if he wasn't going to be at school. No way. School was a road to nowhere and he wouldn't be seen dead holding down a job where he'd be required to wear a uniform with his name stencilled on the left breast pocket. No sir. That was for mugs and Spider wasn't a mug, despite the treatment he'd received in the hands of those fellows. Boy, he was madder than a scorpion. That Mvumbi was going to get his dues. Even if it took him years, Spider was going to get even.

The slight drizzle reminded Spider that it was December; the year was ending. His mind going back to Mvumbi and the men at Ngobese's place, he chuckled inwardly. December was a month traditionally earmarked for settling scores. In the whole of Natal, it was known that the best time to get back at someone who'd wronged you was in the Christmas period.

The street was bustling with Christmas shoppers as well as taxis and hawkers of anything under the sun. Touts shouted above the blaring hooters, advertising cut-price goods to attract the last of the buyers before everything shut down. At 7:00 p.m., under the bright cluster lights that created sharpened shadows, the taxis were doing a brisk trade as they picked up or dropped off passengers, mainly shoppers clutching plastic carrier bags that were stamped with the labels of famous shops. No economist, but familiar with the flow of money in the township, Spider was aware that most of the buyers couldn't afford what they brought home, stuff that would be outdated before the first light of dawn of the New Year.

A yellow shaft of light from a passing car shifted some of the sculpted shadows under a street lamp, some eighty metres from where Spider stood, behind the gate of his uncle's house in F Section. Given form, if momentarily, two of the shadows turned out to be Tikka Joe and someone new in the township, a lanky, clean-shaven fellow whose physique and watchful features marked him for a serious customer. Spider had jumped on people before, all sorts – this wasn't the type to be jumped on. So, he thought as he concentrated his gaze on the newcomer, that's Tikka Joe's meal ticket.

If Tikka Joe had been a woman, Spider would have said that the relationship between the two was sexual. From the body language of the two figures, however, it was clear that something more than hanky panky was at play. For one, this wasn't a favourite spot for *izinkonkoni*, men who preyed on boys and, two, Tikka Joe wasn't associated with that kind of trade. He was a scrounger, a pickpocket and a weed head. His mind racing forward, skipping useless data, Spider decided that this must be about politics. Everyone in KwaMashu knew that something was brewing underground, in *the underground*. Cops were all over the place. Sometimes at night there'd be people trying to conduct stop-and-search procedures, see if you're carrying some pamphlets, which was why he carried a gun. See if someone's going to try and take that away. Okay, it's happened already, with Mvumbi's father's cronies – they must be guerrillas; no one could pull a move like that unless he'd got training from Ruskies. And everyone knew that Russians were from outer space; if you needed confirmation, just tune in to the 6:00 p.m. news on TV1. Even though he knew in his heart of hearts that he was indulging in self-deception, Spider derived momentary comfort from the notion that he had been disarmed, turned upside down and trussed up like a Rainbow Chicken by a force that had come from elsewhere. That aliens had administered the humiliation was somewhat bearable.

He caught sight of Tikka Joe laughing, head thrown back like a big person; boy must be eating well to laugh like that. Something inside Spider found this hilarity at odds with his own sense of self. Without putting his mind to it, while pulling up the collar of his jacket and zipping it up to the neck, he opened the gate of his uncle's house and stepped out onto the road. He waited for a few cars and taxis to pass before there was a break in the flow of traffic. The tyres were already splashing out the puddles trapped in potholes, creating night-time rainbows. By the time he had crossed to the other side, the tall man had left. No bother, he thought. The person he actually wanted to speak to was still at the street corner, now lighting a stompie, cupping his fingers around the flame against the rising wind.

'Tikka Joe,' Spider said. 'How's it hanging, *mfan'omdala*?'

Used to being harassed by Spider and his gang, Tikka Joe's first reaction was to step back and get ready to flee. Then, reassured by Spider's loose and easy demeanour, he relaxed somewhat. 'Heita, Spiderman,' he said. Then he smiled, his brain processing the day's data from the township grapevine – Spider getting mashed up and being shown he was fuck-all. The grin had to be calibrated correctly so as not to give offence; Spider was still Spider.

'We're still here,' he said. 'Waiting for Father Christmas.'

'I thought he lived in your backyard,' Spider said, rubbing a tender spot on his forehead. 'Heard you've come into some jam.'

'Awu, Spiderman, how can you say that?' Tikka Joe protested. 'We're still vying for the crumbs that drop from big tables.'

'Someone tells me you're setting your own table nowadays, Tikka Joe, my boy,' Spider said, his tone freighted with distant menace. 'Just don't forget who really owns these streets.'

'People talk, you know how it is …'

Spider produced a packet of Mills and made a big show of extracting a cigarette out of the yellow box. Noting Tikka Joe's admiring eyes, he could tell from the acrid fumes that the younger man must be smoking some inferior brand, most likely Lexington filter toasted. Tikka Joe flicked the burning stub into a puddle and heard it hiss. The two young men, boys really, lit up together and surveyed the traffic in silence. Unable to contain his curiosity any longer, Spider gave Tikka Joe a sidelong glance.

'Who's Tall Man, *mfan'omdala*?' he asked.

'Tall Man?'

'Tall Man.'

'Oh. That tall man,' Tikka Joe said, deciding it was dangerous to jerk Spider around. 'I don't think he's got anything to do with it.'

'With what?'

'With what happened to you and S'gindayi and Ndosi at the shopping centre …'

'How do you know that?'

'Because Bra Gab ...'

'That's the name of Tall Man? Bra Gab?'

'Ya, but he doesn't want me blabbing his mission ...'

'Oh,' Spider said, 'so he's on a mission,' and imitated the oompah-pah of a dramatic credits sequence of an action film. '*OSS 117 Mission for a Killer*, did you see that movie?' Without waiting for an answer, he asked: 'So, what's his mission?'

'I don't know if he's a cop or something, but he's collecting information on the group.'

'The group at Mvumbi's dad?'

'Yes. I saw them arrive.'

'Does he give you *inyuku*?' Spider saw puzzlement written on Tikka Joe's face. '*Inyuku*. Shekels. Moola. Don't you know the language of nabobs?'

'Nabobs?'

'Never mind,' Spider said, changing tack. 'Who's he working with ... Bra Gab?'

'There are six other people holed up in H Section. I take food for them. They don't come out during the day.'

'Who prepares the food?' This was better than hustling. People in hiding would shell out some shekels for that kind of safety.

'His girlfriend.' He told Spider where the girlfriend lived. Spider was familiar with all the shebeens in the neighbourhood.

'You're a good boy, Tikka Joe.'

'You sure you won't be doing nothing, Spiderman?' Tikka Joe appealed, suddenly very worried. By 'nothing' he meant anything rash.

'What do you take me for, Tikka Joe?' Spider asked, spreading his arms to demonstrate agreeableness. 'I just think that Bra Gab, as a visitor here, needs to help the community.' Which was his way of saying that he hoped to use others to regain his title as a prince of the streets. It would also help his plan to see to it that his enemies got their comeuppance.

At 8:30 a.m. on Christmas Eve, Ngobese was seated with Muzi Thabethe in the last of the tearooms on Grey Street. They watched the bustle of shoppers and labourers through the window. Every shopping bag, even for groceries, carried some reminder of Christmas. Across a traffic island, sounding far off, a man in yellow overalls was busy demolishing a section of the road with a pneumatic drill.

'It was stupid.'

Muzi Thabethe would not let Ngobese off the hook. 'Imagine the scandal if the enemy got to hear of this. They would say we have brought in reinforcements from the People's Army.'

Some minutes before the meeting, Ngobese had stood on the pavement, watching the already-seated Thabethe through the window. Tapping an impatient tattoo on the Formica-topped table, Thabethe exuded confidence, politely waving off a waitress hovering around, indicating he was waiting for someone to join him. Ngobese inwardly cursed his luck to be involved in a mission with Laura's husband. Worse, the man was an ex-prisoner, someone with a heightened sense of self-preservation. More daunting than Thabethe's appearance – small, compact, giving the impression of an energised bantam, a big dome with burr-like black hair flecked with grey, and wide-awake eyes that seemed to pierce anything they rested on – was that, though short, perhaps five-seven, he gave off an effect of bigness. Clean-cut though casual in a navy-blue blazer, a light-blue shirt, khaki chinos and brown moccasins, he could have been a consultant meeting a client. Finally seated across from Thabethe nearer to the exit, Ngobese was reminded of his primary schooldays in Babanango where a schoolyard bully was humiliated by a boy almost half his size. One day he'd ask Thabethe where he'd done his earlier schooling. But first, he had to dispose of the matter at hand.

'They weren't armed when they dealt with the thugs,' Ngobese explained. 'And it was their own idea. I didn't consent to it.' He wanted to question the logic of reinforcements. Even the regime's propaganda could not downplay the inroads made by the forces of the Movement, so why would they call for extra muscle? But he was conflicted with Thabethe. He was his political senior. If he ever got the tiniest inkling that Ngobese was betraying him with his wife, there'd be hell to pay.

'We mustn't let our personal affairs blind us to our task,' Thabethe said, looking Ngobese in the eye. 'Your breakfast is getting cold.'

Ngobese gazed down at his Builder's Breakfast: two eggs and rashers of bacon, a steak, sausages, chips and fried tomatoes – and a small hill of beans. What was I thinking? He was not one to heed the warnings of doomsayers from white clinics who advocated healthy eating, but this was extreme by anyone's standards. Cutting up a piece of bacon, impaling it on a potato chip and taking a bite, he immediately envisioned himself having a heart attack while with Laura. He closed his eyes.

'Are you all right?' Thabethe asked.

'I'm okay,' Ngobese said. 'Possibly coming down with something.'

'I'm led to understand that there's another group of men in KwaMashu,' Thabethe said. 'They could be the ones who killed those men who are survived by your guests.'

'If that is the case,' Ngobese said, 'what is the status of my men?'

'Your men?'

'Our men. The guerrillas in the house.'

'It's not them personally that we're concerned about,' Muzi Thabethe said. 'It's the information contained in the trunk.' He paused, thinking. 'Even in jail we knew – we were told, although in whispers – that the Movement, even the senior structure, had been compromised. The word was that there was a big mamba eating the eggs.'

'Eggs?' Ngobese looked at the two fried eggs on his plate, the unbroken yolks staring back at him.

'The information about the Movement's activities is obviously very valuable to someone,' Muzi Thabethe said. 'When people say someone is selling out they also mean it literally. That person is trading information for money. Pieces of silver.'

'The information in the trunk will tell us who's selling out?'

'It will give us the map. Most of the time these reports are in code and we'll probably need someone to help us clarify things.' Muzi Thabethe rubbed the corners of his eyes and yawned, stretching. 'Chaplain Nerissa is in Johannesburg, but she's been instructed to come down to the coast.'

'She'll help analyse the material?'

'She's one of the best,' Muzi Thabethe said, trying to suppress a stubborn yawn, his eyes watering at the end.

'A rough night, also?' Ngobese asked, smiling.

'You should get married and understand what they mean when they say, *no rest for the wicked*.'

I'd like to have that problem, Ngobese thought, warding off an image that tried to creep into his head. 'The other group,' he asked. 'You think they also have possession of a boxful of information?'

'It's tempting to think that they might have information that could complement what we know. To fill in the gaps.'

'What do *we* know?'

'Who knows?' Thabethe asked. Signalling the waiter over, he drew an air signature. A young woman who was possibly still a student brought the bill and smiled at the tip. His business done, Thabethe got to his feet.

'I'd say bring the men over to my place, but that place is being watched, I'm sure of it. In fact Nerissa will most likely come here to get a report on the situation. She'll have to be given the box. Then the men will be free agents. In the meantime, someone will have to find a place for them. Why don't you try Sonto? She lives alone with her aunt and a niece.'

'Doesn't her relative, Aunt Maisie, run a shebeen?' Ngobese asked. 'Isn't that a little bit too crowded?'

'Those who know,' Muzi Thabethe put in, 'say that the best place to hide is in plain sight. So a crowded place is good. And proximity to shebeens is great for collecting information. It's like when you're screwing someone's wife. It's always advisable to stay close to the husband.'

Ngobese smiled, shrugging, his body language trying hard to say, *I wouldn't know anything about that.* Then he asked: 'What about Bra Zeph? Can you talk to him?'

'I'm a little nervous about Zeph,' Muzi Thabethe said. 'I hear he's surrounded himself with youngsters armed with guns.'

'I didn't know that.'

'It's an explosive cocktail,' Muzi Thabethe went on, 'because he's back on the bottle after a long lay-off. He doesn't know that we know. Booze and unstable political gangsters might be problematic.'

'Shouldn't you have a word with him?'

'I should do that,' Muzi Thabethe said. 'But Bra Zeph has never really accepted that he's not the leader of the Committee here. It rankles that someone younger, me, has to give the orders.' He paused, thinking. 'Laura gets along well with him. Why don't the two of you make time and see if Bra Zeph would accommodate the men? Or even suggest where they could find a temporary hidey-hole while we look for more stable lodgings.'

'Won't you ask her to get in touch then?' Unable to call Laura's name in Thabethe's presence, Ngobese struggled to maintain eye contact.

'Will do,' Muzi Thabethe said. 'I just hope that Bra Zeph will be sober and that the men won't have to end up shacking up with some trigger-happy militant from the self-defence unit.'

He opened a briefcase, which had all along occupied an empty chair by his side, and took out a brown envelope bulging with cash.

'That should cover the expenses,' Muzi Thabethe said, sliding the envelope across the table. 'And give the men a little Christmas box. God knows they deserve it.'

'And so do you,' Ngobese said. But Muzi Thabethe had left.

LOG #1

When she reflects back on it, it's all too late. It's as if it all never happened and she is left with memories, snatches of remembered dialogue, colour, and feeling – especially feeling. Even with the most urgent probing, an interrogation that approximates a session before a panel of torturers, all she can come up with is a series of incidents, all connected to her flesh. She remembers things in terms of her body's recollection of texture, pressure, smell and colour – and, of course, taste. These senses operated independently of her conscious understanding of things. There were times of pain, sometimes pleasure; she was back in those days – in that past in which she had no volition – like the woman she had read about who could only start understanding that she had been violated in a shack somewhere near the sea when she heard the call of seagulls.

Why her?

She doesn't know. On the one hand she feels overwhelmed by the whole experience; on the other hand she is like someone who has walked blindfolded and has only now been able to open the eyes. But, strangely enough, the blindness made her all the more appreciative of pleasure. She remembers a moment, a node, a piece of music composed by the flesh.

And him?

He was like a musician with a favourite instrument, which he had mastered: her body. He was like a masseuse, familiar with every contour, every fold. Now and then, discovering a point he hadn't known, hearing her gasp in appreciation or pain or both, he would chuckle with triumph.

What made her so special, to be targeted by him?

She doesn't know. His comment was that he saw her on the street and had already heard she had ambitions to become a revolutionary. Her beauty must have captivated him; she knew she was beautiful, people had told her so. She had seen the way Johannes Sibisi, Bra Zeph – even Muzi Thabethe, although he might not have been aware he was looking at her – looked at her, and she knew she had some power – or could have some power – over men.

Was she the only one?

There could have been more. He used women. He used men. How did he justify that? He simply said, we are at war. We have to do this, to men, to women. Some come voluntarily, others are unwilling. At the end of the day, all of us, the captors and the captive, are locked up in a huge cage and we have to find a way to get out. As she says this, she remembers feeling him exploring her depths, probing at the base of her stomach where the womb ends and life begins.

Did he ever say anything about his father?

He maintained that his father was respected. His words were, even though he was now a pale imitation of what he used to be, people still held him in high esteem.

And Strella? Did he talk of his connection with Strella?

No, he never just came out and said anything about the people he was working with. But she could remember him saying something about someone who could have been his twin brother. A star in the making.

A star in the making … did he say that?

Something to that effect. She now clams up, not so much out of bloody-mindedness as from a residual sense of shame. Because that afternoon, he was inside her when there was a change in tempo.

You're thinking about other things again, she said to him, aware that he had slowed down. Somewhere, hidden in the folds of her mind was the suspicion that if he started thinking, he might become even crueller. She needed him unthinking, an automaton, a hardened body whose sole purpose – at least for that moment – was to provide pleasure.

Yes, he said.

What's it about? She asked, hoping to engage him in small talk until he could get his mojo back. Her whole time with him was a contradiction; she wanted him strong but not so strong that he would hurt her.

He said: my father.

She wanted to say: imagine him inside me, but that kind of crack would have earned her five against the mouth. I'd like to meet him one day. I've heard so much about him.

Then, his mojo back, he started again. Climbing one more hill, with vigour this time, until she moaned.

When did this happen? Was it at the beginning of the relationship … affair, whatever?

The beginning was the end for me, she says.

Okay. That's all for now.

3

STRELLA'S GHOST

The convoy pulled out of the compound in Mochudi. It was late afternoon on 17 November 1989, and Strella's whole body delighted in the gentle breeze rustling the leaves of the marula tree. Turning to the business at hand, of keeping watch from the vantage point of the knoll, he occasionally brought up his rifle to take a bead on someone walking blithely on. While assorted assassins he'd come to know boasted a preference for machine pistols, Strella found solace in his baby, the Dragunov SVD sniper's rifle, fitted with a set of sights that could pick out a solitary dung beetle rolling a turd five hundred metres away. Not that he ever bothered with insects or animals, except for the two-legged species that had always been the source of problems. Moreover there was no drama about the death of a beast, an antelope or even kudu. They just folded up and expired with docile eyes. Human quarry was different. He remembered the range of expressions on a target's face – or, sometimes, what would be left of it – at the exact moment of impact, when the high velocity, metal jacketed slug slapped the flesh, *pah!* In an instant, the eyes would register the five stages of grief, namely, denial, anger, bargaining, depression, and acceptance.

The long-distance violence, while thrilling in its endorsement of his marksmanship, couldn't match the excitement of close combat, no, correction, intimate killing: pushing the serrated blade into the ribcage, thrusting in that last, pulsating inch, the thrill coursing like an electrical charge down his spine as he would watch life flapping about and then finally ebbing out with a sigh. There was nothing to beat the smell of fresh blood.

The lust for blood originated seventeen years ago in Gaborone, Botswana, in 1972 to be exact. Strella had a visual, almost palpable memory of crossing the Pitsane Molopo in September; being picked up on the other side. There followed an unsettling ride to Gaborone and then a brief sojourn at the Gaborone Hotel before being assigned to the house for refugees in Extension 14. It was all there in his head: the forced camaraderie in communal accommodations, the political lessons – Karl Marx, Lenin, Mao's *Little Red Book*, Engels – the confusion in *Anti-Dühring.*

He remembered a rambling section that still came to him, like a catchy tune or an irritating jingle. *Sublime nonsense in poetry, in philosophy, in politics, in economics, in historiography, sublime nonsense in the lecture-room and on the platform, sublime nonsense everywhere* … what the hell!

On one of the evenings, a Friday early in September 1972, he was alone in the backroom of the palatial home of an academic from the University of Botswana, Lesotho and Swaziland. It all started with the guy's wife, a prim and proper classy bitch with balloon boobs, whom he fucked senseless in the guy's absence. She liked it rough. But, on this evening, she said something smart-alecky, which he didn't understand.

She was acting weird, following him from room to room, like sales assistants for whom every black person entering their shop symbolised diminishing profits. It must have been the time of the month or she was just too tired from making all that money and probably found him boring or something. He toyed with the idea of smacking her on the mouth but that could get him PI'd, and he had seen what happened when people were declared prohibited immigrants. Some were buried in unmarked graves along the stretch between the Tlokweng border gate and Zeerust.

Shrugging, glad he'd acted wisely, Strella set out walking along Julius Nyerere Drive past the Holiday Inn where the over-rouged and loudly dressed client-catchers milled about the entrance like fucking flamingos, waiting to be picked up by expatriates who rocked up in UN agency-issue Land Cruisers or Range Rovers. He walked past Maru-a-Pula, the high school for the privileged of the land. There was a story about how one Grade 12 student, asked to write an essay about her future aspiration, said she wished to become a South African refugee. When asked to explain, she said: 'South African refugees spend the whole day drinking beer and talking English at the Gaborone Hotel, and, at the end of the month they get thirty pula.'

At the gates of UBLS, he debated with himself about going in to check on some of the Swazi students, get a beer, perhaps, but then, it being September, they'd be probably swotting, learning to be scientists and engineers and lecturers who'd recycle their certificated ignorance and then produce clones that would turn out other monstrosities in the next cycle. He also had an impression that something about him made these students uneasy. The women loved him, but he'd come to think that they, too, didn't see a future with him. One of them, in a moment of beer-induced candour, even told him that, glamorous as the South African refugees might be, they were regarded as dead men walking. It was known in Botswana that the South African security was keeping tabs on them. One day, they'd act – and the Swazis didn't relish being caught in that particular crossfire. Fuck it. He resumed his trek to nowhere in particular.

The old cobbler selling cigarettes, shoelaces, bits and bobs ran his booth a little off the main road to The Village. Scattered all around were signs of despairing commercial activity. Ripening marula trees dwarfed empty lean-tos. Most of the shabby cubicles were now shuttered and locked away for the night. The old man in his booth covered with posters and banners advertising soft drinks and ice-lollies had been here for such a long time that he'd become a feature of the landscape. Head down, working at the leather with the light of a paraffin lamp, he seemed in no hurry to get anywhere. The flame from the lamp simultaneously cast a shadow across the wall behind and flickered as if in rhythm to the thump of the hammer. Perhaps, sensing a presence nearby, the old man raised his head and gazed at Strella. His eyes were tired and full of depthless longing. Strella wondered when last he'd had a restful sleep.

'Can I help you?' he asked.

'I'd like a match,' Strella said. 'To light a cigarette.'

'Do you have cigarettes?'

'No,' Strella admitted. 'Could I have two loose ones? Peter Stuyvesant.'

'I don't stock Stuyvesant, loose or in packets.'

'Cavalla Kings?'

'Sonny,' the old man said, 'where do you come from? No one smokes Cavalla Kings any more.'

'Okay. What have you got?' He had a few pulas courtesy of the academic's wife, for services that may or may not have been rendered. 'Anything.'

'Do you smoke?' The old man's hand tightened on the hammer.

'No,' Strella said. Although a counter separated them, Strella could smell the cobbler's sour breath. 'But there's no rule that says I can't try it.'

'Why? What do you know about rules?'

'I know it's a free country and I have the money,' Strella said heatedly.

'That means you must serve me.'

'You from South Africa, aren't you, sonny?' the old man asked. 'One of the fence-jumpers?'

For the first time that day Strella laughed. This was not the first time he'd heard the locals referring to refugees as 'fence-jumpers'. The portrayal always brought to mind lithe, long-limbed duikers springing over a border fence. 'E, Rra,' he said. 'I come from South Africa.'

'And how long do you think you'll stay here?'

'I don't know,' Strella said. 'For as long as it takes to change the situation back home.'

'And you know it won't change by itself,' the cobbler said, going back to his hammering. 'Some of you are selling stolen cars here, others drink and cavort with client-catchers and forget the reason why they left home the first time.' He steadied his gaze as if checking if Strella fitted any of the categories.

'Believe you me, I'll never do that,' Strella said.

'Don't be cheeky,' the man said. 'And with what are you going to fight? Throw stones?'

'I'll probably throw something a little more explosive than a rock,' Strella said under his breath. He was not joking, possibly expressing his hope that the plan of the Organisation of Black Warriors for military training in Libya would come to fruition. Already, everyone in the small cell in the house in Bontleng had a copy of Muammar Gaddafi's *Green Book*. They were all a little skittish as it was rumoured that Libyan instructors didn't use dummy ammunition for training.

Cars hooted as they trundled along the road. A dark-grey cloud of smoke that hovered above the suburbs indicated the preparation of the evening meals. In the dark distance, the cling-clang of cowbells marked the progress of someone herding sleepy cattle to a kraal.

Snorting at Strella's mumbled reply, the old man started packing up his shop. He piled broken shoes into a cardboard box and stowed it in the corner. Then he blew out the flame, plunging the area into moonlit darkness. He used a hooked stick to pull down the flap door, which he then secured with a padlock. He handed Strella one of the two carrier bags. 'Help me with these.' He shoved a drawstring pouch, which possibly contained the day's takings, into an inside jacket pocket. He buttoned up his double-breasted jacket. Strella noticed an irony in the man's physical appearance; he was a shoemaker/vendor, but his left shoe, housing a malformed foot, was fitted with extra layers of leather for balance. Still, he had the jiggling gait of a sailor unsure of the evenness of the deck. He also walked with the aid of a stick.

Together they hiked into The Village, which was quieter than the industrial zone of Extension 4, past the home of an exiled leader of the Movement. The old man, whose name was Mabitla – *Mister* Mabitla to you, sonny – observed that Joe Matthews – Joe Matewus – was one of the smartest men he'd ever known. After years of serious book learning overseas, he was now working in the office of President Seretse Khama. 'And our Tau Tona – the Big Lion as we call our president – can't abide foolish people,' Mabitla said. 'Rre Joe Matewus is very different from most of you young South Africans.'

'How different, Mr Mabitla?'

'He didn't come here carrying a begging bowl,' Mr Mabitla said very quickly as if the idea had always been at the front of his mind. 'He wasn't busy causing a ruckus in the taverns or sniffing after *nyoana* like some of you young hounds.'

From that point until they reached the old man's place – a backroom behind a cheery house where ivy and tickey creepers competed to cover the walls, no different from the academic's house he had fled a few hours ago – Strella decided to keep his silence. Parked on the paved driveway three sedans and four-wheel drives complemented the sound of merriment; in the lounge, sprawled on the sofas, the black hosts and their white guests could be seen through the open windows, glasses in hand. Outside, the safety light came alive, momentarily transfixing both men to the driveway before they made their way to the back. Strella had intended merely to unload Mabitla's bag and make his way back to Extension 4, but curiosity pulled him along.

The air was filled with the smell of growing things, the modest garden behind the house sporting subsistence crops: mielies, spinach, a few pendulous tomatoes and cabbage. Even in the half-light, all the signs were there of a meagre harvest because – even though a city boy – Strella noticed that blight and other forms of pestilence had ravaged the plants. The old man, Mr Mabitla, had no chance.

The condition of the room, the squalor that would defeat any attempts at betterment, cemented this thought. Having deposited his parcels on the narrow iron cot, Mabitla fired a Primus stove and started cooking, his enterprise miraculously producing a passably edible fare of mielie-pap, morogo and chicken wings. Later, drinking tea from an iron mug, he indulged the young man sitting across from him with a face full of questions. 'You heard me, Mr Mabitla,' Strella said, emboldened by the cosiness. 'Where are your kids?'

'Old people,' Mabitla said, wiping his lips with the back of his hand, 'are alive to the fact that their age-mates are popping off every day. The children have gone, looking for a place where there's no anxiety about old age or death. And, do you know what is every – and I mean every – old person's game? It's to pretend that the deaths that happen around him or her don't mean shit. We carry coffins of people five, ten years younger than us but still tell ourselves that they are victims of bad luck. Their number has come up. The patience of ancestors has dried up. Ours is the sin of refusing to acknowledge the evidence of our own eyes. We harbour a death wish.'

'But why?' Strella asked, not really grasping what the old man was saying. He noticed the long-bladed knife, with a black handle, which the old man used to chop the onions for the evening's meal. He'd have to clean the grease off the handle.

'Because,' Mr Mabitla said, his gaze also drawn to the blade, but perhaps staring at something beyond the confines of the room, 'because that's perhaps the way certain things were meant to be.'

After a while, a silence punctuated by the smacking of lips after taking a sip of tea, Mabitla said, 'Come with me. Look out there. What do you see?'

The rear windows of the backroom opened into another backyard, but beyond that was a stretch of a sandy field. 'If you cast your eyes further up,' Mabitla said, pointing with the walking stick, 'there's a graveyard, gravestones that speak to either the richness of the surviving members of the family or the poverty of those who will mount cheap memorials of stone. I know them all. There's the Christian section and the Jewish section. Both are separated by a shared confusion over the real meaning of God. MacArthur, John, born in 1906 somewhere in Scotland … Govan; on the other side, from a gravestone fashioned to resemble a menorah is Markowitz, Julius, born 1907 in Vilnius, Lithuania.'

'How do you know so much?' Strella asked, irritated at the same time that this knowledge, supported by facts and figures, didn't translate into something that the old man could sell. It was empty knowledge like the symbols learnt by Swazi students, which they would take home to confuse the more ignorant of their compatriots.

'Your time will come,' Mabitla said, 'when you'll also stagger under the weight of knowing too many unwholesome things.'

As they got ready to retire, Mabitla decorously placed his jacket along the wall, like someone forced to share a bed with a child and fearing that he might roll and suffocate it. Strella was assigned to the floor, his mattress a bundle of grey UNHCR-issue blankets. Wondering whether the other comrades were aware of his absence, he determined to hike home first thing in the morning. But then, there was the unspoken code among the refugees that, if you struck gold, you must ensure that the rest of the collective also had a sumptuous meal. He remembered the communal fridge back at the residence. It squatted in the middle of the room on the grey-blue tiles. It belched, rumbled and then gave a long squelching sound evocative of a shebeen queen sucking in her teeth.

The noise of the fridge's inner workings rose in direct proportion to the emptiness of its shelves. A hero was a refugee who contributed to the silencing of the fridge, when he or she brought into the kitty something of value. Now and then he'd contributed some of the money from his Sugar Mama, the academic's wife, but it had been nothing really, just change for bubble gum and crisps. Remembering Mabitla's drawstring pouch he suddenly recalled that the landed of the Batswana who plied their trade in Gaborone actually hoarded hundreds if not thousands of pula to repatriate to some *moraka*, a cattle post out in the sticks. And, this evening, Strella wanted to return to his commune and be regarded as a hero, a supplier, and a comprehensive silencer of the fridge.

The noise from the party in the main house filtered into the back-room in waves. It was difficult to catch the drift of the conversation except that it was animated, fuelled, Strella was sure, by booze. He suddenly felt a great emptiness, hollowness in that part of his chest, which, he supposed, was the resting place for his soul. He listened to Mabitla nattering on, cursing his landlord and his bitch wife and how it served them right that they couldn't have babies. God's punishment, Mabitla said in the manner of someone who conducted regular conversations with the Almighty.

'The drought of the Kgalagadi,' he said, 'hasn't got shit on that strumpet.'

Strella imagined he could hear the bitch in question laughing, a trilling, staccato sound that approximated the tinkle of ice cubes into a tall glass. Mabitla's rant segued into a ragged snore and in a few minutes the snores were of a man who wouldn't wake up if you dragged him across the floor and dumped him in the cemetery where MacArthur and Markowitz were enjoying a well-earned rest.

At least that was what Strella supposed. When sure that Mabitla, whose face was skewered by a shaft of light streaming in from outside, must be fast asleep, Strella got up, straining as he felt his bones creaking. Slowly, he cast off the thin blanket and, without putting his mind to it, folded it carefully and placed it on the makeshift pillow on the floor. On all fours now, he advanced to the chair where Mabitla had hung his clothes. Working with quiet urgency, he dipped his fingers into the inside jacket pocket where, he was sure, he saw Mabitla shoving the pouch. His fingertips felt something; an object with a sharp edge and a needle pricked the quick. Cursing, he drew back his hand, his fingers afire as if they had been caught in a toothed trap.

In that instant, Strella realised that Mabitla's inside jacket pocket was lined with surgical blades mounted on a block of wood the size and texture of a single piece of parquet flooring. What kind of person goes to such lengths to thwart pickpockets? What if a grandchild innocently reached into ntatemogolo's pockets looking for a sweet?

As if answering the unasked question, a sniggering Mabitla, who could not have been asleep after all, sprang up from the bed. Effortlessly, he struck Strella across the temple with his walking stick, sending him tottering back in the confined space, his back knocking into the rude worktop. As Strella tried to dodge another blow, everything in the room slowed down by the gloom reminiscent of a theatre, he tripped on the bedding, landing on his back with a thud. 'So,' Mabitla said, dribbling on the supine would-be robber, 'you're just another common thief, after all. A dog that bites the hand that feeds it. Gah!' Hawking up a generous body of phlegm, Mabitla spat.

In that infinitesimal moment of feeling the spatter of warm fluid against his cheek and tasting its awful saltiness, a moment as fraught as the explosion following a flash of lightning, something loosened up inside him. If Mabitla had defiled him sexually, the reaction would have been no less violent. Still, in the throes of an intense seizure, he knew he'd never again be the same person. Much later, in the morning following the blackout, he woke up lying next to the contorted bundle of what was until recently Rre Mabitla. For a crazy moment Strella visualised two corpses lying side by side on mortuary trays. There was blood everywhere, even on the ceiling. What puzzled him was that he had actually found it possible to fall asleep alongside the dead man. He even remembered that he had had a vivid dream whose details, unfortunately, he couldn't quite piece together. His confusion contrasted with the clarity of his actions, his capacity to do everyday things without feeling that something was amiss. He scrubbed himself of the blood. He changed into the old man's clothes. He knew where everything was. Unguided, he found under the bed a shoebox full of bits and bobs and, at its bottom and wrapped in a plastic bag was a treasure trove of banknotes of almost all denominations, even those discontinued by the Botswana government.

Strella was disconnected from the hue and cry that followed the old man's murder, even when Mabitla's eyes gazed at him from the pages of *Dikgang tsa Gompieno* or *Mmegi*, the country's newspapers. Adding its voice to the public outcry, Radio Botswana blamed 'outside elements for the barbaric act'. There was no elaboration as to what agency might constitute these elements, not that it would have made any difference to Strella. In fact, when learning that the police had stumbled on clues that might lead to an arrest, it was as remote from his immediate concerns as if he were being informed that astronomers had discovered a new star to add to the galaxy. Far away and of no consequence.

What Strella did hear early in November 1972, at the height of one of the country's hottest summers, was the steady drone of the aeroplane engines as twenty-two members of the Organisation of Black Warriors flew across the Kgalagadi, en route to Libya. At long last, there was a real possibility for people to get military training without being aligned with the national liberation movement. The break with everything became even more real when they landed at the Tripoli airport. Green flags fluttered in the air. The no-nonsense security personnel hustled the group into trucks, having processed them peremptorily through customs under the stern gaze of the man who saw himself as the sole legitimate leader of Africa, Colonel Muammar Gaddafi.

His image was everywhere on the walls, along the route to the barracks of a training camp in Bin Ghashir, some ten or so kilometres south of the Tripoli airport. The heat, humidity and the bone-rattling drive at the back of the military truck made the journey feel longer. Their temporary hosts, the guards escorting the convoy, were mostly young, clean-shaven and seemingly reluctant to fraternise with their charges. It was possibly the rules. Only weeks later and much farther into a different and tougher training camp situated in the desert did the guards and instructors become more relaxed. Although there was a hierarchy – even guerrilla armies had to observe the policy of command and control – the isolation from the rest of the country and the tough regimen assisted in breaking the ice. Although it did not degenerate into folksy familiarity, the instructors, mainly Libyan or Palestinian officers, loosened up a bit, now and then passing around unsmokable Turkish cigarettes. Outnumbered by the newcomers, the instructors were also intrigued by the cosmopolitan character of the trainees. There were all shades of skin colour from the deep black of the Nubian nationalist fighting the Jaafar Nimeiri government in the Sudan to the palest, almost albinoid recruit from Krasnodar, all united by a commitment to the overthrow of some oppressive regime. The training was harsh, uncompromising, the objective of the instructors to produce fighters as hardy as the desert – and as elusive.

In December 1972, dog-tired and depleted in the most draining place on earth, following a gruelling day of infantry combat training, Strella flopped into his bunk hoping simply to die. Instead, he encountered Mabitla in his dreams. They were so real, these dreams, which had taken the character of visitations. Usually, the old man was, with his hand, trying to staunch the blood gushing from a wound in his neck. Sometimes – a circumstance that Strella regarded as grossly unfair, the dead being overly dramatic – the old man was headless, carrying his own head in his hands while worm-like, fibrous tassels of tissue, muscle and sinew dripped blood and stained the floor. In these nightmares, strangely enough, Strella could tell on some rational plane it was not real, the results of an overheated imagination. But still, it felt real, so real, in fact, that he sometimes woke up in the morning with Mabitla's funky body odour filling the air. It was musty and rank, a mixture of old age and misery. On some of the nights, a part of his anatomy gashed raw and red, Mabitla sat on the side of the bed, his heavy buttock depressing the thin mattress, causing Strella to shift to make space.

On these occasions, Mabitla waxed philosophical. 'And so,' he would ask, 'you still think you can overthrow the Boers?' Even in Libya, thousands of kilometres from home, the dead Mabitla still referred to South African whites as *maburu*. There was no hostility or judgement in the term, it was just the way he called it, possibly the way of the village he came from. And Strella would always respond: 'I have nothing to say to you. You are dead.'

'Isn't that what the struggle is all about?' Mabitla asked, smiling, exposing a toothless cavern. 'The liberation songs … they're all calling on dead people to come up and help you.'

'We sing of Mandela …'

'Dead,' Mabitla interjected triumphantly, 'buried on Robben Island.' His contempt glinted out of his eyes like live coals. 'Even your national anthem is a call to God, another obsolete notion.' His resentment mounting, Strella was mystified by the ghost's disruptive nature. 'Is this the man I killed?' Whenever Strella offered up a leader's name, Mabitla shot it down. It was exhausting. 'You people, you've never even invented matches but you think you can fight the white man. Grow up', he continued, 'and come to terms with the fact that black people won't achieve much.'

Strella remembered a session in one of the political classes in Gaborone where they discussed the different tracts that had informed the philosophy of Black Consciousness. One of the members, whose head was full of eclectic reading, recommended Malcolm X's 'Message to the Grassroots'. This was the section where a revolutionary nine-year-old Chinese girl shoots her father who was on his hands and knees because he was, in Malcolm X's unmatchable prose, 'an Uncle Tom Chinaman'. And then: 'When they had the revolution over there, they took a whole generation of Uncle Toms and just wiped them out. And within ten years that little girl became a full-grown woman. No more Toms in China.' Strella reasoned that someone should have killed Mabitla, this nettlesome old Uncle Tom, a lot earlier. Spoiling for a confrontation with the phantom, Strella went to sleep the following night. The ghost didn't show up. In fact, the nightmares disappeared as dramatically as they had come.

On sleepless nights, Strella found that he missed Uncle Tom, for that was what he'd come to call Mabitla. 'Uncle Tom was here last night,' he'd tell the two of his compatriots who formed the platoon from Botswana. Jethro and Gatsby had come to know of Strella's nocturnal visitor although they were not privy to the finer points of the ghost's provenance or even how it got dispatched into the spirit world in the first place. But the morning exercise in the old and disused tennis court and the half-hour at the noisy canteen where the would-be guerrillas took their breakfast, were incomplete without an account of the escapades involving the broken man from the ancestral lands.

When the visits dried up, so did the stories; in the camp of humdrum life and instances of restricted leisure, the departure felt a bit like a betrayal. 'He'll come back,' said Jethro, a musician in civilian life. It was as if he were comforting someone bereaved. 'Ghosts always do.'

He never did. At least not while Strella was in Bin Ghashir. Soon his attention was diverted when the platoon was introduced to an advanced firearms class. Strella did well, surpassing his compatriots, his aim unerring even when firing automatic weapons from a moving vehicle. His skill was recognised by Adnan Yassin, one of Abu Nidal's commanders, who took him under his wing. 'Such a good eye,' Yassin said, 'the instinct, the patience. Being able to hold your breath and squeeze the trigger is a talent possessed by a select few. Training in small arms and hand grenades, while essential, should not be allowed to corrupt that.' Yassin then took Strella along to practise, first with vintage weapons such as the Lee-Enfield. In no time Strella was allowed access to the more sophisticated range of sniper rifles, like the Dragunov.

Now, a little more than seventeen years later, Strella was back where he started. Experience in various battlefields having heightened his insight into himself, he knew that his arrogance could easily become his downfall. He had no business here in Mochudi; he was supposed to be making his way to the border. A border he'd crossed so often that he could do it with his eyes closed. But he just wanted to have a ringside view of the men he was supposed to kill. And so he studied them, seeing their faces framed in the crosshairs of telescopic sights.

The confidence or arrogance hadn't always been there. Nor had he always been familiar with border crossings. It all changed when he returned to Botswana from his Libyan adventure in December 1973, intent on going inside South Africa to kill himself a few of the oppressors. As luck would have it, it was exactly the selfsame oppressors who, working with Botswana state security officials, surprised him early in the morning while he was sleeping in the backroom in Broadhurst. The local police had been keeping him in their sights, having been tipped off by someone – Strella suspected it was either the academic ex-cuckold or his wife – that he was involved in a car-smuggling syndicate. From the early 1970s to the early 1980s, South African racketeers had been doing a roaring trade spiriting hot cars across the border into Botswana, whence the merchandise, whole or in parts, would find its way into the markets of Lusaka or even as far as Kinshasa. Reluctant to alienate its more powerful neighbour, Botswana decided to rat on the syndicates; when they raided Strella they were simply going for small fry, a petty thief. Being a small place where everyone knows everyone, it was inevitable that one of the Batswana policemen, related by marriage to the late Kgosientso Mabitla, would stumble upon clothes and various artefacts – for instance, the toothed contraption to discourage pickpockets – that placed Strella slap bang at the murder scene. Later that day, in the offices of the Special Branch located at the Ramotswa border, surrounded by a group consisting of Botswana police officers and their South African counterparts, Strella couldn't quite explain why he had hacked Mr Mabitla to death. Even more bizarre was his admission that he spent the night lying next to the body on the narrow bed.

'He was very lonely,' Strella remarked, perhaps suggesting that he was merely doing Mabitla a favour. Led by Colonel Simon Monnakgotla, the Batswana security police were furious that a refugee had murdered one of their own and – since the country still practised the death penalty – they appeared eager to have him stand trial in Botswana. 'We caught him dead to rights with blood still on the murder weapon,' Monnakgotla, a small, dapper man with a military moustache, told his South African opposite number, Colonel Jan Stander. 'We want to teach him a lesson that he can't just go about butchering innocent Batswana.' Asked what would actually happen to Strella, Colonel Monnakgotla, totally without irony, answered: 'We'll give him a fair trial and then hang him.'

'Ja,' Colonel Stander said, reflecting. Tall, with a grizzly beard and a hank of greying hair, he resembled an untidy bear. He rubbed his jaw, the bristles crackling in the room. Outside it was quiet except for the faraway drone of a spotter plane and the lazy tinkling of cowbells. 'Problem is he's needed for a lot more serious crimes back home.'

'More serious than murder?' Monnakgotla asked, his moustache bristling.

'Believe you me,' Stander said. 'Murder is just a walk in the park where this one is concerned.' And to emphasise the gravity of the captive's transgressions, Stander gave Strella a long look of a lion watching a gambolling gazelle. 'We'll need his docket.'

Monnakgotla, possibly conscious of the Geneva Convention protocols regarding the treatment of asylum seekers and refugees – even ones with a murderous streak – said: 'This man came as a refugee. He's a guest, albeit an unwholesome one, of this government. We have a right to protect him. If he's committed a crime on Botswana soil, it's up to us to put him through our criminal justice system.'

Smiling thinly, Colonel Jan Stander pulled himself up to his full height, a superfluous gesture because, even slouched, he'd still tower above his Motswana opposite. His unkempt appearance, reinforced by a rumpled, light-grey safari suit and brown riempies, befitting an individual least concerned with convention and operational niceties. 'Oh,' he asked, 'you'll put him through your system – and then what? He'll probably escape, seeing your prison cells are as porous as loofahs.'

'That's not exactly correct,' Monnakgotla said. This time he didn't disguise his distaste for the South African. 'We have managed to hold our prisoners. A few escapes are normal, common with any penal system.'

Strella had a sense that even though this exchange had a lot to do with him, it also had absolutely nothing to do with him. There was an ongoing tug-of-war between South African and Botswana officialdom. Botswana still hadn't forgiven South Africa for its racist laws, which it even tried to extend to Botswana when Seretse Khama, the leader who would later become the country's first black prime minister, married a white woman in England. The accommodation of refugees from South Africa seeking asylum in Botswana was also an affirmation of Botswana's state of independence. It was a way of the Batswana to differentiate themselves completely from the backwardness of South Africa's social policies. A one-time Black Panther fugitive from the law in the USA, whom Strella met briefly in Tripoli, had marvelled at Botswana's stance.

'That country,' he said, 'is whipping the racists in moral stakes and asking them: "How do you like them apples?"'

'Okay,' Jan Stander said, the soulless smile never once leaving his face. 'Suit yourself. But I'll report this lack of co-operation to Hirschfeld, who's sure to alert Minister Kwelagobe, who will certainly brief the president. And we'll stop our border operation where we've almost halved the operational capacity of South African and Zairian syndicates smokkeling stolen cars into your country. Not to say anything about terrorist activities launched from this country.' He said 'this country' with such disdain as if naming Botswana would somehow grant it a status he wished to withhold.

'There's no need to be hasty,' Monnakgotla said. 'Let me think.'

To help him think, Stander snapped his briefcase open and took out an A4-size envelope stamped OFFICIAL/AMPTELIK. He arranged in a fan-like shape on the desk a series of crime-scene photographs. Bomb victims, burnt to the whiteness of the bone; dead people in various, inelegant poses. A man of indeterminate age lay on the ground, his one foot still on the pedal of his bicycle. There was a dead little girl, three or four years old, with the top of her head sheared off by shrapnel, eyes opened in a moment of great curiosity.

'*Die's jou fokken gedoente*,' Stander said, shoving down Strella's head and forcing him to look at the exhibition. Then he unclasped his holstered sidearm and laid it on the polished desk with a thud.

His head a couple of inches off the surface of the desk, Strella felt rather than saw Stander shaking behind him like someone about to lose control, marvelling at this piece of theatre despite his discomfort. Strella knew the performance had nothing to do with rage and a lot to do with Stander demonstrating that he was ready to commit mayhem if these Batswana tried to thwart him. He was going to execute the prisoner right before their eyes and see how they would explain that. The paperwork alone would kill them, too. Strella just hoped that Stander would not get carried away. A few people had died during such demonstrations, even during training, when the performance went out of control. Strella could feel the cold muzzle of the gun against his temple. '*Jou fokken hond,*' Stander said, growling like the mongrel in whose name he was swearing, his hot breath fanning the nape of Strella's neck. Strella couldn't tell what the real source of Stander's anger was; he was aware of the man behind him, something hard pressing against his buttocks. 'I could spray your bloody brains all over the desk …'

'Whoa, stopstopstopstop …' Monnakgotla was saying, sounding less a police officer than a herdboy struggling to hold back stampeding cattle. 'Whoa, Mr Stander …'

Mr Stander? Strella wanted to laugh but his positioning, half-bent and head down, had caused a crick in his neck. *Mr* Stander … surely?

'Let's talk this thing out,' Monnakgotla pleaded. 'Leave the boy with the other men. Let's get to the other office.'

Colonel Jan Stander marched behind Colonel Monnakgotla. He stopped at the door and addressed some of the men still grouped around Strella. 'That is a trained terrorist,' he said, 'so watch it. If he tries to escape, shoot him on both knees.'

With those words, Strella's fate was sealed. Within a month, he was a full agent of the South African secret police, complete with a new name and a number. In January 1974, he started his training in the SADF's military base in Ondangwa, in South-West Africa (which, he was told, was called Namibia by SWAPO) together with a unit of askaris, former members of the liberation movement who had been captured and turned. Here they were taken on a course in intelligence where they learnt about handling informants, analysing seized documents, counter-intelligence and targeting, designing dead drops, among a range of expertise that would be needed later. More importantly, Strella and the recruits were trained in taking advantage of the kindness of strangers.

Much later, when confronted by questions about his earlier years, Muzi Thabethe could not, strangely, remember what his parents looked like. He remembered with devastating clarity every moment shared with friends and acquaintances. He realised again later that people around him helped broaden his understanding of a confusing time. The mid-1970s in KwaMashu, Durban, were full of turmoil; everywhere, there were voices that sought to enlighten but ended up deepening the confusion. Muzi was therefore thankful for Vukani Majozi. He had inherited the good fortune of being both handsome and popular, with a beautiful younger sister, Wanda. Herself a minor celebrity for having made a cameo appearance on the social page of *Drum* magazine, Wanda had two close friends, Gabrielle Nkosi and Laura Mdunge. Muzi Thabethe was interested in Laura Mdunge; there was something quiet and simultaneously spontaneous about her that made her exceedingly beguiling.

On Friday, 25 June 1971, which was the last day of school at Fundisani High, Muzi Thabethe accepted Vukani Majozi's invitation to the city of Durban, where, together with a few close friends, they would celebrate the end of the half-year term. This acceptance was sweetened by the addition of Laura to the group.

Muzi Thabethe would remember the evening in Durban, the cold Friday night when the group was also joined by Stanley Kekana, one of those personalities, it seemed to Muzi, no high school could do without. Eternally surrounded by a gaggle of admirers, Stanley would regale his audience with stories that mainly poked fun at the authorities. He knew all the spots, as he called watering holes, dotting the back streets of Durban.

Although he hadn't developed a taste for alcohol, Muzi Thabethe tagged along, seizing every opportunity to sit next to Laura as he sipped some brew on offer in a succession of taverns and shebeens around the historic precinct of Grey Street and the Indian Market. Later, around 9:00 p.m., with his shirt collar turned up against the chill, Stanley led Vukani Majozi's group along a stinky lane littered with skips and overflowing bins to a row of silent houses. Even in the cold gloom of the night Muzi Thabethe imagined that a person could almost hear the scratchy sound of paint peeling off as the suburb descended into disrepair.

Stanley paused for a minute before opening a gate that was slap-bang against the pavement. He led them up a short flight of stairs to the front of a three- or four-storey brick building with wrought-iron balconies fronting shuttered doors and windows latticed with burglar bars. Pressing a buzzer, he waited. A raspy woman's voice came through the intercom. 'Who's that?'

'It's me, Aunty Cindy, Stanley.'

'Jee-zus,' Aunt Cindy muttered. 'Hold on, I'm coming.'

'She's not very happy,' Stanley said. Then, looking around, seeing Laura, Wanda, Gabrielle, all still in their school uniforms, and concluding that they must be dying of cold, he softened, smiling like a chastised wolf. 'I know it's past your bedtime,' he said. 'But please trust me on this one. You'll enjoy yourselves.'

And they did.

Aunt Cindy, although grumpy at first, was all smiles as she ushered the group inside the landing after peering at the street to check they weren't followed here. She cautioned them to tread carefully on the stairs, as some of the planks were loose. Muzi Thabethe thought that

Aunt Cindy, who must have weighed over 130 kilos, should be the last person to caution on light-footedness. On the first landing, Muzi started getting a whiff of embrocation and wondered if Aunt Cindy was also running a gym in the bargain. The smell got stronger towards the top of the stairs. Aunt Cindy stopped to check the progress of her visitors, murmuring to the young women that they must be chilled to the bone. 'Come on up and I'll whip up something to warm you up.'

That Friday evening in June 1971 would mark the beginning of a relationship in which Aunt Cindy would extend her own brand of kindness to strangers like Muzi Thabethe. Warm-hearted and open, Aunt Cindy put Muzi to shame for his earlier unflattering musings about her weight. He had thought that she must be quite old. Now that her features were in the open under the ceiling lights, he realised that she was much younger; probably in her forties, with an oval face and full lips whose corners flickered with a ready smile. 'Hey, people,' she said, wheezing from the climb, 'we've got a full house tonight. Come on up, Stan and your friends, and meet the people.'

Once in the lounge, Muzi Thabethe did a double take when he saw exactly who consisted of 'the people'. Men of various ages, sizes and nationalities either sat or lay sprawled on an assortment of bedding. Settees had been converted into beds. Mattresses were spread on the floor. There was even a massage table on which a half-naked man lay face down, his torso glistening. With practised dexterity, Aunt Cindy draped a comforter over him. 'Poor Greg, fell asleep in mid-massage. Always does.'

'Not asleep,' Greg said thickly and began to snore.

Through the window, the moonlit rooftops were grey and ghostly, the chimneys and spires skeletal against the sky. Far off twinkled the pinpoints of lights embedded into the gloomy acreage of the Greyville racecourse, the place where all dreams come to an end, Muzi's father used to say – and then, come next Saturday, he was back at the tote.

All told, there were some twelve people in the lounge. 'Find yourself somewhere to sit,' Aunt Cindy said. 'Girls, follow me.' Stanley joined them.

Vukani and Muzi perched on the arm of a settee and paged through old copies of *Drum* magazine, admiring the fashion sense of the 1950s' socialites, lingering on the sections with bevies of beauties with hourglass shapes – Dolly Rathebe, Miriam Makeba, Peggy Phango. At sixteen, they had reached that age when they thought they knew everything about men and women and, in the same breath, suspected that what they knew counted for naught. And so they gazed at the black-and-white pictures, speculating on what lay beneath the cloth tautened over bulges and depressions marking the female form. Behind the kitchen door along the passage, Aunt Cindy was bantering with the girls. She must have said something funny because the hallway and the lounge were flooded with sounds of womanly laughter. At that moment, both Vukani and Muzi suddenly became aware that they were away from home with women who weren't their sisters. It was around 10:00 p.m. Both Vukani and Muzi cursed themselves for being duped by Stanley and his crazy schemes. What are we doing here? They looked around, sceptical of Aunt Cindy's lame efforts to whip up some enthusiasm from her largely sleepy guests. But her sunny disposition paid off.

Twenty minutes or so later, one by one, the sleepers shook themselves free of slumber, stretched and stowed away their bedding and generally helped restore the lounge to its former state of shabby respectability. With the removal of drowsy Greg and his massage table, it changed from a railway station into a passable lounge where the recently pomaded heads of the former sleepers soaked up the glow from a giant bulb that hung from the ceiling. Suddenly there was music, a hi-fi stereo blasting something funky by Stanley Turrentine. There was food – chicken wings, barbeque sausages, samosas, onion bhaji, roti and rolls, lamb chops – and drink: soft, hard, beer and wine and vodka fruit punch.

'I wouldn't touch that,' said Aunt Cindy from behind, having approached unseen and unheard above the successive thump and wail of the percussions and saxophone. Snatching the tumblers of punch from the boys' hands, she emptied the liquid back into the bowl, handing them instead cans of Seven-Up. 'I don't know where your mothers are tonight, but I'm sure they wouldn't like to see you boys drinking. Would they?'

'My mother wouldn't mind,' said a young man, who'd also sidled up to the little group. 'You see,' he explained, 'my mother ran a shebeen in Clermont Township. And she knew that if she didn't control our drinking from when we were small we'd grow up and become drunks. And so, with every meal, there was wine. That taught me and my brother that you don't have to abuse alcohol to enjoy it.'

'Zweli,' Aunt Cindy said, sternly, 'you don't come here and put nonsense into my children's heads. I know your mother. She was a schoolteacher …'

'And ran a shebeen as a sideline. Like you, Aunt Sindiswa,' Zweli said with a triumphant smile.

'Get away from here, you,' she said with exasperation and rushed off to put out another fire.

Zweli laughed and introduced himself. 'Just kidding,' he said with a grin. 'I don't even drink alcohol.' Then, 'You guys are at Fundisani High?'

As the evening progressed, Muzi Thabethe was puzzled by the presence of Zweli Gama and Frank Nyembe, another young man who emerged out of the crowd of partygoers. They didn't seem to have any real business at Aunt Cindy's place. The rest of the people were worker representatives, shop stewards, from various parts of the country, in Durban for a conference to establish a trade union federation. Most of them, Greg included, had that open, no-nonsense, salt-of-the earth aura about them, people used to hard work and who argued their points in loud, emphatic tones. If they had a disagreement that could not be sorted out via words, they would be the first to invite you to take it outside. And so, as the evening wore on, their geniality or nuisance value increased in proportion to their intake of booze. In contrast, Zweli and Frank were vigilant non-drinkers, somewhat cautious in their demeanour, conversing without moving their lips, like ventriloquists. They were as languid as cats, their eyes more articulate than their hands.

Muzi checked them out, the beardless faces whose complexion spoke of prolonged exposure to the sun, T-shirts under windbreakers, jeans and Adidas shoes, like athletes popping off to relatives for a bit of rest and recreation. Even as they talked about this and that, nothing serious, Muzi had a feeling that they were young men of experience. They had been in situations.

'What brings you here?' Zweli asked Muzi.

'Stanley. It's his aunt's place.'

'Stanley's my cousin,' Zweli confided. 'Although we don't walk in the same circles, I've come to know that he's a fine man.'

'What circles,' Muzi asked, 'do you walk in?'

All four of them laughed and Frank and Vukani edged off to join the mass on the dance floor. Someone had put on 'The Low Spark of the High-Heeled Boys' and the room was suddenly giddy. Muzi saw Laura, her hand twirling in the air like a cowboy about to lasso a heifer, one hand on her hip as she moved to the beat. Seeing her face transfigured by the enjoyable effort of dancing, he wondered what had kept him from telling her how he felt, even though, truth be told, he didn't know how he felt. Everything was mashed up inside his chest. The music pumped on.

Zweli smiled, following the direction of Muzi's eyes. 'That's your girl, isn't it?' he asked.

'Who?'

'Come on, you know who I'm talking about. She's very pretty.'

'I think she's special,' Muzi admitted.

'Now you're blushing,' Zweli teased. 'Ah, that's sweet.'

'Come on.'

During the half-year school vacations of 1971, starting in the last week of June and ending in mid-July, Zweli and Frank became a common feature in the lives of both Muzi and Vukani. Laura Mdunge, now a regular at Muzi's home in G Section, KwaMashu, refused to enter into any discussion that involved Zweli and Frank. 'Those two,' she'd tell Muzi, 'are pure poison.'

'Apart from so-called female intuition,' Muzi would counter, 'on what do you base your charge?'

'Mark my words: time will tell,' was her reply.

But he did appreciate her female intuition, for what it was, for she had helped steer him from harm's way in many instances. She'd suggest a detour, for instance, and he'd heed her advice and hear, later, that a dead body was found somewhere along his original route. Laura never tired of telling him that her grandmother was an isangoma who could see into the future. He was there in her future, Laura said, but there would be a period of great turbulence that would rock their lives. In the three weeks of the school holidays, Muzi would laugh at these predictions while keeping his eyes peeled for danger whenever out alone at night.

In the first week of July Muzi and Vukani got a message to meet with Zweli and Frank in a different house in F Section. Zweli was the one who finally opened up. His opening words were as much an indication of his own vulnerability as of his trust in the two schoolboys. 'After telling you what I want you to help us with,' he said, 'you have a right to say no and we will accept that. We will probably have to pack our bags and disappear.' He paused and licked his lips. 'We are here to kill a man. He's someone who's caused us a lot of pain as the Movement. The decision to remove him has not been taken lightly. We need you to help us with reconnaissance of the target.'

From Vukani's stolid gaze, Muzi knew that his friend was already in on what the two men were about. 'No mission,' Zweli continued, 'can succeed without careful study of the enemy's terrain, his readiness and his weak spots. We are a small part of the People's Army. We depend on people like you to succeed.' It was impossible for Muzi to be outside what Zweli termed the inexorable logic of history.

In days that followed, the four got together and discussed the way forward. Zweli, who was the commissar – and thus the political head – of the unit, would start with a briefing on current affairs, which linked some of the international news to what was happening inside the country. For instance, Zweli informed the group about the death of Papa Doc Duvalier, the Haitian dictator who had unleashed untold terror via his paramilitary force, the Ton-Ton Macoute.

'We live in a dictatorship that boasts the most powerful military machinery on the continent,' said Zweli. 'But all such regimes have their soft underbellies. They cannot outlast the resolve of people to be free.'

On a more personal note, Zweli exulted over the fact that Arsenal had won the FA Cup.

'Is that part of the people's victory?' Muzi asked.

'Not quite,' Zweli said, beaming, 'but close.'

The easy-going style disappeared when he sought history to justify the need to take up arms against a regime no different from the one run by Papa Doc: the National Party coming to power in 1948, which motivated the ANC to adopt its Programme of Action in December 1949, which bore the seeds for the Defiance Campaign. He spoke of events from the adoption of the Freedom Charter in 1955 and the removal of coloureds from the common voters roll to the Treason Trial that dragged on from 1956 to 1961. The tide changed with the massacres at Sharpeville and Langa to the enactment of the state of emergency in 1960, the banning of the liberation movements and the establishment by Oliver Tambo of the ANC in exile. And … and … Zweli looked up from his notes.

'Are you tired of the history lesson?' he asked. Although young, Zweli wore a pair of horn-rimmed glasses with thick lenses, reading aids necessitated as a result of his vision being ruined by reading up close in dim lamplight in the camps. 'The dates and places and names don't seem to make sense?'

'No,' Vukani said. 'It's quite interesting.'

'It gets better,' Zweli said. He glanced up at his colleague, owlish. 'Do you want to take over, Komandir?'

'Proceed, Commissar,' Frank Nyembe said. 'You're doing great.'

Komandir. Commissar. The names were strange, exotic and had a hypnotic lilt to them, like magic incantations. Sometimes, when they wished to converse among themselves without the recruits knowing, the two men would slip into some other strange-sounding lingo. Snippets of it sounded like Russian. It was a language markedly different to the gibberish put out by Radio Bantu serials, which stood for the speech patterns of Russian Communists. Calling themselves a study group, the four tuned in to these serials. They almost collapsed with laughter at the accents. When Zweli was amused, he laughed with his whole body. His sparse frame shook like a scarecrow being rocked by a strong wind.

If Muzi was warm towards Zweli, he was equally cool with Frank, whose small, knowing smile never left his face. Muzi thought he was lazy. There were areas in which Frank was more forthcoming, more diligent (perhaps his perception was merely evidence of the division of labour or specialisation) but still, he felt that the komandir was just cruising, here for the ride.

On one occasion, while the lesson was going on, Muzi had to go to the toilet, which was a brick structure detached from the house. While squatting, he caught a whiff of burning weed. Through the cracks on the wall, even though there was little light, he could clearly see Frank busy puffing dagga from a pipe made out of a broken beer bottle. An occasional smoker himself, Muzi could not, however, reconcile the profound political concepts and revolutionary zeal with a zol. Something just didn't add up. Also, it was known in the township, you just could never entrust your life into the hands of a dagga smoker.

Even when Frank came back and made a lot of sense, Muzi was still unconvinced. He dismissed Frank's lucidity as a fluke, the way some mentally disturbed people would break out into a recital of Mark Antony's funeral oration. He was sure to crack up somewhere and slip up. Already Muzi was not comfortable with the flippant manner in which Frank referred to 'targets'. He'd overheard, for instance, some of the comments, like: 'Do you think we should waste our bullets on that old geezer? He looks like a goner already.' Or: 'That one, I'd do him for free, just to get a crack at his wife.' There was much more that rankled Muzi; he concluded that there was something corrupt and undisciplined about Frank.

It was Frank's roving eye and restless hands that proved the final straw.

On Friday, 2 July 1971, Muzi Thabethe had to meet Frank Nyembe at the appointed meeting place, a disused building that housed an old swimming pool, which was now a crater wild with garbage, algae and smelly foliage. The abandoned structure represented the misguided benevolence of the municipality. Originally built to promote swimming among township youngsters, it was now a 'stadium', a spot for trysting, in the parlance of the township. A favourite haunt for rapists and assorted lowlifes, it was to be avoided at all costs by any self-respecting woman.

Walking towards the spot with Laura Mdunge, whom he had accompanied to the shopping centre and who would be taking the footpath to the house, Muzi heard a car engine purring up behind them. He turned and saw Frank behind the wheel, a smile on his face. Despite the strict rule forbidding public acknowledgement among members of the unit, Frank pulled up alongside and rolled down the side window. 'Come on in,' he said.

'Look,' Muzi said, 'she's supposed to get home. I'll meet you at the spot.'

'No,' Frank said, stretching to open the door, 'Hop in. I'll drop her near the house. Never know what lurks in there.' He pointed at the tall grass covering the path leading to Laura's home. 'It's okay.'

It was not okay, Muzi thought. The tall grass probably hides two-legged snakes like you. The car's interior was stuffy, the stale smell of tobacco having soaked into the upholstery. And, true to form, with Laura wedged between the two men, Frank's hand fumbled as he manipulated the gearstick, the fingers slipping off the knob and lingering on Laura's knee. Laura sat with an unflinching face, suffering the indignity with poise. The smile never left Frank's face, even as he continued with his dagga-induced prattle. Muzi wanted to reach across and punch him on the mouth, but he knew that would not do.

Eventually, mercifully, they were on Laura's street. 'It's best she gets out here,' Muzi said. 'We don't want people to see her getting out of the car.'

Frank stopped, more out of reflex than from a rational decision. Looking blankly at Muzi, while giving the disembarking Laura a once-over, he said: 'You've taken this security thing seriously, haven't you?'

'If I don't,' Muzi said, 'I'll live to rue the day.'

'Rue away, Comrade,' Frank said. 'Let's go.'

In the car, Muzi thought he'd keep things to himself. But he was upset. 'That wasn't cool.'

'What wasn't cool, Comrade?' Frank asked.

'You know.'

'No, I don't know. Tell me.'

'Well,' Muzi said. 'If you don't, then we're in more trouble than I thought.'

'Are you threatening me?'

'I'm doing nothing of the sort,' Muzi said. 'I'm just saying we must treat each other with respect as comrades. That's all I'm saying.'

Frank rubbed the side of his face with his palm. The smile now looked pasted, like the painted smiles of clowns. He was about to say something when he thought the better of it.

Later, at the lunch meeting, the unit sat amid the debris of paper plates piled with leftover potato chips and crunched bones. On the table squatted an empty bucket of Kentucky Fried Chicken next to litres of Coke and Sprite. Sipping from a tumbler, Zweli showed no sign he was aware of the row between Frank and Muzi. He seemed absorbed in thought. 'I don't like it,' he said.

'It's not for you to like, Commissar,' Frank was saying. It was clear that this matter could develop into a full-blown clash. 'We've been given orders.'

'Ja,' Zweli said. 'But we're on the ground here. We can take decisions. We read the situation. And our reading is that this is just pure madness.'

As they conversed, Muzi gathered that they were talking about 'hitting' a certain Brigadier Zimu. Frank repeated his remark about wasting ammunition on the *old geezer*. 'Okay,' he said. 'Consider this my treat. I'll hit the old man. Solo. One ball.'

'I'm still not happy with this.'

'Don't worry. It'll be a dry run for the main job.'

'It'll bring the heat down on all of us and scupper the operation.'

'You're getting to be a worrywart, Commissar.'

Zweli ignored the insult. 'Will you do the recce yourself?'

'Don't worry about it.' Frank was sure. 'I know his every move. He's been fitted with one of those colostomy things following an operation, two weeks ago. So, being a military guy, he doesn't want to do the business in the house, prefers to drive to the municipal office in H Section, where he's got keys to a private bathroom. I'll pop him when he gets into the car in the morning.'

'Wow,' Zweli said, impressed. 'You've really studied your subject.'

'It's the least I can do, Commissar.' Frank revelled in praise. He was beaming from ear to ear.

'Be careful.' Zweli sounded as if he were already dealing with another problem. He sounded far off.

A few days later – on 4 July 1971 – there was a change of plan. The unit, which consisted of Vukani and Muzi (local reconnaissance), and Frank and Zweli (trained special operations commandos of the People's Army) was given a fresh target. A notorious Special Branch officer, Lieutenant Caleb Ngozi, was a former member of the People's Army. He was captured on a cross-border raid on Swaziland, brought back to South Africa, where he was turned into an enemy agent. Others felt that he had been working for the South African state security all along, seeing that his conversion seemed almost immediate. But he was dangerous, having given damning testimony in trials involving one-time colleagues.

'It's hard to forgive someone who betrays a revolution,' Zweli said during the briefing. 'It's better not to have joined at all than to be a collaborator.'

Even though Frank agreed with his comrade, his heart seemed to be not in it. A little preoccupied, he kept on glancing at his watch. Zweli noticed.

'You have an appointment, Comrade?' he asked.

'Not really,' Frank said. 'Just a later meeting with someone I'm trying to bring into the circle.'

'Who could that be?' Zweli asked. 'Speak, you're among comrades here.'

'I think it is Gabrielle,' Vukani said. 'I heard her say she's met someone from outside.'

'Gabrielle?' Muzi burst out. 'Gabrielle knows about the unit?'

'I haven't told her much,' Frank said, defensively. 'Just sketched the outline.'

'Whether you sketched outline or gave her the whole plan,' Muzi said, 'you might as well put an ad in the *Daily News*.'

'Are you trying to tell me I don't know how to handle a recruit?'

'With Gabrielle, my friend, you don't know a thing.'

'Comrades,' Zweli said. 'Let's tone down the drama.'

'Look,' Muzi said. 'I thought secrecy was the catchword here. Now, it seems like the whole of KwaMashu will be in on this ...'

'You heard the commissar,' Frank said. 'Cut the hysterics.'

'... and so,' Muzi continued, getting to his feet, 'I don't see myself participating in this any further, if we're going to be this lax.'

'Sit down, Comrade Muzi,' Zweli said. He waited until Muzi complied. Then he turned to Frank. 'This thing must be sorted out.'

It wasn't.

It occurred to Muzi Thabethe, when he had the luxury of reconstructing the events that had got him arrested, that assassinations were an overrated if misunderstood strategy. In most cases, it served to boost the morale of a weaker force; sometimes this weakness was not so much a matter of military strength as much as ethics or morality. The apartheid state was much stronger but had resorted to assassinations in an attempt to demoralise its opponents. Was the People's Army also losing its revolutionary morality by adopting strategies that had earned the apartheid state international condemnation? Was there a place for such subtleties in the red-hot moments of struggle when women and children were being killed and buried in shallow graves?

In KwaMashu, at the hidey-hole, Zweli explained the official line: 'We must distinguish assassinations by terrorist groups or deranged individuals from what we do,' he said. 'We do not assassinate; we eliminate organisms that cause sickness to our society. These are malignancies that need to be cut out of the body, if the body has to heal. We are no different from pest exterminators.'

'Amen to that,' Frank said.

In mid-July, Durban struggled with unseasonal rains. This was a blessing in disguise for the unit. Cold or rainy weather made it easy to carry weapons on one's person, even sub-machine guns or a bazooka. The two schoolboys were to be unarmed, guiding two armed men to Sheila's on D Section, the shebeen run by Sheila Ndawonde, Caleb Ngozi's girlfriend. Involving young recruits was standard procedure in most liberation struggles, the logic being the need for fresh blood to continue the tradition in case of capture or death of guerrillas.

It was Vukani Majozi who'd discovered that Ngozi would call at the shebeen every Thursday around 7:30 p.m. The regulars knew that they had to drink up and leave early, or finish their drinks on the stoep outside. After supper, about two hours later, Sis Sheila and her man would retire to the bedroom.

It was around 10:00 p.m. on Thursday, 15 July 1971, that Muzi and Vukani joined Zweli and Frank in crawling through a hole in the fence leading to Sheila's. Although they couldn't see the action at the front of the house, they could hear Sheila turfing the stragglers out of the yard and threatening to spray them with a hose. One of them retorted, 'I'll gladly spray you with *my* hose, Sheila,' to which she answered, 'Ja, voetsek, wena Lucas. We know all about *your* little hose without a nozzle.'

Even as Muzi heard the laughter of the men disappearing into the night and the metallic rattle of locks securing the door, he had an impression of everything taking place on an unreal plane. The sights and sounds were from another world: the windows fortified by burglar bars, the light flickering inside the lounge, the man sitting on a couch swaying to something playing on the stereo, snapping his fingers in time to the music. He turned to say something to Sheila, who minutes later handed him a glass, shielding him from view. When Caleb Ngozi next appeared, he was looking straight into the darkness outside, almost as if he were seeking out the men sent to kill him.

'Is that our man?' Zweli asked. Vukani nodded.

And then it hit Muzi Thabethe. When Sheila Ndawonde, now in a nightgown, put finishing touches to the evening, drawing the curtains in the lounge, switching off the lights and proceeding to the bedroom with her lover, the combatants' quarry, in tow, he became aware of the ordinariness of people's lives. Oil lamp in hand, Sheila dimmed the overhead bedroom lights and stood framed in the bedroom window. Drawing the lace curtains, she pulled the drapes halfway across, possibly for natural light. Moments later, illuminated by an oil lamp, presumably to add spice to the lovemaking, the two figures rocked and wrestled on the bed. To Muzi, the coupling was so mundane it could have been a bull and a cow in a field. He watched as Ngozi's stomach heaved, rolls of flesh rippling as he strained against the woman, seemingly nearer to a heart attack than ecstasy. That's when Frank, who hadn't prepared the youngsters for it, raised the Skorpion machine pistol, aimed and fired through the glass, stitching Ngozi neatly from the neck down to the hip, each bullet seeming to unleash the passion latent in the body of the dying man. Seeing Sheila, covered in blood, pushing off Ngozi's lifeless body, her mouth open in a wordless scream, Muzi recalled women keening at funerals; he saw his own mother overcome by grief.

Later, while Frank and Vukani re-enacted the scene of the shooting, Muzi Thabethe asked a question. 'Why is it that we're oppressed by white people but it's only the blacks that the People's Army is killing. Why?'

Muzi was sixteen years old.

Frank and Zweli fell out soon after the killing. Gabrielle was now a regular visitor to the safe house, itself a breach of security. Increasingly, she became a part of the unit, sometimes taking part in the discussions, to Zweli's annoyance. He was concerned that they were hanging around, knowing that each day spent inside the country brought nearer the possibility of arrest. He put it all down to indiscipline, especially with regard to Frank. Then on Sunday, 18 July 1971, a predawn raid by the Durban North Special Branch netted Vukani Majozi, Muziwendoda Thabethe and Gabrielle Nkosi. Frank Nyembe – whose real name was Anthony Blose – was picked up later in the afternoon, holed up in Sindiswa Mabusela's flat on Prince Edward Street in Durban. The police were still looking for Zwelinzima Gama, also known as Zweli, a trained terrorist belonging to the People's Army. A few others, suspected of subversive activities, were caught in a police dragnet around Durban and its environs.

By April 1977, the camp administration and instructors in Ondangwa were confident that Strella could now go on missions. He was secreted into Angola where he was among a platoon of SADF askaris integrated into Holden Roberto's National Liberation Front of Angola (FNLA), which was engaged in a struggle against the dominant People's Movement for the Liberation of Angola (MPLA). Led by mercenaries from most parts of the Western world, Strella, askaris and a ragtag army of Angolans who spoke neither Portuguese nor English, mounted ambushes against the People's Armed Forces for the Liberation of Angola (FAPLA) and Cuban forces. It was no secret that the FNLA received funds from the CIA. Even back at base there was widespread talk that Roberto and his lieutenants, some of them South Africans who had deserted their liberation movements, were simply looting the coffers, helped in this plunder by his brother-in-law, Mobuto Sese-Seko of Zaire. The culture of surviving on ill-gotten gains was widespread. The soldiers in various camps, including the one where Strella was stationed, took to selling miscellaneous merchandise donated by government agencies and their agencies, like the CIA or conservative foundations. The latter were spreading charitable evangelism against what they considered the inexorable tide of communism in Africa. The principle of keeping the fridge quiet in Botswana was also followed in the bush, perhaps even more vigorously; any resource worth looting was looted and anything of value was sold. A visitor to Cuanza Norte, for instance, could be forgiven for assuming that sections of northern Angolan villagers had become zealous supporters of Washington Redskins, stepping out in burgundy-and-gold sweatshirts and tracksuits; all that was needed to complete the effect were high-kicking cheerleaders flashing pom-poms. During the drought, when there was nothing to flog, the troops simply did what comes naturally to most undisciplined armies. They were armed and it was wartime and the peasants, who were called *o povo*, owed the soldiers a favour. They could pay in kind. Some of the men traded their weapons for pombe, caproto or cachaca, the local liquor. In time, however, the FNLA's lack of modern weapons took its toll. A few units strayed off and ended up freelancing as bank robbers, sometimes holding up general dealers and making a nuisance of themselves. It was no different with Strella's band.

It was a ragtag group that crossed the Dange River and marched, unguided, into the town of Sanza Pombo in the district of Uige. The group consisted of Strella accompanied by two askari homeboys. Then there was Jolene, a twenty-four-year-old blonde hard-case who modelled herself on Vietcong women guerrillas. Jolene had taken to marching around the camp with a retooled Mosin Nagant rifle strapped across her back. Adding a rakish element to the gang was a crazy and ageless mercenary called Barak the Greek or Jesus on account of his flowing locks. The group, united by the simple need for survival, considered itself a cut above the rest. They were cosmopolitan, each member having seen the world, and were the epitome of non-racialism.

However far they strayed, the groups would, like homing pigeons, always return to camp at nightfall a day or two later, some with stories to tell, others with silent, bloodshot eyes that spoke volumes. One platoon had been separated from the main detachment when they went out foraging for arms and ammunition, food and water after weeks of fighting, and never came back.

It was late in the afternoon of Sunday, 24 April 1977 that Strella's team moved into the outskirts of Sanza Pombo from the northeast part that still bore signs of earlier fighting, the corrugated roads littered with debris. Here, a burnt-out armoured personnel carrier; there, rondavels with the thatch shorn off by fire. There was an abiding smell of death, which meant that the bushes still hid unburied bodies. A steady drizzle fell and Strella hoped it would wash away the sins of the day. The ripe stench of runny sewage and death drove the group away from the road, over a ditch towards a broken-down cluster of adobe huts that were daubed in optimistic hues. The splash of unexpected colour leavened the grimness of the area while somehow hinting at imminent danger.

The suggestion of peril was disregarded as the group scrambled to find shelter from the rain that was building up steam, and wait out the night. They ruled out a night trek, knowing they would invariably come across an MPLA checkpoint. Hiking in the woods was asking for trouble. All the warring parties had made it their business to plant landmines, to the extent that Angola was now setting world records in amputees. The small town was deserted, not a soul on the road.

'This place gives me the creeps,' Jolene said and shivered. Strella marvelled at how much she had changed. She had come into the training camp in Ondangwa a huge blob of pink flesh, weighing in at 120 kilograms, with a self-destructive attitude ingrained through years of abuse. Overlooking her size, pretending that she was just another boeremeisie from the Orange Free State with a messed-up sense of self, the trainers put her through a regimen designed for troops in special ops. She took whatever they gave her without a whimper and got a reputation as someone you messed with at your own peril. Jolene was like a woman demented, running the daily six hours of fisico, the field exercises simulating military combat, across the sun-drenched plain of loose rocks and treacherous sand, returning to the camp lobster-red during the first months. Much later, leaner, blonder, she was almost unrecognisably brown. Her nickname, on top of her travelling name, was Attic, for her outburst in a close-quarters-combat class, when Stander, preaching absolute alertness, reminded the platoon that people tended to overlook basements. 'What about attics?' Jolene asked, and the name stuck.

Here, on the trail, hundreds of miles from Ondangwa, she had a run-in with Barak the Greek. The charred trees and burnt things that had once been valuable to someone, most likely someone dead or in a desperate situation, were reflected in her dark glasses. 'Barak,' she was saying, 'this is fucking madness. This town … we should get out of here, now.'

'Look,' Barak the Greek said, 'someone will have to assume the role of commander. Otherwise we're fucked.'

'I'm not talking about leadership, Barak,' Jolene said, with devastating patience. 'I'm talking about this town. We'll die here. Listen.'

At first there was nothing, just the ambient sounds of a dead town, but then, slowly, the distant rumble of artillery, like unenthusiastic thunder, carried over the humid air.

'Yeah, sure,' Barak the Greek said, his tone downplaying the implication of the detonations. 'That's the Grad-P, about five clicks away.'

'Yeah,' Jolene said. 'We're within range.'

'We might be, but we've got a mission here.'

'Oh?' Jolene said. 'That's a new twist. I thought we were here looking for what we don't have. I didn't know we were on a mission.' She drew quotation marks in the air around the word *mission*. 'What's this mission?'

'The higher-ups ordered us to hole up here.'

'I don't recall the higher-ups, whatever that is, saying anything of the sort,' Jolene said. 'Everyone was scrambling for a place of safety. The higher-ups are just concerned about saving their backsides.' She paused. 'Hole up here to what end?'

Strella laughed, imagining the combined size of the big brass's backside. 'That artillery,' he said, 'has nothing on the blast of those farts.'

Some of the men laughed nervously at Strella's unruliness. They shrugged; it was just typical. Jolene regarded him for a moment and then burst out laughing.

'Don't tell you been smoking that weed again, Strells?' If she liked you, Jolene had a habit of suffixing your name with an S, so much that the South Africans in the group such as Macaco or Gabela had to cock their ears when Jolene, who hadn't lost her thick platteland accent, lapsed into an affectionate mode and called them Macs or Gabs respectively. She never attempted to change Barak's name however.

'Really, Strella,' added Macaco. 'Not after all the warnings?' He had a quick, simian alertness about him, which had earned him his *nom de guerre*. 'Man, we need you to have a clear head here.'

'Come on, Macaco,' said Gabela. 'You're the last one to speak of clear heads here. Just look at you.'

And everyone turned to look at Macaco, gaunt, crouched like he'd be springing onto the nearest tree, his eyes sunken into their sockets. It didn't take a genius to know that he was a smoker.

'All of you, relax,' Strella said. He wanted to say that Macaco looked no different from anyone in the unit, well, except for Jolene, it being a universal law that women took longer than men for the toll of drug taking to show. All of us are users, he wanted to say, but turned instead to Barak the Greek. 'Barak? The lady asked you a question. What are we here for?'

'We have to wait a few hours,' Barak the Greek said. 'For nightfall.'

'And then what?' Strella asked. Jolene wrinkled her nose.

'We've got to collect a package,' Barak said. 'For the Old Man.'

'I don't like this,' Jolene grumbled, but still trailed behind Barak the Greek. 'We could be walking straight into an ambush.'

'That would make me a spy for the MPLA or the Cubans, right, Jolene?' Barak the Greek asked. 'I've heard it said that mercenaries cannot be trusted, that they owe their loyalty to the highest bidder.'

'I don't care who's got your loyalty,' Jolene said. 'I just know I want to get out of this fucking thing in one piece.' *Die fokken ding.*

'In that case,' Barak the Greek said, raising his voice. 'I'd appreciate it if you all just shut the fuck up and did as you're told.'

'Yes, baas,' Jolene muttered with bad grace.

Evening was fast approaching as the group marched past the debris towards a ruined adobe hut. The site they picked was off a track in a field overgrown with grass and weeds that choked wild flowers in bloom. It was shielded from the main rugged thoroughfare by abandoned huts, cannibalised sheds and rusting skeletons of tractors and various scraps that spoke of a dead farm. Looming over the field from a distance of one hundred and twenty metres was a ruin of a house, whitewashed once upon a time but now a sick grey and pockmarked with bullets. Like almost all Portuguese houses, it was fronted by a veranda, the wrought-iron gate of which was still, miraculously, intact, the windows hidden behind shutters like eyes unwilling to reveal their secrets.

It must have been a farm that had fallen onto hard times ending in ruin, the livestock gone and the vegetation mangled by the combined assault of neglect and pitiless elements. Cassava, which had been one of the main crops by the sight of its dead roots, was now a mere memory, the mangrove-like stalks as useless as fossils to a starving traveller. The group paused before a structure, perhaps a debilitated silo. On the one wall out of four that were almost undamaged, someone, a village artist perhaps, had painted a crude though fairly accurate portrait of MPLA president, Dr Agostinho Neto. Scrawled in ink that had withstood the elements, above the bespectacled, presidential face and alongside 'vivas' and 'abaixos', was a thought bubble enclosing the words, 'RESOLVER

OS PROBLEMAS DO POVO'. The portrait seemed to annoy Barak the Greek because he swung his rifle and seemed set to fire a burst when something checked him, perhaps the knowledge that they were low on ammo and wasting it on an image, however reviled, was plain stupidity. Behind him Jolene shook her head in a gesture typical of women witnessing the capacity of men to act like idiots.

Strella remembered one of the tips he had picked up back at the training camp in Ondangwa. His instructor had said that it was useful – at a certain, desperate moment – to trust one's instincts. He'd said: 'Listen to the little voice that warns you of danger.' Strella could swear he was hearing that voice once more and he wondered whether it wasn't Mabitla leading him into a trap, where he'd chortle while Strella writhed on the fishhook. If it wasn't Mabitla, then, he'd better stay awake.

Barak the Greek, somehow assuming that his status of mercenary was a badge of leadership, had started giving orders, allocating the watch for the night, assigning sleeping places. Better armed with the Belgian FAL rifle held at the ready, Barak the Greek was a picture of soldierly perfection, which belied his unreliable temperament. Dressed in a soft cloth cap, jungle jacket, and trousers tucked into his boots like a musketeer, he was the only one with a fragmentation jacket worn over his dappled camouflage uniform. He came kitted out with standard webbing consisting of suspenders, ammunition pouches, complete with a holster containing a 9 mm pistol strapped to his side. In contrast, the other men, Macaco and Gabela, were outfitted with recycled SWAPO or FAPLA-issue camouflage uniforms, Chinese AKs, perhaps one or two defensive hand grenades. Their shoes – mainly trainers – had seen better days, some so ragged that mischievous toes peeked out of holes in the side of the canvas. Everyone had lost weight and for this reason men took to hitching up their pants on the trot, like prisoners divested of their belts. Only Jolene, who had learnt to be fashionable under adverse conditions, looked like those women Strella had seen gracing the covers of *Soldier of Fortune*, which men would pass around for some solitary manual relief in the latrine.

They now lay with their backs against oil-drums cut in half lengthwise and used as troughs for animals, gazing at the approaching night, the first stars flickering in the sky. It was a strangely peaceful moment, beguiling in its placidity. On Strella's side and smoking a roll-up cigarette, Jolene sighed.

'This isn't a country,' she said. 'It's a crime scene.'

Even though he never wanted to agree with anyone, Strella thought that what Jolene was saying was true.

'True. Nothing makes sense here,' Strella said. 'When do we go in to check the house?'

'When the *baas* says so,' Jolene said.

'You don't like him. Do you?'

'There's no rule that we must love one another here.'

'I can hear you people,' Barak said. 'You're plotting your little mutiny. You'll fucking get yourselves into trouble.'

Strella shook his head. Nothing was real here; even Barak the Greek sounded unlike his usual self, because, in another time, someone would be on the ground, bleeding from the mouth and counting his teeth. Although Strella carried out orders of the FNLA commanders and participated in hot, sudden fights where his side sometimes took heavy casualties, he still felt eerily cut off from it all. Engaging in battle, spilling blood, watching comrades dropping around him or a headless body running a few metres before tottering to the ground, was as intimate as sexual activity – and as bewildering. But he was experiencing it all as if it were happening to someone else. This worried him more than the numbness he had felt after stabbing Mabitla. Being unmoved in the midst of death – causing death; seeing green flies buzzing over bodies bloated in the sun; his handiwork and that of his compatriots; the smell – indicated a quality in him which he couldn't quite accept. It was like the trembling moment, a revelation that faces someone who suspects that he or she is capable of committing heinous crimes.

Am I crazy? Black people regarded insanity as the most abject of human conditions – perhaps white people, too, but as he'd never been white he wouldn't know how *they* processed stuff. It was an affliction worse than death. The feeling of not belonging anywhere further complicated the distance, the deadness. In his short life he'd had to do so much in strange lands, starting with Botswana. Then he was in Libya. From there, he was in the hands of aliens led by one Jan Stander. There was Ondangwa, a dustbowl of tents and scrub. And now here, in a country which had a patent on violent death. He was a South African fighting in a foreign land against an enemy he could never have imagined encountering back home. He had no beef with Angolans or Cubans or even some of the People's Army fighters who were in the units with FAPLA. He had trained in Libya to fight the racist regime, Mabitla's invincible Maburu. But it had all changed. He was now part of the Maburu, doing their bidding. They had trained him and broken him the way some men broke wild horses or the nubile women they turned into prostitutes. He was their prostitute, their bitch; any time they had an erection they were at liberty to fuck him in the ass, the way he had fucked the academic's wife. Finally, though, she had fucked him up royally. Look where he was now. Not in a real country but a scream of pain, a sweltering armpit full of fetid malarial swamps and bugs and creepy-crawlies that laid their eggs beneath one's skin, regenerating themselves in pustules that thrived in moist and hidden places. It was a cauldron of hot sun and hot rain where the body was marinated in the toxic juices of the elements. If he were Angolan, he wouldn't be fighting for this land. If anyone wanted it, he would have willingly ceded it to the invader and wished them good luck with the wasps and the snakes and the red ants and swamps and illiterate peasants whose pot-bellied toddlers were always sauntering around naked on thin, stick-like legs, thumbs jammed into their mouths.

Barak the Greek broke out some weed, a handful of maconha ground with hashish into a crazy mix, and passed the pipe around as if participating in some ancient ritual. Through the cloud of smoke, Strella regarded Barak the Greek, seeing him sprawled as if there was no war or need for vigilance, his rucksack forming a pillow. The last of the day's light flickered and Strella became aware that although the Greek carried himself like a young man and had perfected the swagger of youth with his shaggy brown hair tied with a bandanna under the floppy hat, he was quite an old man, perhaps in his fifties, one foot already in the grave.

'How old are you, Barak?' Strella asked, a wave of peacefulness washing over him, the distance returning but unthreatening this time.

Barak the Greek pondered the question. 'I could be your father, Strella,' he said. 'Matter of fact, you can regard me as an ancestor.'

One of the men, Strella's homeboy with a forgettable name, laughed, sounding as if he were on the other side of a canyon. Small, sinewy, the AK-47 looking very heavy in his hand, he was watching the smokers with an amused expression, like a parent. 'You, Barak?' he asked. 'An ancestor?'

'Why not, Gabela?' Barak the Greek said. 'Ancestors are getting younger by the day. Very few people die of old age nowadays.'

'And us? Thina?' Gabela asked. Perhaps this was the only question he ever wanted to ask. 'Are we going to see old age?'

'I wouldn't count on it,' Barak the Greek put in cruelly. 'In any event, why would you want to grow into an old fogey?'

'Why?' Gabela asked. 'So that we'd also experience what you've experienced. Eat the food you've eaten ...'

'And sleep with the women you've slept with,' said Macaco, the other South African who'd kept his eyes trained on the road from the moment they entered the hut.

'For fuck's sake, just get back to your post,' Barak the Greek said. 'You're still a virgin.'

'You bastard,' Macaco said. 'It's your mother who's a virgin.'

'Of course, you're spot on,' Barak the Greek said. 'Didn't you know my other name's Jesus? I'm a product of immaculate conception.'

'Fuck you,' Macaco said.

The men laughed. Yes, that was Macaco, all right, with his stock insult. Like clockwork, whenever affronted, Macaco would be sure to bring someone's mother into it. Your mother this. Your mother that. Had he had it in him, he would have shot Barak the Greek on the spot. However, his back rigid with indignation, he elected to step over the broken wall and proceeded to keep watch from behind a nearby shrub.

'My, my,' Barak the Greek said. 'Everyone's a little touchy this evening. Could it be my wee pipe?'

'I wouldn't advertise that so proudly if I were you,' Jolene said.

Strella suspected that the two had a history together, hence the ill feeling. He thought of the academic's wife, far away in Botswana and wondered bleakly what had become of her. Everything was unreal.

He shrugged off a disagreeable thought that was knocking at the door of his mind and instead listened to the darkness as it shrouded them like a living thing, a blanket. The pipe now glowed like a one-eyed animal, moving from hand to hand. 'When do we go in?' Strella wanted to know.

'Now,' Barak the Greek said, glancing at his watch. 'We go in now.'

'Zulu hour,' Jolene said. Then she giggled and became the little girl she once was. 'I've always wanted to say that … Zulu hour.'

There was no giggling, Zulu hour or no, after they had entered the house. The hallway smelled hideously. Rodents scuttled across the wooden floor. The electrical lamps flooded the passage leading to the lounge with light. Household articles, clothing items, books and papers littered the floor, pointing to a hurried orgy of looting. The house looked like a squatted house after students had been served with eviction orders. Anything that could be carried had been taken, the wallpaper bearing rectangular discolouration marking the spots where paintings had hung. The glass display cabinet stood empty, some of the crockery smashed on the floor, not so much in an act of vandalism as in suggestion of haste. The raiding party had carted off the Telefunken hi-fi radio, leaving behind tendrils of confused wiring. Someone, almost as a malicious afterthought, had smashed the heavy speakers with a hard object, most likely a rifle butt. Similar care and carelessness marked the plunder in the bedrooms.

The big surprise lay in the dining room. Here, a reverential attitude had applied and the bodies of the family had been left untouched – by human beings, that is. Huge rats scampered off at the introduction of light, while their braver cousins lingered longer to nibble on the human remains. Four dead bodies lay slumped and eyeless as they putrefied at the dining table. This family consisted of a mother, two daughters in their teens and the man who must have been the father. A bullet had removed the top of his head, a bottle of red wine half-full and the meal, also rotting, so covered with mobile maggots it seemed to have a life of its own.

'Did they just sit there and let him kill them?' Jolene asked.

Strella wasn't sure if her voice was choked with fury or disgust. 'Probably shot them very quickly, before they could see what was going on.'

'No,' said Macaco. 'Look at the wine glasses. The three have sipped from their glasses. The glass of o mais velho looks full.'

'Poison?' Jolene asked. The three bodies had no bullet wounds.

'Yep, poison,' Macaco said. He lifted the glass beyond the reach of dead fingers and brought it up to his nose and sniffed it. He put it down with a look of satisfaction at having been proven right. He had after all been a police officer in South Africa and knew about these things.

'Who was he?' Strella asked Barak the Greek.

'The Old Man's collector,' Barak the Greek said. 'Some kind of chief enforcer in a countrywide protection racket.'

'So,' Jolene asked, 'what are we? Cogs in a big extortion wheel?'

'Extortionists,' Macaco said, swirling the syllables around his mouth. 'That's who we are.' He sounded amazed at the journey that had taken him from being an upholder of the law to an armed breaker of one.

'Well,' Strella said, 'he's not enforcing anything at the moment.'

'Okay,' said Barak the Greek, the commander, straightening up. 'We have our orders. Let's get cracking.'

'What we're looking for,' Strella asked, 'how do we know the others haven't already found it?'

'Because the dining table hasn't been disturbed.' Barak the Greek knew where everything was. He had a map.

Jolene refused point blank to help move the table with the dead bodies on it. In fact, when Barak, Strella, Macaco and Gabela went about carting the table and chairs, trying without much success to cause as little disturbance as possible to the dead, Jolene stepped out into the dark outside. Strella heard her strike a match and soon the sharp tang of tobacco smoke wafted into the dining room, mingling with the pervasive odour of death and decay.

It didn't take them long to find the trapdoor under the square of carpet on the wooden floor. The locker, wrapped in a shawl that looked like an heirloom, was itself a worthy item that could have brought a tidy sum in the market. It was a wooden box with steel-plated metal corners and brass studs, wrought-iron hasps and pendulous padlocks securing the lid. Dragging it out proved difficult, as its hiding place was a deep hollow square that could accommodate only one person. And so, Macaco had to make a huge effort to lift the box and hoist it above his head for Strella and Barak the Greek to haul up.

'Where's Gabela?' Strella asked as they laid the box on the side of the table, the dead now forgotten. The moment he asked the question, he knew that something was wrong. It was the momentary suspension of sound, itself an interruption to the rhythm of a discordant night. It was the loud silence of the dead members of the family, their stillness under a candelabra dangling from a high pressed ceiling that spoke of long-gone luxury. It was the fact that this was a house occupied by ghosts that objected to the ongoing thieving.

As if conjured by a bad dream, Gabela burst into the dining room walking backwards, arms raised. Reversing also, arms up as if doing a fatigue exercise, cigarette burning in her hand, the prized Mosin Nagant rifle now jabbing her midriff, Jolene seemed to be performing a complex dance routine whose central motif was a double-shuffle.

The group that entered, rifles covering Strella's unit, consisted of masked professionals who knew how to take control of a dwelling, disarming the Ondangwa products while two or three of them swept through the house with lightning speed. They conducted their operation with minimum use of language, communicating through gestures and signs, until Barak the Greek shot out the light from a prone position, forgetting about the pale light of an inconvenient moon that made nonsense of the darkness. The room's silence was shattered by a salvo of gunfire, most of it directed at Barak the Greek. In the half-light, Strella could see his body jerking spasmodically. He had to be superhuman to survive that. Strella wanted to ask, what the fuck's the matter with you, when a sledgehammer slammed into his chest and he knew that the body armour to absorb that impact had still to be invented. Accepting that he was dying, he thought: hey, that's the way it goes, children. Then he was pulled into the embrace of a warm and enveloping darkness, the sticky moistness under him, which he knew was his lifeblood, spreading and radiating warmth, generously, like a drink of chai on sentry duty at an outpost late at night. He thought he heard Jolene scream, a shriek that formed words. Zulu hour, *die fokken ding*.

He woke up on Saturday, 30 April 1977, in the casualty ward of the military hospital in Luanda. A Cuban doctor was asking him questions. He was unable to respond because the pain was as big as the universe. Much later, bones knitting together but still unable to move his arms, he was told that his upper body was shattered but there was no damage to any of the vital organs. You're one lucky hombre, they said.

Night after night the chaplain, Nerissa Rodrigues, came accompanied by men whose faces looked vaguely familiar and whose demeanour convinced him he was better off dead. They asked him questions that caused his head to throb. Where did you meet Barak the Greek? Do you know he's actually a Phalangist from Lebanon, a friend of Bachir Gemayel? No, I don't know. Okay, tell us about Jan Stander. He knew that the questions would not stop until he gave them something.

He was discharged to serve time in the Movement's camp for dissidents and captured enemy agents, UNITA, and given a different name – no, a number. His left tibia was fragmented, endowing him with a limp like Mabitla. The old bastard must be doing a jig in the grave. You thought you're something, but you're nothing, boy, just a common piece of shit. Six months later, he found himself a prisoner in a fetid cell in Sector 37, where he received harsh treatment at the hands of the People's Army's security. Etched as if with acid on his brain was the face of one Nozishada. He discovered the thin line between pain and pleasure, how Nozishada's visits were opportunities for the jailer to tell the prisoner what was being done to Jolene. So, she was alive, also in the camp prison. On one occasion Nozishada, animated by an undefined madness, flourished his fingers under Strella's nostrils, enjoining him to get a whiff of Jolene's genital juices. And then, one night, he was brought into the cell with her, Jolene's own eyes as round as saucers, showing the terror he didn't know a human being was capable of suffering. Later, they used his marksmanship, his skill, getting him to kill while they had a gun trained on him. Nozishada and Stander, he found, were one and the same thing, two people born worlds apart but as alike as two peas. Later, unleashed on the world, Strella became convinced that the touch of another human being could transcend political loyalty.

Reinforced now by five men carrying guns fitted with silencers, on 17 December 1989, Strella rode shotgun beside the driver known as Doctor on account of his knives that were honed to the sharpness of surgical scalpels. Sikwane, the border village straddling South Africa and Botswana, was still as if taking a siesta. A hundred metres away, a boy herding a single goat stopped and looked at the van passing. Strella watched the side mirror as the bush sailed away, the scrub trailing behind, wondering if Doctor had seen the boy. Everyone feared Doctor; Strella was sure that he was one of the most effective killing machines. For him, killing or maiming was just another day in the office, executing his task with the detachment of a surgeon removing a tumour. The car pulled to a stop beside a camouflaged encampment and the men waited for the night.

At the right hour they filed out. Having checked their weapons and affixed silencers to the gun barrels, they donned the night goggles. 'It's time, *madoda*,' Strella said.

LOG #2

At first he asks her to strip and then, overtaken by an alien emotion, he strides across the small bedroom, naked, and starts to undress her. 'Have you ever done this before?' he asks, hard against her back. 'No,' she says, fearful and curious, never having heard him express doubt before. 'I've never wanted to do it,' he says. She studies his face in the mirror across the room, trying to read if he's sincere or taking her for a ride. So many men have done that. But then she gives him the benefit of the doubt, bending over, he hiking the dress over the mound of her buttocks and then, slowly, the strange feeling of being more naked than when she had absolutely nothing on. The head going in first, probing, then the shaft slowly sliding in, the faint, distant odour of sulphur and then her insides unravelling.

Later, he tells her about his mission. She's amazed and at the same time not surprised. He would always represent the duality of good and evil, right and wrong, pain and ecstasy. 'I want you to do something for us.'

And late at night he takes her along to meet the contact, a young boy who does his bidding, runs errands. She remains in the car while he gets out and hears him voicing surprise when he comes across the young man in a leather jacket and a haircut sported by streetwise youngsters. 'But you're not Tikka Joe,' he says. The young man answers with a respectful tone that, however, still holds a trace of cockiness. 'There's been a change of plan Tikka Joe's no longer part of this deal,' he says. 'My boys and I are at your service.'

She senses rather than sees him tensing as he digests this information. The way his back is rigid, she knows that he is angry. He doesn't like diversion from routine, especially if he isn't the one instituting the changes. Sensing this, the young man speaks hurriedly. 'My name's Spider and we're called the Nabobs.'

'Nabobs?' Even to her the name sounds ridiculous, something plucked out of an illustrated storybook or heard in a movie, and it convinces her of the boys' utter lack of seriousness. Then Spider says: 'I know the house where the people you're looking for are. Ngobese's place.'

'Did Tikka Joe ...'

'He didn't tell me anything. But I'm resourceful.'

She laughs at the word. Resourceful. How can a teenage tsotsi be resourceful? But then her skin crawls when she thinks of what all this means. And she's powerless. She isn't at all resourceful.

'Okay,' she hears him saying. 'Let's see what the Nabobs can do.'

4

CONNECTIONS

At 11:00 a.m. on Christmas Day of 1989, Mchinda, Django, Pomegranate and Stinkwood enjoyed a brunch of cake and tea, trying to cheer themselves up. There was news of fighting between a group sponsored by the government, called Imbokodo, and comrades aligned to the freedom struggle. A young man was shot dead not far from Ngobese's place. The guerrillas, although sure of their capacity to defend themselves, started to understand that coming home could be another foray into enemy territory. It was an unseasonably cold morning, defying the weatherman on radio who had promised a scorcher. Perhaps later in the day, it would improve.

'Us sitting in the sun like this,' Mchinda said, 'reminds me of those people banished in places like Sekhukhune. Nothing happens there. They wake up in the morning, follow the sun and at night they go to sleep.'

'They cannot work?' Pomegranate found this impossible to grasp.

'No,' Mchinda said. 'The banishment order forbids them from being in the company of more than one or two people at a time. Bosses can't hire someone who's condemned to being a loner.'

'Apart from that,' Django said, 'no one can give a rabble-rouser a job. Might influence the other workers.'

Stinkwood had been lost in thought. 'What we're doing is wrong.'

'What's eating you?' Django asked.

'We left our comrades in Zeerust.'

'Ja. But there was nothing we could do.'

'We could have given them a fitting burial. Not leave them in the cave.'

Pomegranate, who was somehow always obliged to agree with Stinkwood, said: 'Perhaps all we need to do is tell their folks that their sons are dead.'

'Or,' Stinkwood said, brightening up, 'at least that we know where their bones are.'

'What use is that,' Django asked, 'knowing where their bones are? Are you going to mount an operation, travel more than three hundred miles – with what?'

'We don't have to go there,' Mchinda said. 'We have to know who those comrades were, their real names and then tell their folks.'

'Do you realise that we're in this country illegally?' Django asked. 'We are still on the wanted list of the security police. We are trained guerrillas, terrorists, in their eyes. If we got caught here we'd sit for a long time. Or even hang.' He could feel that he was losing the argument. Even Mchinda sounded sold on the idea of extending the mission beyond its original remit. 'We're likely to get caught.'

'Who would rat on us?' Mchinda asked. 'It's Christmas time, everyone's in a jolly mood, no one's looking out for guerrillas. Furthermore, we haven't heard anything on the radio.'

'You seriously expect security police to put out an all-points bulletin for us using the public media? Grow up, you people.' Django was getting angry. He had a feeling of being sucked up into something he wouldn't be able to control. 'What happened to the vigilance of the commandos?'

'We are still the commandos,' Pomegranate said belligerently. He looked round at the others, to get a corroboration that they were still worthy of the designation. 'Right?'

No one answered him, letting him sweat this one out. Mchinda said: 'Okay, let's broach this with Ngobese. See what he advises.'

'Ah,' Django said. 'So, Ngobese is now your new chief of intelligence. You all go ahead and talk to Ngobese. Maybe he'll suggest a quicker route to the Fisher Street police headquarters.' He paused. 'I'd understand if we asked him to put us in touch with Chaplain Nerissa or any of the comrades from the senior structures.'

'That's a good idea,' Mchinda said. 'Chaplain Nerissa.' He nodded. To Django he said: 'See? All it took was just a little pressure and here you are now, coming up with a solution.'

'Comrades,' Django said. 'We've got to think this one through.'

'If there's anyone who can help with this one,' Mchinda said, 'it's you, Django. You worked with the *gatas* and came across people's biographies.'

His use of the derogatory term for the security police suggested Mchinda's own unfinished battles. He shrugged: even though unwholesome, he accepted that someone had to do the job.

'Even under the most ideal circumstances,' Django said, 'it takes time to do a comprehensive match. There's a lot involved in the verification process.'

'It doesn't need to be protracted,' Mchinda said. 'You just have to match the name – the *nom de guerre* – to the real name, which might be in records somewhere.'

'When I joined the People's Army,' Django said, 'it was always important that a record should be kept of comrades who died. We needed the information: who, when and how. The one question never asked was "Why". Everyone who joins the Movement, especially the People's Army, does so fully knowing the reason why. That's why I stayed close to recording officers and the commissars – and, much later, the chaplain: to ensure a record was kept of the location of the graves.' And so, with the recent mission – and the deaths – in the Western Transvaal, he knows, it's almost automatic, that the parents, the next of kin, of the men who fell, should be told.

But how to obtain their true true names? pondered Django. Guerrillas are so secretive. Sometimes they embraced their alternative identities to the extent that some had been known to forget their given names.

He recalled a Nyirenda in the camp in Sector 37, who kept a record of everyone who ever entered the gates of a training camp in Angola. Where would Nyirenda be, now? Possibly still in Angola or Zambia or somewhere in Europe – or even inside the country, on a Special Operations mission.

'Where do we find the records that Nyirenda had collated in the camp?' Django asked Mchinda.

'Chaplain Nerissa left with some of the records,' Mchinda said. 'I know. I was there.'

'Do you think she kept them?'

'She's smart. Maybe converted them to some easier format,' Mchinda said. 'I can't see her lugging around files with people's names and biographies.'

'How do we get to ask her?'

'Ngobese is our pointsman here,' Mchinda said. 'We give him the trunk; he finds a way to hand us the records. A fair exchange.'

'You think he'll like that?'

'What's not to like?' Mchinda laughed. 'It's Christmas. The parents of the men need something to cheer them up.'

'Here comes Ngobese,' Pomegranate said. To Django: 'You tell him.'

'I should tell him?' Django was scandalised. 'Are you crazy?'

'He's right,' Mchinda said with a straight face. 'You handle this, Django. You're the commissar. Apart from that, Ngobese has a lot of respect for you.'

'Fuck you, guys.'

Thinking about it on his own he saw that it made emotional sense, even though he hadn't even remotely considered getting in touch with his own family members – most of them hailing from these parts, actually in D Section of KwaMashu Township – who must have worried about him from the first day of his disappearance into exile. What would members of the Zimu household know of exile? For them it was so abstract it could be in another galaxy. His father must be an old man now, in his eighties, his mom – and this was one thing that had shaken him – passed away in 1982, some strange illness, and he never got a chance to bury her. Of all the sins he placed on the doorstep of the regime, the one that stood head and shoulders above anything, as unforgivable as betrayal, was his being barred from saying goodbye to his mother. In a sense, it was this single death that spelled a complete rupture with his family. In his mind's eye he saw the perplexed, wounded look on the faces of mourners, all of them asking silently: what kind of son was this who couldn't attend his own mother's funeral? His younger sister, Norah, got married to Kelelo Mabitse, Django's one-time friend; they relocated to the greener pastures, if there was such a place, of Johannesburg, during his absence. Their kids, Django's growing tribe of nephews and nieces, must be past adolescence by now. His brother, Eustace, was a sales rep at Smith & Nephew, in Westville, Durban. Who was this Smith and what did his nephew look like?

His father was a minister of religion, a status that Django viewed with the greatest suspicion, railing against the old man for worshipping a god that must have held black people in low esteem, else why were their lives such a pile of shit? Thinking back to the Reverend Matthew Zimu, he wondered if he had reached a higher level of self-delusion in his old age. Or had the events of the last decade, during which the regime outdid itself in cruelty, introduced a more critical attitude? He doubted it. In his father's eyes, white people were God's representatives on earth. Next in line on the rung of sanctity was a black prince who shared his father's view that to be white was to be blessed. On leaving home, turning his back on his father's house, Django was heard vowing that he dreamed of a day when he'd bring to his father the head of a white man on a tray. Django had heard of Poqo members in the Transkei who were hanged for killing white people.

Much later, when some of his comrades died in various parts of Africa, especially in Angola, Django was seized by a fear that the deaths meant the disappearance of something important, history, maybe, that connected the deceased with what was going on way back home. He hated the thought that these lives could easily fall into a void, emptiness the likes of which was encountered in a nightmare. It was also obscene that some of the recording officers, members of security, were callow youths who didn't seem overly exercised with the need for continuity. Some of them, when taking down the biographies of newcomers, played down the importance of what their ears heard and their pens scribbled on lined notepaper. This of course was their own defence against breaking down, for young people, far from home, could only steel themselves against the pain by sheathing their feelings within the skin of callousness. Working briefly with Nyirenda in the camp in Sector 37, Django had determined to remember each face, each name; he memorised the stories of the men and women, ensuring that he would be able to recall everything in the documents that passed through his hands. He wept in the privacy of his bunk in the dugout, the fortified trench, which was also the officers' quarters, when he replayed in his mind the day's quota of woe, for instance the account of a recruit who'd left home on the same day of the burial of his child or his father or his mother. That same evening, on the radio used to monitor the news, Django caught a moving rendition of 'The Circle Won't Be Broken', and couldn't go out until the night of the following day.

He informed Ngobese of the guerrillas' proposal. Ngobese didn't like it. 'Couldn't you guys have bought me a Christmas card or something? Or a gift from a camp … this?' He waved a hand in the air like a wand with which to transform all the evil conspiring to make his life difficult, on Christmas Day, no less.

'What's difficult about getting the information?' Django asked, unsympathetic. His was a mixed attitude to Ngobese; he had allowed his son too much leeway. If a child looks like you, he thought, you have a duty to make sure he grows up into something that would make you proud.

'For one, it means checking with Muzi Thabethe.' Ngobese paused, contemplating the injustice. 'Why do you have to be a bunch of social workers … I thought you were guerrillas.'

What we're doing is observed by fighting men the world over, Django wanted to tell him, edify the bastard. 'Why don't you want to check with MT?' He had a sense Ngobese had been drinking. 'Have you been drinking?' Then, cruelly: 'Drowning the sorrow.'

'Just this once,' Ngobese said. 'She's wasting time with him.'

Django knew it must be a woman. 'With Muzi Thabethe?'

'Who else?'

'Is that who you were thinking about in the car when we rode down here?' Django asked. 'Muzi's wife … what's her name?'

'Laura.'

'You have a right to love someone,' Django said, seized by an anarchic spasm. If the price of getting information about his slain comrades entailed aiding and abetting the sin of adultery, well then, so be it. Also, wasn't it that, when all was said and done, the source of adultery was love, however misdirected? 'Mr Ngobese,' he said, 'it's also love that makes us do what we have to do.' He meant to say that it was love for his people that would have spurred him or any other patriot to join the struggle, but it all came out wrong.

'So we're all lovers?' There were tears struggling to break out in Ngobese's stammer.

'Sure, Mr Ngobese.' Shit, the man was drunk. 'The hell with MT, just go straight to Chaplain Nerissa.'

'You'll back me up?'

'We're guerrillas. That's all we're trained for.'

The following afternoon, on Boxing Day, which a hungover Mchinda declared to be a day for boxing the ears of noisy people, the guerrillas confirmed to Ngobese that he had their support. He must ensure that Chaplain Nerissa came to Durban. 'On second thoughts,' Ngobese said, while reassuring Django that he was not chickening out, 'I have to fly this past the Committee.' He told them that the Committee consisted of Muzi Thabethe, Zephaniah Zwane, known as Bra Zeph, Johannes Sibisi and Nomasonto Sokhela. They didn't try to dissuade him. They understood that there were structures.

'It's not correct,' Muzi Thabethe said. He was alone in the bedroom. The people waiting for him were in the lounge. Laura was fixing them snacks. Yes, Christmas was a time for orgiastic feasting, when his wife sponsored a week-long feeding scheme. Earlier in the day, runny-nosed urchins peeped over the fence. Anyone suddenly on your doorstep had to be given something: tea, coffee, cookies and sweets; kids yelled for ice cream as if the fridge had unlimited capacity. Even Jehovah's Witnesses showed more consideration.

It was evening. Somewhere in the distance they could hear the sound of firecrackers, the people welcoming the approach of 1990. Boxing Day simply meant that it was not even a week before people would be shouting, '*Happeeee*!' There was no happiness in the room, much less in Muzi Thabethe's face. The clock chimed the hour in the lounge: it was 9:00 p.m.

The truth was that Thabethe was not a people's person. He got nervous and uncomfortable when in the company of more than two people at a time; for him three was not just a crowd but a crowd that filled him with dread, a sense of being swamped. People held inane conversations, starting with long exchanges about the weather, the change of seasons, even if there was no discernible change anywhere, and then went on to enquire about the health conditions of so-and-so, while wondering about the state of the country, sighing at the heavy burden on the shoulders of each and every black person in this blasted republic. He hated this even more when it extended to his own comrades, the dominant principle being that every point, no matter how banal, had to be couched in bombast aimed at elevating the contributor's standing in society, or wherever. Nowadays, for some unknown reason, people had adopted certain hand gestures, slicing and vigorously jabbing the air with the index finger, pursing their lips and supporting their chins with their fists while adopting expressions of rapt attention, when he, Thabethe, knew that what they were thinking about was the probable number that would come up a winner in the fah-fee stakes that night. And then the aping of mannerisms of some of the Movement's guiding lights, addressing one another as 'Chief' and broadening their vowels in feeble approximation of a continental African accent. He'd even heard rumours of some of his compatriots being tutored in pidgin English by Nigerian immigrants. 'Wetin de happen, Chief?'

Here they were, now, filling his lounge, actually fouling up his lounge, on a holiday when he would have preferred to watch sports on television or put his feet up and try to finish reading *War and Peace*. Jesus, sometimes he wished he were back in prison; at least people there knew when to leave you alone.

'Are you well, baba?' Laura said, having come up behind him like a ghost, scaring him damn near out of his skin. He'd retreated into the room so as to compose himself, gather his thoughts. Laura, who seemed more animated in the presence of other people, also irritated him. Throughout the day, she'd been in her normal, housewifely clothes, but, quick as a flash, when the people arrived she'd changed into a matching denim suit and high heels, attire that accentuated both her height and backside. He didn't like it when she towered above him, making him seem puny in other men's eyes. He even caught a whiff of perfume and remembered glancing through one of Laura's magazines and reading about how some Japanese guy would bring out a new women's fragrance in September 1989.

'I'm well,' he said. 'Nice perfume.'

'Ah,' Laura said dismissively, 'that … I would feel more comfortable if I'd had time for a bath. Baba, your guests are waiting.'

'Okay, I'm coming. They know I've seen them.'

In truth, though, he knew that her beauty made him look good. He had caught a glimpse of her effect on the visiting men when earlier she had opened up the door as he stood behind her in the doorway, watching over her shoulder. She hadn't changed then and was still in her flat shoes. But still, the four men's eyes had widened in appreciation. Ngobese, their escort, had looked away pointedly as if avoiding eye contact with both host and hostess. He wondered about the wisdom of pairing her with Ngobese to negotiate with Bra Zeph.

He appeared after a few minutes, smiling. 'I'm sorry for my rudeness back there,' he said. 'I had to take care of an urgent matter.'

Ngobese did the honours, rattling off strange-sounding names of trees until one of the men, Django, put up a hand.

'I don't think we still need all this cloak-and-dagger stuff. My name is Django, real name Ezekiel Zimu. I was called Hickory until recently. I used to be a photographer a long time ago, but am now just an unemployed guerrilla.' He gestured in Mchinda's direction.

'I'm Mchinda. It's a name I'm comfortable with although my real name is Sidwell Zondi. And I dare anyone to call me Sidwell.' He glared at a snickering Stinkwood. 'I first went by the name of Thabo Stone and then I was called Sassafras, for some unknown reason … Now that Django has blown our cover, I'm hoping to know the real names of Pomegranate and Stinkwood.'

Standing at attention, Stinkwood said: 'I'm Rex Mabena and I left home together with Pomegranate, who's back at base, in 1974. For anyone interested, Pomegranate's also known as Styles at home. His real name is Refiloe Mokoena. He was still a student when we left home for exile. I was a taxi driver.'

'Now that I look at you,' Mchinda said, 'you do resemble the guy who threw me out of his taxi in Soweto.'

'You probably didn't want to pay.' Rex Mabena even talked like a taxi driver.

They all laughed. The ice was broken. The group still hovered around the entrance.

'Come on in and sit down,' Muzi Thabethe said. 'And I'm Muzi, an ex-political prisoner, husband to one Laura, Mr Mdunge's only daughter.' Dressed in loose khaki trousers and a simple white shirt and sandals, Muzi was almost relaxed. At his side, Laura Mdunge smiled but didn't say much beyond the usual words of welcome. She disappeared somewhere into the house.

Ngobese trailed behind, taking in the lounge, which he has seen numerous times before, failing to shake off the feeling that he was out of place. Guilt gnawed at him like a persistent mouse and he wondered if Laura had it in her to enclose their little secret inside a steel vault. Even as he got the faint wisps of her perfume still lingering in the air, he was struck by a fatalistic notion that no secret went undiscovered for long.

'You're awfully quiet today, Ngobese,' Muzi Thabethe said as he ushered the guests to their seats. 'Rough times, hey, this Christmas period?'

'You know how it is,' Ngobese said, easing his bulk into the settee. He did feel tired.

'Well,' Muzi Thabethe said, 'I have just the cure for you.' He chuckled at the irony. 'A medicine for our ailing inyanga.'

Over drinks, including a concoction designed to address Ngobese's hangover, the men discussed the war currently gripping Natal and the collusion of the state with elements of the Zululand Bantustan administration. Shuddering for effect, Ngobese related the horrors of necklace killings that had become the favoured method of punishing people accused of betrayals. Night gathered. Delicately, Ngobese raised the issue of the guerrillas' intention to pay their respects to honour their fallen comrades by visiting their families.

'But,' Muzi Thabethe asked, 'what will it solve? You'll just be exposing yourselves.' He didn't voice this, but 'yourselves' seemed to include the operations of the Natal underground machinery.

'That's a tragedy,' Django said, 'because this is very important to us.'

Sensing trouble, Ngobese chipped in. 'It shouldn't be a black-and-white issue. We must find a compromise.'

'How do you expect the Movement to come to a compromise, Medicine Man?' Muzi Thabethe asked, half-jokingly although there was no mistaking the steel in his tone. 'The men were supposed to bring the trunk from the Western Transvaal. There was no discussion about paying respects, whatever that is.'

'Do you know what happened in the caves of Zeerust, Mr Thabethe?' Django asked quietly. Without waiting for Thabethe to answer he launched into his speech. 'We arrived, ready to defend the Movement. And in our own way we defended the interests of the Movement, of the people of this country. And our comrades died in the process of doing their duty.'

'Listen,' Muzi Thabethe said. 'I also served years in prison for the Movement …'

'Ja,' Django put in quietly, 'many people served the Movement and serve it daily, without expecting to be rewarded. We're not asking for special treatment. We're here in this country illegally. If we were to be arrested we'd serve life imprisonment, if not hang. So, don't go telling us you served in prison. We respect the leadership, but it has to respect us back.'

'What Django means, Mister Thabethe …' Mchinda started. Muzi Thabethe put up his hand, a man used to being taken seriously.

'*Comrade* Thabethe,' he said.

'… *Mister* Thabethe,' Mchinda continued as if undisturbed, 'we are going to make our way back to Ngobese's. But you – or the Movement – are only going to see the trunk the day you enable us to pay our respects to the fallen men. The comrades deserve no less.'

'Who would have such information?'

'General Palweni or people working with him,' Django said. 'By now they should be in the country.' He paused. 'I think they may also be looking for the trunk.'

'Else,' Mchinda said, 'Chaplain Nerissa. That might take more time, but she's always been able to access information.'

'How do you know her?'

'That's the impression I had of her in Angola,' Mchinda said. 'So you'll do it?'

'We'll see.' Then: 'How do I know the trunk is even there?'

'It's there,' Ngobese testified. 'I saw it with my two eyes.'

'You're dealing with guerrillas, Medicine Man. They can disappear in a wink of an eye.'

'The trunk is there, Comrade Muzi,' Rex Mabena said. 'Pomegranate … Refiloe Mokoena is at the house, guarding it. It's not been opened or anything. Still in the original form.'

'Good,' Muzi Thabethe said. 'I don't have the authority for this, but we'll try to get the information. Then I want to see the trunk here, in this house.'

'You'll see it,' Mchinda said.

'It's like in the radio show,' Django said, 'Money or the Box?'

'That just shows you,' Ngobese said, unable to resist the gibe, 'how long you've been gone. That show came to an end a long time ago.'

They heard the car pulling to a stop outside. Laura Mdunge crossed from the kitchen and opened the door before the rest of the visitors could reach the entrance.

'Baba?' she told Muzi Thabethe. 'Sonto, Johannes and Bra Zeph are here.'

Even though no social animal, Muzi Thabethe seemed to be enjoying himself among the comrades – even the truculent ones, who earlier called him *Mister*, imagine the nerve – now dancing up a storm in the lounge. Even though they were all as different as four men could be, Muzi Thabethe was also struck by how they shared common traits. For one, there was no doubting that they were at the prime of their health, as fit as fiddles, even Django whose every step sought to belie the nature of his injury. He must be on the mend. Mchinda was a hard case, his shaven head showing two or three old scars that must have been acquired in serious scrapes. Mchinda was also the most volatile, with a cruel streak that was not hard to recognise. Rex Mabena, the former taxi driver, was much younger, but in his youthfulness Muzi discerned miles and miles of experience, not all of it gained in propitious circumstances. Distantly, he wondered if there was any sexual activity among the guerrillas. Were any of them lovers? He quickly banished the thought. Did love exist in a state of war?

As the music throbbed, rattling the sideboard, Laura Mdunge's pride and joy, he looked at his wife, standing outside the circle of revellers, laughing with her head thrown back, taking part in the merriment but still maintaining a distance. He had observed how she had a default mode that allowed her to retreat into a private world all her own, a world in which he felt unwelcome even when she told him that she loved him. Love was a quaint notion as intangible as the wind. He suspected she was seeing someone. A woman who exploded with the passion that resided in Laura's heart couldn't be expected to pay allegiance to just one person. He wondered who it could be, perplexed momentarily at the possibility that she might fall for one of the guerrillas. He caught Ngobese giving her a long, speculative look, but Ngobese was … Ngobese, a scheming bumbler, eager to please. Muzi even suspected that for all his vaunted manliness, Ngobese might be impotent. The only women he saw were the impressionable township washerwomen who sought the medicine man's counsel on domestic matters. But, then, this was the liberation struggle, where you were forced to work with what you had, with all sorts. Laura, though, seemed drawn to Django; he, on the other hand, appeared oblivious to his magnetism. And that, Muzi Thabethe knew, was the secret; it's what drew him to Japhet Makhunga in prison. Makhunga was strong, able to stand his ground even under the assault by warders armed with truncheons. Distantly, he wondered how the man was faring.

'Nice place you have here, Comrade Muzi,' said Rex Mabena, who'd come up from the settee to stand next to him. They had their backs to the drinks table, facing the small crowd.

'I was lucky,' Muzi Thabethe said. 'It's thanks to Laura that the place looks like a home.'

'A woman's touch,' Rex Mabena said. 'I wonder what my home looks like now.'

'Where's that?'

'Orlando East. Soweto.'

'Boy, you're far from home.'

'I know. We're people of many homes.' Rex Mabena considered his own statement. 'And then, at the same time, nothing, really, is home. I still feel a need to go back to Angola, which was a difficult place more than three thousand miles from here.' He shrugged, perplexed. 'It's far but at the same time … you know what I mean?'

Muzi Thabethe thought he knew what he meant. He had felt the same way in prison. He still missed aspects of confinement. 'Aren't you scared? Of being discovered?'

'I don't know. What's the date today?'

'Boxing Day or 26 December 1989.'

'I just feel that things are coming to a head,' Rex Mabena said. 'They released Tata Sisulu and eight long-term political prisoners in mid-October and since then things have never been the same. The country is in turmoil. Getting arrested now wouldn't faze me, really. It's not like we're careless or actively courting arrest. It's just that … we're home. We've been dreaming of this for years … decades.'

Two spent dancers – whom Muzi Thabethe had christened Mutt and Jeff because Bra Zeph, tall and gangling, towered over a shorter and more thickset Johannes Sibisi – took a breather from the dance floor. Earlier, Bra Zeph had just stood there, swaying to the music, looking at the more frenzied dancers, content with being a spectator. Johannes, younger and possibly fitter, had tried a combination of dances, doing the pantsula and the funky chicken, which had elicited a few laughs from Sonto and Mchinda. Ngobese joined in the festivity although his heart didn't seem to be in it, shambling around like a dispirited hippo and then slumping back into a chair, probably too much to drink last night. The soul of the party was of course Sonto. Nomasonto Sokhela, small but full-figured with an oval face dominated by huge eyes that were accentuated by her short-cropped hair, was lost in a vigorous dance with Mchinda. Their gyrating hips appeared on the verge of uncoupling themselves from their torsos, their hands clapping in time to the bass drum up above their heads, now and then getting down to their haunches while, miraculously, their feet managing a rapid shuffle.

Laura, after watching from the sidelines, joined in, making a grab for her husband, who demurred, smiling, edging back. She signalled Django over with a jerk of her head. Despite the limp Django joined her and led her in a kizomba dance, whirling her around and then gathering her in his arms; he noticed with a smile that she strove hard to match his step. Getting a wisp of her perfume, he felt her softness pressed against him and, sensing an erection, gently stepped back and told her that the dance was popular in countries such as Angola, Congo and Mozambique. She said it was a sexy dance, full of latent energy and he was about to volunteer to teach her when, from the corner of his eye, he caught Muzi Thabethe giving his wife a strange look.

He wondered whether Ngobese appreciated the trouble he was in. The woman was as volatile as gelignite; her grip spoke of something waiting to be unleashed. Her depthless eyes, gleaming hair and satiny skin whose hue reminded him of Curtis Mayfield's tune, 'We People Who Are Darker Than Blue', amounted to a formidable conspiracy against any male resolve. Ngobese, poor sod: he'd better stop whatever he was doing with this woman. Mercifully, the song came to an end but Django still felt her fingers in his hand long after they had both stopped dancing and drifted off into the small crowd standing and chatting. Sonto was holding court and Stinkwood – Jesus, he couldn't quite get used to the name of Rex Mabena – and Mchinda were hanging on to her every word. '… and so they slung a tyre filled with petrol around his neck and struck a match …' She fixed her eyes on her audience as if to check that they were adequately horrified.

They obliged, eyes bugged out in feigned expressions of horror. Mchinda recalled once being part of a small unit patrolling the outskirts of Cacuso when the commander unadvisedly hoisted himself out of the hatch of a BTR60 armoured personnel carrier. There was a sound like a watermelon cracking open on a pavement, followed by the crump of a mortar round before the commander's severed head plopped on Mchinda's lap. He suppressed an urge to inform Sonto that a human head weighed the same as a five-kilogram bag of mielie meal.

At around 11:00 p.m., with everyone gone, Pomegranate (who didn't know that from that point onwards he was he was going to be known as Refiloe Mokoena) left the cottage and installed himself in Ngobese's lounge where he popped a video cassette into the VCR. While experiencing a pang of guilt at abandoning his post, he justified the indulgence on the basis of having stood guard for two hours at a stretch, scanning the terrain for likely intruders. Nothing abnormal detected, just the sound of the township having a ball on Boxing Day. Here and there were intermittent bursts of fireworks. A varicoloured cluster mushroomed up and illuminated the dark-grey sky; a few salvoes painted parabolic arcs, like tracer fire. Nothing more.

He'd stepped outside when he heard a car idling for what seemed an inordinately long time and saw a low-slung Nissan Skyline cruising past. He had heard that these were the friends of Ngobese's political connection, Bra Zeph, kids with guns who were otherwise harmless. He supposed that since the introduction of television in 1976, most of the young people fashioned themselves on some of the TV stars. He had left home just as TV was being introduced, with the most boring programming. In fact on the day he left, a Sunday, he remembered with perfect clarity the daytime programme featuring a symphony orchestra conducted by Herbert von Karajan. It gave him a bad feeling, the music, like something to which people could commit suicide.

But now for something different, he told himself. He didn't know where he'd heard that line, but there he was, ready to enjoy himself.

Plopped on the settee, the television set on the sideboard and the AK-47 on the floor, Refiloe Mokoena watched the antics of cops and robbers in a recorded episode of *Cagney & Lacey*. There was a frenetic car chase where a hoodlum got his comeuppance as his vehicle wrapped itself around a lamppost. Refiloe heard another car pulling up in front of the house and, momentarily disoriented, wondered if the adventure on the box had come to life. Getting to his feet and without paying it too much thought, Refiloe picked up the gun and peered through a corner of the window. He noticed the twin-cab parked across the way. Muzi Thabethe and the Committee must have cold-shouldered the delegation, he mused, or they wouldn't be back this soon.

Eager to return to the interrupted action on the television screen, Refiloe Mokoena opened the front door and tottered back from the force of the door crashing inwards from a tremendous force. Before he could regain his balance, a fist as hard as rock slammed into his jaw and he could feel his teeth loosening and the metallic taste of blood in his mouth. It was surreal, the beating, because he recognised his attacker, taking in the trim, muscled figure, the cap still at the familiar jaunty angle on a shaved head, the eyes watchful; it was as if the men were back in the bush. The attack, then, had the quality of something happening elsewhere in another time and to someone else. *Where's the box?* He heard this question being posed from behind a mist, which he soon recognised to be his own blood blinding him as it flowed from a cut above his eyebrow. *It's at your ma's place*, he said, grinning, knowing that his teeth must be stained red with blood. *I don't need the help of a quisling*, his attacker said almost to himself. It was his signature characterisation for an enemy agent en route to a firing squad. Pulling a pistol out of his waistband and pointing it at Refiloe Mokoena, the attacker shot him in the chest. *I'll find it myself*, he said. Dying, Refiloe Mokoena experienced a great need to inform his killer that he'd never been a quisling. And never would be, but it was already too late as he drifted into a cloud that had dissolved from red to black.

On Friday, 29 December 1989, Ngobese had to take decisions. Someone had died. No matter how closely kept the secret, people gravitate towards the household of the deceased. Because Ngobese was well known around the area, and some insomniac had actually broadcast the news of the killing of the inyanga's nephew from Stanger, a stream of visitors headed for the house. These killings were not unknown, it being the Christmas season, a time for settling scores.

The remaining guerrillas hoped that the killer would return to check his handiwork. They were certain the murderer was someone with military training, perhaps one of their own, most likely from the group that wreaked havoc on Mahogany and his unit in Zeerust. So, they sat, watching at first from a concealed position and then later openly, knowing that it was always better to hide among people. They examined each person as the mourners made their way to the house, hoping for a face that seemed out of place. They knew that the face would be familiar, from a past experience. Some of the visitors were genuine neighbours out to show support for the awkward if secretive inyanga. There was also a sprinkling of Mvumbi's curious friends who hadn't yet come to grips with their buddy's hasty retreat to the sticks following the episode with Spider at the shopping centre.

It was actually a neighbour, Mr Ambrose Maseko, a pot-bellied and moustachioed middle-aged car mechanic who had proposed that Ngobese put up a tent in the yard. Hesitant at first, Ngobese did not wish to draw attention unto the house and by extension the business of the guerrillas. But Muzi Thabethe and Bra Zeph prevailed on him, with Sonto and Johannes putting in their two cents' worth. Clandestinity worked best in circumstances of ordinariness.

'Someone's been shot dead in your house,' Bra Zeph said. 'Some Good Samaritan or nosy parker, take your pick, has spread the word. It's therefore expected that some ritual should take place.' Also, given Ngobese's status as an inyanga – an authority on matters concerning ancestors – he should be the last person to deny the living the opportunity to give full vent to their emotions.

'But,' Ngobese had argued, 'what about Refiloe Mokoena's identity? Won't we bring attention to this place where the murder happened?'

'Don't worry about that,' Muzi Thabethe said. 'We'll fix that.' And fix it they did. First, a detail of workmen went about making repairs to the house, ending up by covering the hole on the door with a piece of planking. They short-circuited the red tape to procure the crucial police report and death certificate for Refiloe Mokoena, the second child of Thulasizwe Ngobese's sister in Stanger. They arranged space in the mortuary and a plot in KwaMashu cemetery. So, now, here they were, the worshippers from the Wesleyan Methodist Church. The men were sombre in dark suits and the women, almost celebratory in red-and-white tunics and black skirts, added to the mix. They jostled for pride of place with the congregants from the Zionist Christian Church. Clad in white robes with a blue cross appliquéd to the fabric in the back, this group had an added advantage. The men carried the shepherd's staff with a hook at the end, for clobbering the Evil One, which could come in handy in an altercation. Two of the visitors in plain clothes alighted from a police van with Z P plates, Zululand Police. Oblivious to the steely stare of the mass of people, they made their way to where Muzi Thabethe and Thulasizwe Ngobese conversed with their lowered heads nearly touching. The cops were unaware that their arrival had hastened the removal of the three surviving guerrillas to the cottage. The location of the cottage was a stroke of genius on Ngobese's part. Even Refiloe Mokoena's killer or killers, who turned the house upside down looking for God-knows-what, hadn't considered to go across to the back, especially since the fowl-run between the two dwellings reinforced the corrugated iron fence as a convincing barrier. The two police officers – one much older, bulkier and taller with an appropriately mournful look, and his younger junior partner with wet eyes – stood respectfully on the side.

'I'm Warrant Officer Brian Khumalo,' the older one said, showing his identification. 'This is Sergeant Mzukisi Booi. We're both from KwaDambuza Police Station. Please accept our condolences and those of our station commander.'

'Thank you, Mntungwa,' Ngobese said, using the cop's clan name. 'How can we help you?'

'We're a little puzzled,' W/O Khumalo said. 'Intrigued is the right word. Without alerting my superiors, I checked with a contact at the Stanger Police Station if they have a Refiloe Mokoena on their records, you know how it is with the young people. Turns out there's no such. The only Refiloe Mokoena, also called Styles in Pimville, is on a list of wanted terrorists. Booi, this young Xhosa boy and me …' he went on, giving his sidekick an avuncular thump on the upper arm with his meaty hand, which must have left the younger man with a bruise, '… took his prints from the mortuary on Gale Street. He's after all a gunshot victim and that's what we do routinely.'

'Routinely,' Sgt Booi echoed, nodding.

'And the database gives us a positive match,' W/O Khumalo continued. 'Normally we're not even supposed to talk about these cases, just refer them straight to the Security Branch liaison on Fisher Street. But we thought we could do this differently.'

'We're breaking the law as it is,' Sgt Booi said. Someone, one of the Wesleyan Brothers, started a song, which faltered while others struggled with the pitch of his voice. But since a tragedy normally united communities and different denominations, the Wesleyans and the Zionists meandered through tonal confusion until a soprano as clear as a clarinet provided the frequency onto which all of them could hang their voices.

'Okay,' Muzi Thabethe said, using the tough tone of one taking control. 'What do you want?'

'We're just saying that people must be careful,' W/O Khumalo said. 'Contrary to popular belief, we are also part of the community. Do what you have to do but not in a manner that would force our hand.'

'"We"?' Muzi Thabethe asked. 'Who's "we"?'

'A number of police officers,' Sgt Booi said. 'There are a few of us.'

'What does this "few of you" want?' Muzi Thabethe asked.

'The person or persons who killed your friend …'

'Refiloe Mokoena,' Khumalo explained.

'… Yes, Mokoena,' Sgt Booi continued, 'we'd like to be the ones that arrest him. Them.'

'Why is that so important to you?'

'Can we speak candidly here?' Khumalo asked. He had hesitated for a minute, someone struggling with a huge decision.

Muzi Thabethe nodded. 'Of course.'

'A few police stations have come under attack,' Khumalo said. 'Most cops don't appear in public in their uniforms as they're targets. We could kill two birds with one stone. If we make the arrest, we increase our value in the eyes of our superiors and you are assured that your friend's killer is brought to book.'

'What does increasing your value do for us?'

'We get privy to more operational information,' Khumalo said. 'Surely, that could be valuable to you …'

'Why don't you just join the Movement, then?' Ngobese asked. He had long realised that he and Muzi were engaged in a crucial negotiation with the police.

'It's not that simple.'

Emboldened, causing Muzi Thabethe to look at him askance, Ngobese made a request. 'We need you to help us.'

'How so?' Khumalo asked.

'We understand,' Ngobese said, 'that the SBs have a database of people who left the country. The list is complete with photos.'

'The point being …?'

'We'd like to be provided with a copy.'

'What for?'

'Some boys died at the border,' Muzi Thabethe said. 'We want to verify their identities.'

'I suppose it's impossible for us to be given more details …'

'We ourselves have just the bare bones of the circumstances,'

Thabethe said, shivering at the unintended pun. 'We only have their travelling names.'

'It's going to be hard,' W/O Khumalo said. 'SBs guard their records.'

'Thanks to the SBs, I served fifteen years in prison.'

'You be careful,' W/O Khumalo said by way of goodbye.

'You too.' Muzi Thabethe softened somewhat. 'Thank you.'

W/O Khumalo waved as he and Booi departed. 'Until later,' he said.

Other unexpected visitors arrived. Mostly dressed in hooded sweatshirts and jeans, they were Bra Zeph's connections – their word – and wished to pay their respects. During the interminable services, marked by sermons and singing, they participated, now and then turning the hymns into liberation songs by transposing the names of Jesus or any of the biblical heroes to names of struggle heroes. They rattled the rafters with their energetic dances, doing the toyi-toyi and simulating with their gestures the firing of machine guns or bazookas. Their leader was simply called Lucky or, as he preferred it, Comrade Lucky. A lanky lad who was once a household name in pantsula dance competitions, he did a frenzied jig. Just as he got down on the floor, his pistol rolled out and landed on the dusty ground; without batting an eyelid, Lucky continued dancing, the action of retrieving the gun off the floor and relocating it inside his jacket being incorporated into the dance routine. The other members clapped and spun around, showing enjoyment as part of bidding a guerrilla goodbye. As they took their leave, Lucky confided to Ngobese. 'Bra Zeph is our man,' he said. 'He's told us about you. We patrol the streets at night, so you're safe.'

'Many thanks,' Ngobese said, wondering why this reassurance left him feeling somewhat insecure. When Ngobese briefed the guerrillas on the encounters of the afternoon, Mchinda told him that Comrade Lucky's outfit must be a self-defence unit. 'You fuck with SDUs,' he said, 'and they sling a burning tyre around your neck.'

It was the first time that Ngobese had heard Mchinda voice anxiety. I hope to God, he thought, that they stay on our side.

On the morning of Saturday, 30 December, the guerrillas remained at home and mourned their comrade in quiet contemplation. Since they couldn't go to the burial grounds, not during the day anyway, they delegated to Ngobese, Thabethe, Bra Zeph and Johannes the responsibility to convey their goodbyes. Muzi Thabethe reported that Sonto had sent her apologies as she had to take care of her sister and Aunt Maisie, who were both down with flu.

There was a lot of anger. The men knew that anger was useful and useless in equal measure. After the funeral, Muzi Thabethe intended to return so that the guerrillas could hand him the trunk, formally. He promised to call Chaplain Nerissa and brief her on the developments.

LOG #3

Suddenly, she's open to life and its possibilities. She intends to surprise him, go to his hidey-hole in KwaDambuza, a warren of shacks, some with coy pretensions to nobleness, the majority having given up any attempt at improvement, narrow tracks, unpaved roads, sewage gurgling and spreading into the ground, getting mixed with the household garbage and kneaded into biological specimens by feet, hooves or wheels of various agencies with any business around the plot. There is a pervasive smell of organic matter that has become a signature of the area, which is less than one square mile. A gaggle of pot-bellied and half-naked toddlers playing in the dust seem as oblivious to the smell as they are of their surroundings. Ditto with the dogs that scavenge in the garbage heap. Taunting them, children throw stones, lisping: 'Voetsek!'

Her feet seem to carry her along the road, running between shacks without numbers, appalled at the lack of privacy. From the road she can see into people's rooms, the bedroom that doubles up as a kitchen, which is also a lounge where a small television set broadcasts the news or a soap opera to animate the unemployed.

And there they are, the unemployed, lounging on doorways, hunched in a circle over a game of mrabaraba or draughts, using bottle caps as counters. Others sit huddled, individually or in groups, staring into the air or sharing a bottle of illegal brew, two or three listening to the radio. Her appearance animates some of the younger men, who whistle or make kissing sounds; it's all good fun during the day but, she knows, it would be edged with menace come nightfall. Others give her a look that is at once quizzical and knowing as if they have a fair idea of the destination of the owner of those exquisite legs. Those in the know give her a quick glance and look away. There are certain women it's always best to leave well alone.

He's surprised when he opens the door to her although she doesn't know whether that's a good thing or a bad thing. She has a feeling that he disapproves of surprises. The room is in darkness, the bed already made with the sheet and blankets perfectly aligned, the corners taut and sharp, better than hospital beds. He opens the curtains. She realises that today he's shaved off all his hair, not that he had much to start with, but it looks somewhat ritualistic; maybe someone important has died.

'You can come out now, Dad,' he says.

A toilet flushes. A man wearing a singlet, shorts and sandals appears. Even though thin now and diminished by illness, it's quite clear he was once a strong man. 'This is my father.'

'Pleased to meet you, sir,' she says, taking the hand that has the texture of sandpaper. She's face-to-face with Captain Mkhukhu.

Captain Mkhukhu gives her a guarded if absentminded look, an old prisoner still wary of the land of the free. He retreats to the other room, leaving behind the smell of a hospital ward.

His son smiles, grim and full of concern. Suddenly, she feels scared.

He knows where she stays with her aunt, who took over when her ma died, and her twelve-year-old li'l sis, Thembani, in Standard 5 at Zamazulu Secondary School in H Section, KwaMashu. In her unguarded moments she speaks of Thembani and the plans she has for her, to take her out of the township into a better place, once her ship comes in. She likes that phrase as it makes her feel all grown up and older than her twenty-three years.

When your ship comes in, he says one day, smiling but not mocking her, what would you really like to do? I mean, apart from taking Thembani to a better school. What do you want for you?

She thinks for a moment. One thing she's come to realise is that it's frustratingly difficult to think while completely naked. And with him, she's naked almost all the time. If she's not naked with him, she's thinking about being naked with him. When naked with him, she's already plotting when next they're going to be naked together. The hours they spend exchanging fluids with limbs entwined always feel woefully inadequate. What would I want for me? Yes. I don't think it's proper? What – the question is improper? C'mon, everyone wants something. We're not talking obvious things like money here, she suggests. He shakes his head. No, not money: consider money as something that we can provide, you and I, together. I'd like to feel safe. This is a fucked-up township. No one is safe here, especially if you're a woman. I'm concerned for Thembani, that someone could rape her and we wouldn't be able to do anything, the house is just full of women. He says, quickly: My father can ensure that you're always safe. He says, you know that? She answers: Of course, but we can't have a normal existence with some bodyguard lurking around. It's also kind of creepy.

I'll provide you with a weapon. In fact, he gets up and picks up his pair of jeans, neatly folded atop his trainers, and his hand reappears with a 9 mm Beretta. He hands it to her. She hefts the weapon, surprised at its weight and, something else, its presence. There's nothing as alive as a gun in the hand, and as stirring. That afternoon, he enters her, forcing her to hold the gun in her hand, the cold steel an accessory, the muzzle unblinking and bearing witness to her rapture.

Later, he has a request. I need a place, a quiet and safe hideout. Got some men who wish to stay out of the limelight. The word makes her smile with its connotations of showbiz. Are they actors, the men wanting accommodation? You could call them circus performers. Really? Yes, he says, smiling at a distant memory. I have seven men, lion-tamers, trapeze artists, knife-throwers, sharpshooters, and experts in fire.

She has an idea what these people might represent. At the same time she curses herself for asking. To know is to understand; to understand is to accept and take responsibility. She has a place in mind – one of Aunt Maisie's relatives lets out a four-roomed house in H Section, not far from Thembani's school. It's got a nice breezeblock fence and should be okay for the circus troupe.

5

TWO WOMEN

On the same Saturday afternoon of 30 December 1989, almost exactly at the time of Refiloe Mokoena's burial, two women reviewed a past that held a key to their future.

'Well,' Chaplain Nerissa said, 'it all starts with excitement and ends up in silence.' The report to the President of the Movement, typed up neatly and collated, sat on the small table beside her. 'I'm done.'

She and Georgina Smith were sitting on the stoep of their house on Regent Street in Yeoville. She had her back to an electric fan that was whirring noisily behind, blowing gusts of air before rattling off on its axis and then swinging back. Meaning to be helpful earlier, Georgina had made the mistake of adjusting the knob so that the blades would blow the wind in one direction. Nerissa had almost bitten her head off, saying she needed the flow of the breeze – the term she used was zephyr. 'My dear,' she had said, 'the zephyr must caress my back and hasten the healing process.'

Who talks like that nowadays? Georgina Smith thought – healing process, my foot. And a zephyr is a make of car. Although miffed, she determined to indulge the older woman her little whimsies. And for good reason. Even though she had seen it so many times, Georgina still couldn't get over the sight of Nerissa's back. For a while it was crisscrossed with angry scars from a parcel bomb blast injury sustained some sixteen weeks ago. Approvingly, Georgina had noticed that the latticework had now become less discernible and a lot less raw. Wondering if her brother had helped accelerate the healing, Georgina remembered when the wounds were so reminiscent of bloodied spaghetti that she had contemplated becoming a vegetarian. Earlier this afternoon, then, while releasing the knob of the fan, Georgina had asked: 'How's the zephyr treating you now?' Nerissa had responded: 'It's fucking great,' and both women had burst out laughing.

The pair had now lapsed into reflective seriousness. Even the three-quarter empty bottle of Chenin blanc, cracked up to enliven any social occasion, had failed in its mission. Absently, Chaplain Nerissa toyed with her glass, tilting it as if about to pour the wine on the flowerbeds. Looking up at her friend, she asked: 'You don't agree?'

'I don't agree that Mandela's release will, as you say, plunge us into confusion,' Georgina said. 'We might not be ready for it but I believe we have a self-correcting gene in our DNA.'

'I don't want to argue,' Chaplain Nerissa said, arguing, 'but from what I hear from the people from Lusaka, things are still a shambles. The pressure is on for people to come back in an orderly way. But they are coming back to structures that are a bit chaotic. The young people here have not grown up enough to avoid being victims of their own anger.'

'I don't think you should be worrying too much about structures,' Georgina said. 'Your concern should be about getting better. Stronger.' She paused, took a sip of her wine, gazed at the street below, the people milling about, black people of all shapes and sizes, oblivious of their impact on history.

'Look at them,' she continued. 'They might have heard at the rally for Walter Sisulu et al that it's just a matter of time before Mandela is released. For them that will mark liberation, one man symbolising the best of humanity. But would that be true?'

'People don't give a damn under which banner they celebrate their freedom. Mandela. Papa Doc Duvalier. Take your pick.' Chaplain Nerissa was at her dismissive best. 'The only thing that shouldn't happen is for De Klerk to take credit for ushering in a new dispensation.'

'De Klerk was the Minister of Education when the children were slaughtered in 1976,' Georgina said. 'Even if he spent the entire rest of his life feeding gumdrops to schoolchildren he'll still be the inveterate racist we know him to be.'

'Isn't that a bit harsh?' Nerissa asked, smiling, now playing the devil's advocate. 'He's put some reforms into place.'

'Pull the other one, Nerissa.' She looked at her friend and lover. 'If Mandela … I mean, *when* he is released, it will be on the basis of his own strength and the fortitude of the people. It will have nothing to do with De Klerk or his cohorts.'

'I agree with you,' Nerissa said. 'That says very little for our faith in the goodness of human beings.'

'Faith is important for you …'

'It should be. For all of us.'

'We should drink to that.'

'Problem is, Georgie,' Chaplain Nerissa said, 'we'll all be so gung-ho about the future, I have a niggling feeling we'll be caught with our pants down. There are just too many unresolved issues in our lives, so many unmourned corpses, so much destruction. And the poverty will be the undoing of any government that takes over this mess.'

Turning her eyes to the five o'clock traffic on the road, she nodded at something in harmony with her inner world. Settling her wine glass on a tray atop a rollable drinks table, she got hold of her crutches, props for getting around the house, which she sometimes left behind when going out. 'Be a dear and get us a bottle of something real,' Chaplain Nerissa said as she hobbled to the toilet inside. 'This wine's given me a headache.'

The light was slowly fading, the darkness pressing its advantage, inhabiting corners and sucking into its maw the throb of the suburb. The new occupants of Yeoville were night people. They were also unafraid, unlike in the past, of disporting themselves along the daytime streets in clothes that were somehow at odds with their bodies. The women wore colours that called attention to the owners' imperfections. The men, usually immigrants whose suits might have been a hit once upon a time on the streets of Bamako or Harare or Yaoundé, evinced a shabbiness that matched their shame at being destitute so far away from home, where some of them were perhaps feted as princes. Only the Nigerians or the occasional Somali proceeded along the street with the calm and purposeful gait of people who'd somehow find a market to corner anywhere on God's earth.

In truth, however, it was becoming more and more difficult to distinguish a black South African from someone from beyond the borders, the immigrant, or, in the parlance of the hour, the alien. Already the trouble that daily trudged up the stairs to her stoep, where someone deferentially asked the domestic helper – herself a Zimbabwean – for the chaplain, pointed to the tension that hung over Yeoville like a pall. In many of the cases of people who felt hard done-by and sought redress, the common denominator was tension between black South Africans and a foreigner. Privately, Nerissa had no time for her fellow men and women's attitudes towards foreigners; she had suffered hideously, a two-year stint for being suspected – suspected, for fuck's sake – of terrorism and a spell of detentions and then, of course, being maimed by a bomb. But she still maintained her people were just crybabies and knew fuck-all about hardship. And so they got their jollies out of tormenting the poor foreign Africans just because they couldn't punish the whites. 'These people,' she'd say, 'sheltered us and paid a huge price for that

– and we pay them back with what? Attitude? No.' She'd shake her head so that her sharp chin would seemingly pave a way for her sharp, un-African, nose to follow. During these outbursts, Georgina Smith usually kept her own counsel. Sometimes, it was a little bit too much.

'Maybe,' Georgina once said, rather unkindly, after getting an earful of Nerissa in full cry, 'it was actually your comrades and not the Special Branch that sent you that parcel bomb, just to shut you up.'

Back from the toilet, Nerissa sat down and looked at Georgina in profile, noticing with surprise that she'd never really seen how closely she resembled Yusuf. She thought of making a snide comment but thought better of it. Georgina doted on her brother.

Now the two of them were staring at the gathering night, perhaps thinking about a momentous year edging to a close. 'Muzi called me this morning. There has been a change with the men.'

'What's their situation?' Georgina Smith asked. 'I think you told me that one of them was injured?'

'It's worse. One was killed. Shot dead a few days ago.'

'That's not good. Any idea who?'

'No one knows. They are burying him today.'

'You have to go there, I suppose.'

'Yes. And this is the country Mandela's returning to.' A shadow fell across her face. 'I wonder what he's thinking.'

'Who?' Georgina Smith asked, although she had an idea about who it might be.

'Nelson. Tata.' Something caught in Nerissa's throat.

'You should know,' Georgina said, 'how a prisoner feels when he's about to be released. You've been there.'

'Ja, but ours was a short time, a blip, really, compared with the men on Robben Island.'

'I saw the picture Uncle Walter brought of him from the inside. He still looks good,' Georgina said. 'Tall and lean … Looks kind of Chinese, almost.'

'If I didn't know your preferences,' Nerissa said, 'I'd have said you've got the hots for him.'

'Even if,' Georgina said, 'which I don't, but, even if … I'd be shit scared of Winnie.' She gave a theatrical shudder. 'She's pretty, though.'

'Ja,' Nerissa said. 'But then who is she to say anything, playing footsie with those footballers.'

'You think Nelson suspects something?'

'He knows. Everybody knows.' She paused and then laughed. It was empty, mirthless. 'And here we are, two old struggle crones, demolishing people's reputations …'

Georgina Smith, adept at avoiding engagement, asked: 'When do you leave for Durban then?'

'Early. I don't even know if there's a Sunday morning flight to Durban.'

'Do you want me to take you to the airport?'

'Who else?' Nerissa asked. 'The people in Durban are in a kind of a tizzy since the boys returned from Botswana. We might as well get down and do an inventory of the material they brought with them.'

'What's the rush?' Georgina asked. 'Shouldn't we be focusing on the Committee?'

'The Committee will be falling all over itself trying to create opportunities to cosy up to the leadership in Lusaka before Mandela's release.' Chaplain Nerissa looked around her. 'I have to see what Muzi and them are doing. I have a feeling the guerrillas might want to cut everyone out of the deal.'

'But that would be mutiny.'

'Well,' Nerissa said, 'they've just lost one of their own in violent circumstances. I would also mutiny in their place.'

'Lordy, Lordy.'

'Dead right,' Chaplain Nerissa said. 'When you come back from dropping me tomorrow, please make sure you treat my little children with kindness.'

'Your little children?'

'Yes, *die arme skepsels* – the poor buggers that come here for advice.' A cloud flitted across Chaplain Nerissa's face. 'People need hope. Most of them are far from home.'

'Are you trying to outdo Jesse Jackson?' An impish smile on her face, Georgina raised her fist. 'Keep hope alive!'

'Something like that.' Chaplain Nerissa looked at her friend for a while. 'You just need to grow a moustache and work on the accent. Otherwise you'd be a dead ringer for Jesse.'

A lie, but it was still a favourite game of the two women, neither of whom bore any resemblance to African American clerics. Both in their fifties, they kept their grey-streaked hair either braided or cosseted inside colourful scarves. Whether on business or going out, they favoured formal two-piece suits. Sometimes, in acceptance of their status as middle-aged, sophisticated and politicised women, they didn't hide that they were devoted to each other. However, they drew a line at appearing in matching outfits, even if the sameness was unplanned; someone would have to go back and change before they'd venture out. On these occasions, which called for a test of wills, Georgina, more adept at passive aggression, came out the winner. Today, however, they were in tracksuits and trainers, attire which made them look younger, the effect of the wine smoothing out some of the lines on their faces. Although relaxed, Nerissa now and then showed strain, wincing, possibly as a result of her injuries. Watching this struggle, Georgina feigned a lack of concern, although her affectionate nature couldn't quite pull it off.

She worried that Chaplain Nerissa worked too hard. The counselling she conducted from the lounge of her house must take its toll. None of her clients – destitute war veterans, vagrants, *arme skepsels* without hope, violated women escaping violent marriages, troubled kids fleeing their own excesses – had two pennies to rub together. Even the NGOs that referred the cases complained of a shortage of funds. It was always manana, kusasa, tomorrow, which never came. So, she and Georgie pooled their savings to keep the service going. Worse still, with regard to the future, Nerissa would have rather died than registered for a pension, all thanks to an abiding superstition. Resigning oneself to the status of pensioner, it was believed, quickened the journey to the grave.

Georgina was also concerned with Nerissa's drinking, never an issue before the bomb. The bomb, it seemed, had loosed demons that had lain dormant for all these decades and were now expressed through the biting humour, the swearing. Georgina smiled at her own hypocrisy; Nerissa's use of four-letter words had in fact struck a chord with her. It made her feel virtuous by contrast and allowed her space in which to curse like a sailor. We are old tannies, she thought, and we should be allowed these little lapses.

'You know,' she told Nerissa, 'we're the only two old people who have time for each other.' They were now inside the house, in the lounge.

'How do you come to that conclusion?' Nerissa asked.

'It just occurred to me,' Georgina said. 'Old people can't stand the elderly. It reminds them of the journey they don't want to think about.'

'One thing good about being in the struggle,' Nerissa said, 'is that age doesn't really bother you. You live a life of danger. When you celebrate one more birthday it's a real surprise.'

'A bonus,' Georgina said.

'The young aren't having it any easier.' Nerissa said. 'One of the reasons – which very few people know about – that I ended up in the cooler, was leaving South Africa in 1976 and touring southern Africa: Gaborone, Harare, Mbabane, Maseru, Lourenço Marques had just changed into Maputo – and of course Lusaka. In no time I was on a TAAG airline to Luanda, Angola, where I did firearms and explosives training in one of those underground houses in Miramar.'

'Why are you telling me this?' Georgina asked. 'I could recite your exotic journey back to you … even those parts you skipped.'

'Of course,' Nerissa said quickly. 'But the part you'd miss is the real reason for the flight. I couldn't stand my younger brother, Zenzo, and his wife, Shalimar, who were blessed with an autistic child, my nephew, Abdul. For some reason, since Abdul was a toddler, he would creep back into his head, which I imagined to be a confused and dark space of swirling things, but as soon as I made an appearance, he was as excited and as communicative as any normal child. I felt guilty, then, possibly thinking that somewhere in me was a key to his wellbeing. That was exhausting. But nothing as devastating as seeing Zenzo and Shalimar struggling.'

'That's the reason you left?'

'One of the reasons I left.' Nerissa said. 'I broke with the security protocol in the People's Army and became the chaplain. Everyone, from the chief of security, the regional commissar, the people from the High Council, thought it was a good idea. I guess the distance from home and the heat and excitement of Angola must have gone to my head, because the idea that I'd one day return home was so remote; it had gone straight out of my head. And so I put my training at the ecumenical centre to good use. In a strange way, too, being anchored to some belief system comes in handy in that crazy place. I found a lot of bewildered youngsters who needed counselling. But in truth, the whole deal was to counsel me.'

'And you managed to forget Abdul …' Georgina said. 'And Zenzo and Shalimar.'

'It was not so much a case of forgetting them. How could I forget them – or the people of this country? Perhaps it's closer to the truth that I was reinvesting them with different values, dimensions, characters or qualities.' Nerissa fumbled for the right words, 'I suppose it's like carrying a mould for a sculpture along with you. And then something happens to it. Something difficult, violent, maybe it gets smashed to pieces and you have to recreate it in another terrain. You have to carry the image in your head and reproduce it, not to the dimensions of the original, but to something grander, huger – more heroic.'

And so in approaching the young men and women who had left home to join the People's Army, she was addressing what was wounded and infirm among the people she had left behind. The young men and women singing their songs repeatedly represented an Abdul who was infinitely more robust. In addition to being statements of affirmation, the liberation songs became anthems of a liberated land, no longer a hope but a reality. The dust billowing up into the air during the one hour when the whole camp rejoiced did not put anyone's teeth on edge but was instead transmuted into the free terrain, christened the firm trench of the revolution – a *trincheira firme da revolução* – by President Agostinho Neto. Almost thirty years ago, on 4 February 1961, organised armed resistance to Portuguese rule began, when urban partisans of the Popular Movement for the Liberation of Angola (MPLA) attacked the São Paulo fortress and police headquarters in Luanda.

This evening, the air in Yeoville crackled with energy, an atmosphere reminiscent of the Highveld following a thunderstorm. Something about the day and the report from Durban had put a weight on the two women's shoulders. It was the feeling that huge changes were happening but it would be long after the women's bones were bleached white before today's generations fully grasped the significance of these changes.

Strolling along Yeoville's Bezuidenhout Road, Nerissa and Georgina negotiated their way through the crowds drifting to various points before everything closed at 7:30 p.m. Shoppers were en route to the OK Bazaars for cheap stuff that was usually past its sell-by date long before it hit the shelves; others to the market, butchery, numerous food outlets or liquor joints – all along Rockey Street. The women hastened to hairdressing salons whose creations were advertised on posters along the cluttered pavements, where pictures of delicate Nilotic models either in straightened hair or in weaves set the standard to be achieved.

Nerissa regretted turning down Georgina's suggestion that they take the car as she struggled up a short flight of stairs. She was, however, grateful she'd given in to Georgina's bullying about bringing the crutches along. She paused, heaving and balancing on the awkward supports, still maintaining that she was just out of breath – a lack of fitness that had nothing to do with pain.

Her friend's wilful challenge to pain reminded Georgina of the stories of Nerissa's conduct when arrested by the Special Branch. On 16 August 1984, Nerissa was captured in a group of People's Army fighters that clashed with the raiding party of the SADF during a cross-border incursion into Maseru, Lesotho. Bound and blindfolded, she was groggy and disoriented from the bone-rattling journey at the back of a Land Cruiser. The smell of blood fresh in her nostrils, she thought she could hear the groans of wounded comrades and, eerily, the silence of those who hadn't made it. By the time the convoy reached Bloemfontein, she had passed out.

She would insist to Georgina whenever an opportunity presented itself that she hadn't really set out to be brave. 'The regime did me a favour,' she said now, as they proceeded to an unoccupied booth in The Roque Santeiro. The small, modish restaurant catered for a clientele nostalgic for authentic Portuguese cuisine, none of that ersatz stuff from the colonies, where flavour was buried under rivers of oil. The interior of the restaurant suggested a classiness, which, at the same time, seemed to be engaged in mortal combat with sleaze. Along the wall and fluttering lazily above an eclectic mix of framed black-and-white, daguerreotype or colour portraits of Portuguese notables, were banners of the coat of arms of the House of Braganza. Nerissa noted that a new addition to the gallery rewarded each of her absences from Roque Santeiro. Now, the dictators, rouged opera and Fado singers, heroes or villains, had been joined by Henry the Navigator, Vasco da

Gama, Antonio Oscar Carmona, the tenth president of Portugal and Eusebio, the Mozambican-born soccer legend.

Waiters and waitresses in red and green uniforms flitted to and fro to take orders from the customers seated at tables covered with bright red tablecloths. Piped, scratchy traditional Fado music featuring Amalia Rodrigues wafted through the lounge, deepening the nostalgia.

The dishes on offer were represented in graphic detail on the menu, the name Roque Santeiro printed large in intaglio script. The restaurant's unoriginal name, inspired by the famous Brazilian telenovela, was a stroke of genius by Mozambican businessman Luis Bernado Muchave, for it attracted a clientele whose appetites went beyond the mere culinary. His restaurant did a brisk trade in Brazilian CDs, DVDs, vinyl records and – for the worshippers of exotic flesh – skin magazines, books and artefacts that would have been frowned upon by the publications control board. But then the law, whose vigilance was characterised by a blind eye, protected these establishments. Now and then a young and haunted mulatta led a paunchy patron with restless eyes through the side door that opened onto a courtyard. Looking for a ladies room on one such visit, Nerissa had gone out through this exit and stumbled upon two mismatched couples headed for the barracks-style backrooms, under the incurious gaze of people scavenging in dustbins.

Slipping inside the booth, thankful for the opportunity to take the weight off her feet, Nerissa looked around for the state agents, whom she could smell a mile off. Nada; there was no sign of the paid voyeurs among the diners tucking into dishes of calulu fish, vegetables, funge or farofa. The hatted young man with a weak chin strumming a guitar and crooning about the love that deserted him in Baia Farta in Benguela couldn't be mistaken for anything but a cuckold in the making.

Four tables away, his back to the food stands in the centre of the room, Luis, tall, skinny and bearded, and as dark as the night, made a big show of espying both women exactly at the moment that they, too, became aware of him. It was a necessary pantomime people performed, as it gave each party that breathing space to fill platitudes with meaning. Giving *desculpas* as he threaded his way through diners hunched over their food, Luis continued towards the women, his arms already spread for the revolutionary *abrazo*. Careful not to give Nerissa a hard squeeze, he murmured words of endearment. 'Ah,' he said, 'just the beautiful ladies I need to add grandeur to …'

'… a taste of paradise?' Nerissa teased. 'Isn't that what you once called this joint?'

'Ah, Senhora,' Luis protested, 'that was my predecessor, who had a way with words.' He turned his large eyes towards Georgina and bowed. 'And this is Senhora Georgina I have heard so much about.'

'Pleased to meet you,' Georgina said. 'Nice place.'

'Senhora Nerissa should have brought you here much sooner,' Luis said with an arched eyebrow. 'But then certain pleasures become much more consequential when delayed.'

'We're just old women, Luis,' Nerissa said tiredly. 'What on earth could we ever do with pleasure? It would be wasted on us.'

'Old? No.' Luis was at his flirtiest best. Then a cloud flitted across his face as he surveyed their unserved table. 'Have you been offered drinks, yet?'

'It's okay,' Georgina said. 'It gave us time to talk.'

Luis would have none of it. 'This is unacceptable,' he complained, slapping the lapel of his jacket as if he'd taken a blow to the heart. He intercepted a waitress crossing over to the bar. 'Manuela!'

Manuela, a sloe-eyed, olive-skinned beauty who looked even younger at close quarters, regarded Luis with disdainful respect. This seemed to add to his irritation. 'Why have these ladies been ignored?' Manuela seemed about to explain but perhaps saw the futility of it all and decided to stand stock-still. Her face didn't change as Luis dressed her down in rapid-fire Portuguese.

The two women lowered their eyes at this demonstration of outrage, which was disproportionate to the sin. At last, Luis ran out of steam.

Manuela turned and left having taken the drinks order. Luis turned on the charm again. 'Could I interest the ladies in my specialty, a caipirinha cocktail? On the house?'

'No,' Nerissa said. 'I need a clear head tonight.'

'We've already had something to drink at home,' Georgina said, softening the blow.

'A pity,' Luis said. 'I prepare them with my own hands.'

'I'm sure it's a bomb,' Nerissa said. Then: 'Perhaps we can have a little chat later, before we call it a night?'

'Of course. Could I know what it's about?' His face was guarded, almost closed, but still managing not to give offence.

'A doctor friend said you'd be of assistance. It concerns storage.'

'Ah. Perhaps before you leave? I'm at your service,' Luis said. 'Now, if you'll excuse me …' As he departed to tend to his customers, he paused. 'And,' he said, 'my congratulations for the good rumour regarding Nelson Mandela.'

'Good man,' Nerissa said. Georgina wondered whether this referred to the prisoner or was praise for one Luis Bernado Muchave. In a way it didn't matter.

Their drinks arrived. Their order of langoustines and veggies followed. The women dined in friendly silence, listening to the mournful songs of ancient mariners.

Paying and getting ready to go, Nerissa caught Luis Bernado Muchave's eye. The latter glided back to their table.

'You wanted to chat,' he told Nerissa.

Nerissa decided to get to the nub of the matter. 'People I know have quantities of Portuguese memorabilia. Paintings, objets d'art, repossessed during the fighting in Angola.'

'And you wish to liquidate all that,' Muchave said. 'How genuine is the merchandise?'

'As genuine as it gets,' Nerissa said. 'From what I know, it's all appraised and certified.'

'And why me?' Luis Muchave asked. 'I know next to nothing about art collections.'

'Exactly because you look like an honest man,' Nerissa said. 'And the collections might be of sentimental value to some of your patrons.'

'Is that really it?'

'Because I have friends among the police,' Nerissa answered. 'And they assure me that if I've stolen stuff from thieves, you'll help me. It's all part of restorative justice.'

'Ah,' Luis Bernado Muchave said, 'like Robin Hood. I'm to help Robin Hood find a banker.'

'Something like that.'

'I have a few people who might warm to the idea,' Luis Muchave said. 'You see the man there? Sitting with that woman at the table near the bar?'

'The old man with a shock of white hair?'

A striking dark-haired woman in a black dress at that moment joined the couple. Even from the distance of Nerissa and Georgina's table, the cocktail dress seemed to fit her like a glove. 'Wow,' Nerissa said, 'that woman is beautiful. Who's she?'

'*Minha noiva*, my fiancée,' Luis Muchave said, hardly able to contain his pride. 'Mariela. Just flown in from Lisbon. We get married in March.'

'And the couple with her,' Nerissa asked. 'Your in-laws?'

'Mariela's mom and dad,' Luis Muchave said. 'Keeping an eye on me.' He laughed.

'I noticed them as we came in,' Georgina said. 'The woman has on a necklace of pearls. I thought they were fakes. Plastic.'

'They are real,' Luis said. '*Minha sogra e meu sogro Juan de Matos*.'

Chaplain Nerissa supposed that the in-laws must mean a lot to him for the formal way he referred to them. Even the accent had become more decorous as if he were in court, ministering to a duke of the house of Braganza. Nerissa, however, didn't get a chance to voice this rather unkind view, as Luis Muchave was again off to minister to his clients like a fretful pastor. Most of the patrons didn't look at all well heeled but that was usually how the moneyed discouraged scroungers, by dressing down and looking as dowdy as courtroom clerks. Except of course black people. The poorest darkies, she mused, would step out dressed to the nines even though they couldn't afford a square meal. They'd go to bed on a rumbling belly and wake up in the morning to step into Florsheim shoes and Brooks Brothers suits. They'd lay-by expensive stuff in stores, for twelve months, ending up paying far more. They believed in easy terms. Those easy terms made easy money for retailers. Blacks were the only people who didn't seem to realise how expensive it was to be poor.

Nerissa and Georgina watched and waited while Luis, carrying with him a whiff of perfumed decadence, stooped over the fleshy woman of indeterminate age and her white-haired escort, the recently introduced Senhor and Senhora Juan de Matos respectively. Muchave's white teeth flashed handy insincerities. The woman's thick fingers seemed almost weighed down by glistening valuables disguised as knock-offs, the highlights from the jewels accentuating the shadows under her eyes. The man, the lines on his face adding maturity to his good looks, gazed up at Luis, listening attentively, now and then craning his neck to survey the other diners before focusing on Chaplain Nerissa and Georgina's table.

'I don't trust Luis's father-in-law,' Georgina said. 'Senhor de Matzos.'

'De Matos.'

'Whatever.'

'Scepticism is good,' Nerissa said. 'Means you'll have a long life.'

'At my age that's almost like a curse,' Georgina said. Then her eyes widened. 'Uh-oh, he's coming over.'

Senhor de Matos's handsomeness diminished with each step taken towards the women's table. Closer, now seated following a courteous self-introduction, his warm baritone voice was a subtle pointer that he must have been a lady-killer in his heyday. Sadly that had passed. His black eyes were sad. It was a sadness that might have had nothing to do with the weight of memories. Deferential, in a manner that made him endearing, he apologised for his English, which he confessed to be not too good.

'Our Portuguese,' Chaplain Nerissa lied, 'is not anything to write home about, either.'

'Oh, I doubt that,' said Senhor de Matos. 'That's not what I've heard.'

'Oh,' Georgina said. 'What have you heard?'

'Johannesburg is a great telephone exchange,' Senhor de Matos said. 'It's a telephone exchange in a marketplace where the real currency is information.'

'And is Senhor de Matos a rich man, then?' Chaplain Nerissa asked.

'It depends,' Juan de Matos said. 'Sometimes what you think is important can be … zero.' He punctuated his statement by forming a circle with thumb and forefinger.

'And this place is a marketplace?' Georgina pressed on.

'I like it here,' Senhor de Matos said. 'My wife and I have been married for over fifty years. We like places which remind us of the old Portugal and, would you believe it, you can only find old Portugal in Africa.'

'Maybe,' Chaplain Nerissa said, 'Africa is very good at preserving what isn't naturally African?'

'Perhaps,' Senhor de Matos said, with a shrug. 'Perhaps Africa looks to the West for answers. But the West hasn't been a great exemplar. It has been terrible to its own poorer children, which has meant losses that could never be recouped. We, the Portuguese, depended on NATO and became a laughing stock when we couldn't retain our colonies. Even the revolutionary from Guinea-Bissao, Amilcar Cabral, mocked us, saying we're so poor we don't even manufacture toy aeroplanes. But we were maintaining these colonies for the West. For them.'

'Maybe you should count your blessings,' Chaplain Nerissa said, wondering what had occasioned this outpouring of guilty regret. 'It's a real burden to keep a whole lot of people under the boot. They tend to throw you off, sometimes not very gently.'

'I'm just happy to get out of that Western bus, so to say.' Senhor de Matos gave a rueful smile as if relief from being divested of colonies was a form of heresy. 'In any event it gave the world a list of memorable dictators – and a taste for genocide.'

'Which means,' Georgina said, 'we must be careful of what we borrow from you?'

'Especially since the interest rate might be very high.' Senhor de Matos gave out a long sigh. 'I must go back to my wife and daughter.'

'They're both very beautiful women,' Nerissa said with feeling. 'You must be proud.'

'I am,' Senhor de Matos admitted. 'But at the same time I'm filled with trepidation. South Africa seems to have a hard edge against women – sometimes women and children. The administration has to play its role in ensuring their safety. My wife and I are going back to Lisbon. So, if you have any control in the changes to come in your country, please keep an eye on my Mariela.'

'We'll do that, Senhor de Matos,' Nerissa said. 'Thank you.'

'*Até amanhã, obrigado.*'

She mulled over the old man's words, which sounded like a warning, all the way from the plane to the meeting point inside the lounge of Louis Botha Airport, DBN. Catching sight of her reflection in one of the mirrors, which she knew was an observation mirror servicing concealed offices occupied by the Special Branch, Nerissa accepted that she looked run down. For the occasion she had dressed casually in a pair of Terylene slacks, a lightweight beige jacket over a lemon top and low-heeled light-brown pumps. To anyone watching, she surmised, I'm just another Indian businesswoman. In the South African political imagination Indians were harmless, more concerned with business and being left alone, until, of course, some spoilsports like Phyllis Naidoo, Billy Nair, Mac Maharaj, Ahmed Kathrada, came onto the scene and blasted that sedate impression to smithereens.

She thought of sharing last night's encounter with Muzi Thabethe, who stood waiting in the company of another man, later introduced as Thulasizwe Ngobese. On the way back home after dinner, Georgina, a sponge for titbits of information normally missed by most people, said that Senhor de Matos's brother, or Mariela's uncle, had a reputation as a big mamba in one of the Portuguese syndicates operating in southern Africa. They owned just about every asset from Bedfordview, through Kensington and Jeppestown down to Ferreirasdorp.

'If that Luis Muchave doesn't do right by Mariela,' she said, 'he'd best watch out for Angelo de Matos and his gang.' Nerissa had heard of Angie de Matos but hadn't made a connection. In any event, this didn't concern her. She was already thinking about Muzi Thabethe and the guerrillas.

Even though the two were on a mission, comrades in arms, and no matter how energetically they sought to demonstrate what South Africans termed 'braskap' or brotherhood, there was something about their interaction that immediately signalled to Nerissa that they were working together purely out of duty. It wasn't in anything done or said; perhaps it was in the silences and absences in gestures. Muzi looked older and thinner, and she prayed he wasn't struggling with something. The concern was tempered by the expression of joy on his face as he embraced Chaplain Nerissa.

'You still look good,' Muzi Thabethe said. He took her overnight bag and handed it to Ngobese. The latter watched with the tight smile of one relegated to a lowly status.

Ngobese took the wheel. Chaplain Nerissa shared the back seat with Muzi Thabethe. Ngobese kept his eye on the road, now and then glancing at his passengers in the rearview mirror. Caught off guard when he found Nerissa's eyes on him, Ngobese decided to focus entirely on the road.

Even though it was morning, the December air whooshing into the car promised a scorcher. She remembered Angola, where heat was suggested in the dewless lawns and parched insects that raised Cain from dawn to sunset. Here, trucks belching acrid smoke trundled along the highway, their emissions effectively cutting off any breathable elements in the atmosphere. It brought back memories of the journey to unload tankers at the dockside in Luanda, the choking stench of things rotting in the water, the grease and sweat under an unblinking sky. The reward, though, was well worth the discomfort, when the platoon of men and women would detour, barefooted, along the unspoilt section of the beach before enjoying *o copo de cerveja* in any one of the cantinas dotting the seaside. And: the great gusts of air, the breeze wafting from the Atlantic, iridescent droplets of surf and spume providing a visual and aural feast. In those moments in the shade, all memory of evil and discomfort disappeared as thirst was slaked, the beer tasting like nothing on earth; Lord, let me die now. We will never appreciate beauty until we've been exposed to the threat of its absolute elimination.

Looking out the window at the city unfolding before her, the morning looking glorious and promising, she experienced a sudden kinship with Durban. Durban to her was like Luanda; a coastal city, claiming and being claimed by the restless expanse of water. It was in Durban that she was trained in the craft of document analysis; encoding and decoding – the new technologies that became necessary when she went on a mission for the President. That was a long time ago.

'What time do we arrive?' she asked.

'Soon,' Ngobese said.

It was such a quintessentially South African answer Nerissa burst out laughing. She knew, now, that she was home.

'The man who was injured,' she asked. 'How is he now?'

'Django?' Ngobese asked, glad to be part of the conversation. 'He's strong. He's pulled through.'

'Was it your herbs that did the trick?' Nerissa asked.

'His herbs …' Muzi Thabethe snorted. 'It was the white man's medicine … isn't that right, Ngobese?'

Ngobese went quiet for a few hundred feet, someone mentally counting off seconds, before clearing his throat. 'I don't advertise my services, Comrade MT,' Ngobese said quietly. 'But if you want to know whether my treatment is good, perhaps it would be better to ask others.'

'Others?' Muzi Thabethe sounded mystified. 'Like who?'

'You've cracked many mysteries,' Ngobese said. 'This one shouldn't be too difficult …'

'Comrades,' said Nerissa Rodrigues excitedly. 'Look!'

Characteristic of a city that revelled in some form of mayhem, the streets of Durban suddenly played host to a continuous carnival. Coming out of intersections along the highway, from under the bridge where they had thronged, pilgrims en route to a miracle, hundreds of people were marching and there wasn't a cop in sight. New Year's Eve, Sunday, 31 December 1989, was alive with colour and sound, music and voices clamouring to make sense of a country that was trying to distil five centuries into a moment of triumph. Some of the demonstrators carried ghetto blasters, which played music that Nerissa had not heard in a long while. Some of the songs prohibited by the state were now being broadcast with abandon. Hugh Masekela was singing lustily about his wish to see Nelson Mandela brought back home to Soweto.

'I wonder,' Ngobese said from the front, 'whatever gave Bra Hugh the idea that Mandela wants to be brought back to Soweto. He might want to settle somewhere else.'

'After Robben Island or Pollsmoor Prison,' Muzi Thabethe said, 'anywhere – Soweto, Gugulethu, Langa, Nyanga, KwaMashu, eMlazi – any rathole seems like paradise.'

'Those are places that helped us grow,' Ngobese said, all jocularity gone. 'You can't disrespect them like that.'

Her suspicions about the undercurrent of animosity confirmed, Nerissa kept quiet. They would work out their issues, whatever they were, in time. I don't have a dog in this hunt, she thought.

Out on the freeway, crowds clogged the traffic, the blare of horns and radios challenging the laryngeal chants of revellers. Here and there, along the tarmac and flowing over to the edge of the thoroughfare, butting up against the breezeblock barriers, people had broken out with placards and banners inscribed with messages calling for the end of the prohibition of liberation movements and the speedy release of Mandela. One banner read: MANDELA OUR AFRIKAN KING! EVERYWHERE YOU ARE WELLCOME!

'True that,' Nerissa said. 'The man is after all the future president. He's going to be spoilt for choice.'

The traditional mercilessness of the December sun yielded to allow brief showers that failed to dampen the ardour of people demanding freedom. After all, rain was a libation for the gods. Rain was a stamp of approval by ancestors.

The tarmac sent up clouds of vapour and the marchers seemed to emerge out of a mist, like ghostly creatures coming out of water, in children's storybooks. Ngobese made slow progress, inching the car forward, pulling to a stop, moving forward again. It was understandable and therefore bearable.

Uneasy, Nerissa remembered that her dressing was due for a change. Mingling with the general bad breath emitted by a coastal city and its unscheduled crowds of demonstrators and cars spewing diesel fumes, she thought she caught a whiff of her own lack of freshness. It was a strange sensation, this awareness of the crumbling of one's tissues, the dissolution where various elements of her body were slowly breaking off in a unilateral declaration of independence. This was what ageing was all about. The dressings and plasters, much like Zimmer frames and pacemakers, were mere measures, largely manmade, to stem an inexorable march to the grave.

Nerissa shivered, remembering how tall Mandela had seemed as he walked into the gates of prison, to serve his life sentence – a proud, healthy man. His gait said it all. Towering above his escorts, he was the freest man on earth, freer, certainly, than his captors who'd have to wrestle with their souls as cat's paws of unjust power. She knew. She'd heard how prison preserved people, the regimen adding years to their lives, provided they didn't contract something deadly inside. But most people, on getting out, became prey to the fatal impact of freedom. There were these thousands calling for Mandela's release – Wel*come*! The thousands would probably swell into millions on the actual hour of release. How many more would be at his gravesite, when the hour arrived for him to kick the fucking bucket? There was something deliciously naughty in thinking of Mandela, a faceless saint, in such earthy terms. She felt a tug at her bladder. Nerissa fought back the need to use a loo. Lord, she prayed, don't let me fixate on running water. Her internal eye was filled with the visions of ghosts from the past.

The group turned, finally, into Moore Road, a confluence of exits and ramps, which could take them onto the main drag to Berea, Stanger or Pietermaritzburg. Two police cruisers were parked under the bridge, the occupants young, in dark glasses. Seeing them, Nerissa felt something coiling up inside her, like a distant warning of a birth. There was all over an abundance of concrete, breezeblocks, and bricks, cement slabs that seemed ready to be deployed as barricades along the sides of the carriageway. This impression of hardness continued, as the stony rubble became a filling station on the left and a courthouse-cum-police station on the right. As Ngobese nosed the car deeper into the city, the effect of being closed in deepened in Nerissa as the crowds, Sunday people, examined the car and its occupants. The revellers and seemingly aimless walkers were all black, not a white face in sight, not even those long-haired adventurers who wore socks with their sandals and drove colourful VW Kombis, hoping to score an exotic variety of Durban Poison. It was just a stream of black people, milling along the road, coming in and out of the high-rise flats, a few swigging from quarts of Castle, Lion or Black Label lager. The earlier camaraderie of the crowds was now inflected with wariness, while the faces that scanned the small car and its occupants were open, it was also as if a shutter had come down. Some of the younger men walking bare-chested with low-slung jeans were evidently looking for trouble. Someone banged on the roof of the car.

She'd been through it all in her fifty-three years, in tight spots. She remembered the smell of cordite and propellant. It had happened before that people had died from being at the wrong place, recriminations later paralysing the progressive movement. She didn't want it to be like that for her. Suddenly, sitting up straight from the easy sprawl of a traveller recharging life's batteries, she thought of Georgina. She thought of her nephew, who was a child no longer, Abdul, and of her brother, Zenzo, and his wife, Shalimar. It had become crucial for Nerissa that all of them were okay. The crowds, possibly recognising Muzi Thabethe, flagged them through.

They had to find a working phone somewhere. She needed to ring Georgina and get her to call the others.

'Comrade Ngobese?' Nerissa called from the back.

'Yes, Chaplain?' Ngobese said.

'Get us out of here.'

At around 4:30 p.m., they booked Nerissa into the boutique Hotel Serenade on Prince Edward Street, which was central and unobtrusive at the same time. Its location was ideal, near shops, transport and a few minutes from Umgeni Road, the thoroughfare they would later take to KwaDambuza. The hotel manager, Rajesh Mohan, had from time to time conducted business deals with the Movement via both Nerissa and Muzi and kept a special suite ready for Muzi's visitors. A battery of car guards and street-kids were primed to alert the hotel to any threats, which might consist of breakers or upholders of the public peace.

Inside the suite on the third floor, which Mohan vouched for with his life, Muzi, Nerissa and Ngobese discussed the urgent matter involving the guerrillas. They all listened, ears pricked, as firecrackers started up. 'Someone is jumping the gun about New Year celebrations,' Nerissa said. Then she looked at Ngobese. 'The Committee here consists of you, Muzi, Johannes, Bra Zeph and Nomasonto Sokhela.'

'Sonto, yes,' Ngobese said.

'Do you know everyone very well, including Sonto?'

'If you mean, did we do a thorough check on her, the answer is yes.'

'Yes?' Nerissa insisted. 'But …'

'Well, there's always a possibility one has missed a few details …'

'Let me put this delicately. Do you know anything about her love life?' Nerissa probed. 'I hear she's quite a beauty …'

'I didn't think to delve into that terrain …'

'That terrain, quote and unquote, is usually the most important. Love is what makes all of us vulnerable.' She turned to look at Muzi, who had one eye on the television screen where footballers flitted silently with the volume turned down. 'Wouldn't you agree MT?'

'About love, you mean?' Muzi Thabethe asked. 'I only know that love makes the world go round.'

'It also makes the world go gaga, mark my words.' Nerissa remembered Jolene. 'Comrades, please check if this young woman has got a clean bill of health. We're heading for very dangerous times.'

'Why, Chaplain?' Muzi Thabethe asked. 'Have you heard something about her?' He was actually thinking of Laura. Who can be said to be absolutely guiltless in this dirty struggle?

'I just know one rule of life: rather safe than sorry.' Nerissa asked

Ngobese, 'Has she seen what's in the trunk?'

Ngobese laughed. 'Chaplain, no one's seen what's inside the trunk. All of us were waiting for you, or anyone from the Senior Council, to direct us. I'm therefore happy that you are here.'

'Aren't you curious about what's in the trunk?'

'You want to know the truth?' Ngobese said. 'I fetched the men from Zeerust. I accommodated them, nursed them and fed them. One of them, a young man with spirit and humour, was shot dead, in my house. In a word, all the malevolence trailing the people comes from that trunk. I don't want to know what's inside. I just want it out of my house.'

'It will be done,' Nerissa said. She had a sense that Thulasizwe Ngobese might be burdened with his own secrets, but there was no mistaking that he was a good man. 'We'll see to it.'

'I'll be grateful.'

LOG #4

'Bless me Father for I have sinned. My last confession was, oh, a couple of months ago. Things have happened which have left me confused, unhappy and afraid.' The priest is silent during her recital. When she pauses, he says: 'These are difficult times. You say, "things have happened" instead of "I have done this-and-that", where you take ownership of the wrongdoing, the trespass. You are young and have a glorious future ahead but you must be able to help others take responsibility. But it all starts with you. You have to make sure your acts do not endanger your loved ones because they are innocent.' After this counsel, he gives her absolution, offers her the sign of peace and sends her on her way. It's the beginning of the year and there are sinners lining up who haven't seen the inside of a confessional booth in a long time.

She ponders the priest's words, their weight and prophecy. She is young but she knows that her future might not be as glorious as the priest imagines. The blind eye of the seers, she thinks, a bleak thought. The Sunday people pour out into the streets, most of them in colours of their denominations. Methodists, Anglicans, Catholics, Zionists, robes, costumes of sanctity, coats of many colours, like Joseph's – all on the streets, some thumping their bibles and hymnals, praising their God.

She wonders if Refiloe Mokoena had ever seen the inside of a church. What was his last thought?

Even though she can't prove this, she knows in her bones that her lover, for that's who or what he is, is implicated in this killing. It's not in anything he says; it's in all the things he refrains from saying. She told him, for instance, that Refiloe was shot dead and he started saying something about Pomegranate before he stopped himself. How did he know that name? Wasn't the knowledge of these names limited to the occupants of Ngobese's house? She thought that maybe he hadn't said it, that her imagination was running away with her. So she said something inane about Ngobese and he said: 'Ngobese? Who's that?' From that time he's been cagey about saying anything.

It's when he's silent that she knows that he knows she has him pegged and no number of orgasms will eradicate this disturbing fact. She's caught him out.

He's a killer. He started with Refiloe Mokoena. He's harbouring killers in the house in H Section.

Who is next?

If she is in danger, she'd better get out of here. Somehow, as this thought occurs to her, she knows it might be too late.

He picks her up at midnight. Outside the township is alive with people thronging the street welcoming the New Year. 1990: what's the New Year going to bring? They drive out of KwaDambuza and cut through KwaMashu Township. The streets are littered with remnants of jubilation, upended garbage cans, burning tyres, crackers that had exploded along the pavements, their entrails still smouldering. Looking up at the township swirling past, she reads the names of the streets and realises, as if for the first time, that they tell an incoherent tale of struggle and worship of heroes. She wonders if the authorities were aware of this little act of rebellion when they gave the citizens the right to suggest the naming of their places. She knows, having heard her aunt declaim with impotent fury, that there are few townships that black people inhabited out of love. Almost all of them are a result of the grand scheme of making way for white people. And so townships, no matter how many names of heroes were emblazoned on their streets, are simply evidence of how thoroughly the white world holds black people in contempt. And so, here, she sees a road called Sandlwana Drive, after the victory of the Zulu regiments over the British in 1879. It's January 1990 and she's twenty-three years old. The Battle of Isandlwana, like the One Hundred Years War, has just become an obscure detail about life forms in another galaxy, one of the questions posed in a multiple choice history exam.

The township named after a sugar baron recedes from memory as the solitary car heads to the highway, sugar cane fields a swathe of darkness on the left. On the right, she knows, are the blocks of houses for hostel dwellers, izimpohlo, which township residents have nicknamed 'obhejane', the rhinos. In the township, the despised have their own pecking order and sugar-cane workers, mostly migrants from the Eastern Cape, are at the bottom of the pile. She wonders what their fate will be when – and if – freedom comes.

But, for now, everything is quiet as if last night's revellers are readying themselves for the morning. The occupants of two or three police vans cruising by, dome lights off, give his car a cursory glance and go about their own business. She imagines that she saw a flicker of recognition in the face of one of the cops, but that could have been her imagination running away with her. She wants to ask him what he thinks of the struggle, where he fits in the whole scheme of things. This, because she can sense that he knows a lot more than he lets on. His dexterity with the weapon, stripping and assembling an AK-47, for instance, or taking off a pin of an F-1 grenade and inserting it back, rendering it harmless, that set of skills belongs to a soldier. In all their conversations, he has adroitly sidestepped any question that might trap him into elaborating on his experiences. So, to her, he is a man with a past that's better left in the past. But she knows – she's heard some wit stating it – that while the future is certain, it's the past that remains unpredictable.

Minutes later they are on Umgeni Road and she wishes they would stop so that she can take a look at the river. But he drives on in the direction of the beachfront. Soon enough she reads the signs and sees the black-green fenced-in expanse of the Umgeni River Bird Park. He drives off the main road onto an unpaved roadway that cuts through a dense grove where she can identify the spiky strelitzias and the water myrtle, whose dark-purple fruit must have been a bounty for the monkeys. She fears snakes and hopes that her companion has strategies against reptiles as part of his impressive repertoire.

What are we doing here? she asks. Above a sighing silence, she can hear the crash of waves nearby. Be patient, he says.

Then he pops the boot open and, crazily, she thinks that it is going to be one of those romantic gestures she has read about in women's magazines, where supposedly adventurous lovers evolve games, playacting, to spice up the bedroom antics. But this is no bedroom and what emerges out of the boot are two young men, both hogtied and gagged. It's quite clear that they have been roughed up because their faces are puffed and their clothes are speckled with blood, which looks eerily dark under the light of the moon.

As if in a dream, she watches as he takes out a gun from his belt and motions the young man she's come to know as Tikka Joe, a kid, really, and the other unknown boy, kneel down, facing the direction of the sound of the churning sea.

This boy, he says, pointing at Tikka Joe, came to me and threatened to tell the people at Ngobese's house.

She listens to the explanation, which sounds a little like a judgement recited by a judge before a person is sentenced to death.

And the other boy? she asks. Was he also going to rat on you?'

His friend, called Boy-Boy. He sniggers as if the very name qualifies the boy for execution. I can't afford to have my operation compromised.

But kill them?

That's just how it is in the revolution.

Are you really going to do this? she asks, more afraid now than at any time in her life. She wants to say: it's wrong, but something in his eyes tells her that it would be unwise, not now. But then she asks:What is it really that drives you to be – she pauses, searching for a language that will not give any offence – this way?

You mean, a killer?

If that's how you see yourself …

I don't see myself in any light, he says. Every time I go back in years, I see myself full of optimism and trust. I came into the struggle like all the young people of my time.

Like the young people here, she says, pointing at the condemned young men.

Like them, sure, but I was caught in a trap when I came back after a crash course in Maputo. It was in 1977 and we were armed with limpet mines. We were to attack a petrol refinery in Wentworth, but I was caught along Hopkins Road in the Bluff, someone shopped me. I was tortured and told to work for the enemy or else they'd release a transcript of the session where I confessed and gave them names of another cell that was operating in Durban. On top of that, my father was released from prison and they threatened to circulate a rumour that he was their man all along. It was their trap. I couldn't bear that. I went back into exile with a story of having escaped.

But this one … Tikka Joe is too young to have been involved in any of that stuff …

I had my eye on him from the very beginning, he says. For one, I know no one will miss him. Two, he knows too much already and has shown weakness, being bullied by Spider like that. That calibre of person will break and shop me …

But you broke and shopped others, she wants to say, to point out the irony, but holds her tongue. This is not the time to show how sharp she is. But the Movement … you owe allegiance to the Movement? At least she can ask that one question.

The Movement deserted my father. The structure that was supposed to be funded by General Palweni, which would ensure our people inside got their welfare, supplies, etc., it simply disappeared with the money. People were supposed to give him money for his medication. You saw that he's not well. You might not know this, but my father contributed with his life in the struggle for freedom. His own Movement deserted him when he came out and he had to eat out of garbage cans. Everyone says that the Movement was strapped for cash and was fighting the war on many fronts, many needs and couldn't afford to become a welfare organisation. But still, the fat cats of the Movement were salting away huge sums of money and living high on the hog. My father's luck only changed when I came back from exile, secretly, to find him like this. My mother had remarried and took my little sister with her to the Northern Transvaal. I don't know where they are, but I'll find them one day.

What about the men in Ngobese's place? She asks, wondering if she's used up her quota of queries. They were your comrades?

They also have something of mine, he says, looking suddenly weary. They don't know this but I suspect that the files in the trunks contain information that might end up exposing me. Exposing some of the men I work with. I fear that they'll bring someone who'll break the codes and uncover the agents in the Movement. I don't know some of them but I bet you there are big ones in the senior structures.

And me? She knows now that her own survival hangs by the slenderest of threads.

He looks at her as if surprised by the question. You, he says … you are my comrade in arms. My support. But enough.

Without seeming to aim, he shoots Tikka Joe in the back of the head. Soundlessly, the young man who has been petrified throughout topples over and lies face down in the sand.

Then he says to her: You want to be a revolutionary. In a revolution, people kill. It's kill or be killed. No one wakes up in the morning and says, I want to be a killer. The situation gives you no alternative. But killing has to be learnt. You have to be clinical about it. You learn to kill by practising on dogs, cats, vermin and later on useless people, on the enemy. This is the enemy. I cannot give you a crash course in developing a stomach for killing. I am doing you a favour, teaching you how to kill. I gave you a gun. Use it. We are in this together.

For a moment, which seems like an eternity, she hears the sea crashing in the distance and feels insignificant in the immensity of forces that drive the levers of the universe. Some night bird, a witness, squawks and flaps away as if escaping the explosion that is sure to come.

Go on, he says. Once you do it you will realise how enjoyable it is to have that power. You'll thank me one day.

Knowing that if she refuses this will never end, she takes the gun from his hand and aims without looking at the last man, who's gurgling futilely against the tape gagging his mouth. She gets a whiff of churning insides and knows that he has soiled himself. She pulls the trigger.

6

THE ELOQUENCE OF BONES

On 31 March 1985 – a day remembered clearly because, even in the liberation movement, it signalled the beginning of the financial year – she was summoned to a house in the Lusaka suburb of Kabulonga. To her surprise, she found the President of the Movement waiting for her. Dressed in a blue-and-white tracksuit and sneakers, he took his time telling her and the few people in the lounge, what he wanted done.

'All my life,' he said, 'I've been fascinated by the process of rebirth – of regeneration. When I wasn't herding our scraggly goats and cattle, my schooldays in Bizana, in Pondoland, were spent studying the patterns of life, the journey taken by organisms from dust into life and back to dust. In the church, the sermons were delivered with much fanfare and bravura, without giving us an explanation of the miracle that nature provided and displayed every living day.

'I did a bit of service as an altar boy,' he went on, 'to try to get a ringside seat to the unfurling wonders that held our people spellbound. Even much later, at the University of Fort Hare, some of my colleagues scoffed at my preoccupation with the trajectory of life. It is a trajectory blasphemed daily by the policies of apartheid, where our people groan under the yoke of oppression, the denial of our humanity. The women sitting at the lip of a grave wailing – sometimes silently, without tears – while a loved one is being laid into the ground.

'The men died early,' he said, in full cry. 'Life expectancy was low, from the bottle, illness, knife, gun or the rope, but mainly from despair. I joined the Movement as a boy. It was not a conscious act the way you enrol into a class of Physics. It was something that had claimed me long before I could say I am a member of the Movement. After that it didn't seem as if any reality could exist without the Movement. And life before that seemed like no life at all.' Here he looked Chaplain Nerissa in the eye and she was surprised that his eyes were black but ringed with brown, irises that seemed infused with an energy that was tormenting its owner.

He said: 'And so it pains me that there are zealots among us whose practices are inimical to life. They are menacing the Movement, which has, throughout time, preached the sanctity of life. I hear of torture of prisoners – South Africans – by our people.' He paused. 'We might even have our own dead, whose remains were not handled with dignity. I have cast around in my head for someone with the necessary qualifications and it all points to you. I want you to find out what is happening in our camps, especially our camp in Sector 37.'

Chaplain Nerissa wondered what these necessary qualifications were. Her religious training, which had earned her the sinecure job of chaplain? Which liberation movements still had chaplains? It just meant that the President wanted someone who'd know what to do with the bones of the dead. She shook her head. Nerissa had heard the rumblings, especially that some of the comrades abused women and that people had been locked up or even executed for minor infractions. She had no illusions that the camp admin would welcome her with open arms. But she was an old hand at dealing with stonewallers.

She thanked the President for placing his faith in her. She left.

Her impression of Luanda – a city whose power to beguile had never failed to amaze her since the seventies – was that the cloudless sky dominated everything, bearing down on the tall buildings and resting gracefully on the edge of the ocean. The weather was cool and fine, despite the fact that early April was in the rainy season. It could not, however, counter the humidity, which had pasted the fabric of her tunic against her back. The plastic seats of the jeep, a Lada Niva, helped trap the heat inside.

'You okay?' Almon Jonas, the People's Army regional commander, asked, giving her a sideways glance. 'It can be hot here.'

'You don't have to apologise for the weather, Almon,' Nerissa said. She shifted to the right-hand corner, the better to stretch her legs. Paranoid about thrombosis, she remembered her near-three-hour flight in the cramped seat where she was wedged between large business types in safari suits who had probably woken up too early to attend to personal hygiene. And they wouldn't swap seats with her, preferring to carry on the dialogue between the window and the aisle. She felt chuffed when one of them seemed to experience a problem with a customs official at the arrivals lobby of the Quatro Fevereiro Airport, where the larger-than-life picture of Dr Agostinho Neto gazed down on travellers.

The jeep was proceeding slowly along the packed Revolução de Outubro, signalling left towards Rua de Heróis when, drawn to something past Almon Jonas's head through the window, a vendor perhaps, Nerissa noticed the smile on her companion's face. It was a sad and painful smile that took her to Dr Neto's reluctant grin. What was it about Angola that introduced ambivalence towards life that etched itself in people's faces? Along the road now, asserting the heroism of MPLA, she tried to read the expressions on the faces hurtling past. The women, proud, their skin tones ranging from the deep black of Nubia to the milky white of the Caucasus, reflected the play of shadow and light from age-old encounters. There was watchful animation on the faces, laughter that sounded very close to tears. Young men in colourful shirts suited to a carnival, bantered with their counterparts, mostly soldiers in camouflage, guns slung or carried in gestures of casual readiness.

Inside the bustling hotel lobby, on Rua Rainha Gingha, Almon Jonas finished doing the registration, flirting in Portuguese with a strikingly beautiful thirtyish-year-old receptionist behind the desk. Red hair piled on top of her head and hazel eyes harmonised to set off her caramel complexion. Wearing a simple cream blouse and a beige skirt, she was an example of practicality, down to the variegated silk scarf adorning her neck. The name on the gold pin fixed to her blouse was Katya, leading Nerissa to wonder if this exemplar of efficiency with the bearing of an airhostess had Slavic roots. Handing him the keys, Katya flashed a grin that dimmed somewhat when she became conscious of Nerissa's scrutiny. 'Have a good day,' she said in accentless English. 'Enjoy your stay.'

'*Obrigada*,' Nerissa said.

'You're from Brazil.' Nerissa said, latching on to something that suddenly appeared in the accent.

'*Sim, eu sou brasileira.*'

For Nerissa there was nothing more alluring than hearing Brazilians enunciating the name of their country. She'd never come across people more in touch with the spirit of their land, a pride deeper than patriotism. When they said 'Brazil', the syllables rolled pleasurably across the palate, like cool water over pebbles, *bra-zooe.*

'You need such people, ears on the ground.' Almon Jonas told her as they stood on the balcony of her room on the third floor. A cool breeze ruffled the palms that stood marking out the property of the hotel. Beyond the broken treetops rose spires and domes and the higgledy-piggledy skyline that was softened by the blueness of the ocean.

'Those are very pretty ears on the ground,' Nerissa said wryly, unscrewing the second of the vodka miniatures from the mini-bar, emptying them inside a glass and splashing some orange juice out of a carton. She stirred the drink with a teaspoon, the ice clinking in the glass. Almon Jonas settled for a Coke. He turned his eyes to Nerissa.

'Despite her appearance,' he said defensively, 'Katya is from a working class background and I've alerted her to know what comprises important information. She coordinates the activity of other hotel workers in the neighbourhood. There's Globo just over there; the Tropico on Rua de Missão is frequented by big wheels, lots of information swirling around there.'

Nerissa felt the fist of the liquor hit the pit of her stomach and she realised she hadn't had anything to eat since last night's supper. She loved food but had drawn a line at aeroplane fare. Listening to Almon Jonas, realising that he'd lost a lot of weight but still wore his pre-weight-loss fatigues, she was chastened by his humility. The women he trained were an asset to the Movement; they in turn, being women and therefore able to penetrate areas that were impermeable for males, recreated themselves in others, it being a woman's job to swell the numbers of functional people.

'It's helped us keep tabs on the comings and goings of important people.' Jonas gazed into the sky as if weighing up what to tell her and what to keep secret. He shrugged. 'We learnt a painful lesson from Mozambique and Lesotho – in fact, from the front areas – the likelihood of tragedy if we relaxed our vigilance. The Boers would, of course, like to get us kicked out of Angola. They've threatened the Angolans and even mounted aggression in the south. At one stage they were very close to Luanda before they were beaten back.'

It was happening with nauseating regularity, South Africa making inroads into Angolan territory, until the Angolans brought in the Cubans. 'They didn't need any inviting,' Almon Jonas said. 'Fidel Castro was always wanting to give the Uncle Sam a bloody nose. He was only too happy to *stick it* fully into the racist stand-in.' He punctuated the phrase 'stand-in' with a gesture most Angolans considered obscene, slamming the open palm of one hand into the thumb-and-forefinger side of his fist. 'For him, apartheid is an abomination and he was passionate about it being removed from African soil, *ja acabou*!'

As if self-conscious at his sudden outburst of emotion, Almon Jonas stepped back from the balcony and put more ice into his glass. On a Wednesday afternoon, the first week of April, life continued on the streets below, music weaving through the air. Knowing that the afternoon might stretch into an uncomfortable evening of drinking and God-only-knew what else, Nerissa crossed the balcony into the air-conditioned lounge. There were sandwiches and fruit and a bottle of wine on a silver tray on the table, covered in lace against the flies. When she shouted to Almon Jonas if he wanted anything, he said no.

'Who else is around?' Nerissa asked, chewing an inedible cheese and ham sandwich. They should have toasted it.

'From the leadership … General Palweni is here, at the Rez.' This was the Movement's official residence on Rua Anibal de Melo in the suburb of Villa Alice. There were underground houses in Miramar and São Paulo and a transit camp in Viana, some fifty kilometres east of Luanda.

'Is he going to the camps?'

'I'm not privy to that information,' Almon Jonas said. 'What I know is, he wants to see you.'

'For what?'

'He knows you have the ear of the President. People are a little nervous when they hear of someone from HQ. They know there's uneasiness about the existence of a big leak among members of the Senior Council. Otherwise how is it that the Boers seem to know our moves as we infiltrate people inside the country.'

'Educated guesses?' Nerissa asked. 'Inspired second-guessing of our commanders? A good intelligence that maps out variables based on our public strategy documents? We do tend to boast long before we mount our operations.'

'That might be,' Almon Jonas said. 'But the recent spate of arrests at the border with Swaziland, those have the hallmark of inside information. In high places.'

'But Palweni shouldn't be worried,' Nerissa said. 'He's got a cast-iron reputation, one of the best in preparing ordnance and propaganda material for infiltration. I hear he's the one who came up with the idea of operatives from home bringing reports hidden in soap powder boxes.'

'Ja,' Almon Jonas said. 'That didn't last long though; the Boers started wondering who might be having so much laundry in front areas.'

'Or they were concerned about money laundering …'

'Or washing our sins away …'

Nerissa, laughing, realised she was fast getting drunk. 'We need to get something to eat.'

'Okay. But remember,' Almon Jonas said solemnly. 'The mission regarding Sector 37 should start with you going through all the files, if you can find them. I hear, for instance, that some reports involving captured agents, South Africans running together with UNITA or FNLA, might have gone missing. That's where you might track the patterns that will take you to the big mamba selling us out.'

'How?'

'If we've been penetrated to the very top,' Almon Jonas explained, 'there will be pointers as to who the handlers are. I suspect there are a few of them. There will be a uniformity of language, the thing that happens when people have been briefed.'

'Meaning?'

'Let me give you an example,' Almon Jonas said patiently. 'When we skipped the country all those hundreds of years ago, we landed in Botswana. That time it was still Bechuanaland, a British Protectorate.

We'd been coached by the Movement what to say to the cops. The phrase that we used when questioned about why we were in Botswana was that we were fleeing apartheid persecution and we regarded Botswana as our second home. When taking down our statements, the Botswana police would be able to write the whole thing down, before we even opened our mouths. They'd have fun at our expense, trying not to laugh as they waited for us to say the magic words …'

'… about regarding Botswana as your second home …'

Jonas chuckled. 'That's right. The Boers too will have slotted in choice keywords, signatures that you'll find peppering some of the biographical reports that people were required to write when joining the Movement.' Eyebrows knitted, Jonas glanced at the visitor like a doctor checking if the dosage he prescribed was having an effect on a patient. 'Follow the files, Comrade Nerissa. The answer to all our questions lies in them.'

'Including the infiltration at the top?'

'Especially the infiltration at the top.'

Two weeks later, she was in Quibaxe. It was a town where the asphalt on the main road was in patches, the tonsure of a playful barber, before disappearing completely beyond the town limits and deteriorating into a potholed track. The neglect was a by-product of war and a preoccupation with life-and-death matters by successive administrations. The buildings, some once plastered models of Portuguese architecture and stonework, were now mostly dust-coloured and scarred by firefights and bombings. Miraculously, splashes of colour emerged through the layers of dust and broken stone to expose meticulously calligraphed storefront signs. There was evidence of a life that was once vibrant and productive, an ancient bakery here, a *floreira* there. Atop rubble, strewn across the floor of what was once a bridal shop, beneath a lopsided sign announcing *o roupas do casamento*, sightless and limbless mannequins lay in different poses of surrender. The empty and unamused faces seemed to register the anxious progress of passersby.

A town of absences, Quibaxe was a dance of shadows, where unseen phantoms gazed at themselves in shattered glass. Where a pavement once ran was a crater that some civic-minded soul had tried to fill with debris and which had now become a convenient spot to dump garbage. The townsfolk walked along, patiently. Some of the women toted bundles of merchandise on their way to the market. Very old men in castoffs and boys and girls of school-going age all stepped aside onto the non-existent pavement for the steady stream of military vehicles, mainly jeeps and Kraz or Zil trucks topped with canvas, ferrying heavily armed men. In the middle of the woods loomed a washed-out greyish shell of a building that might once have been stately. The empty holes that used to be windows, now gutted and charred, looked out on the road.

'What happened here?' Chaplain Nerissa asked her driver, a young man with old eyes, in a FAPLA camouflage uniform and Czech boots. The security detail at the back of the Niva 4x4 kept a respectful silence. Chaplain Nerissa knew that the question was pointless.

'The fighting, Comrade Leader,' the young man said. His answer explained everything.

Chaplain Nerissa turned and looked at him, judging him to be no older than her nineteen-year-old nephew, with a jaw that was only now reacting to the churn of hormones. 'What's your name?'

'Thabo,' the young man said. He turned and faced her, his unlined face showing first signs of worry as if he were panicked about possibly offending her. 'Thabo Stone, Comrade Leader.'

'Don't call me that,' Chaplain Nerissa snapped. 'I'm not Colonel Gaddafi. Call me Chaplain or Nerissa. Can you manage that?'

'Yes … Comrade Leader … Chaplain.'

'That's more like it.' After a few heartbeats, she asked: 'Don't you have any curiosity about who I am, what's bringing me here, and so forth?'

'No,' Thabo Stone replied. 'It's none of my business.'

'What's your business?'

'Taking orders. Driving.'

'How long have you been at this camp?'

'Eighteen months. I was in Hoji ya Henda before.'

'You like it here?'

'I have to serve.'

'Even if you're required to shoot someone?' Chaplain Nerissa asked carefully, knowing that the silent wraiths behind were listening with bated breath. 'Would you do it? Just like that?' She snapped her fingers.

'Not just like that', Thabo said with spirit. 'But if it's an order I have to carry it out.'

'Do you know why I'm here?' Chaplain Nerissa asked.

'It's none of my business.' Thabo Stone said again. He turned to the men in the back. 'Right, *madoda*? It's none of our business.' *Biznis*.

The men in the back seat mumbled assent. It was none of their biznis. Their reticence was born of both respect and wariness.

'At the end of the day,' Chaplain Nerissa said, suddenly weary, 'it's all our business.' She wanted to confide in the young men, in all the men in the car, that the President had sent her to oversee interrogations of enemy prisoners captured in ambushes. Much more, it was to record the living conditions of the People's Army's own prisoners – the ne'er-do-wells classified under the rubric of enemy agents, that included spies, saboteurs, internees charged with insubordination or for miscellaneous breaches of military discipline. She knew that it would be premature to disclose the full nature of her business. She had to check her instinctive amiability towards Thabo Stone. Certain knowledge could compromise him.

More than two hours later, it was the singing that told her that they were approaching the camp of the People's Army. The singing, coming in waves, appeared to electrify the dark northern Angolan bush so that it, too, crackled with energy. The headlights penetrated the imposing black wall of verdant growth. It parted like the sea cleaving for Moses' passage, exposing a track.

'Here we are,' said the young driver in FAPLA camos.

The welcoming committee, consisting of the commissar and the recording officer, was waiting for her. The young commissar, Bafo Bopape, looked well turned-out in his pale-green Cuban uniform and a peaked cap from some socialist country. Executing a crisp salute, '*Bienvenidos, camarada Chaplain*,' he apologised for the absence of the camp commander who had been called to an important meeting in Luanda. 'But the few of us here will do our best to help you.'

'Ah,' Chaplain Nerissa said. 'I appreciate that, Comrade Commissar. Could I perhaps worry you for a cup of tea?'

'No problem, Chaplain,' Bafo Bopape said. 'Let's all get to admin.' As they walked down the paved path, they came across a pretty woman in her early thirties, her skin brown and shiny, the complexion set off by her camouflage uniform. Stepping aside, she executed a smart salute and waited until the big brass passed.

'Who's that?' Nerissa asked as they resumed their walk.

'Comrade Viola,' Bafo Bopape said. 'She's a medical doctor, trained in Cuba, specialising in tropical medicine.'

'It's great that women play significant roles here.'

'Well,' Bafo Bopape said, 'we couldn't have it otherwise.'

Nerissa caught a wistful lilt in Bafo Bopape's tone and wondered if the poor guy wasn't a little in love with this one.

'Here's the admin,' Bafo Bopape said, pointing at the pre-fabricated block, consisting of two, one-storey rectangles. From her short spell in various People's Army establishments, Chaplain Nerissa had become familiar with the jargon. Admin meant the officer's quarters, where the camp commander and the camp commissar kept their stash of the good stuff. Tea, called can-can for some obscure reason, real instant coffee rather than that chicory crap that tasted like bilge water, decent biscuits, beer, meat and various creature comforts that made the life of a soldier somewhat bearable. The variety of cigarettes stocked could be found only in the diplomatic shops: Marlboros, Winston, Benson & Hedges or Camel. It was a far cry from the bitter smoke produced by Populares, the Cuban brand. Chaplain Nerissa was often struck by the irony of symbols of Western consumer culture oiling the anti-imperialist struggle. The twist in the tail, of course, was that these luxuries had their side-effects, however long they took to manifest. A guerrilla leader dying of lung cancer simply joined the pantheon of heroes in a place unaccustomed to issuing death certificates.

Looking up from her exquisite cup of can-can, she caught the commissar and the recording officer, Nozishada, exchanging a look. She knew – she had known this long before setting out – that they would try to turn her around. They respected the President of the Movement and commander-in-chief of the People's Army, but they'd be damned if they'd allow the demonisation of their camp. Wondering if she wasn't chasing phantoms and at the same time, aware of the culture of secrecy underpinning the struggle, Chaplain Nerissa decided to let them know there was no need for paranoia.

'I'm not,' she said, 'out to get you, Commissar.'

'I know that,' Bafo Bopape said. 'In fact, we wouldn't think there's a reason for that.' It was the kind of statement any commissar would make.

'But truth is,' Chaplain Nerissa said, 'I've been sent by the chief to ascertain if what he's heard is true.'

'And what would that be?' Nozishada asked.

'That you're torturing prisoners.' Play it straight, she told herself. They expect you to dissemble, but these are the biggest bullshitters in the game. 'Here, in this camp in Sector 37.'

The singing outside ebbed and flowed like a river. Beneath the tune, at once mournful and triumphant, was the rhythmic beat of feet thumping the ground, doom-dum-de-dum, causing the walls to shake.

'Chaplain,' Nozishada said, 'with all due respect, we're in Sector 37 exactly because this is a military region. There's a war going on. And we are doing the fighting. Enemies of progress, imperialist agents, FNLA, UNITA working with CIA, the Boers are trying to annihilate the emergent Angolan democracy. To that end, the People's Army is allied with the Forças Armadas Populares de Libertação de Angola …' rattling off the long name with practised ease.

'FAPLA,' said Bafo Bopape, being helpful like a good commissar.

'*Obrigado*, Commissar,' Nozishada said. He turned to Nerissa. 'Our work is made more complex by our own homegrown traitor …' His voice trailed off. 'You look unconvinced, Chaplain. You don't believe we have agents running around here?'

'I'm sure you do,' Nerissa said. 'I'm just puzzled why people would risk life and limb to infiltrate the People's Army. For instance, it makes little sense for someone to go through the perils of crossing a fence into a neighbouring country, join the Movement, go through the screening process, which I know is quite rigorous and then, hey presto, turn out to be enemy agents in Angola.'

Nozishada smiled as if he'd been expecting such a comment. 'The regime,' he said, 'has invested huge resources in cultivating agents. They recruit people from inside prisons, who are serving time. They target vulnerable wretches who have a lot to lose. More than that, they hold people's families to ransom.'

'In any event,' Nerissa said, 'I suppose it's agreed that I'll start inspecting the cells tomorrow.' She yawned. 'Right, Commissar?'

Bafo Bopape glanced at Nozishada before answering. 'Of course.' Then: 'I've prepared the guest quarters for you. You can freshen up and we'll all have something to eat.'

The singing swelled to a crescendo as the two men and the woman crossed the courtyard to the guest lodge, an old guard house repurposed as a self-contained accommodation unit. Ranged in concentric circles around a handful of guerrillas leading the chants and dances, the company seemed to get more and more animated with the approach of the camp leadership. Nerissa wondered whether this was a good thing, a stamp of approval, or something to the contrary. She did not have long to wonder, though, because Nozishada, a forceful and confident kind of leader, led his commissar and the visitor deep into the centre of the throng. Strutting like a cockerel, and appropriating the territory immediately around him, Nozishada began the toyi-toyi, lunging forward and rearing back, feinting to confuse an envisaged enemy, stamping his feet, raising dust and crouching with one shoulder angled for his arms to point an imaginary rifle. It was a performance that won admiration from the soldiers. They egged him on, clapping and ululating, the black prince of their time. Now spent, with rivulets of sweat down his face, Nozishada did a small pirouette of stylised rapture before joining Nerissa where she stood with Bafo Bopape.

'I want you,' Nozishada said to her, 'to join our royal fellowship.'

She couldn't tell whether the remark was made in disdain or out of a genuine need to enlist her comradeship. Nozishada was a man of ferocious strength and grace, a warrior resplendent in battledress with a shiny holster in which nestled an officer's pistol that lent grandeur to destructive power. But as she looked into his eyes she encountered arrogance so deep as to defy classification. Nerissa knew that any prisoner unlucky enough to land in Nozishada's manicured hands would find no pity.

Nerissa found it easy to fall asleep despite the ongoing singing. But at around 3:00 a.m. she woke up with a distinct feeling that someone was in the room. Unarmed, she was surprised that she experienced little fear of being murdered. Perhaps it was the knowledge that anyone who wanted her dead would have killed her a long time ago. Like any woman, however, she dreaded being raped.

'Who is it?' she asked and fumbled for her bedside lamp.

'Chaplain. It's me, Bafo. Commissar.' It was as if Bafo Bopape wasn't too sure of his own identity. 'I need to talk to you.'

'Couldn't it wait until morning?' Nerissa asked.

'Pardon me,' Bafo Bopape said. 'It's urgent.'

'Turn around,' she said. 'Let me put something on.'

A minute later, they sat in the half-dark, the moon glow providing adequate light, sculpting objects into shadows. He had brought along a flask of tea. 'I know you like can-can', he'd said, putting it on the table like a peace offering. She sipped the hot and over-sweetened tea, gazing at the swirl of steam framing Bopape's face. Head cocked to the side she could sense his nervousness as he unburdened himself.

'We've tried,' he said, 'to alert the regional command to our need here. But I suppose there being a war and all, with most people concentrating on the Eastern Front campaign against bandits, the concern of a single camp becomes nothing more than a nuisance. The SADF is massing in Namibia and already we know they have their forces not too far from here. And so people regarded as enemy agents are given short shrift …'

'Whoa. Hold it there, Bafo. Commissar,' Nerissa said. 'What do you mean, "short shrift"?'

'It's absurd,' Bafo said. 'Soldiers have come back from the Eastern Front. Some with wounds, others with memories of comrades who died on the battlefield. And all they want is to go and fight at home. Now, that wish – with the People's Army totally unprepared to infiltrate hundreds of men and women inside South African borders – that wish is simply unsustainable.'

All wishes are unsustainable. 'But the Movement can't be that incoherent.'

'The Movement is not fractured,' Commissar Bopape said. 'The President has performed a miracle by keeping it all together, so to say. The Movement speaks with one voice. A policy position articulated in Lusaka is delivered to Kuala Lumpur or New York. But its weak spot is here, in the camps. I have a feeling something's brewing and it will explode in front of our faces.'

'Like what?'

'This push to go home, the fact that cadres are hungry, they are starving.'

'You all look well-fed to me.'

'The stores are empty. If nothing comes up in the week, we might as well retreat to the bush.'

'You are in the bush, remember?'

'A bigger bush.' Commissar Bopape appeared momentarily distracted. 'It's a bush in which populism has no place, unlike here. I've tried to speak to the soldiers and to give them a realistic view of the situation. But they shout me down. The jazz hour you saw last night …'

'The jazz hour?' Nerissa was puzzled. 'What's that?'

'The song and dance on the square,' Bopape said. 'People sing revolutionary songs. They invoke the names of Mandela, Dadoo, and Kotane. They sing their hunger. Of late the songs have taken on a more ominous tone. They now sing how they're going to get rid of obstacles to their march towards Pretoria.'

'Do they understand the terrain they have to cross to reach South Africa?' It suddenly dawned on her that the regional commander, Almon Jonas, had the world's most unenviable job. 'Luanda is more than three thousand kilometres from Johannesburg.'

'You bring that up as a commissar and they tell you of the Long March.'

'Do they know that of the eighty thousand marchers only about eight thousand made it?'

'That doesn't mean anything.'

'And your chief recording officer?' Nerissa asked.

'Nozishada?'

'Yes. Nozishada. Where does he feature in all of this?'

'In the songs,' Bopape said, 'Nozishada is the anointed commander at the head of the procession that will storm the Union Buildings.'

'Does he know about all this?'

'Sometimes, sometimes I suspect that he actually composes this crap.' Bopape laughed grimly. 'Isn't it funny? People want to go home and fight. Their leaders get jailed for agitating for the return. The only person gung-ho about their imprisonment is the same one who promises that he'll lead them home. Only it's got to be done his way, the man with a plan.'

There was something sad and unattractive about Bopape's impotence. Nerissa felt like getting hold of his shirtfront and shaking him. He was, after all, the most powerful man on the ground. South Africans, she had come to realise, weren't very assertive when it came to exercising the power they had. Bleakly, distantly, she despaired for the future dispensation in a free country if this trend weren't nipped in the bud. At the same time, she wished to cradle Bopape in her arms and assure him that everything would be all right. The visiting woman and the young man gazed at each other, both shaking their heads at the situation facing them.

'I have faith you'll achieve something,' Bopape said, a leave-taking as heavy as a curse. 'People tend to hide things in the open.' Shortly thereafter he bade her goodbye, stopping at the doorway to snap her a crisp salute.

The time was 6:00 a.m. It was still a little dark and a steady drizzle deepened her laziness to get ready for the day. She opened the window and watched the company getting down to its pre-breakfast exercises. Droplets of water sprinkled her face, the lukewarm rain of the tropics that brought to mind holidays in forgotten climes. Donning a tracksuit, she tried to match the activity on the square, running on the spot, squatting and stretching. But the soldiers were fit and she couldn't keep up with them. Out of breath, she called it quits. 'No need for a heart attack.'

A somewhat subdued, although well turned out, Nozishada sat at the back of the Niva as Nerissa was collected from her lodgings. Thabo Stone got out and walked round to open the door for her and invited her to share the back seat with Nozishada. The latter shifted to the farthest end to give her more room. The greetings were perfunctory, soldierly, Nozishada acknowledging he was in the presence of his political superior. In the People's Army's credo, politics trumped military might.

Nerissa kidded around with the driver. 'I forgot to ask you yesterday, how long it took you to get used to driving on the wrong side of the road.' Both Nozishada and Stone smiled politely.

'Where is the commissar?' she asked.

'Ah,' Nozishada said, 'he's been called to Luanda.'

'Like the commander?' Nerissa asked. 'Must be some serious doings there.'

'That's just how it is, sometimes,' Nozishada said. 'Many are called but few are chosen. You get summoned; you jump to it. Right Thabo?'

'Of course, Komandir,' Thabo Stone said, studying the plants on either side of the road.

It was a short drive to the admin building, an L-shaped, one-storey brownstone that bore signs of age. The structure incorporated a clinic, an armoury and a kitchen. The place looked different from the night before, bereft now of the throngs that had sung with abandon and conviction. A few guards snapped to attention at the entrance. The rain had let up. The heat was rising, the damp adding to the humidity in the air. Far off, Nerissa could hear the sound of platoons jogging off to fisico, tactics or firearms drills.

Inside the main admin office, the heat was more bearable; the blades of a small Sony fan recirculated the close air, ruffling some dockets on the rough desk that supported a few books – Alexandra Kollontai, Nikolai Ostrowski, and Maxim Gorky. Two or three other volumes were open, face down, their spines unreadable. Nerissa wanted to pick them up and straighten them, but decided against it. Even though Nozishada was an example of rectitude and affected a distant affability, she couldn't quite shake off an unsettling feeling about him. Last night's impressions of him still lingered, at once real and as intangible as a dream.

'You don't approve of me,' Nozishada said, taking her by surprise. Before she could answer, he added, 'In any event, it is not important. We're here to serve the Movement and the freedom of our people should be our first love. How we feel about each other doesn't matter.'

'I'm just here to do a job, Comrade,' Nerissa said. 'Nothing personal.'

'Truth is,' Nozishada said, 'this is a long struggle. It has many chapters. It's a big book. We don't count. We might think ourselves important but at the end of the day our contribution to this big volume is not even this little tiny sentence.'

'You know,' Nerissa said. 'You're quite right. My concern right now is about people, South Africans, once someone's children, who might have been charged with some wrongdoing – and sentenced, God-knows-to-what. That's the kind of place where I want to see the word "sentence" used. All else is smoke.'

'In a word, you're looking for justice?'

'Justice, perhaps,' Nerissa said. 'But what I'm really asking you to help me with are files with names of people who might have been regarded as unimportant and therefore treated as unimportant. That's all.'

'I'm instructed to give you all the assistance you require,' Nozishada said, smiling at his own impotence. 'Seems you have some friends in high places …'

'The files, Nozishada. Where are the fucking files?'

'On the desk there,' he said. 'More are being collected from various centres for your reading pleasure. Happy reading and when done, you'll find me in the other office.'

He stepped out. Nerissa found that she had been holding her breath throughout the exchange. Sitting down at the desk, the humidity swirling around her, she started leafing through the binders, randomly reading through the biographical accounts of those comrades accused of various offences. True to his word, Nozishada had left a foot-high stack of files that now jammed one of the drawers. Taking them out one by one Nerissa added them to the bundle on the desk.

She couldn't tell what she was looking for. So she just flipped through, at first distracted by the mundanity of it all and then finding herself increasingly absorbed in the lives of people who were mere ciphers. It was this anonymity, however, which fed her imagination and she could freely conjure up images of faces she had come across in her life. It was like breathing flesh and blood into skeletons, animating a collection of nameless phantoms. In most of the accounts she could gather from the consistency of language that the recording officer had guided the subject. It was the usual dismal tale of people forced into the struggle by poverty, by injustice.

One young woman, a child, really, who should have been a charge of social workers, escaping abuse that was aided and abetted by her own parents, landing in the arms of another shrewder abuser who introduced her to drugs and prostitution until she was recruited into the Movement by an old schoolmate. There were young men with tales of woe, who'd had to leave hurriedly, some of them following clashes with fathers who were partial to alcohol and to using the boys' mothers as punching bags. The majority, however, were motivated by their disgust with the regime and wished to take up arms, sometimes to avenge grave injustices against people they knew and loved.

She smelled a rat; it was all too easy. There were no accounts or reports about people locked up in the camp. There was no mention of Sector 37 as a security zone. Through her training in document handling, she knew about censorship and redaction.

She wasn't aware of the passage of time until, three or so hours later, the first platoon jogged back to base, singing. She got to her feet and watched the men and women whose khaki fatigues were stained with the red of the earth and the black of the swampy water they had forded as part of their manoeuvres. She listened to the lyrics:

Sobashiy'abazal'ekhaya
Saphuma sangena kwamany'amazwe
Lapho kungabikhon'ubaba nomama
Silandel'inkululeko.

She was moved beyond words by the simplicity of the message about young people leaving home for unknown lands in search of freedom. These people represented the best hope for the country. We have no right to dupe them into thinking that freedom will come tomorrow from the barrel of a gun. Freedom will come, as it must. No force will stand in its way. But these young people did not deserve to become cannon fodder any more than they deserved incarceration. What was really happening?

In the evening, while Nerissa got ready to take the short walk to the dining hall, looking forward to her second supper in the camp, Nozishada knocked on her door. 'Good evening,' he said. 'I know I'm supposed to join you for supper. Point is, we're going hunting. People are tired of the regular stuff they've been eating.'

Behind him, looking somewhat impatient in the gloom, stood the ever-present Thabo Stone and two other men, one who she thought looked familiar but whose identity she couldn't quite place. Each man carried, in addition to the AK-47 that seemed an extension of the limbs, a sniper rifle slung over the shoulder. Nerissa admired the polished stock and burnished barrel of one of the guns, attracted and yet repelled by its fatal beauty.

'I'd like to come,' she said suddenly.

'Are you sure, Chaplain?' Nozishada asked, discouragingly.

'I'm sure,' Nerissa said, feeling rather than seeing the shrugs of irritated acceptance of the rest of the men. Only the man whose face she couldn't quite remember stayed blank, striving to blend with the darkness. A phrase came to her: 'I don't have a dog in this hunt.' The man, who carried himself in the hunched, apologetic manner of someone familiar with the weight of chains, didn't have a dog in that particular hunt.

'Yes, I'd like to come along.' She felt the need to reiterate her intention and spoke in clipped, impatient syllables, remembering the way her own father used his tone of voice whenever unsure of his ground around neighbourhood skollies. Perhaps, she thought, the unspeaking man who seems like someone I've seen before is going to get killed. It could happen that I'm his only hope. She remembered seeing, in old issues of *Drum*, grainy photographs of victims of firing squads in Ghana or Nigeria.

'Have you hunted before?' Nozishada asked. 'It's quite complex.'

'I haven't. But I've heard women are supposed to be bad luck in a hunt. Women and salt are taboo. But, this being the People's Army where sexism, superstition and backwardness are challenged, you might just want to turn all that obscurantist crap on its head.'

'Shoo!' Nozishada said with resigned admiration. 'You certainly know how to get your way, Chaplain.'

The forest at night was like a river. It was quiet, brooding, unmoving although the absolute silence meant that living things were there, holding their collective breath. A river could be dark, its depths seductive and deceptive, which, to Nerissa, were one and the same thing. Sometimes in their stealth, walking in Indian file, trying to tread as gingerly as possible on the unseen boot impression of the one in front, the hunters would be startled by a sudden flapping of wings as some giant bird, disturbed from its perch, would take off and hover momentarily before landing elsewhere, probably, Nerissa would conclude, to warn other animals of the approach of danger. Was there communication between different species, for instance, game and birds? Weren't they united by the simple fact that man found their flesh tasty to his palate?

Even though Nozishada was the commander, leader of the hunting group, it was the tracker at the head of the single file who influenced the progress. If he ducked his head, all followed suit. If he straightened up or signalled for absolute silence, it was done. He was the one who'd flash an admonishing look that would chasten them all, Nozishada included. Behind him, the strange man who was at first unarmed but who now lovingly cradled his own sniper rifle, seemed to anticipate the tracker's every action, giving guidance to Nozishada, Thabo Stone and Nerissa.

'Who's our mournful gunner over there?' Nerissa asked.

'Ah, that's Strella,' Thabo Stone said, giving her a look. 'Best shooter in Sector 37.'

'Is he one of ours now?' Nerissa asked, remembering a wispy detail from the discussion with Almon Jonas, something about captured FNLA fighters who had been trained by Colonel Jan Stander. There was also a Strella, so long ago, who'd lain wounded in the hospital ward in Luanda. Was it the same man? She had thought of that Strella in the past tense. Had he graduated from shooting his enemies to sustaining them?

'I'm not authorised to talk about that,' Thabo Stone said.

'Shh, *silencio, camaradas*,' Nozishada said.

In the hush that followed, counterpointed by the crackle of each twig underfoot, and the chittering of insects which transformed the forest into a feral concert hall, Nerissa felt far from home. It was a feeling that had never come upon her, even on the most distant shores. She had not felt this estrangement in Vietnam or even in Bolivia, mainly because – she supposed – the blend of bloods from Africa, Asia and Europe coursing through her veins spoke to almost all the peoples of the world. But here … She loved the country, loved its history of courage, but she knew she would never come to terms with it.

She felt the night pressing down on them, on her, the indifferent sky dotted with stars that winked knowingly about something that lay in wait, something that would astonish the gazer. To her, it seemed crazy, unreal, that the beast or beasts whose hour of reckoning was nearing, would also have marvelled at the mysteriousness of the night, the uneven landscape, treetops and the brilliant sky.

Just then, out of a smoky mist it came, striding as if willed by Nerissa's musings. It was a kudu, black coat glistening in the dark and weighing in, she estimated, at more than two hundred pounds, the horns stately in their span. Even from the distance of less than three hundred feet, its eyes were visibly large, giving her – she was sure the beast could intuit her in the dark – a gaze at once proud and knowledgeable.

POW!

She hadn't noticed Strella change position so that he was now a step behind Nerissa off to the side. She was still mesmerised by the kudu that was staring back at her as if to establish rapport when the gun went off. While she had anticipated it, she also hadn't expected the sheer unbelievable loudness of the report. Her heart lurched and she got to her knees exactly as the animal tottered, the forelegs first and then the massive body crashing to the ground. Birds screeched and flew off. The sounds of war, which had displaced them from one part of the forest, had returned to trouble them again.

Nerissa couldn't quite remember the journey back to the camp, except that on the jeep she'd taken a long draught from a flask someone had handed her.

She woke up at around 3:00 a.m. Still fully clothed, she was aware that something of great importance had happened to her. The room reeled as if she were underwater, the floor now and then swaying as if to collide with the ceiling. Steadying herself on the bed, she heard that some celebration was in full swing out on the square.

At first she was convinced that her eyes were playing tricks on her. Arrayed on a long trestle table were cans and bottles – even the much-loved dumpies – of soft drinks and beer, the main brand being Carlsberg, and earthen flagons of wine. Off to the side the kudu was roasting on a spit, the fat dripping into the fire and shooting up into the air. Gone was the majesty of the kudu as it had now been reduced to a carcass – trussed up, skewered and strung up with wire like a hog. Using long-handled ladles, two cooks wearing aprons over their fatigues, continually basted the browning flesh, the flames now and then causing them to rear back.

She saw Nozishada standing in the middle of a circle, holding court, gesturing volubly in a manner that told Nerissa this was just a performance for her benefit. He turned and regarded her as if from a great height, a smile across his face.

'Ah, the chaplain,' he said. 'Come on over, Chaplain, and have a drink with us. God knows you've earned it.'

Putting on her sweetest smile, Nerissa approached the circle of Nozishada's supporters. 'So that's the end of the kudu?' It sounded banal to her but she had to say something.

'The way of all flesh, I suppose,' Nozishada said. 'If we hadn't killed it, someone else would have. Or some poacher with a vicious trap, in which the bull would have suffered.'

'Our method was humane, you mean?'

'As humane as it could get under the circumstances.'

'It's a lot of meat,' Nerissa said, sweeping a hand in the general direction of the spit. She was aware that the others were listening and, unable to enter into the conversation, they kept a respectable and companionable silence. Also in the group, standing stiffly, Thabo Stone was like someone unsure of his level of sobriety.

'We'll be sending some of it to other camps,' Nozishada said.

'And the booze,' Nerissa asked. 'You'll get them some of that, too?'

'No,' Nozishada said. 'That's ours. We appropriated a huge consignment from FNLA.'

'Ja,' Thabo Stone said. 'That was a mission and a half.'

'Is that where you got Strella?' Nerissa asked, conversationally, eyes fixed on Thabo Stone.

There was a long silence. Thabo Stone smiled guiltily, glancing at Nozishada. 'She asked me during the hunt, Komandir.'

'And what did you say?' Nozishada was suddenly businesslike.

'What was he supposed to tell me?' Nerissa asked. 'Or, rather, what was he instructed *not* to tell me?'

'Mchinda,' Nozishada said, 'you were way out of line.'

'Thabo Stone?' Nerissa said. 'You're also known as Mchinda?'

'That's another one of my many names,' Thabo Stone/Mchinda, said.

'I'd keep quiet if I were you, Mchinda,' Nozishada said.

The soldiers who had formed part of the circle of admirers sidled off, two of them mumbling something about getting a couple of beers, the rest discovering a pressing need to visit the loo.

'You're a soldier, Mchinda,' Nozishada pressed on. 'There are things that don't get told to civilians.'

'If I were a civilian,' Nerissa said, 'I wouldn't be here.'

'You're here,' Nozishada started off heatedly, 'because some educated civilian sissy from Lusaka …'

'Did you just call the President a civilian sissy?' Nerissa asked. She suppressed a bubble of laughter that was building up inside her.

'I didn't mean to attack the President.'

'He's not a sissy, Nozishada,' Nerissa said. 'And neither am I. You don't know me.'

'She's a soldier,' Mchinda said. 'The People's Army is guided by the political direction of the Movement.'

'Ah,' Nozishada said. 'You're now another commissar?'

'I am a commissar,' Mchinda said with quiet defiance. 'All PA soldiers are commissars. Even commanders.'

'The army could do with less bleeding hearts and more real soldiers,' Nozishada said. 'We're in a new phase. The guerrilla of the past is gone, as is the soldier of the past. We're not fighting in the Second World War here.'

'The sacrifice of common soldiers in the Second World War,' Mchinda said, 'laid the foundation for the democracy we're striving towards.'

'Aw fuck off, Mchinda,' Nozishada said. 'I've had it up to here with that Aleksandr Matrosov rubbish.' He snorted. 'Common soldiers …'

And then all hell broke loose.

Much later when she recounted the attack, it seemed as if it never actually happened. Quick, lightning fast, the raid was impressive in its precision. Afterwards, chronology was in a jumble; she couldn't tell with clarity what had come first, the loud explosion from a hand-grenade nearby or the mortar, a few hundred feet away. But she recalled a whump that sucked up all the air and the next moment she was flat on her stomach, her face pressed against the dust. Bothered by the effect of the first drink in the jeep, which had been later fortified with a glass of brandy and Coke she'd had on the square, Nerissa feared she'd throw up. This always happened whenever she was on the verge of losing control. Her gorge rising, her nostrils were assailed by the smell of roasting meat. The earth began to rumble as if in the throes of an earthquake. When she got to her knees, she saw that the camp buildings were on fire. There were jeeps careening to and fro, flattening the hedgerows and chewing up chunks of the lawn while soldiers who looked like white men, tossed smoke grenades. Then trucks mounted with artillery rolled in and the thunder, which had initially been far off, became deafening, the guns shaking on the beds of the trucks, eliciting screams from the combatants and trainees scampering across the square.

The camp went dark, the lights cut off, fused or destroyed, leaving a darkness that outlined the objects last seen in the final moment of illumination. The dark gave way to music, a soft melody dominated by a piano. Then there was a bass clarinet solo, long and tremulous like courtship, which Nerissa, even in that moment of confusion immediately recognised as Eric Dolphy's. What was the tune? 'India', she thought, just as something crashed a few feet ahead. A reddish flare arced across the air and landed on the lawn. Resembling one of the township crackers, it whooshed up from the ground, illuminating the backs of fleeing figures.

It was a night of lights and silhouettes that danced on the walls. One of the shadows, Thabo Stone – Mchinda – took cover behind a waterless stone fountain. That pause allowed Nerissa time to gain on him. She followed him into the barracks, sprinted along the corridor where she crashed into a bunk. Rubbing her numbed thigh muscle, she hobbled behind Thabo Stone, trying to keep up with him. He stopped. 'I'm over here, Comrade Chaplain,' he said. He sounded emboldened by something, fear perhaps. The volume of the music increased, a crash of cymbals counterpointing the insistent baritone saxophone. Getting to his haunches Stone thumped the floor with the butt of his rifle until he was rewarded by a hollow sound. He gave a satisfied grunt. 'A trapdoor,' he said, his eyes alive in the near darkness. A sudden flare of light, red-tinged and dangerous, illuminated his face and she noticed beads of sweat ringing his upper lip. Putting the gun to the side, he unsheathed his bayonet and started hacking into the wood to access the embedded metal hasp until the locking assembly, still padlocked, was wedged to stand shining at 45 degrees. Pushing the lock, still attached to the metal plate securing the trapdoor closed, Mchinda's efforts were rewarded by the sound of a sharp click – something snapping – reminiscent of the slide of a gun being cocked. Mchinda smiled or showed his teeth as he raised the metal plate a few inches off the surface of the floor. Sitting back, he kicked at it with the heels of his boots like someone attempting the Russian squat dance. Eventually there was a muted crunch as the ruined hasp clattered back. Raising the trapdoor, which opened into an even darker square of darkness, Mchinda climbed down until his head disappeared, followed by the one hand that had held on to the edge of the cavity.

The noise of war abated, momentarily and then carried on with renewed ferocity, the explosions ear-splitting, even from the shelter of the barracks. Unhesitating, Nerissa clambered into the void, her feet encountering a rung, and then one, two, three steps down before her feet found the ledge. The underground shelter, called a dugout, was illuminated with paraffin lanterns placed randomly on the floor and the rough table next to which stood a 1950s Blaupunkt Hi-Fi stereo, the source of the music. Strangely, the helter-skelter crash of drums, Alvin Jones, no doubt, complemented the boom and crackle of explosions aboveground. Had John Coltrane and Eric Dolphy, both mystics, rehearsed for this particular apocalypse? Other figures that harked back to a legendary past were displayed on posters and pen-and-ink drawings tacked to the wall, all seeming somewhat lifelike in the flickering light of lanterns. Even in a moment of panic, she registered a gallery of images depicting historical icons of struggle from John Langalibalele Dube with his trademark handlebar moustache, past the nattily dressed Sol Plaatje, through to Charlotte Maxeke, Dora Tamana, Florence Maphosho, among many faces she couldn't immediately place.

The place brought back memories of her father's church, where, as a child, she would often fall asleep in the midst of evening prayers. Nerissa remembered the spookiness of the spacious building, the holy idols of Mary and Jesus, the latter with arms spread out and a heart pierced by a crown of thorns dominating the chest area. Despite years in a seminary, Jesus' eyes blazing like blue coals in the dark still haunted her.

The music segued into a series of wails, which Nerissa couldn't place at first, the mind tricked into conjuring images of the up-tempo holy dances in her father's church. When she became fully conscious of her surroundings, like someone waking up still disoriented from a narcotic stupor, Nerissa saw that she was in an underground chamber. Constructed out of sturdy timber, the roof rested on strong pillars.

The cavern stretched away into an unlit area, sectioned off by steel bars, the people behind them unseen but heard. At one point, the picture contrasted so forcefully with the earlier images of redemption it all seemed like the work of a malevolent painter, Hieronymus Bosch, perhaps. Redemption and damnation butting up one against the other. Here they were, gaunt faces and skeletal limbs, holding on to prison bars, almost all clamouring to speak to Nerissa and, simultaneously incoherent. Thabo Stone looked at Nerissa. She, in turn gazed at the faces of about sixty people crammed into two adjoining cells, men and women.

'Can you open?' Chaplain Nerissa asked Thabo Stone. 'Please open.'

'Yes,' he said. 'Stand back.' He aimed his rifle at the lock.

'You don't have to do that,' someone said from the other side of the barrier, a voice that doubted the rightness of the very act of speaking. It was Strella.

'Strella?' Chaplain Nerissa said. 'Weren't you at the celebration? Enjoying the meat of the kudu you shot?'

'No,' Strella said with a wry smile. 'I am always the gunman, shooting people or animals, on orders of the big men. When done I get locked in here with the rest.' A pause. 'This door just needs a crowbar.'

Thabo Stone put the bayonet to use. To Nerissa, it seemed to take the whole of eternity. Then a bit of a stampede ensued as prisoners poured out of the cell. A few hobbled out looking wildly about them. In their confused hurry, some bumped into both Thabo Stone and Chaplain Nerissa. The air, which had been stuffy and close, was now heavy with the odour of unwashed bodies, human waste and infected wounds. Is this who we are? What we have become? Strella merely stood aside while some of the prisoners dawdled inside the ill-lit cell, like children unsure if the bell that had sounded meant they should go out and play.

'What's wrong?' Chaplain Nerissa asked.

'They don't know what to do,' Strella said. 'Some have been here for a very long time.'

Nerissa and Thabo Stone followed Strella, now armed with a torch, into the cell. The breezeblock walls were scrawled and etched with evidence of previous inmates. A group huddled on the floor in the corner: three women, two black and one white, the latter shielding her eyes from the light. She was young, with yellow hair shorn to the scalp. Dressed in a ragged khaki uniform she seemed the most naked woman Nerissa had ever encountered. The nakedness was in the eyes that must have witnessed everything unnameable under the sun. She cowered as Strella neared, the beam of light on her face. 'Jolene?' he said.

'Strella?' Her response was soft, hesitant.

'Jolene?' Strella said again. 'Why are you not getting out?'

'Jolene?' Chaplain Nerissa said, looking at a woman who was the nearest thing to a human coat hanger, the boniness covered by a tunic and baggy trousers tied with twine to a non-existent waist. 'She was with you in Sanza Pombo.'

'Yes,' Jolene said. Then she started to cry, shoulders shaking. Nerissa held her briefly. This pale child will die on us, she thought.

'It's going to be okay.' She didn't know why she said that or what was going to happen next. They'd broken into Nozishada's holy of holies and he wasn't likely to take that lying down. She hoped there was additional information in the documents she hadn't seen.

Ensconced at a compound for Cuban volunteers in the outskirts of Quibaxe, Nerissa was able to communicate with Almon Jonas by radio and told him of her mission. Jonas would arrange transport to Luanda. Just wait, he said, hearing how disappointed – and scared – she was.

Jolene, who had seemed in poor health, rallied, the improvement evident in her appearance. Her hair started to grow and her pallid complexion improved. Nerissa was conflicted in her attitude towards Jolene, on the one hand divining a depthless cunning and, on the other, a damaged core. She knew that to get to the bottom of the woman's story would take some time, time that wasn't a luxury in Angola. Over a few days, Jolene told her story, about her recruitment, ending up in Ondangwa, the poor self-image, the need to prove herself among the men. All over, she declared, the men in power used women; the worst treatment had been in the camp in Sector 37. She was curious about Nozishada; at the same time, she didn't really want to know his whereabouts.

'Strangely,' she told Nerissa, 'I don't want them dead.' It was a week later and they were just leaving the checkpoint at Dondo, halfway between Quibaxe and Luanda. Sharing a bottle of water after visiting the latrine and stretching their muscles, Nerissa and Jolene sat at the back of the truck surrounded by youthful FAPLA soldiers, who feigned indifference to the two women. Because, even though Nerissa was old in the scheme of things, past forty, which, in the reckoning of these youngsters, meant she already had one foot in the grave, she knew she was a woman in a world of men at war.

The issue of women in the camps needed reviewing. Some of the commanders tended to pull rank and there was always the possibility of abuse. Of course, she thought, there were also genuine instances of love and relationships and all that, but in the main, it was not very healthy. And Jolene's own fate at the hands of the men, led by Nozishada, supported this. Sometimes she couldn't walk for days after they'd been through with her, fucking enemy cunt, white bitch!

'A prick is undiscriminating,' she told Nerissa. 'It shoots jism into every hole it encounters, big, small, deep, shallow, black, white, yellow or brown.' Wrinkling her nose, Jolene's freckles bunched up into a mauve patch across her face. It was a girlish and yet ageless quirk, leading Nerissa to wish to wrap up the young woman and shield her against the wound caused by her own vulnerability. And there, in the back of the truck, shaven and shrunken in her wrinkled fatigues, now and then nodding off to sleep, there was no mistaking that, once upon a time, someone, a boy at school, perhaps, had found Jolene desirable.

'Am I still under arrest?' Jolene asked, looking beyond her own memory of the moment. 'I mean, *jy ken mos*.'

Jy ken, mos. You know. The informality of Jolene's language meant she was relaxing somewhat. At the same time it also spoke of a stubborn connection with her origins. She would never lose touch with her roots. Despite her time in Ondangwa and latterly Quibaxe, Jolene would forever carry Calvinia with her. 'It's a dorpie on the Oorlogskloof River,' she'd earlier told Nerissa. 'Lying at the foot of the Hantam Mountains.' Then, fixing Nerissa with her eyes, asked: 'You know what Hantam means?'

Nerissa shook her head, no.

'It's where the red bulbs grow in the language of the Hottentots.' She smiled, looking at the road, the trees flitting past, the boys in uniform. 'The high street has a few shops, like Sanza Pombo, no Kentucky Fried Chicken, no OK Bazaars, no Foschini's – just a lot of pharmacies because people are sick and tired of the place.' *Want mense is siek en sat van daardie plek*. 'It's hard to forget.'

'To forget what? Calvinia?' Nerissa was suddenly irritated, figuring that Jolene's frightened innocence was a sham. It upset her that such perfect lips could also utter hurtful words. But does Jolene understand that calling people Hottentots is a no-no? She'd already confided in Nerissa that in her career as an agent trained by one Col. Jan Stander, she had already killed people. How many? She couldn't tell, shrugging. They were just kaffirs, darkies, of no consequence. No wonder, Nerissa thought now, these despised people were so diligent in inflicting themselves on you, fucking all that whiteness out of you. Jolene saw the flicker of hatred in her saviour's eyes, as hot as coals.

'What's the matter?' Jolene asked. *Wat makeer?*

'*Wat makeer*, my dear Jolene,' Nerissa said cruelly, 'is that I have to check with the Regional Command what to do with you.'

'And Strella?' Jolene sounded at a loss, like a child attempting to address a class of know-alls at primary school. In her trembling, it was quite clear that Jolene liked Strella, perhaps excluding him from the unholy fellowship of black rapists. This tentativeness on the part of the younger woman, her conflict with herself when it came to the elemental questions of love and hate, disarmed Nerissa. Jolene was more than just another corn-fed, platteland meisie. She was a human being, another woman's child, damaged but still worth saving. That's why, she thought, Jolene cared for Strella, another monster, a South African corrupted by men into becoming a thief of lives. Nerissa thought she'd share with Jolene some of the information she had about the role of the SADF in the destabilisation of the region. She wanted to tell her about people like Stander, their capacity for unleashing untold horror on an unarmed public. What, though, would be the use? Moreover, it would be well nigh impossible to turn Jolene and train her as an agent of the Movement.

'We don't know what happened with Strella,' Nerissa said. 'Soon as he was out of the camp, he hightailed it off into the bush.'

'Strella is a good warrior. He'll come right.'

'Well, out there are wild animals and patrols and bandits of every stripe. To say nothing about the landmines.'

'He'll come right.' Jolene scratched her scalp, an unconscious reflex from prolonged interaction with head lice. Then: 'You think I'm a racist?'

'You're what you are, Jolene.'

'I'm not.'

'I guess now's the time to tell me some of your friends are black?'

'No. There're black people as well as white people that I loathe,' Jolene said. 'In Ondangwa I had a black partner, a Mukongo from Angola.'

'Oh wow. I bet he rocked your world.'

'You mock me,' Jolene said. 'But it is true. We went out for a while in the limited way that camp rules allow. And then they poisoned him.'

'Killed him?'

'No. They poisoned his mind. Brainwashed him.' Jolene was quiet for a moment. 'He'd gone away for a bit and came back a changed man. When I tried to resume our relationship, he told me that, even though the white government of South Africa was our sponsor, white people were the devil. What we were doing was wrong.'

'And Strella?' Nerissa asked. 'He took over from the Mukongo guy?'

'You make light of this,' Jolene said, her eyes flashing. 'Strella should have been the commander, instead of Barak the Greek. His only wish is to get the treasure that was taken from us by the People's Army in Sanza Pombo. Nothing more.'

'He's not interested in women?'

'I don't think so,' Jolene said. 'Not in that way.'

Jolene didn't say in which way, knowing she wouldn't be able to explain the violence that throbbed in Strella's breast. 'He went through a tough time in the training.'

She related the brutality of the commanders, who were mostly acting on Jan Stander's orders. The askaris, former fighters of liberation movements who had been turned, were not trusted. On many occasions they were sent on missions to test their loyalty. Stander had hit on an idea, which he thought quite ingenuous, of supplying these former guerrillas with battle-dress armed with hidden devices that could be detonated remotely. 'Like a suicide-bomber's jacket,' Jolene said, 'only without its wearer knowing.'

Jolene went quiet and Nerissa had the impression she was possibly falling asleep. She wanted to hear the rest of the story – wasn't the whole point of the mission to get as much information as possible?

'What happened?'

'Many times,' Jolene said, 'Strella found his colleagues exploding left, right and centre, and lived with the knowledge that his turn would come one day.'

'Couldn't you … someone just … kill him?' Nerissa imagined someone sticking a knife in Stander's chest and twisting it all around.

'Even thinking that way would have been pure suicide. Stander was … is a god.'

It must have been around 8:00 p.m. when they reached Luanda and drove through the city without meeting a roadblock. In the suburb of Vila Alice, which the Angolans pronounced as '*Villa Lissi*', Nerissa and Jolene were escorted to the gate of a nondescript residence of the Movement's chief representative at the end of a tree-lined street. It was at the gate that Nerissa noticed how heavily guarded the place was. Ushered into the house by two young men in bulletproof vests over their uniforms, they were assigned a bedroom on the upper landing and shown the location of the kitchen. One of the men said curtly: 'The chief is not here. He'll see you in the morning.'

'Who's the "chief"?' Jolene asked, when the two of them were settled in the room. There had been an initial moment of awkwardness because there was only one double bed, but it quickly passed when a now-sombre Jolene gestured towards it, saying: 'I guess this is my last night here. And, as we have a lot to talk about, let's *sommer* sleep here.' Then: 'I promise I sleep like a log and won't kick you, tossing and turning.'

'Promise?' Nerissa was aware of a sadness in the young woman. Perhaps everything is becoming real, she thought.

'I promise. Who's the "chief"?'

'He arranged the escape. Almon Jonas is a good man.'

'Unlike Strella, you mean?' Jolene asked with a trace of bitterness.

'I didn't say that. Although, in the scheme of things, Strella cannot be called a good man.' Nerissa paused. 'Nor, for that matter, Nozishada.'

'But you,' Jolene said. 'You're a woman of God, aren't you? You're supposed to see human beings in their totality, as God's creations.'

'Ja, but you have to draw a line with monsters. I'm not one of those who believe God's grace should extend to the Standers of the world.'

Nerissa felt a great weariness enveloping her and she wondered, distantly, what had given Jolene a second wind. It then struck her that the young woman was scared for her life. She was in the hands of the enemy and had had a taste of its brand of retribution. But then, she told herself, Jolene was a master manipulator. 'Should we switch off the light?' she asked once they were both in the bed.

'Nozishada said he didn't start out like that.'

'What?' Nerissa was suddenly wide awake. 'When?'

'Nozishada had been part of a mission inside the country,' Jolene said. 'He was captured and tortured. His torture was different because Stander ... Stander again, said that they would not kill him if he refused to work for them. Instead, they would make life a living hell for his father and he'd have to live with the repercussions. His old man had just come off Robben Island and was in poor health.'

'He became an agent to save his father?' Nerissa was taken aback, wondering if this could justify selling out. 'He told you this ... Nozishada?'

'He was fucking me then ... *hy het my verkrag*.' Verbalising her experiences in her mother tongue suddenly brought it all home to Jolene. Her face rippled across a welter of emotions and finally settled on a hard smile of acceptance. 'He must have thought I'd never live to tell the tale.'

'You could have told someone in the camp?'

'You've no idea what our life was like in Camp 46. We could not speak. Just being alive was like we were being done a favour. We were not allowed to look officers in the eye. All the time we had to keep our gaze fixed on the floor.' She snorted, shaking her head. 'Speak to someone ... Jeezus.'

It is my Movement, its armed wing, the People's Army, that's in the dock here, Nerissa thought as exhaustion tightened its grip on her. Here we are, being lectured by the daughters of the architects of obscene systems, just because we've sacrificed our humanity on the altar of expediency.

Nerissa, who could have lived comfortably elsewhere, had committed so completely to a life of struggle towards the freedom of the African majority. How was it that certain elements from that majority found it possible to be a barrier to that freedom and turn their backs on history? Sell them down the river? What turned people into traitors? But Jolene had asked her a pertinent if unanswerable question. How could she, a chaplain, advocate murder and mayhem in pursuit of a political objective when she had a mission to save souls? Were the souls of marauding beasts like Stander, Nozishada or Strella saveable?

'No!' Her reverie was broken by Jolene's scream. She had fallen asleep quietly beside Nerissa and had been jolted awake by a nightmare.

It took Nerissa a while to quieten her down. She got out of bed and padded off to switch off the light. The humidity of the day still lingered – and in the sudden darkness, the nocturnal sounds, muffled at first, became more defined. Somewhere in the house a radio played church music before two excitable individuals launched into a debate about Africa and independence.

Whether in sleep or half-wakefulness, deliberately or by design, the two women – separated by age and allegiance – held each other, at first like survivors of a storm and, much later, like lovers. Their bodies, unfamiliar to each other, turned into terrains to be explored. Both knew the house could easily become a prison, with guards outside patrolling, all their senses alert to an attack by the SADF or their proxies, UNITA bandits.

In the still, sultry night, carrying undying remnants of the day's heat, they listened to the distant murmur of the sea, which echoed the thrumming of blood in their veins. Somewhere in the vast and stammering distance, a vessel departing from the quayside hooted in an expression of valediction or welcome, it was hard to tell which, except that it happened in the night and left an aural after-image of itself. Somewhere in the house someone mumbled in sleep. They hoped it wasn't one of the guards.

The two women exchanged stories of life and death. Jolene recounted a hunting raid when they clashed with guerrillas of the South West African People's Organisation, the gunfire and explosions and the bodies that lay rotting in the heat, the putrefaction diminishing human beings and making it impossible to look at life with a straight face. And Nerissa, seeing women who came from different climes trying to help others mourn and bury the remnants of victims slain by the South African military: 'We don't believe a soul has found its place of rest until the dead has been mourned according to custom,' she said. Some of it was quite ridiculous, really: the young people dead in the snow in Novgorod or Novosibirsk. Was it possible to thaw the body and warm the soul? Some of the women who came from London to bury their estranged men in Lusaka, forced to wrap themselves in shawls and sit on mattresses under the tropical heat – what sense was there in that?

They talked about the liberation movements, the South African support for UNITA and the involvement of Americans, the CIA, Savimbi and Roberto and Mobuto and apartheid. 'It's not true that Savimbi was a revolutionary,' Nerissa said, 'because people knew – there were documents – that he was an agent of the Portuguese, the same Portuguese he pretended to be fighting.'

'And Neto?' Jolene asked, flaring up momentarily like a match struck in the darkness of a cave. 'How could he claim to be a nationalist when he was married to a white woman, a Portuguese white woman at that? Can you fight against that which makes you reach an orgasm?'

They decided to agree that they would never see eye to eye. The only reality was that they were in this house, under a mosquito net, both alone and somewhat afraid. And then, in the dead of night, entwined into a ball of mobile limbs, the women cried out, each realising the liberating power of surrender. Sweating in the torpid heat of restless mosquitoes, they lay back. In the morning, as Nerissa was going down the stairs to see about breakfast, a unit of six members of the People's Army security department strode past her and up the stairs without so much as a glance in her direction. They took Jolene away.

7

MANIFESTO

The meeting of the big brains, men and women with political muscle and influence got underway at 7:00 a.m. on Friday, 29 December 1989.

It was an important date for Bobo Jones. Almost a hundred years ago, exactly on this day in 1890, the US Seventh Cavalry massacred over four hundred men, women and children at Wounded Knee Creek in South Dakota. Although cited as one of the last major conflicts between Indians and US troops, for Bobo Jones this information kindled a great yearning to have been a warrior at the time. It marked the beginning of his activism. Not only did the blood of ancestral Sioux warriors run in his veins but his mother, a peripatetic poet who dragged her son from meeting to meeting, told him he was meant for great things. This expectation, that he was somehow special, led him to join the Black Panther Party. By the time he bade goodbye to the Badlands, he considered himself a fully-fledged international revolutionary.

But a revolutionary without skills was useless. Exploiting his father's connections in the military – Robert Xavier Jones was a senior enlisted advisor at the Goodfellow air force base in Texas – Bobo ended up specialising in intelligence analysis. When he upped and left and joined the Panthers, he wasn't your run-of-the-mill Afro-wearing, sloganeer but someone with skills that came in handy in thwarting Uncle Sam's counter-intelligence and disinformation programmes.

He had been living in exile in many countries, Cuba, Algeria, Zambia and latterly South Africa, and was convinced that he'd got a hand in the momentous developments unfolding in his newly adopted country. He hadn't been granted citizenship, having to traipse over to Home Affairs in Randburg once every two weeks to freshen his alien's permit and to be ignored by African clerks who must find his status rather odd. And he knew that he was under constant surveillance, both from his hosts and the spooks from the US Embassy here. Even though he found South Africans hard to figure out, they still intrigued him, and Bobo Jones was all about intrigue. It didn't matter that they hid their secrets behind a cloak of openness. It was a friendliness that was a far cry from the wariness of Algerians, who were perhaps true revolutionaries in the classical sense – if classical was dependent on definitions espoused by Fanon, Sartre or Camus – and who had fought a bitter war against the French colonists. But now, they, too, had joined the league of romanticists, their upper classes having become faithful clones of exactly the power they once sought to overthrow. In Zambia, Bobo Jones had been bored shitless by the intellectual claptrap at the Pamodzi Hotel or the second-rate arts scene dominated by drunken South African dilettantes at the Ridgeway Hotel or at the University of Zambia. He felt that South Africa was different. He was entranced by the idea of the struggle, which was real, palpable and violent. It was evolving into a new country on the basis of all that blood. It was blood – the Bloods – that had introduced him to the Panthers. He had been captivated by the eloquence of Bobby Seale and Eldridge Cleaver and had come full circle to Africa via Malcolm X's depiction of the African Revolution. He remembered meeting Rap Brown and that South African poet, skinny, short motherfucker with a beard and an impossible name, Willie … Willie Kgositsile who introduced him, *him*, an African American, to the Last Poets. He liked that poem with the lines 'to every birth its blood' … that was how Bobo Jones saw himself then, a midwife, bloodying his hands in the rebirth of a resurgent Africa. That was why he was now in league with proponents of the kinetic energy that was poised to fashion a new country. Bobo Jones liked the ring of it, *the new country* – he only had to continue coming up with new ideas for the new dispensation. Bobo Jones knew that the new dispensation, a futuristic view of South Africa, had become a buzzword, bandied around by the opportunists and carpetbaggers. He accepted that he might himself be regarded as an opportunist, but he believed he had rare skills to offer. And he was looking beyond the future that was envisaged by scenario planners and commentators. It was a foregone conclusion that the Movement and the People's Army would form the new administration. They would take over from the current bunch of racists. But would they follow a truly revolutionary path or would they be so burdened by a need to compromise and mollify the Western powers that were pouring funds into their coffers? He knew – he had heard it – that the US and the UK were preparing to take credit for any changes that would take place in South Africa. So, he said to himself, we're in for another social democratic regime where the gains of the revolution, the blood, sweat and tears will be sacrificed on the altar of trade-offs. To this end, then, Bobo Jones had been forced to look beyond the current, orthodox leadership, and cast his lot in with forceful leaders like General Palweni. For the sake of his own future, Bobo Jones had to ensure that General Palweni remained happy. Palweni struck him as the kind of guy you didn't want to get ticked off.

As it happened, General Palweni was far from happy. Everywhere he looked, people had fouled up his plans. On 17 December, he had sent men inside the country, with two sets of consignments of money and material. Now, he had briefed his lieutenants, first in Lusaka and then in Mochudi, that the first group to go in consisted of suspected or known enemy agents, same thing, really, when you came down to it. At that time, the Movement was still reeling from a series of body blows, including its ouster from a few of the Frontline States and the unrest in some of the camps in Angola, which made it insuperably unsympathetic to the cause of anyone suspected of being an enemy agent. That was Palweni at his best, weaving an elaborate story that invariably situated him at the head of those seeking solutions. The suggestion, which was carried, that the first group's mission inside the country would have to be verified by a second unit, was originally Palweni's but came out as a collective's decision. One commander, freshly arrived from Luanda and tucked away in the safe house in Mochudi, went by the name of Nyirenda. Speaking eloquently and passionately about the dangers of allowing armed enemy agents access to records and resources, he volunteered to lead the second group. For some unknown reason, he would call the unit the 'second detachment'; he and Palweni would put their heads together regarding how it would be constituted.

Nyirenda's second detachment was a motley crew of askaris, mercenaries, and miscellaneous malcontents cobbled up into a platoon by Colonel Stander and given a home by General Palweni. Strella, Doctor and six other men, all graduates of the People's Army prison cells located in Sector 37, headed the group's senior command structure. Even though they knew Nyirenda to be their real commander, they suspected they owed their lives to General Palweni, who had integrated them into the unit.

But for all their accumulated know-how and training, Palweni fumed, the second detachment truly and thoroughly botched things up. For starters, they allowed some of the members of the first unit to escape; they had also picked up the wrong trunk. Talk about snafu. No one in the first group was supposed to survive; people killed inside South Africa, who had crossed illegally, would have remained anonymous, unclaimed. The animals and elements would have obliterated their identities. And now, Strella, Doctor and Nyirenda had disappeared, most likely acting as freelance agents in the propagation of terror and mayhem in the land.

Now there were survivors and they had the trunk containing some damaging reports that, in the hands of a good analyst, would point to his collusion with Stander on a variety of operations. The Movement would simply not forgive the fact that he had been working with the enemy for a long time. Even in the new dispensation, that would cut him off at the knees. He'd have no role.

He knew that the first person everyone would be looking for was Chaplain Nerissa, who had liaised effectively with both internal and external structures. A hard nut to crack, she had survived a bomb blast; he personally didn't know its source, there being other psychos like Craig Williamson, who got their jollies from sending women parcel bombs. Nerissa must never have access to the trunk.

From what he knew now, the cache was in Durban, KwaDambuza of all places, for God's sake. He shook his head and looked at the sickening wallpaper, the framed photographs of dead oppressors ranged along the wall, their eyes gazing down at the oval boardroom table, complete with place mats stencilled with the crest of the Primrose Hotel, Johannesburg. There were water carafes, matching glasses, rinky-dinky bowls full of mints, alongside little notebooks and pencils. For fuck's sake, who uses a pencil nowadays? He was angry, in fact, madder than a black mamba and as murderous. In his more normal life he was calm and hardly ever used profanity but boy, just get him riled up and he would swear like a sailor. And it didn't end with merely cursing. When General Palweni was angry he was likely to stomp on someone or at least kick him or her halfway round the hall. No gender equity here, boom, a size fourteen boot right on the keester.

General Palweni's rage could also be traced to the fact that he had heard that the High Council had already alerted the machinery inside the country that Palweni had sold out or at least, had dipped his fingers into the coffers of the Movement. And so, in the last week of December 1989, accompanied by Sizwe Ndawo, he had also crossed the Pitsane Molopo into Zeerust, armed with a few thousand rand and a Makarov 9 mm pistol. He had been relieved that there'd been no sign of a patrol. He imagined that Sizwe would be carrying heftier financial resources and scarier weapons. Sizwe wasn't known for taking chances. Once inside the country, Palweni had felt vindicated as he could now lord it over some of his leadership colleagues who'd speak longingly about going home but wouldn't dare leave their cushy desk jobs in Lusaka, or wherever. Here he was on terra firma, at home in the fatherland, alive and kicking and ready to redeem himself in the eyes of his peers. If the Movement were a listed entity on some stock exchange, he'd stand to amass a pile of hefty shares; if it were the Mafia, he would be accorded the status worthy of a made man.

He was in a reflective state when they were safely in the car, one of those ancient Cortinas invented for the sole purpose of torturing passengers. But it had a stout engine and, although it conked out twice or thrice along the route, it had stood its ground against the potholes and unevenness of secondary roads. Somewhere, again once or twice, Palweni thought he saw the terrified eyes of some small animal, a jackal, perhaps, caught in the headlights, followed by a yelp and a crunch. Palweni hoped there were no deer or bigger ungulates that would simply turn the little jalopy into a crumpled mass of metal. He smiled to himself, appreciating once more another irony: surviving exile and all its dangers only to get wasted by some fucking Bambi. He wondered if his companions in the car harboured any anxiety. Sizwe Ndawo – could you believe this? – was snoring on the side, his chest going up and down. The guide was the only one who tried to engage Palweni in conversation, pointing out invisible landmarks, signs of progress, a mine here, a dam there, just the proud chatter of a country cousin for whom anything manufactured with the aid of machines signified progress. The driver, bulked up against the highland extremes, never once took his eyes off the road, even when he would curtly respond to the guide's observations. He only spoke up on the track where Malatsi had guided the guerrillas to the caves.

'He was my cousin,' he said. 'Our village is still mourning him to this day.' And then they passed some villages in the dark where not even a dog barked. Later, they reached a stately, old rambling house surrounded by a high wall in Swartruggens. The driver flashed the group a rare smile, a man proud of his successful delivery of valuable cargo to its destination. As soon as the gate rolled shut behind the car, the lights in the house came on. Two young men came out of the house and helped with the luggage and signalled Palweni to follow. Sizwe took the driver and the guide to the side and Palweni imagined a quick confab where money changed hands.

Safe at last. The return was exciting, but nothing earth shaking. No one's done me any favours.

'You're no longer beholden to your *verdomde* Movement,' Colonel Jan Stander told General Palweni over the phone. 'I'm just sorry you had to go through the indignity of jumping over the border like a common *letlolaterata*.' That was Stander for you, always showing off his facility with languages, even the derogatory word, which means a fence-jumper, used by some Batswana for refugees. Palweni remembered him in the September of 1987. It was during a complicated prisoner exchange that took place in Maputo, Mozambique, involving Angolan soldiers; anti-apartheid activists, Klaas de Jonge, a Dutch anthropologist and Pierre Andre Albertini, a French university lecturer; and Major Wynand du Toit, a South African officer captured in Angola in 1985. At the exchange of prisoners at the Maputo airport terminal, Stander had bidden '*Adeus*' to the 133 newly freed Angolan prisoners and '*Welkom terug*' to SADF officer Major Wynand du Toit.

'I'd grown fond of the men,' he told Palweni. 'We were happy to hand over that prick, De Jonge, a right royal Dutch pain in the neck.'

'We were also happy to be rid of Du Toit,' Palweni confided. He didn't explain why. But this was where the two men, enemies, established rapport. Stander could report to his superiors that he had found a senior Movement official who was ripe for nobbling. In Lusaka, Palweni crowed of his own coup on the tarmac of the airport in Maputo.

'We owe each other something,' he said to Stander. 'That's way above political affiliations.

'Amen to that,' Stander said. 'It's your call.'

The brief moment of recollection ended with the sound of a timorous knock on the door. A scrubbed and uniformed female hotel clerk came in, followed by a man in whites wearing a chef's hat and wheeling a trolley laden with an assortment of fruit, sandwiches, muffins and various breakfast eats and teas and coffees. Young but exuding an air of agelessness in accordance with her office, the woman bent to present General Palweni with the bill, which he signed without checking, knowing that he was in any event being ripped off.

'Thank you, sir,' she said and departed, as soundless as a wraith.

And that was another thing that got his goat. Nowadays, he thought, you pay for everything. Had they been able to put breathable air in cans, these bastards would be peddling it at a premium. Everywhere, you're faced with a meter. A taxi from wherever and whatever the distance clicks like a cash register. You can almost hear the banknotes hissing out of the wallet. You need service; people glance at the clock, their meter. They even tell you, the barefaced cheek, that they need their tips. No, not need – want; they *want* their fucking tips. Everyone. It's likely that when Dr Chris Barnard transplanted hearts here he must have got into a little sideline installing meters alongside the pacemakers, two for the price of one.

And now that he had called a meeting, he must of course feed the nation of attendees. No one could think on an empty stomach. From his jacket pocket, Palweni took out a box of assorted tablets, arranged them up along the calico napkin like multicoloured drugs waiting to be chopped into lines. Making sure to take the series for high blood pressure first, he followed up with the course for cholesterol. There was no logic to this chronology. It was just a quirk, his personal superstition. Either way, his arteries were hardening and with each step taken he could feel his sixty-two-odd years squatting on his shoulders like a rucksack of sand. Today he empathised with the poor wretches under punishment who were forced to run up and down a hill in Malange. He looked at the clock on the wall, 6:47 a.m. Let's see, he thought, if anyone's going to be punctual today.

Bobo Jones, like a Caribbean hurricane, burst into the boardroom, pursued by a flustered female clerk, who seemed unconvinced that anyone dressed in a dashiki of lurid ochre, red corduroy trousers and tan San Remo boots could possibly have any business with the general. She pulled back when she saw the men performing the revolutionary greeting, which entailed a clinch tighter than a lover's embrace. She could almost hear the percussive collision of shoulders, an action that could liquefy the bones of weaker mortals and which ended with another wrestling hold. Whereupon the men, hands still interlocked, inspected each other's faces.

'My brother, my brother,' Palweni said, eyes flicking over the friend's attire and blinking a couple of times as if in the presence of an optical illusion. 'I see you haven't stopped wearing pyjamas to meetings.'

Used to being ribbed about his clothes, Bobo Jones laughed. 'Man,' he said, 'these are my stepping-out rags. You should see my pyjamas.'

They laughed and settled down. Bobo Jones poured himself a cup of coffee and loaded a Danish and a croissant onto a side plate. Then he spooned sugar into the cup and drank it black. The general took a sip of an infusion of herbal tea and honey. 'Disorders that come with responsibility, my brother,' he said, apologising for his sugarless breakfast.

Then they got down to talking shop. 'Did you have trouble coming here?' General Palweni asked.

'My papers are okay, for now. You?' Bobo Jones last saw the general in Lusaka some months ago. As far as he knew, Palweni was still in exile.

'I have a special status,' Palweni said. 'The security people know we're here. Now and then they'll pick up one of ours and rough them up. But it's all posturing. Their party is over.'

'Is it true?' Bobo Jones asked, *it* being the rumour doing the rounds about Mandela's imminent release.

'I hear it's any day.' Palweni had had it up to here with rumours of Mandela's release. Why, just two years ago, the world media, TV cameras, all types of long-haired creatures and journalists of all stripes, camped outside the Movement's HQ in Lusaka, on Independence Circle, hoping to get a glimpse – just because someone had said that Mandela was going to be released.

'They'll make the announcement soon?'

'Yes,' Palweni said. 'I got it from a reliable source.' He debated with the thought of telling him that the source was actually Jan Stander. Although not very definite, Stander had got it from someone in De Klerk's inner circle. It was important for Palweni to be seen to have unlimited access to secret information. But boasting could have its downside. As a child his mother would regale him with folk tales from the Batswana of Kimberley. One concerned a songbird that lost the meat to a fox on account of pride. However, trusting Bobo Jones with the knowledge about his secret connection with Stander would be like believing a hound would guard one's chickens. In Lusaka, the Movement people regarded Bobo Jones as a CIA agent; they would either feed him titbits of half-truths, which they hoped would finally end up confusing the enemy or simply give him a wide berth. Using a pseudonym, he had become quite adept at raising funds and networking for left-leaning organisations, exploits that were published in a little subscription newsletter. The newsletter, which grew from strength to strength, would find its way into the post boxes if not the bejewelled hands of opinion-formers, bankers and powerful lobbyists in the US. He had promised to profile General Palweni the same way his media competitors had transformed Jonas Savimbi from a leader of a ragtag guerrilla army into a household name. Staying close to the general, Bobo Jones would announce, would also help him collate data for a definitive biography. Palweni looked forward to the biography, for the sake of posterity, but he drew a line on wholly opening up to the American.

'What's going to happen?' Bobo Jones wanted to know.

'Well,' General Palweni said, 'we're now on the home stretch. The Movement will surely put pressure on the call for talks with the government.'

'Do you have any leverage,' Bobo Jones asked. 'Personally?'

'I don't get you.'

'It's simple, General,' Bobo Jones put in. 'When the roll is called up yonder, what's going to happen to you?'

'You're obviously influenced by storefront preachers, Brother Jones,' Palweni said. 'It's possibly important, but it makes no sense to me.'

'Okay,' Bobo Jones said warily, noticing the general's eyes narrowing. 'From what I've heard, you've had a little falling out with the Movement. Aren't they likely to go on without you?'

Unseen but certainly loud enough to be heard, a radio newscaster recited the weather. The headlines reiterated the main news of the day: another massacre in some outback of Natal; a man's body transformed into a lump of charcoal following a necklace killing in KwaDambuza … a litany of horror.

'Mr Bobo Jones,' he said, no 'brother' or any title of endearment this time, 'we got into politics knowing full well that, like Moses, we'd do our bit leading the Children of Israel out of Egypt but might not get to see the Promised Land.' He paused. 'Right now, we're near Mount Sinai, where probably we'll work towards a Covenant, the agreement, which should lead us to elections and cobbling together some unifying constitution. That's when we'll say we're approaching Canaan.'

'Well, I'll be …' Bobo Jones said admiringly. 'So you're well versed with your Old Testament.'

Palweni waved a hand airily, unmoved by the praise. 'I know I might not get to Canaan,' he said. 'Just as I know when someone's feeding me a pile of patronising bullshit. But I'll have you know, there're folks out there who are ready to fling their very bodies into the fire to protect me. To ensure that what I stand for is also given room on the negotiating table.'

'So,' Bobo Jones asked. 'What's the deal? The country will burn so that you get a place at the table?'

'For you to be taken seriously,' General Palweni said, 'you've got to set something on fire. Wasn't it you guys who exhorted us, burn, baby, burn?'

'I think you're crazy,' said Bobo Jones. 'Are you content with going down in history as a warlord?'

'I'm sure you know about Genghis Khan.' General Palweni said.

'Of course.' Bobo Jones studied Palweni's face. 'What's the point?'

'What about Sultan Jalal al-Din?'

'You got me there,' Bobo Jones said. 'Who's he?'

'He was defeated by Genghis Khan, a powerful man in his own right,' Palweni said. 'But few people, not even scholars, would recognise his name. Point is, in the beginning Genghis Khan was a warlord, but in the scheme of things he ended up a ruler of a huge empire. I'm not comparing myself with him, except I think he was a good commander and knew a lot about weapons, which is also my speciality, if I might say so myself. But these are modern times. We have to use modern means to meet our objectives. If that makes me a warlord, so be it. In my heart of hearts, though, I see myself as a patriot.'

'I'm not too sure about patriotism,' Bobo Jones said. 'But I can smell a lot of ambition in the air.'

'Sit in the meeting,' General Palweni advised. 'Be a spectator and let yourself be educated. At the end, see if what we're all about is just ambition or pragmatism.' He wanted to expound on the theme of the warlord, the fact that almost all nation building of the past happened via the fire and the sword of one-time warlords. There would be time for that later. Right now, duty called. And, looking over Jones's shoulders, Palweni's eyes brightened. 'Here come the patriots.' It was 7:00 a.m.

They filed in, two middle-aged men in black as if bound for the Wailing Wall, followed by another pair whose youthfulness didn't match their world-weary eyes, wearing ill-fitting brown suits as if blind to current trends. And then a stocky, bald, courteous type in a grey summer suit, accompanied by what seemed like two close acquaintances, both in safari suits fashioned to accommodate shoulder holsters. Bringing up the rear two women, who bore a close resemblance to each other, sisters, perhaps, high-stepped in pinstriped power suits while pulling bulky briefcases on rollers. Something about their stride conveyed a confidence that nothing could stop them. The last to enter was Sizwe Ndawo, the general's aide-de-camp. Carrying notebooks and a miscellany of stationery, he handed each person a file with a nametag clipped to the top corner. Some of the guests proceeded to fasten the laminated tags to their breast pockets. Having done the rounds, Sizwe Ndawo made sure that the double doors to the boardroom were closed before striding across the floor to take a seat off to the left behind his principal.

Dressed in a loose guayabera and a pair of black chinos, General Absalom Palweni cut an informal if practical figure, a nod, possibly to casual Friday. There was nothing casual, however, about the way he conducted the meeting.

'You're all here,' he began, 'because of self-interest. Much as altruism is worthy, it is a dying tradition. Present here are interests of big business, civil society, security, that is the military and the police, and of course, organised religion. The latter to make sure that, while we safeguard the material welfare of all, our spiritual wellbeing is also accommodated. Otherwise we become no different from bandits.'

He smiled, possibly to reassure the meeting that he was no bandit. 'I am sure you'll be interested in the various scenarios that will be unveiled today. We'll start with the gentlemen with the crystal ball.'

The two men in question were dressed like undertakers. Messrs A Ross and S Flintoff arranged their papers before them. One-time futures analysts, they'd turned their hand to scenario planning. Their slogan was *a country without vision is a country without a future.* Without much ado, they took turns explaining the possible impact of Mandela's release from prison.

'There's no doubt,' Ross said in a sonorous voice that brooked no opposition, 'that Mandela's release will unleash unrealisable expectations. I will use the analogy of the imminence of Christmas time for different communities. In the black household, where a father has to scrimp and scrape to meet the expectations of wife and kids, this period is a royal pain in the arse, if you'll pardon my French, ladies. For the kids, it's a time for custard and jelly, goodies everyone does without in the course of the year but miraculously available in the one week of the year. The father has to create this miracle. Mandela is expected to perform a feat that would confound the most surefooted trapeze artist.' He took a sip of water.

'Then there's the violence,' he went on. 'There's no guaranteeing that people are going to lay down their weapons, mainly because, in a country awash with firearms, few would feel safe disarmed, especially since our law enforcement agencies are themselves linked to the bloodletting. The continuing state of flux means that warlords could consolidate their gains and entrench themselves. A state of war is usually incredibly profitable for the shrewd ones profiting out of misery, the arms dealers, the crooks, the money launderers – it's a bonanza.'

The vision of the apocalypse in most people's minds wavered momentarily when one of the lookalike women raised her hand, interrupting the speaker, whom she addressed as Mr Roth. She observed that the meeting was called to discuss the fallout from – emphasising *fallout*, and not *impact* – following Mr Mandela's release. Would Mr Roth explain the sudden diversion, or was it a mere case of semantics, and so on.

First of all, the speaker had to correct the lady. He bent down to scrutinise her nametag, Ms Cecilia Bartle. His name was Mr *Ross* and not Roth, although he'd always found that mix-up flattering, as he was an admirer of novelist Philip Roth. 'Be that as it may, fallout and impact could be used interchangeably, but hey, knock yourself out, we'll stay with fallout if that rocks your boat.'

The other sister interjected that she resented the tone used by Mr Roth, Ross, whatever. 'It's so fucking condescending, all those homey, folksy putdowns typical of you people.'

Mr Flintoff rose at this moment to ask: 'Which people?'

'You people, you know.'

At this point, Absalom Palweni banged his fist on the table and called the meeting to order. 'Continue, Mr Ross. Anyone else who feels like starting a rebellion, there's the door.'

'Thank you, my general,' Mr Ross said. 'We represent very powerful individuals of this country. Organisations and corporations and well-heeled interests want a new South Africa. This South Africa is ailing, economically at the ropes, if you'll pardon that folksy turn of phrase ...'

'Go on, Mr Ross,' Palweni said. 'Cut out the commentary.'

'Okay.' This came from Mr Flintoff. 'Even though the picture painted by my colleague is somewhat gloomy, there's a silver lining to all this. South Africans will be offered an opportunity to reinvent themselves. The prognosis is that a new South Africa led by Mandela – because we're sure no other person will have the moral authority to lead the country – the new South Africa will thrive and all that goodwill from countries will translate into investment, projects and a healthy budget. But that will happen seamlessly only if Mandela comes back as a supreme leader, the father of the nation, if you will, whose loyalty is only to the country as a whole and not to one political party.'

'If he leads a party,' Flintoff continued, 'his stature will be diminished on account of his having to share the light with personalities tainted by engagement in struggle. The struggle, by its very nature, means people have to take decisions that compromise them in the long run, which are inimical to their ethical beliefs. Mr Mandela has been hermetically sealed off from controversy for the last thirty years. The leaders, who've spoken to us, have suggested that General Palweni must somehow find a way to communicate to Mr Mandela that he needs to see himself as standing head and shoulders above the fray. My partner and I will have more details for the general on how to implement a plan that could be presented to Mr Mandela.'

Bobo Jones raised his hand. 'You mean to tell me,' he asked, 'that Mandela will be required to jettison his political movement to become a friggin' figurehead without any political support, some mahatma, a peacenik without a power base?'

Mr Flintoff bristled. 'You're twisting my words …'

'Your words are *twisted*, buddy,' Bobo Jones charged. 'What kind of plan is this, where a man spends twenty-seven fucking years and is then scammed into becoming a political eunuch?'

'Mr Jones?' General Palweni warned, 'you're here as an observer. Please control yourself.'

Bobo Jones retracted into himself, a butterfly covering its core with colourful wings. The grey-suited stocky man spoke from his seat, looking around him, a man not used to interruptions.

'My name's Colonel Jan Stander,' he started. 'I sit here, General, listening to people who don't seem to understand our purpose here. Our purpose here is not to show how intelligent we are but to deal with an urgent situation.' He paused. 'The general hasn't told you that he is not here by choice. He has to be here and his mission has to succeed. I won't bore you with the details of how we came to be allies, suffice to say, in the bigger scheme of things, people will recognise that we had vision.'

Because he knew that the group would do its own research and finally get the whole truth behind his association with the general, he drew a diagram on the flipchart. It was a schematic representation of the development of the conflict in Angola and how that finally entailed the involvement of the South African military. He spoke of the different warring parties, UNITA, led by Jonas Savimbi, *our friend*, allied tenuously to FNLA, our bigger friend, against MPLA, definitely not a friend and run by communists and aided by Cubans and Soviets. A jewel in the crown, of course, was South West Africa, which was being menaced by SWAPO.

'It's clear,' Stander said, 'that the dominoes are falling, despite the murmurs from Messrs Reagan and Crocker and their constructive engagement. Our boys at the border are returning in body bags, inside sealed caskets. Our responsibility, in a word, is to make sure that even if the Movement wins, we should be the beneficiaries of that victory.'

He told them that the future would belong to those capable of flexing their economic muscle. The general had been given the task of establishing units that would mount bank heists and hijacks. We'll have to think of creative ways to introduce drugs – *yes, drugs* – into the market, simply because, to take over an economy you have to first undermine its capacity for sustained survival.

'And then, of course, there'll be violence,' Stander said. 'We'll build on the framework already set by the Movement itself, where it exhorts the youth to render the country ungovernable.'

He chuckled, not a pleasant sound to Bobo Jones's ears. 'We'll show them exactly how to achieve that one.' He paused, letting it all sink in.

'Are you saying,' Bobo Jones asked like someone ill at ease with long silences, 'that you've already brought into the country the … resources?'

He ignored a disapproving look from one of the women. He had come across such people, part of some bank or corporation, sending women out as scouts to see which way the wind blew.

A look of irritation flashed across Stander's face, a man used to dominating an interrogation. Questions were not in the script. 'As happens in these cases,' he said, 'the material was hijacked in a heist by others.'

'Others?'

'Yep. People we'd trained.'

'Where is it now,' one of the combative women asked, 'this fortune?'

'In KwaDambuza, is what we hear,' Stander said. 'By the way, I'm responsible for the original unit sent to procure the trunk from Angola, before it was ambushed by the People's Army in Sanza Pombo.'

He thought of launching into an explanation about how he had assigned a unit led by Barak the Greek to procure assets from Sanza Pombo and how members of the unit had been killed or captured. He wanted to tell them about the elaborate plan to bring some of that material back to South Africa under the guardianship of General Palweni and two of his operatives, Strella and Nozishada. The whole plan had gone awry when the unit, which was not supposed to survive, survived, even though depleted. Even more galling was that the survivors had the trunk in their possession.

But his plans for disclosure were interrupted.

'So,' Mr Ross asked, 'your partnership or alliance with the general – do you think it will last?'

'Let's just say,' Stander replied, 'that war creates enemies sworn to annihilate each other and peace produces enemies whose continued existence is based on co-operation. We have to coexist to survive.'

'But why would you still want the general in your camp?' Mr Ross's puzzlement spread to the others. There was suddenly a murmur of voices. Sizwe Ndawo, like a dog anxious with tension, half-stood, nervously looking from face to face. Without seeming to move, Absalom Palweni signalled his assistant to relax. But Jan Stander was still on the floor.

'We were on the opposite sides in the war. When I learnt of General Palweni's exploits, I knew that this would be the kind of man I'd be proud to serve under. The reason is simple and clear. General Palweni is organised. The military is about organisation. A good general also knows when to advance and when to retreat.' He paused as if picturing stock war footage depicting lives squandered by reckless command.

'We made contact when it became clear that his own side would kill him. He had something we wanted and we have something that could save him. Simple. But,' Stander said, 'we're now moving into uncharted waters and I can tell you that the future is black, whatever you might think. A time is soon coming when being white won't be enough.'

He let those words hang like a curse in the room. Outside, the traffic hummed like a refrigerator. Then one of the men who had come in with Stander suddenly got to his feet as if responding to an urgent call of nature, reaching for his beeper. Returning a few minutes later, he proceeded to whisper something into Stander's ear. A cloud flitted across the colonel's face. Stander then addressed himself to General Palweni.

'General?' he said. 'Seems Strella and Doctor have been at it again.'

'What is it this time?'

'I gather they might have been looking for Chaplain Nerissa.'

'Who's Chaplain Nerissa?' asked Bobo Jones.

'Someone,' Palweni said, 'standing between us and our vision.'

'She's got the trunk, then?'

'She's likely to be roped in to analyse the contents of the trunk.'

'You sound kind of …' Bobo Jones snapped his fingers looking for the lease offensive characterisation.

'Nervous, maybe?' The prompt came from one of the sisters.

'Yeah,' Bobo Jones said, giving the woman a grateful look. 'Nervous, that's right. Does she give you the willies?'

Colonel Stander and General Palweni conferred for a moment. Then, a decision taken, Stander tapped a fork to the side of a water glass decanter to get everyone's attention.

'Mr Bobo Jones,' Col Stander said, 'and this goes for everyone in this room. We're adjourning until further notice. We'll regroup later; you'll be informed. Everything said and heard here is confidential.'

Outside, the sky was overcast on the last Friday of 1989. A newspaper headline asked: WHAT WILL 1990 BRING? Reading this, Stander thought to himself that the year was mostly oblivious of its importance. He asked Palweni, standing next to him, what he thought of the release of Walter Sisulu and other leaders who had been imprisoned on Robben Island. Palweni, though, was engrossed, looking at the faces of the denizens of the city Johannesburg. They were tramping the streets, clutching their handbags close to the body in Braamfontein, a suburb that had proven hazardous to the careless walker. Outside the Primrose Hotel, there was the general bustle of a public preparing for the New Year. Taxis honked, trying to rustle up a few fares among customers waiting their turn to bulk-buy liquor from Solly Kramer's on Jorissen Street.

Coming up the steps leading from the basement car park, Angelo de Matos headed straight to where Stander, Palweni and Bobo Jones leaned against the stuccoed wall of the Primrose Hotel building.

Almost six-feet tall, in his late forties, De Matos managed to look bearish in a brown jacket over a poplin button-down shirt, a pair of jeans and brown moccasins. Unlike Stander's uncultivated stubble, which gave him a feral charm, De Matos's growth, black and peppered with grey, conspired with his receding hairline to making him seem scruffy and harried. Bobo Jones had seen such men around homeless shelters.

But Angelo de Matos's bearing was of a proud and angry man. Gesticulating wildly, he told Stander his men had done a terrible thing.

'And for this,' he said, 'I hold you responsible.'

'Whoa, whoa!' Stander said. 'Tell these men what happened.'

Angelo de Matos's black eyes hovered over the faces of the two black men and something inside him crumbled. He looked like he wanted to cry. He was so angry. When he was finally able to talk, he said, 'I have a car down in the basement. We have to get to Norwood immediately. My niece, Mariela, reports that your killers have struck.'

'Strella and Doctor?'

'Those two,' Angelo de Matos said. 'Hurry.'

8

RENDEZVOUS

Some drunken fool shouted, 'Wotcher, cousins!' It was 12:41 p.m. Strella couldn't seem to get a station that broadcast any sense today, everyone still full of the spirit of the New Year. He now fiddled with the tuning dial of the car radio, searching for a music station, any kind of music, pop, rock, gospel, although he drew a line at classical jazz. He remembered hearing strains of music, Charlie Mingus or Thelonious Monk, playing in the lounge of the professor from the university in Gaborone. The woman, the guy's wife, she was mad about jazz, collecting books and albums and had even internalised the nonsense from musicians, which passed for wisdom. One day, she told him that Monk was a genius, supporting her claim by reading the liner notes of his album, urging Strella to listen, just listen to what the man was saying: *Sometimes it's to your advantage for people to think you're crazy*. Then snapping her fingers in time to some complicated piano riff, eyes closed in rapture, going yeah, yeah, a feline hepcat, scatting. To each their own.

On the radio, however, he couldn't find any ambient music, just a lot of talk. South Africans, it seemed, had suddenly found their vocal chords; everywhere someone was making a ponderous point about nothing, really.

He recalled one of the Palestinian instructors at the camp in Bin Ghashir, expressing doubt over some Black Panthers who wanted to do military training. 'Watch out for him American Negro,' he said. 'Him hair slick, him tongue smooth. Him talk more jive than radio.' Today, Strella would have told Salim al Hamadi that a black American couldn't hold a candle to a South African with an idea.

There they were, loud in the land, talking heads going blah, blah, everyone coming out with an instant solution to problems as old as the mountains, sometimes coming up with ingenious ways to solve problems that were still to be invented. That was how brilliant these jokers were. The anchors were the worst, most of them prefacing their gilt-edged baubles of wisdom with the phrase: *from where I'm standing*. Strella wished they could all go and find real jobs somewhere, preferably where they'd be forced to remain standing until their feet developed bunions, the women as waitresses and the men digging a ditch somewhere, see how they'd like that.

'How long are we going to sit here?' Doctor asked, 'listening to this incessant chatter? Can't you find something more in line with concerns of real people?'

'Doctor?' Strella asked, 'why are you always complaining? And what do real people want to hear?'

'Game shows and quizzes?' Doctor put in quickly. 'People love programmes that confirm their ignorance.'

'Ja,' Strella said. 'Isn't it funny that the last speech of 1989 from a minister tells people to wait. I thought you'd comment on that.'

'And say what?' Doctor couldn't hide his irritation. 'Ministers are always telling people to wait. It's their job. Just as ours is to get that bloody box and go our separate ways.'

'Why separate ways?' Strella asked. 'Isn't there strength in numbers?'

'People who spread that kind of rumour are simply cry babies scared of being alone.' He paused, prising dirt from under his fingernails with the tip of a sharp blade. 'Just about how much are we each getting?'

'Will you stop that,' Strella said. 'Makes me nervous.'

'The knife or the manicure?'

'Both. Knives make me nervous. And I keep on expecting you to slice your fingers.' But Stella couldn't tell Doctor that his first big crime was with a knife on an old man and every time he saw a blade, he experienced a heady feeling, no different from the sensation some people get when standing at the top of a high place. It was as if he wouldn't be able to stop himself from using a knife once it was within reach.

'All right,' Doctor said, the sharp rustle of the blade sliding into the sheath. 'Now, you switch off that stupid radio.'

'Okay.' The car was now quiet.

But Doctor couldn't sustain it. 'You know that we've been sold out?'

'What do you mean, Doc?'

'We've been left to hang out to dry,' Doctor said. 'Otherwise, how do you explain that Stander and the general are now the best of buddies?'

'They could have been buddies all along.'

'Ja, but I know they were enemies. Stander was with us, the general with the People's Army. They're now as thick as thieves. I know this.' Doctor slammed a fist on the dashboard.

'How do you know all this?'

'They are meeting today,' Doctor said. 'Don't ask me how I know. I know.'

'I'm the commander of this unit, Doctor. You answer to me.'

Resuming the operation on his fingernails, Doctor gave Strella a sidelong glance. 'Let's not go there, Mfo. We're on our own out here. And when this gig is over, we'll be even lonelier.'

'You mean alone?'

'No. Lonely.'

Outside, on Regent Street, the restless Yeoville crowds went about their business. Whether strolling or hurrying past, no one seemed to pay attention to the powder-blue Toyota Cressida parked between delivery vans near the corner with Fortesque. Two men in the car kept a watch on the house across the road. Built on ground raised slightly above street level, it was a stone and red brick structure with high windows and a great, polished oak door. Fronted by a formal garden, the house was surrounded by a breezeblock wall topped with an electric fence and rigged with a sliding steel gate.

'How much?' Doctor resumed the questioning. He would not be sidetracked. 'You know I did everything I was supposed to do. Look at my hands. Today I cut up a poor *grigamba*.'

'You're complaining again, Doctor,' Strella said.

'It's all right. I'm just kind of tired.'

'Okay,' Strella said after a minute. 'This will be the last job.'

'Who is it, this time? Another Mozambican?'

'No. And don't keep on talking about the grigamba.' Strella was clearly unhappy.

'What really happened?' Doctor asked. It was not clear who he was addressing.

'You killed a man, Doctor.' Strella looked at his colleague, sitting in the passenger seat, a half-jack of Mainstay Cane Spirit nestling between his legs. Now and then Doctor took a swig and passed the bottle to Strella, who shook his head no.

'Killed a man, huh?' Doctor asked wonderingly. 'Isn't that something?'

'Something you're not only good at,' Strella said, cruelly, 'but also something you seem to relish doing. I don't understand the bleating.'

'I'm not bleating, Strella,' Doctor said. 'I'm just sad that you won't have a drink with me.'

'After the job,' Strella said. 'After the job.'

They both lapsed into silence.

Earlier that morning, at around 6:00 a.m., Strella had steered the Toyota Cressida down the pockmarked road whose surface resembled the wall of a firing squad, and stopped in front of a gate, where two guards pretended to be alert although they must have known that they looked hungover. This part of Norwood, where houses that dated back to the 1920s stood in defiance of more recent dwellings, was bounded by Scholtz in the north, Algernon in the east, Frances in the west and Grant in the south. Even though it was early, some people were already pounding the pavements, some with sprightly determination and not a few dragging themselves as if already returning from a long day's slog at the salt mines.

With Doctor a step behind, Strella opened the gate that led to a narrow lichen-ridden passage separating houses, the gym bag knocking against the gatepost once, the metal tools inside giving a telltale clink that set the guards scampering off. At the corner of the plot, on the way to the back and down the aisle, a dog of doubtful pedigree glanced at the intruders with near-human eyes and whimpered as it sat on its lowered tail. With unhurried precision, the two men pumped a jack, rigged up under the grille door, until it creaked off the hinges, its locking apparatus snapping off and clattering to the step. Lifting the heavy door, they stood it against the wall. They waited for a minute to ascertain if anyone had heard them. No sound from the house; outside birds chirped as they darted from dustbin to dustbin, excited at the sight of rotting peels. Satisfied that the coast was clear, Strella and Doctor quickly jimmied the back door and entered the kitchen.

It was a splendid kitchen befitting a restaurant owner. Modern chrome fittings, a double-door aluminium fridge, cookers that could have provided for a hungry platoon and mod cons including a range of Le Creuset cast-iron pots and saucepans. There were various kitchen items, coolers and a coffee maker, knife sets still in their original packing boxes. Somehow, the range of branded items seemed arbitrary, nothing matched.

'Somebody ripping off the stuff,' Doctor said, sounding indignant. 'Your boy is a fence.'

'Also an aspirant revolutionary,' Strella said, eyeing old pamphlets and lapel pin badges of Frelimo, laminated with black-and-white images of Samora Machel and his predecessor, Eduardo Mondlane. Absently, he took a pin badge and put it in his pocket. 'But where could he be?'

They didn't have long to wonder. From under the floor they could hear muted scrabbling and footfalls until the trapdoor in the floor swung open and banged on the boards, sending Doctor backwards into a two-step shuffle. Strella had a déjà vu moment, taken back to Sanza Pombo. Luis Bernado Muchave, his eyes like saucers, caught between screaming and pulling the flap closed, opted for the more prudent option of mounting the steps one by one, his hands raised level with his shoulders.

Dressed in a cream tracksuit with blue-and-red piping running down each side seam, and Reeboks, he cut a healthy figure, a man checking his stock before setting off on his morning run. 'What's the problem, comrades?' Luis Muchave asked. 'If it's money you want …'

'We're looking for Nerissa,' Strella said. 'Chaplain Nerissa.'

'I don't know where she is,' Luis Bernado Muchave said. 'She spoke of going to Durban.'

'She was in your restaurant?'

'Who with?' Doctor asked. 'I gather people don't eat alone any more.'

'She was with a friend,' Luis Muchave said. 'Georgina. Georgina Smith.'

'Is there someone here with you?' Strella asked.

Luis Bernado Muchave hesitated, looking up at the ceiling. 'No, *estou sozinho*. I'm alone.'

Strella gave Muchave a long look in the eyes and the Mozambican met his gaze for as long as was proper between a homeowner and an armed intruder. Then he dropped his gaze, deferentially, in line with tips to survive South African home invasions.

'What have you got down there?' Strella asked, jerking the muzzle of the gun towards the opening of the trapdoor.

'Lots of stuff,' Luis Muchave said, desperation flitting off his face. He was dealing with common robbers, after all, looking for something to flog.

'Nerissa never said anything about a trunk from Angola?'

'No.' Then: 'No, camarada.'

'You're not hiding anything from me?'

'No. Not at all.'

At which point Strella said to Doctor: 'I'll go do a recce downstairs. Make sure he doesn't make a move.'

'Okay,' Doctor said, looking around. 'Do you have any booze here?'

'It's not a good idea to drink this early, Doc,' Strella said, going down the steps into the dimly lit basement.

At some stage the cellar had been converted into a bunker. Luis Bernado Muchave and whoever must have helped had constructed an underground storage and supply centre, down to cots with stacks of flat mattresses, a refrigeration unit that would have sustained a besieged family for weeks on end. A small generator powered the underground, where yellowish bulbs allowed for minimal illumination. Air flowed in vents in unseen corners, a regular drone of an engine speaking of power being used.

He searched, seeing paintings still in their frames and sealed in cardboard and bubble-wrap, evidence of plunder somewhere, but nothing remotely like his – *his* – own treasure trove. No trunk. There were two or three kists and footlockers laden with linen and stuffy trinkets that looked like Portuguese artefacts, religious icons and heraldic insignia. Perhaps this Luis Muchave had once served in some Portuguese regiment, which would be very funny because it would mean that he had been on the right side of the war.

He thought of all the faces whose features had been obliterated by time and fear and desperation. The night he escaped from Sector 37, tramping in the unbelievable nights, where he negotiated their inky stickiness by putting his hands out and following the void like a blind man. For the first time he wished he were blind for he might have had a better chance of surviving. The expected-though-unexpected bone-rattling fall into stony gorges, the choking slides into swamps, until he reached deep inside himself and called up the survival training at the cruel hands of Arabs. They believed that every part of a human being should be trained to predict and identify the source of danger. 'You must grow eyes on your nose,' Adnan Yassin had said. Five days of tramping through the terrain of Angolan treachery, his nose woke him up to the muzzle of a R4 rifle, the AK-47 and bayonet, Thabo Stone's parting gift as they left him at the end of the road out of Quibaxe, and Thabo's last words: '*I don't know what brought you here, and I don't need to know, but take care of yourself.*' Jolene's face, pale and fearful in the back of the Jeep, Nerissa urging Thabo Stone – Mchinda – to hurry. He, Strella, rushing off into the shadows with an image of Nozishada framed inside the sights of his rifle, *Nozishada,* the name pulsing repeatedly like a prayer in his mind, and now, waking up to a gun. In his sleep he had heard the helicopter circling above, but it had been in a sleep so deep he could easily have been in a coma. A Chinese-looking pilot and medical orderlies that were part of the crew told him he was in Gabela and he thought about Sanza Pombo and his comrade, Gabela who had either been killed or captured together with Barak the Greek. What happened to all those people? He tried to open his mouth and they told him to keep his mouth shut. What about Jolene, the lady of the Attic?

'Jolene,' Jan Stander had told him when Strella was finally safely ensconced in the infirmary in Ondangwa, 'is the one who saved your life and told us you were still alive. She found a radio in one of the People's Army residences and radioed here. I was surprised she still had the coordinates.'

'Hey, Strella,' Doctor shouted and brought him to the present, his voice bouncing against the contraband. 'Are you still there?'

'Coming,' Strella said. Perhaps they'd need a bigger crew to trawl through the stuff here, but he was sure this was a wasted trip. The only prize info was Nerissa's whereabouts. He looked forward to seeing her again. Exactly at that moment, he came face-to-face with Mabitla, now almost totally unrecognisable in decrepitude. 'You're going to shit,' the old ghost said, employing a Setswana idiom as ageless as mountains. 'You will finally discover your real nature.'

'To hell with you,' Strella said. But this time he was really rattled. The old man's comments struck a nerve.

'Hey, Strella, man,' Doctor asked, somewhat nervously. 'You've gone loco or what? Who are you talking to?'

'Don't worry about it,' Strella said, perceiving a distant illumination that could only spiral out of a premonition. Instantly, he sensed that this foray into the Mozambican's house was a mistake. Stander had sold them out. He was now swimming in the pool with the big fish. Everyone had sold them out, Palweni too.

But something was bothering him, something more immediate. Doctor's tone, the cadence of his speech, something was wrong. It was a wrong day, weighed down by the burden of so many expectations, everyone having his or her version of what the future should be. As he took another step up, he heard it, the wet thud of a knife hitting flesh, once, twice. He shouted, 'No!'

No. That's what Mariela de Matos heard as she stood, hiding behind the heavy curtains covering the window of the upstairs bedroom. She knew it was all over for Luis. Luis, Luis, why is God so cruel? They only had a few days left before the wedding in Lisbon. Seized by a defiant impulse, she thought of marching down the stairs and confronting the robbers – and to hell with it if they killed her too – but, she reasoned, dead, she was useless to Luis. No one would have any information about the two intruders. Strangely, when alerted to the sound of a car pulling up in front, something had told her to go to the window. She'd sensed that these were messengers of death – their walk, the heft of the gym bag, the downcast eyes – until they entered the property and then she could see them, the arrogance of people who had already taken power with impunity. Now, hearing the door close, hearing the silence, she knew that she would have to inform Angelo, her *tio* in Kensington. He would know what to do. She knew her uncle's fits of anger could be explosive – he wasn't *o anjo zangado* for nothing. But whatever happened, anything, would give her a measure of satisfaction. At the back of her mind, as she took the steps down to the kitchen, Mariela had already started to feel the weight of the survivor's guilt.

Thirty minutes later Strella pulled up at a BP filling station on Louis Botha Avenue, a long street that passed through numerous suburbs, including Alexandra Township and Corlett Drive. They filled up and drank coffee while the petrol jockey checked oil and water and tyre pressure. In the passenger seat Doctor was reticent, his cap pulled over his eyes as Strella laid into him, telling him he was a total fuck-up.

'Why did you kill the man?'

'Because I thought he was going for his gun?'

'Going for a gun – a man in a tracksuit?'

'Look, Strella,' Doctor said, smiling mirthlessly, foxy cunning. 'You're just sore because you had your eyes on that swish tracksuit, I know you.'

Strella was about to cry out: 'Tracksuit? Tracksuit, Doctor? What fucking madness is that?' But then he noticed a police van pulling up behind their car. Two cops, both black, both young, one tall and lanky, the other one paunchy and a head shorter, emerged from their car and sauntered confidently towards the entrance of the shop, greeting the petrol attendants. They stopped, the taller one giving the Toyota

Cressida a once-over, muttering something to his partner, who also stopped and made an undisguised appraisal of the car.

The two men, now with pistols cocked and ready, concealed, looked on as the cops entered the shop and stood at the counter where they bought coffee and sandwiches – and made their way back. The tall cop approached the Toyota on the driver's side, his two great arms on the roof as if ready to be frisked. His face was even more youthful.

'Nice car,' he said to Strella. 'Been looking for something like this for a while.'

'Oh ja,' Strella agreed. Get the fuck out of here.

'Three-litre engine, huh?'

'Yep,' said Doctor, who knew a little more about cars. 'Want to take it for a spin?'

'Nah,' the policeman said, shooting a quick look at his partner, who'd started on his sandwich. 'Busy day with the news, maybe, that Mandela will come out.'

'Pity,' Strella said.

'Pity what?' the cop asked. 'That Mandela's coming out?'

'Of course not, officer,' Strella said. 'Pity that you can't take this for a drive.'

'I know what you meant, just pulling your leg,' the policeman said, being a sport. 'Well, take care of yourselves. My name's Steven Mabe, if you ever want to get rid of this baby. I'm at the Yeoville Police Station.'

'We'll stay in touch, Officer Mabe,' Strella said. He didn't introduce himself. Mabe gave them a final look before waving and walking back to the van.

They watched the uniformed man join his partner in the van. After a minute it executed an illegal U-turn and headed up the street towards Berea.

Mariela was right to fear her uncle's reaction. Luis's death became a crusade. After placing a call to Colonel Jan Stander – it being a universally accepted fact that organised crime couldn't thrive without the assistance of an enterprising constabulary – Angelo de Matos sent his men to make sure his niece was safe and to help the police in preserving the crime scene. The men also had to latch the basement and sanitise what needed sanitising. He recalled grimly the death of one of the old geezers in a flat in Berea, when Berea was still a respectable neighbourhood, before the invasion of the savages, God-knows-from-which steaming jungle. That his niece had been engaged to a black man didn't matter. Luis was Portuguese, he had refinement and style. Anyway, they went to this dead old man's place, opened up, dumped incriminating stuff into black bags. Then Angelo opened the door of the bedroom cupboard and simply collapsed under the kaleidoscopic shower of skin magazines and videos, some imported. Where did the old man find the time to perve on all that material? To each his own.

Luis wasn't like that. He was solid. A member of the family, trusted with the inner workings of things – and now this. At 8:00 a.m., it already felt like he'd put in a whole day's graft. Stander had given him something to go on, the names of the animals and he had the description of the car they were driving. It must be a stolen car, so the contacts at MVR in Langlaagte wouldn't be much help, except that cops were forever on the lookout for three-litre Toyota Cressida or Nissan Skyline models, especially ones with black occupants, as they had become the vehicle of choice for hitmen in taxi wars. Angelo de Matos put out his own version of an APB on the car among the connections, official and informal.

At 1:00 p.m., twenty minutes since the stakeout, the two men hit the jackpot. Taxis careened up and down the road, stopping to unload or pick up a boundless supply of God's creations, men, women and children, loud colours, some sharp-looking ladies with sharp legs, some double-sized (bet they were made to pay double!) and schoolboys, kicking a ball and actually bouncing it against their car. And sauntering off, switching their backsides, their flannels swung low to expose the ribbed waistbands of their shorts. It was a work day, and this was evident in men in navy-blue Telkom overalls, others in yellow, some wearing hard hats. For Strella, this was still a new country and he felt like a stranger. It didn't help that his colleague was getting drunker by the second from cane spirit. But it was Doctor who spotted Georgina.

'There she is,' he drawled.

'Okay,' Strella said, shoving his pistol in his waistband. 'You wait here. Let me deal with this.'

'Why?' Doctor asked, eyes glazed. 'Because you think I'm drunk?'

'Because I know you're drunk. Now stay put.'

'You don't give orders, Strella.'

'Here, on this mission, I do.'

He stepped out of the car, checked the road, looked right, looked left, looked right again and quickly crossed the street, like he'd been taught in his schooldays. He saw Georgina getting out of the car, leaning inside, and retrieving a few parcels from the back seat. Quickly zipping up his lumber jacket to conceal the weapon, Strella strode across to the small woman. Just when he was about to whip out the gun, he held back, seeing Georgina rushing to the other side to unbuckle a little girl of about five on a booster seat. 'Come, Toni,' she crooned. 'Let's take you to your mama.'

Then, sensing the intensity of the stare from the man on the other side of the car, Georgina, possessed of an instinct honed in numerous close shaves in confrontations with the enemy, decided to squat as she unharnessed the little girl and patted her twice on the back while firmly nudging her forward.

'Run, little Toni,' she whispered urgently. And then her lungs opened up in a scream shriller than a lunch-hour siren.

'What did you make of those fellows, Cliff?' Sgt Steven Mabe asked. They were studying the menu at the counter of Zeco's, the fast-food outlet on the corner of Corlett Drive and Louis Botha. Sgt Clifford Mkhize's unerring early warning system, the stomach, had already alerted the cops that it was fast getting to lunchtime.

'Which ones, Sergeant?' Mkhize asked. Then, knowingly: 'Or should I say "Inspector"? I hear you're up for promotion.'

'Nah,' Mabe said. 'I think that's just talk.'

'I don't think so, Sergeant,' Mkhize pressed on. 'Anyway, which guys are you talking about?'

'The guys at the filling station with the Cressida.'

'Those twerps we saw back there? They shouldn't be in any filling station. They should be in a police station, answering questions.'

'Or filling forms,' Mabe said, making a face.

'That would fix them.'

'Something about those two, huh?'

'Yep. We'll probably meet them in a line-up someday.'

They got their orders, burgers and chips and gallons of Coke, and took the paper bags back to the car.

'Watch out,' Mabe said. 'Don't park your butt on my lectures.'

'What are you studying anyway?' Mkhize picked up one of the folders. 'Chester Himes: Studies in Anger.' He glanced at his partner. 'Shouldn't you be doing police science, rather than studying anger?'

'I love Chester Himes,' Mabe said. 'His two detectives …'

'Take a look at that!' Mkhize pointed with a greasy hand at a well-dressed young woman. 'Wouldn't mind showing that to my mama.'

'Then you'll have to sleep with one eye open,' Mabe said. 'Unless you want to wake up swimming in a bath of boiling water.'

They indulged in a favourite pastime of cops on an uneventful day, checking out the women to see if beneath the voluptuous exterior there lurked a dangerous criminal with malevolent intentions. They watched the men, young and old, classy or shabby, speculating on the vagaries of fate which had elevated some to stellar heights while condemning others – a great many – to life on the treadmill. Mabe, younger and therefore normally more enthusiastic, felt unaccountably low today, watching his partner take a swig of Coke, his Adam's apple bobbing up and down like a kalkoen's. He admired Mkhize, who had an uncomplicated take on life, everything being black or white, never getting bogged in the mire of greyness.

'What do you think will happen to the force once Mandela's out?'

'They'll need a bigger force,' Mkhize said, adjusting his bulk to look at his younger partner as if suspecting that he'd just been asked a trick question. 'The force was there long before Mandela was born and will be there long after he's gone to meet his ancestors. The black power crowd, which unleashed all those kids in Soweto in 1976, led to law and order being seriously undermined. So did Oliver Tambo when he encouraged people to make this country ungovernable. That's good and fine if you're preaching from Lusaka. At home, though, it's a different kettle of fish. All that will come back and haunt us. These kids are saying no education before liberation and they burn down the schools. They have committees and meetings. You ask, where's your seven-year-old, and you learn he's gone to a meeting. Worse, he's out there addressing a fucking crowd. And what's more, people are actually listening to this brat who's barely finished with potty training. South Africa is going to need a lot more policemen simply because there have to be armies of us with umbrellas and shovels when the shit comes down.'

Sgt Mabe was still shaking off a visual image of bucketfuls of dung raining down on an unsuspecting populace when the radio crackled into life. Mkhize listened to the control station issuing orders and co-ordinates and then indicated to Mabe to step on it, mfo.

'Emergency incident in progress,' he said. 'Man with firearm.'

'There goes my afternoon,' Mabe said. 'What was I thinking?'

For Mkhize, Johannesburg-driver behaviour should be a compulsory module for anyone involved with emergency services. He thought

Johannesburg drivers were up there with the most selfish, suicidal bunch with whom he'd ever had the misfortune to share the road. The siren meant fuck-all; it was just another sound to disturb the drivers' enjoyment of Keith Moon's apocalyptic drumming or Hendrix's impossible guitar solo. It never ceased to amaze him, whenever he'd get attitude from some pony-tailed brat, forced off the road. Nowadays he tended to open a channel through the traffic, to Mabe's mortification, simply by waving his non-police-issue .357 Magnum at non-compliant drivers. That usually resulted in the formation of a clear route, though one characterised by dire imprecations and aggressive gestures and a few bashed bumpers. But all that would have ceased to be Sgt Mkhize's problem. Mabe likened him to Chester Himes's blind man with a pistol, who, creating havoc on the streets of Harlem, dismissed the screech of tyres and screams of rage as signs that the roads were full of bad drivers.

Today, for some reason, the Friday traffic was rather compliant, as if the city dwellers in their powerful machines wanted to reach 1990 in one piece. Looking out at the scenery flashing past as the police car raced along Louis Botha Avenue, Mabe registered that Johannesburg was truly living up to its reputation as one of the world's greenest cities.

The trees and hedges forming hedgerows that demarcated properties all the way from Birnam, Birdhaven, Melrose Estates, the Killarney Country Club, along St Andrews Road and down to Raleigh Street – places with names that harked to a forgotten time – added to the beauty of the area, while giving it a brooding edge. As a policeman, Mabe knew all too well how this greenery could become a haven for prowlers.

In a cloud of smoke and dust, the police car turned into Fortesque. Even the most daring dawdlers, even the patients freshly out of the clinic, recognised the urgency of the siren. Mabe had an impression of people frozen as in a tableau, the air still. In the soundless moment, the Cressida registered as just another element in a painting, a still life, before Mabe pointed it out to Mkhize, who then took out his gun. *Inganono*, he had lovingly dubbed the .357 Smith &Wesson, a corruption of 'cannon'.

He leapt out of the moving car, shoe leather beating a tattoo on the pavement. Just then one of the suspects opened the passenger door of the Toyota Cressida, coming out, a knife in one hand and a pistol in the other. Mkhize fired once, boom, and an iridescent red spray formed a halo above a non-existent head, a second before the body flopped inwards into itself as if the frame that had held it together had yielded. The crowd, growing bigger by the minute, sent out a shout as if at a fireworks display.

'Watch out,' someone yelled, a woman, the elderly matron trying to run and duck at the same time. Startled by the sound of the shot, the second man – the driver Mabe had seen earlier at the filling station – was briefly caught between taking cover and responding to the new source of danger, perhaps snapping off a shot. The result, a compromise, was a wrestler's crouch with the gun held level with his head. When he eventually took in his partner lying lifeless in a widening pool of blood, Strella let out a howl as he drew a bead on Sgt Mkhize.

Two guns went off almost at the same time. Rooted to the spot, his foot on the running board of the van, Sgt Mabe saw the shooter snapping off a salvo of rounds in quick succession until the pistol clicked emptily. The gunman tossed the weapon and sprinted forward as if intent on ramming the reeling policeman. Sergeant Clifford Mkhize sank to his knees and then lay on the road, curled like some African American pilgrim kissing the tarmac on landing in the Motherland. Sgt Mabe fired his own shot at the young man, missing, missing again until, feeling numbness in his fingers, he realised that he'd also been hit on the upper arm. Why hadn't Mkhize thought of wearing body armour, he asked himself, feeling a great tiredness coming over him. From a distance came the sound of sirens, loud and urgent. He thought he was saying something, knowing he was mumbling, trying to spit out the nauseating taste of salt and iron in his mouth. Hearing voices.

'It's okay, I'm Colonel Stander,' someone authoritative was saying.

'Yes, this is Angelo de Matos, Special Units … we'll take over from here. This man has to go to hospital. The others … get the mortuary van.'

'Where …?' Sgt Mabe asked, meaning to enquire after the shooter who had killed his friend. Also, the gun – *Inganono* – what happened to it? What happens to weapons of fallen cops?

'We've got it all under control,' Col Stander said.

Bobo Jones was still a little disoriented from the flurry of activity at the Primrose Hotel, where the two military men, Stander and Palweni were sweeping him up in their particular storm. He was already skittish from the discussion, which had swayed and yawed like a boat in choppy waters and became even more vertiginous when Angelo de Matos entered the scene with his own tale of woe. Following that, De Matos, Palweni and Stander had hightailed it out of the hotel, leaving him to pack.

He'd almost composed himself, sipping a G & T from the mini-bar in the room, when, hours later, General Palweni and Jan Stander burst into the room. They helped him cram his remaining clothes into a suitcase and almost frogmarched him to the lift, where he finished dressing. They went down all the way to the basement parking where he was again introduced to Angelo de Matos, the white guy who looked like what South Africans call a 'coloured'. De Matos had a lethal-looking rifle trained in the general direction of the body of a blood-spattered young man who lay still in the back of a red Toyota 4Runner.

'You always wanted to see the country, Bobo,' General Palweni said. 'Now's your chance.'

'Move to the back,' Stander said, opening the door and pushing Angelo de Matos from the driver's seat where he had moved after shutting the back door of the vehicle. 'I'm driving.'

Although red in the face, De Matos complied, settling into the back seat. Seeing that the prisoner was still out for the count, he propped the rifle between his knees. Bobo Jones looked on, wondering what would happen if they hit one of those famous South African potholes.

'Where we going?' he asked.

'Durban,' Palweni said. 'The kingdom of the Zulus.'

'Your ancestors,' Stander said. The two men up in front start laughing like a pair of geriatric hyenas. Bobo Jones didn't think it all that funny.

LOG #5

It's around 2:30 a.m. Instead of returning to KwaDambuza they drive southwards in the direction of Port Shepstone. Along the coast they maintain closeness to the sea, the rasp of the tyres on the tar road complementing the hoarse sigh of the wind. It feels, this ride, like an escape from the world, from the blood and gore and bone shards, the vast expanse of unseen water providing a possibility of baptism. Thunder crackles in the distance, the sky glowing, coaxing the rainclouds into action. Although young and struggling with the complexities of good judgement, she knows that no amount of water – not even a deluge – can cleanse her of her impureness. The combined smell of cordite and excrement refuses to leave her nostrils, nor will she ever exorcise the memory of the kid toppling over, alive and abject one moment and totally dead the next.

You chickened out, he says. She's not sure if she's being censured. You didn't hold your end of the bargain.

We'd never agreed on anything of the sort, she says. In her defence she continues: I tried to fire at the kid but I missed.

Stop calling him a kid, he snarls, the first real show of emotion. It was a man, an enemy. You missed because your heart was not in it.

Can a heart ever be in committing murder?

There you go again. That wasn't murder. It was an execution.

One day, perhaps, you'll educate me on the difference.

You're getting ahead of yourself, he says. It spells trouble if we start flouting the chain of command. I lead. You follow. No accidents that way.

He is quiet for a while. And then: The man who survived is now your responsibility.

How is that?

By missing, he says. It would have spelled bad luck for me to kill him. So you saved him. He owes his life to you.

I don't want that responsibility. You let him go, not me.

He's too scared to report anything. But, you're responsible for a number of lives, he says. Your actions can determine their fate.

Which lives?

Your aunt and your little sister: you have a role in the direction their lives will take.

Is that a threat?

You can read it whichever way you want. Truth is, whether you pulled the trigger of not, you are also implicated in murder. He corrects himself. In the execution. The gun used to shoot Tikka Joe has your fingerprints. There are a number of very virile constables who would salivate at the prospect of grilling you overnight.

What do you want from me?

The group at Ngobese's house, he says. I don't have all the information about their situation. I have an idea that one or two of them might be injured. You must tell me. The weapons they have – what kind; do they have any grenades, plastic …

Plastic?

I mean plastic explosives, detonators, fuses, caps, and the whole damn shoot. I know they have the trunk …

The trunk? What trunk?

He shakes his head and waves a hand dismissively. Don't worry about that. A trunk is a trunk, with things inside.

You don't have to patronise me. I'm not an idiot.

Sorry, but this is urgent. I need the information. He pauses to think for a minute. And to check if they expect any people to join them.

How would you know I would have access to Ngobese's house?

Now it's you patronising me, he says. I know.

It might be tricky, she says.

These things are always tricky, he says. But it could be even trickier for twelve-year-old Thembani doing Standard 5 at Zamazulu Secondary. These girls grow up so fast. Before you know it, a child has become a woman. That alone should help you think of a plan.

She thinks he's as subtle as a shot in the head, but, for once, she won't let him know how his words chill her. She asks: You say you know the people there … at Ngobese's place?

I know there's Sassafras or Mchinda, a.k.a Thabo Stone, real name Sidwell Zondi. I wonder if he knows who he really is. There's Hickory or Django, real name Ezekiel Zimu; there was Pomegranate … Styles, real name Refiloe Mokoena, but he snuffed it. And then there's Stinkwood, Joe Mabuza. I'm not sure if he's ever used another pseudonym.

She asks: Who killed Refiloe? She berates herself for the impulsiveness, knowing that now she has played her hand, whatever it is, rather unwisely. I know you won't tell me that. But you could tell me, how do you know so much about them?

Let's just say we were all once one happy family, he says, showing his teeth. But now we've all gone different ways.

What will you do with the information?

You know I can't answer that.

Should I fear for my life?

No, he replies, looking out the window at the darkness.

She knows he's lying. They always lie.

She wonders if there's a way she could send a message to her Aunt Maisie who runs a shebeen at the corner of Ndonga and Khuzwayo streets, and tell her to collect Thembani and get the hell out of KwaMashu. Get out and go where? And hide in which hole? Is there a place that could be regarded as safe? In fact, she knows, the first stumbling block would be Aunt Maisie herself. She can just see Maisie standing, arms akimbo. Girl, what do you mean run? Look, I'll never leave this place for some bundu where there's no possibility of a livelihood! Run from a man? Look, the Special Branch and the police caused trouble for all of us, but did we run? Hell no. We are staying. We're not moving. And I always warned you against these black power types. She imagines herself remonstrating that he is not from the black power movement. What is he, then, an exile? He's something like that. Aunt Maisie would look at her with a frustrated though indulgent expression: Girl, didn't I tell you, keep away from exiles? They are broke, they might even give you STDs and they've got their noses in the air because they've been fucking white women in Russia. Pah!

She falls asleep in her seat, the rhythm of the drive like the rise and fall of the waves transporting her away from the troubling day. In her short dream the world is sunny; there is no need for her to protect her little sister or her aunt from harm. She wakes up as they are driving on a side road, one of those torturous tracks where high-speed stones ricochet against the undercarriage of the car. Perhaps it is the dark, the diminished visibility, but she feels as if they are in another country. First, a wide acreage of farmland, farmhouses and barns, even a windmill, some farm animals, cattle or horses – it is not possible to make them out clearly in the diffuse light. Then the stones knocking the underside of the car become bigger and the electrified fences that protect and set boundaries are taken over by wobbly strands of barbed wire holding down wooden stakes all the way to some unconvincing gate. There are a few more houses and open fields in which shells of dead cars rest on piles of stones, like offerings. Curious dogs get up from their curled up positions and approach, the headlights giving their canine eyes a scary glint.

She wants to ask him about the whole point of this journey but the question would make it hard to hide the unease pumping in her breast. This place looks like the set of a horror film, ruins, a warehouse, tumbledown houses bracing a dark street, trees more suited to muggers than lending charm to the area. She's seen a few places like this in Durban, deteriorated from decent suburbs into squats for vagrants and drug users.

I'm hungry, she says, realising that she hasn't had a bite in almost eighteen hours. After witnessing the shooting, she was overcome by nausea and heaved against a bush. She remembers now how he snickered and said he was surprised she had no stomach for these things. Well, the stomach she didn't have then is now running on empty.

We'll probably get something at Kheswa's place. He's a medicine man, friend of my father's. The car rolls slowly along with his neck jerking this way and that way, scanning the doorways for a number or familiar markings. Someone's given these houses a facelift, he says, just to confuse the enemy. Ah, he says triumphantly, here we are.

The car pulls to a stop at the gate of a little house that bears no special characteristic. A lone bulb glows dully on the veranda, highlighting sections of a polished stoep. Out of the car, he comes round to her side and taps on the window and motions for her to roll it down.

Wait here, he says. It won't take a minute.

Hurry back, she says. Place makes me uneasy.

You have a gun, he says. Don't miss the target this time.

Fuck you, she mutters under her breath, but she shouldn't have bothered with the precaution because he is already out of earshot, taking long strides to open the gate and proceed towards the door. She laughs out loud when she sees him momentarily put off his stride as a huge dog, an Alsatian, comes from the side of the house and lunges at him. A leash attached to a chain fastened to a stake restrains the huge animal. Its frustrated bark alerts someone. Lights immediately flood the perimeter. A shadow darkens the curtain. Who that?

It's me, Malume, he says.

Who's this 'me'? There are lots of 'me's' around here …

I'm Makhunga's boy. Please open up.

Is your father all right? What are you doing here this time of the night? There is a metallic rattle, a clickety-clack of various locks being unbolted. Then an elderly man, Kheswa, in an oversized T-shirt and drooping pyjama trousers leans against the door jamb, in silhouette in the open doorway. Watching the tableau through the window of the car, she has a sense that Kheswa might have a gun. Is the panoply of security measures his vote of no confidence on the protective power of muthi?

Someone in the car? The old man is pointing.

Yes, he says. My girlfriend.

Ah, uMakoti! Bring her in. Can't have women alone out there.

Unamused by Kheswa's bestowal on her the unwanted honour of a bride-to-be, she gets out and joins them on the threshold. She greets the old man, who's much shorter and stockier and follows him into the lounge, a space cluttered with stuffy furniture that seems to span various generations of ownership. Sofas and divans with scuffed upholstery take her back to her grandparents' home in Groutville. A framed portrait of a grim-looking couple, probably Kheswa's own parents, attracts her eye. Either hanging from hooks or mounted on the wall are heads, tails and mysterious body parts of animals. Drawn to the beasts' dead eyes, she has a feeling they share a past with those of the ancient couple in the picture. Suffusing the room is the heady smell of animal fat, herbs and incense.

Would you like something to drink? Kheswa asks.

Water will be fine, thank you, she says, suddenly no longer hungry. Her companion stands, watching Kheswa, deferential. She senses he wants to say something to her, but she avoids giving any signal that can be read as friendliness.

Come with me, Kheswa says to him on handing her a glass of water, and tell me what's troubling you. Before the two disappear behind a door, she gets a glimpse of a gloomy corridor. Be back now-now, he says.

Take your time, she thinks, settling into the sofa, wishing she had brought a book to read.

Hours later, on their way back, she asks: What was that all about?

My name is formally Nozishada, he says. The ancestors have changed my name.

9

VIBRATIONS: NEW YEAR'S DAY

'Is that what he said? They've got it all under control?' Nerissa asked, her voice breaking from the static such that Georgina had to keep the receiver pressed against her ear. 'Did he say who "they" were?'

'Nerissa?' Georgina said, 'I almost got shot. No. Correction: I was shot at, the bullet going past my ear, *zzzzit*! And you want me to give you the lowdown on an SB? Of course it was Stander, I would know that voice even in my sleep. And I also saw him with my own seeing eyes. And I don't know who "they" are, although I can give you one or two guesses.'

'And they bundled the gunman into their van?'

'Yes. I think he was also wounded. He had blood all over him.'

'It wasn't the blood of the dead policeman?'

'No,' Georgina said. 'I think the Portuguese guy and Stander roughed him up a bit, cuffed him and bundled him in the back of a squad car, you know the one where you share a space with a dog in the back.'

'The Portuguese guy … who was he?'

'He's another De Matos. I thought I heard Stander saying that.'

'What else did you hear?'

'They called the gunman Strella. Seems he and the other dead guy killed someone this morning.'

'Who?'

'Guess?

'They killed Muchave,' Nerissa said. 'I don't know how I know this. But if you have Angelo and Stander, it's clear they killed the guy.'

'But why?'

'Perhaps because they think he knows where I am.' There was a long silence. Then Nerissa asked: 'Was Palweni there?'

'Nah,' Georgina said. 'Just the two killers, two black cops and Stander and his Portuguese sidekick.'

'Don't be racist.'

'I'm not,' Georgina said. 'If Palweni was there he must have stayed inside the van when all that mayhem was unleashed on us.'

'Okay,' Nerissa said. 'Take care of yourself.'

'You too, girl,' Georgina had to have the last word. 'You're the one I think they want to kill. Me? I'm a small fry.' She sounded a little put out.

Nerissa hung up the phone. It was 2:30 p.m., the first day of creation.

Ngobese waited for Nerissa in the foyer of the hotel while she made her phone call in a tickey box. Like most black South Africans, he couldn't feel at home in hotels. They were usually patronised by people who didn't seem connected with life as he knew it. The male of the species exuded an aura of arrogance of those who had arrived, who didn't conduct business anywhere but in boardrooms where their dealings were serenaded by piped music. The women were usually haughty, untouchable, from another planet. He watched one young representative of indeterminate origin, thin as a rake, striding on impossibly high heels, one crooked arm swinging a leather handbag while a long cigarette held in taloned fingers went back and forth between ruby lips and an imaginary ashtray. It was still early on New Year's Day, around 2:45 p.m., and, taking into account her yesterday's clothes, she must be returning from an all-night party, which had spilled into the best part of the following day. Disdainfully, the woman took a long drag of her cigarette as she strode to the bank of lifts. Ngobese often wondered how such women avoided stumbling, as they always seemed to be walking through a cloud of smoke.

'Isn't she something?' someone said at his side. Having finished making her call, Nerissa had returned unnoticed. Her glance forced a guilty smile from him and she could see the boy he once was. 'Not that I blame you – she's pretty, if you go for that kind of thing.'

'She's too thin for me,' Ngobese said, chancing it. They were heading out to the car, parked illegally behind a line of sleek German models.

'Ah,' Nerissa said, getting inside the car. 'Another one of those who likes their women to cast a wide shadow.'

Ngobese laughed. 'A little meat doesn't hurt, Comrade Nerissa.'

'I don't know if that's your standard line in flirting or something that answers the question why black South Africans are forever suffering from gout.' Suddenly, she felt lightheaded, possibly from the cool breeze blowing from the sea, her zephyr. 'You remember I told you about Strella?'

'The sharpshooter in Angola.'

'Yep. He's here. In Durban. Or at least on his way.'

'I'm sure the men know him. They'll know what to do.'

'I sincerely hope so,' Nerissa said. 'Losing Refiloe doesn't fill me with a lot of confidence, but, hey, you guys are on the ground. Look.'

Ngobese noticed her face brightening up. He followed the direction of her gaze. 'Look.'

Streaming towards West Street were scores of people. Singly or in groups, they were almost all in a variety of beachwear. The kids carried plastic buckets and spades and some of the adults were laden with cooler boxes, picnic hampers, throw rugs, grass mats and towels. Nerissa imagined she could get a whiff of sunscreen oil wafting in the wind.

'The annual pilgrimage to the beach,' Ngobese said. 'Happens every New Year's Day. People used to have all-night parties on the beach, see the dawn of the incoming year. They stopped the practice when it became dangerous.'

'Well,' Nerissa said. 'I do think we're living in times that are getting increasingly dangerous.' She peered into the side mirror. 'Like the car following us ... it might spell danger.'

Maintaining a sedate speed of forty kilometres per hour Ngobese kept behind a stream of cars going southwards to Umgeni Road. He checked the rearview mirror. A reddish-brown Chevrolet Caprice with tinted windows came up steadily two cars behind. 'When did you notice them?'

'When I came out of the phone booth,' Nerissa said. 'The car was parked on the other side of the street, in the shade of a palm tree. I noticed the government licence plates, a large radio aerial mounted in the back, extra lights, which could become flashers inside the front grille and remembered the pattern from the time I saw them in the police station parking lot when we were brought up for detention.'

'Just from the plates, aerials and lights?'

'Insignificant details sometimes make a difference between life and death.' She thought of adding that cop cars, even unmarked, had an air about them that distinguished them from civilian vehicles. But that would be showing off.

At the interchange, Ngobese took exit 165, keeping left and following signs announcing the N2 in the direction of Stanger. The Chevy overtook an articulated truck on a hard shoulder and got behind the car immediately behind. Ngobese noticed that even though somewhat reckless, whoever was pursuing them knew how to drive.

'Why were you detained?' Ngobese asked.

'The usual question people ask is, "How long were you inside?"' Nerissa said. 'Which is misleading because it is the nature of the experience inside that matters. You might be in for 180 days and nothing happens to you. And then of course you might be detained for a week, 168 hours of pure hell. I was in for six months, 180 days, and I can remember every minute of that time. Every minute, that is, when I wasn't passed out.'

All the questions roiling in Ngobese's head condensed into one idea. *They shouldn't get away with it.* The men in the car behind, who had been trying with little success to overtake two panel vans, one towing the other, should not be allowed to lay their hands on this woman. He glanced sideways at his passenger, taking in the ascetic face in profile, the aquiline nose that was more Middle Eastern than African. Her dark eyes, fixed on a point far ahead shone like polished onyx and accentuated the olive complexion. The face was largely unlined although the hairline cracks that radiated from the corners of the mouth suggested either advancing age or lips given to reprimanding fools.

'You're staring,' Nerissa said. Then, reassuringly, laying a hand on his arm, she told him the situation was not unusual. 'I'm always with the wrong people. That's why I end up attracting attention.'

'Wrong people?' Ngobese asked. The Chevy had managed to overtake the articulated vehicles, making no pretence that it was in hot pursuit of Ngobese's double-cab VW pickup. Gingerly, he increased speed, hoping that Nerissa wouldn't notice and get spooked. This was a dual carriageway with a verge in the middle, which ruled out an evasive manoeuvre like a U-turn. Moreover, he was on the far left with other cars zooming past along the fast lane. Stretching to the horizon were undulating cane plantations, the sprinklers creating rainbows. Seeing a gap in the fast lane, Ngobese nosed the pickup to the right, causing the driver behind to slam on brakes and press the hooter. The Chevy slowed down a bit, almost getting wiped off by a truck before swerving into the right-hand lane. Some four hundred metres ahead, over the T-junction, buses bound for Inanda or the Phoenix settlement came to a stop to pick up passengers. Some people got out and waited for transport to KwaMashu and KwaDambuza.

'I grew up in Newlands East, which is actually not far from here …' mused Nerissa, trying to defuse the mounting tension.

'I know Newlands East,' Ngobese said. 'The aunties there thought any one of us was a garden boy …'

'Exactly. My folks were no different. My father lived under a huge delusion, believing he was white.' Nerissa laughed grimly at a memory. 'The usual stuff: booze, some dagga, and too many kids, all of different colours, my brothers and sisters. Because I was fair-skinned – at least in the eyes of my father – I was the favourite. He took me everywhere he went. On the buses, he forced me to ride with him in the section reserved for white people. He often got into fights with white people, which was sad because he regarded them as kith and kin. He had no time for his darker-skinned children, much less for black people.'

'What happened?'

'To him? He died. By then he was no longer living with us. Just as well because he was spared the sight of the apple of his eye always running around with the rough kids from KwaMashu or Ntuzuma, stealing sugar cane from the fields before KwaMashu grew into the monster it is now.' She looked at the time: 3:10 p.m. 'Are they still behind us?'

'Yes, but it is high time we lost them.'

'Here, you're the commander.'

'Brace yourself,' Ngobese said. Ignoring the traffic on the left as he shot across from the fast lane, he had a glimpse of wide-eyed passengers in a minibus flitting past and nearly smacking him broadside. Fighting against losing traction, he swerved hard into Malandela Road and trundled along a shallow grassy ditch. The rear wheels spun for a spell, throwing up mud before they got a grip on the squelchy surface and he navigated the car back onto the tarmac. Edging into the KwaMashu-bound traffic, he heard excited shouts behind – and a siren.

'Think we lost them?' Nerissa asked.

'I don't know. I don't think so. But we might have bought ourselves enough time to phone a friend.' He pulled into the Shell garage, hoping the telephone box hadn't been vandalised.

Bhekisisa Luthuli, like any businessman, believed in protecting his turf. His decision to operate from Kwam'shayazafe Men's Hostel in B Section was born of practicality. Having been a scene of bloody battles between warring political factions, Kwam'shayazafe had become a veritable no-go zone for non-residents, mainly the township dwellers who were reviled and called *izakhamizi* or citizens. Luthuli was therefore able to run his businesses undisturbed. Even the less commercially minded of the inhabitants shared this feeling of protectiveness towards the hostel. Although stung that *izakhamizi* held them in contempt, viewing them as uneducated bumpkins who did menial work, their hostility towards the outsiders paled into insignificance when it came to the police. During the heyday of petty apartheid, when being caught outside of one's magisterial district meant arrest followed by deportation to the hopeless reserves, the hostel dwellers, mainly migrant workers, bore the brunt of those inhumane policies. The men respected the law but simply stipulated that the police should never encroach on their terrain.

Resembling more closely an unkempt university campus than a hostel, Kwam'shayazafe consisted of a number of small, three-storey apartment blocks whose exteriors needed a serious paint job. Since women were only tolerated as visitors, the preponderance of men meant very little attention was given to sprucing up the grounds. It was worse following last night's merrymaking. Empty quart bottles lay on the reddish earth, empty crates were scattered along the walls. Here and there a conscientious soul had tried to introduce order by stacking up a few of the boxes but had probably been overwhelmed by the effort.

When Bhekisisa Luthuli got Ngobese's call, he was contemplating assigning the more sober of the men to organise schoolboys to clean up the yards for a small fee. Jesus, today's children and money! Anyway, distracted, he listened to his cousin, ending up by telling him he should come through. Immediately, he called his trusted men and readied them for action.

As an induna of Kwam'shayazafe and known for his ferocity in battle, Luthuli was feared even by his homeboys from Msinga, who were in their own right hardened warriors (witness the faction fights that flared up in the Tugela Ferry come Christmas-time). The fighting sometimes spilled over into the cities, where men dispatched one another without a thought as to the source of the vendetta. To date, the battles had somewhat abated but the reputation and the instinct for secretiveness still lingered around the hostel. It was well secured, surrounded by a six-foot breezeblock fence, topped with broken bottles. From the wooden guardhouse, a liveried guard armed with a pump-action shotgun regulated the flow of vehicular or pedestrian traffic at the boom gate. An enemy foolish enough to venture inside the gate usually wouldn't have control of the condition of his or her departure.

And so it was with a wolflike eagerness that Luthuli waited for the approach of the *led Chevlolet Caplice*. A few minutes later, around 3:30 p.m., Ngobese's pickup arrived. The guard directed it towards the back, behind the apartment blocks. Luthuli joined them there.

'*Awu, Mzala*,' he said, eyeing Nerissa, '*manj'usushaya ngamaNdiya* – now you're into Indian women?' Then, asked: '*Umshiyeph'uLola* – where's Laura?'

Ngobese was caught between laughing at his cousin's difficulty with Laura's name and keeping Nerissa in the dark about his extramural activities. She introduced herself. '*Ngingu*Nerissa Rodrigues.'

'*Hawu*,' Luthuli said, '*bengingaz'ukuth'uyakhuluma*, Neliswa – I didn't know you speak our language.' He had christened her Neliswa.

'I don't advertise it. I enjoy the sight of people squirming when I confront them after they've been saying nasty things about me, taking me for some dumb Indian madam.'

'Is your husband Portuguese – Rodrigues?'

'We're from Goa originally, a Portuguese part of India.'

An Indian Portuguese woman who spoke isiZulu! Bhekisisa Luthuli had heard it all. Shaking his head, he strode off to see how the welcoming committee was doing. Nerissa turned to Ngobese.

'You didn't answer the man,' she said. 'Where's Lola?'

'I don't know what you're talking about,' Ngobese said.

'You know only too damn well. Laura? That's MT's wife, isn't it?'

'Please ...'

'MT will slaughter you.' Nerissa gave him a long look and shook her head. 'A comrade's wife ...'

'I didn't mean to ...'

'What was it? A slip of the penis?'

'It's nothing like that. I'll explain.'

'I'm no puritan, Ngobese. But this ... it can wreak havoc on a political campaign. And we're at a sensitive juncture as it is.'

'I hear you. Here comes Bhekisisa.'

He had shepherded them into a room on the third floor, which provided them with a wide view of the grounds of Kwam'shayazafe. Beyond the grey asbestos rooftops, empty lots and patches of woodland in which Ngobese had in the past actually foraged for herbs, ran the highway. The traffic was unhurried as if the drivers were wary of haste so early in the New Year. A siren, which they'd heard before, heralded the arrival of the law. The guard opened the boom gate and waved the Chevy Caprice in. Some thirty metres into the hostel grounds, the car stopped, its nose almost obscured by the roof of the market below where everything from eggplant to exhaust pipes was on sale. The two men, both tall and rangy, obviously wanted to be recognised as policemen, from their tan suits with oversized, buttoned-up jackets to house shoulder holsters, to the cocky gait as they got out of the car. Ngobese wondered absently if they had ever brushed shoulders with the two black cops who had visited the house after Refiloe was shot. Not a chance, he thought, knowing the hierarchical relationship between regular cops and SBs. Foreshortened, as they weaved through the human traffic moving up and down the courtyard, the Special Branch officers appeared somewhat comical. Passing around a tin container, called a *skaal,* of sorghum beer, a group of hostel residents, mostly shirtless or in singlet vests, sat under a corrugated-iron veranda. The policemen approached.

'Recognise either of them?' Ngobese asked.

'It's difficult,' Nerissa answered. 'It also happened a long time ago.'

'Sure?' Ngobese had an idea she was keeping something back.

'Sure.' There they were, as large as life, Captain Jakob Stroewig and Warrant Officer Ben Hattingh. She'd told a lie because she couldn't bear to acknowledge their existence for, notwithstanding the number of years that had passed, the very mention of their names filled her with dread. To see them in the flesh …

Despite herself, though, Nerissa Rodrigues focused on the action below. Bhekisisa Luthuli, accompanied by another group of men, surrounded the policemen, all of them, the police and the hostel dwellers seeming to engage in a courtship dance. And then, everything was happening with furious haste while, paradoxically, all action slowed down. It was surreal, an enactment of a violent scenario without sound. The dance became more energetic. After much waving of hands and pointing, with W/O Hattingh jabbing a finger into Luthuli's chest and getting shoved back in return, a gun suddenly flew into the air and quickly disappeared in a forest of hands.

Now, even though they were about twenty feet above, a distance compounded by the fact that everything they saw was distorted by the glass of the window through which they watched the fracas down on the ground, both Nerissa and Ngobese actually winced at the soundless blows raining down on the two officers. In a moment, the sound carried to their observation point at the window. Someone shrieked, in pain or triumph, which segued into an urgent wail of sirens. The cops must have radioed for reinforcements on the way to the hostel. In a second, the courtyard was empty save for two naked men lying prostrate on the ground. Gone, too, was the reddish-brown Chevrolet Caprice.

Her first sense on entering the lounge of Ngobese's house was of an inexplicable sadness. It was as if she were reliving the moment of leaving the country secretly, the cramped and – undeniably – unhygienic conditions of the houses of refugees in Botswana, Zambia or Tanzania. She recalled the hand-to-mouth existence that had brought tears to her eyes. Here, too, the smell of death still lingered, directing the eye to the spot on the floor where a brave effort has been made to scrub out Refiloe Mokoena's blood. There was no detergent powerful enough to erase the traces.

She recalled, also, the destroyed houses and the maimed survivors, the women with shamefaced grins confiding that they were having difficulties with deliveries of sanitary towels. But it was exactly the rush of all those memories, the images of devastation and deprivation that competed for dominance in her mind, which become overlaid, as in a printing process, with a series of vivid montages.

She gazed into the faces of the young men who had spruced up Ngobese's place and prepared a supper of lamb stew, pap and potatoes as a token of welcome. She experienced a pang of self-reproach as if she'd somehow been lax in her commitment. For, she reasoned, the day's events, the ride from the airport, the drama at Kwam'shayazafe Hostel, the fact that she still enjoyed a good chase, all pointed to a country on the cusp of reinventing itself. All the setbacks, drawbacks, defeats and humiliations of the past took a back seat, what the fashionable ones called putting things on the back burner. Pain was on the back burner. All that privation had been grounding for this breathing moment.

'I am very happy to meet all of you,' she said, meaning it. 'Ngobese told me that Mchinda is also here. You'll pardon my failing eyesight, I'm after all, what the kids call an old *magogo* ...'

'That's not true,' Mchinda said, smiling. 'That part of you being a *magogo*. I think once we catch up on those good old days in Quibaxe, you'll remember.'

'Good old days, hey?' Django said. 'I thought you hated Quibaxe ...'

'It was a hell-hole,' Mchinda admitted. 'But things changed somewhat after the chaplain.'

'I thought,' Rex Mabena chimed in, 'the camp went up in flames.'

'It was a mock attack,' Mchinda explained. He turned to Nerissa. 'After you left, when we returned from Luanda, where we gave a report to the Regional Command, lots of changes took place in the whole of Sector 37. Nyirenda was relieved of his post and served his punishment in Malange.'

'Jesus,' Nerissa said, remembering. 'I was wondering what happened with him.'

'What happened was that he allowed power to go to his head.' Mchinda thought for a minute. 'It was brave of you to conduct that mission.'

'I thought guerrillas aren't supposed to be fluent in flattery,' Nerissa said. 'Shows how uninformed I am.'

Watching this exchange, Ngobese manoeuvred Rex and Django to the side, leaving Nerissa chatting with Mchinda. 'Comrade Muzi is on his way. He's not happy with the way things turned out today.'

'What things?' Django asks.

'Some trouble on the way here, with the cops.'

In fact, later that afternoon, the joy of reunion for Nerissa Rodrigues and Mchinda was tempered by an understanding – a dread, almost – that the proverbial shit was due to hit the fan. Warrant Officer Hattingh succumbed to his injuries; Captain Stroewig was in a coma the last they heard. 'They won't take this lying down,' Muzi Thabethe said. *They* of course were the state and its coercive power.

'I wish I'd been there,' Rex Mabena said. He regarded Nerissa and Ngobese the way neophytes welcome the return of pilgrims. 'What was it like?'

'Comrades?' Muzi Thabethe was furious. 'What's this? Hero-worship of folly?' All the time glaring at Ngobese.

'Hey,' Ngobese said, putting up his hands as if to ward off a blow, 'I'm not the one who assaulted the policemen.'

'You're the one who detoured to Kwam'shayazafe,' Thabethe said. He laughed ruefully. 'Do you know what the name of the place means?' Before anyone could respond, he answered his own question. 'It means hit him until he dies. That's what Kwam'shayazafe means.'

'Would you rather I'd brought the cops here?'

'Yes,' Rex Mabena added. 'The comrade had to take evasive action.'

'Maybe,' Django said, 'it's the cops who should have taken evasive action. They wouldn't have wound up dead or injured.'

'What is this?' Mchinda asked. 'Are we now the Salvation Army, bleating about the police? They are the enemy, for God's sake.'

'Okay,' Nerissa said. 'Enough.' She turned to Thabethe. 'MT? There was no way we'd have made it anywhere without being cut off by the SBs. Ngobese did what he had to do. The only mistake was involving Bhekisisa, who's got his own problems.'

'Well,' Thabethe said with bad grace, 'we're now saddled with those problems. Thanks to the genius of our host here.'

An exasperated Ngobese started to get to his feet. Nerissa shot him a warning look. *Don't.*

Muzi Thabethe's frustration came from knowing that, apart from Nerissa, who'd suffered torture in detention, not a single person in the room understood prison. Exile, or even the camps couldn't, in his mind, compare even remotely, to prison. Prison was the nearest approximation of hell on earth. And the way things were going they were all sure to end up in the cooler, if not cold stone dead.

For him, it was not at all surprising that Ngobese could be so reckless. He'd never liked Ngobese, but politics, after all, made strange bedfellows. It had never been Thabethe's wish to work in such a sensitive mission with people like Ngobese; but the higher-ups obviously saw something in the man, one of life's enduring mysteries. It was no different from seeing a beautiful woman being swept off her feet by a thoroughly unattractive suitor. The struggle drew into its orbit all sorts of misfits.

However, Muzi Thabethe was still a little taken aback by Nerissa's conduct. He'd have thought she'd have shown a little more sense than let Ngobese wriggle out of facing disciplinary action or even take control. Many a prisoner doing time was incarcerated on account of someone else's mistake. Personally, Thabethe was done with other people's cock-ups.

The rain came, early in the evening, trapping everyone indoors. Nerissa had a sense that the downpour heightened everyone's feeling of being cooped up.

Mchinda was holding court. It seemed to rub Muzi Thabethe up the wrong way that Nerissa appeared to be hanging on to every word that fell from Mchinda's lips. Watching him, Ngobese smiled and looked away, thinking that it was tough to be a revolutionary when you could be upstaged by a bunch of young guerrillas.

'When a person like Refiloe gets killed,' Nerissa asked. 'What do you think happens?'

'What happens?' Muzi Thabethe repeated, his voice somewhat strained. 'What happens in that circumstance is what happens when anyone of us dies. People mourn; they bury and forget. That's what happens.'

'I disagree,' Mchinda said. Django, hearing the clipped remark, anticipated trouble. 'I disagree completely …'

'Because?' Muzi Thabethe had put on his serious face, on the settee, leaning forward with his hands clasping the knees.

'Because guerrillas are special,' Mchinda said. 'They are usually black people with guns, something that's bound to screw up the imagination of any oppressor. They embody something rare and dangerous and unknown. They even the odds.'

Muzi Thabethe smiled. It was a knowing smile that might have otherwise been overlooked in a normal situation. Noticing it, Nerissa shot a quick look at Django and found him staring intently at Thabethe.

'You smile, Comrade Muzi,' Django said. 'Did Mchinda say something funny?'

'Evening the odds?' Thabethe said. 'I thought people learnt politics in the camps, rather than the stock of clichés that you've been trotting out since you came here …'

'Comrade Muzi …?' Nerissa said, raising her hand like an obedient kid in class. But Muzi Thabethe was just getting started.

'Guerrillas,' he said, 'are supposed to be the armed section of a political movement. The emphasis is on "politics" rather than "armed", but you people have been strutting around, beating up little boys, no discipline …'

'What fucking discipline do you want?' Django asked, getting to his feet off the sofa. 'Do you know what we went through, making our way here to give you the trunk?'

'Hey, Django,' Rex Mabena said. 'Cool it.'

'We cannot cool it,' Django said. 'We have lost a comrade already, in this house no less – and you want me to cool it.'

The early evening was descending into a free-for-all involving guerrillas and a former political prisoner, the biggest beneficiary being the host, a healer who had opted to stay silent. Nerissa had a sense of impending disaster.

'We're doing the enemy's bidding,' she said quietly. Outside the rain pelted down. For a minute there was silence in the house. Then Rex Mabena stood up and went to the window.

'We've been docile for too long,' Rex said. 'We've lost a comrade while waiting. He was a friend of mine and I have to account to his parents in Jozi.'

'What course of action do you propose?' Mchinda asked, turning away from his squabble with Muzi Thabethe.

'Go back to Joburg.'

'You step out on your own and you'll be in jail in no time.'

'So, you and Django come with me.'

'I know we've always worked as a unit,' Mchinda said patiently. 'But this is probably the most dangerous time for all of us.'

'Look, we've got weapons. Maybe there's some stuff in the trunk, which we could *trocar* for cold hard cash.' Rex Mabena's frustration increased. 'Don't tell me you and Django are really into this civilian shit.'

The disagreement carried over from the lounge into the bedroom, where Rex Mabena started to stuff his unwashed laundry into a plastic bag. Ngobese and Nerissa decided to join Mchinda and Django, augmenting the strength of the negotiators.

Django cleared his throat.

'Rex?' he said. 'Remember that Mchinda saved all of us. In all the ambushes in Angola, his instinct came through for us. In Cacuso, remember? Or in Sanza Pombo … you and I would be food for wild animals and worms, or buried in some shallow grave in Uige by now.'

'So? This is South Africa,' Rex Mabena said. 'If I can get a car I'll be in Soweto first thing in the morning.'

'And do what, there?'

'I'm a guerrilla, trained … I can survive anywhere.'

'I'll tell you what will happen to you, Rex,' Django said. 'You'll get your car and some guns and probably manage to get to see Refiloe's folks. I don't know what you'll tell them, because we haven't even started discussing how we'll help others deal with their losses. In fact, I don't think that even you, Mchinda or me have any idea what has happened to us. Every night before I go to bed, I have to fight consciously against thinking about certain things, the way we dispel frightening thoughts so that we are not visited by nightmares in our sleep. But one day, I know they'll come and crowd out my defences.'

'Rex, you're a soldier, a fighter for the Movement,' Mchinda said. 'We won't allow you to go off and end up robbing banks and holding up payroll vans. You can't end up like the bandits we fought in Angola. I know this, man.'

'He's right,' Django added, softening. 'It's frustrating. But we have to do this right.'

Rex Mabena listened, head cocked to the side; outside the rain had become part of the everyday sounds of the season. Even as they plopped back onto the couch for the strategy meeting with Muzi Thabethe, Thulasizwe Ngobese and Nerissa Rodrigues, Mchinda and Django suspected that Rex Mabena might already be lost to them.

Unbeknown to anyone, Bhekisisa Luthuli's luck ran out at the crack of dawn. He woke up to an excruciating stomach pain, which, for him, always presaged trouble. Lying face-up, tracking the flight of a wasp, which flitted across the room, landing on a rafter, he wondered whether this was a visit from the ancestors. He should get up and go to the back of the ablution block and take his bucketful of a potent emetic, *uzifozonke*, the healer of all maladies. The stomach ache, after heaving and emptying whatever was wrong and poisonous inside him, would then be a mere memory of a spell of weakness. All men were fated to experience these inconveniences that reminded them they were still members of the human race. He was bent, on all fours, heaving, and the contents of his stomach washing down the drain when he felt a blow on the back of his head. Although a strong man, he lost control of his muscles, his head now under a running tap. There was another wrenching pain as both his arms were pulled backwards and he felt the handcuffs encircling his wrists.

The Special Branch brought him to the headquarters on Fisher Street. As they rode with him along Avoca, they told him, the young policemen with fair hair and fresh chins sporting acne and erratic shaves, that whatever he believed, they would prove to him that it was all a lie. They told him in no uncertain terms that he was a dead man. True to their word, much later, he lay on the floor, naked, folded like a pocketknife, his face and body smashed to a pulp. The interrogators, who had to rope in African members of the Branch for ease of communication, did not hide the fact that they were pressed for time and needed quick answers. Who had lured the two men to the hostel of Kwam'shayazafe? Was Bhekisisa a member of the Movement? What was the role of Thulasizwe Ngobese and Nerissa Rodrigues? Was Muzi Thabethe part of an underground cell? Tell us! And because Bhekisisa Luthuli was big and strong and could fight back, roaring like a bull, they brought big and strong former rugby scrumhalves. Having punched and kicked him until blood was coming out of his mouth, one of the men looped a forearm around Bhekisisa's throat and hoicked him up so that his legs dangled some few inches off the floor. Warrant Officer Brian Khumalo watched as the man's hands jerked up to dislodge the brawny arm to no avail and soon dropped to the sides, the legs also losing tension and a faecal odour filling the cell. He had seen people die before but there was something about the death of a naked man that sent him to the toilet where he heaved and heaved into the bowl until he had emptied himself.

Later, huddled inside the unmarked police sedan, listening to the now-softened pitter-patter of raindrops on the roof, Ngobese and Booi listened to Khumalo's account of his death. Impotent, Ngobese wished for his father, Vezi, who would have augmented the son's stock of knowledge about the rites and rituals that would have to be performed for Bhekisisa Luthuli's soul to be transported honourably to the final resting place of heroes. Suddenly, he was weeping, not so much for Bhekisisa Luthuli as for the loss, the absence of all that energy, the optimism and the capacity to live life and give joy to all the people around him. The loss – the gaping hole – reminded Ngobese of all the unmourned deaths that had stalked him from as far back as he could remember. Khumalo, sensing the man's sadness, but wondering why all these deaths seemed to revolve around the healer, tried to reassure him: 'These deaths are becoming so commonplace, even the young ones have lost the fear of death,' he said. 'But the killers will be brought to book. And we'll try to make sure there are regular patrols around here.'

'I appreciate that,' Ngobese said.

'It's the least we can do.' Then Khumalo asked: 'Do you know the kids in the Skyline? One of them was at your house?'

An image of Lucky on the floor, doing a pantsula dance at the funeral service for Refiloe, flashed across his mind. 'Lucky and his boys … What's he done now?'

'Not "done",' Khumalo said, quickly. 'It's what he's likely to do that's a little worrying.'

'They are Bra Zeph's friends,' Ngobese said, knowing that the cops probably had this information already. 'They just want Bra Zeph to recognise them as useful people.'

'They are armed,' Khumalo said. 'Guns invite guns.'

'Let's hope it never comes to that,'

'Unfortunately,' Khumalo said, starting the car and giving Ngobese the cue to jump out, 'hope alone is no longer enough for this country.

Later, Ngobese watched the police car standing at the corner of the road, waiting for a break in the traffic. It turned left and disappeared. I hope Lucky knows what he's doing, Ngobese thought.

LOG #6

The young man reads to his father: 'When I return from the land of exile and silence, / do not bring me flowers.' He lays The Penguin Book of Modern African Poetry face down on the side table. He gazes at Japhet Makhunga reclining in his chair, the tray on the table holding remains of breakfast. 'You'll resume when we come back, Gabriel,' he says.

'Yes, Pa,' says Gabriel. It is a daily ritual. He might read a piece of text followed by a chat, if Makhunga felt so inclined. On certain mornings, he'd just wave his hand, unwilling to exercise himself. Today, he is somewhat sprightly, a light in his eyes. But then a teenage boy knocks and whispers to Gabriel that the old man is wanted at the shop. 'Argh,' he complains, 'just when I thought I'd have an easy morning.'

'No rest for the wicked, hey, Pa?' Gabriel puts on his jacket.

'In the Island we had these fellows reciting poetry,' Japhet Makhunga says. 'They were amazing, having memorised so much and able to regurgitate chunks of wisdom and inspiration. That's what gave me this energy to carry on. The fact that, even when things were so bleak, they had time to dabble in beauty. It just meant we could overcome so much.' He glanced at his son. 'Was that the same in the camps?'

'What,' his son asks, 'the poetry?'

'What do you think I'm talking about?' Makhunga asks. He reaches for his walking stick of ornately crafted ebony wood. The handle is a snake's head complete with prominent eyes, fangs and forked tongue. He sees Gabriel looking at it, fascinated. 'Kheswa gave me this stick, to beat the lies out of rascals.'

'Well,' Gabriel says. 'I'd never lie to you.'

'Is that true?'

'It's true,' Gabriel says. 'Are you ready? The car's waiting outside.'

In the car, a few minutes later, Makhunga asks: 'What did people do for recreation? In the camps.'

'We also had poetry,' the young man says. 'Poetry: Agostinho Neto, Antonio Jacinto. Tchicaya U Tam'si is my favourite. But for the most part we had music … dance. I see people doing the toyi-toyi; this was the staple of our dances. But …'

'But what?'

'We sometimes used it … we called it Exercise Number Nine,' Gabriel says. 'As a fatigue exercise, to discipline some hard-case.'

'Are you proud of your time as a soldier?'

'I haven't thought about it, Pa.'

'If you haven't thought about it,' Japhet Makhunga says, 'then there's a problem.'

'Meaning?'

'In matters of soldiering, where you have to take orders, things are more clear-cut, black and white, than a lot of people think.' Makhunga pauses. 'In the life before prison, there was always the real possibility of taking lives, sometimes – most times – lives of black people, people close to us. But if you did that as a clear instrument of advancing the struggle, then you went to bed with a clean conscience. I think the complexity is when you get involved with a betrayal, something that conflicts with your own belief in yourself. When that happens, you're in trouble.'

'Are you trying to suggest,' Gabriel asks, 'that I might have gone against my own beliefs?'

'Have you?'

'I've done nothing that I cannot justify.' Gabriel is irritated by his own vehemence.

'I named you Gabriel when you were born,' Japhet Makhunga says, with a touch of sadness. 'An archangel never betrays his mission, which is to spread the word of God. Or, if not God, then, at least be an agent of good. Of what is right.'

'I don't know,' Gabriel says, 'where this God talk comes from. I believe that we all have our responsibilities on this earth. Your generation had to pave the path for our generation to push towards victory.'

'What victory, Gabriel? Where do you see it?'

'When we take over. People's power.'

'People's power …' Japhet Makhunga says. 'Clichés and slogans, Gabriel, that's what I expect from smaller people, not from a son of mine. It's not what I raised you for.'

'What did you raise me for, Pa?'

'The other day,' Makhunga says carefully, 'I learnt that there are young men, mostly men, some of them former members of the People's Army, who thronged the shop, looking for you. I learnt that you've organised them into a group. To what intent?'

'People are not as forgiving as you, Pa,' Gabriel says. 'These people returned from exile. Some were part of the underground. They sacrificed their youth, giving up the possibility of furthering their education, to be soldiers, to take up arms, to fight. They came back, some were arrested and a few are broken men. No support. No welfare. The fat cats who did fuck-all are in the pound seats.' He pauses, his chest heaving.

'And you're their saviour?'

'I'm not. I just channel their energies …'

'How? By getting them embroiled in the violence in Natal?'

'It's better that they have found a purpose,' Gabriel says. 'They were hungry, drunkards, diseased, a good number of them stricken by HIV and AIDS. Some are homeless; they can't even go to their families because of shame. You know what one of them said, the other day?'

'What?' Japhet Makhunga is fascinated despite himself.

'He said that he'd get a gun and go after white people.'

'I hope you stopped him.'

'Of course I did. We're not fighting white civilians. But he was saying that our lives have become a big, unfunny joke …'

'A joke?'

'Yes. He said that in all the deaths that have happened, you could fit all the white people who died in the struggle in a school bag and still have room for the Holy Bible and a bottle of ink.'

'I can't have my son linked to senseless violence,' Makhunga says. 'If there's a group, dismantle it immediately. We don't need that. Not now.'

'What do we need, Pa?' Gabriel says heatedly. 'Look at these shacks, waterlogged houses. The despair. People shovelling shit against the tide …'

'Watch your mouth …'

'It's true. And we still go cap in hand to the Movement …'

'I suffered when I came back from prison,' Makhunga says. 'But I never turned my back on the Movement. It's that sense of loyalty, of knowing that victory takes a long time, a generation even, before it can start to make sense, to take effect. You're not struggling for short-term, dramatic gains. This is my word to you. And I am your father.'

'Yes, Pa.'

'Do the right thing. Do the right thing with that woman you brought to the house. What's her name?'

'Sonto Sokhela.'

'The very fact that someone took the trouble to give her a name,' Makhunga says, 'means that she's someone's child. Remember that.'

10

THE CITY OF MANGOES

'We found a shoes and a blood. Our heart is very much broken.'

— A RELATIVE OF A MURDERED WOMAN

It was 7:00 p.m. when Colonel Jan Stander drove slowly along the main road of KwaMashu Township, carefully threading his way through evening commuters coming down the bridge that spanned the Tembalihle railway station. Disrespect for vehicular traffic was no longer limited to the youth, who tended to go against the traffic lights. Now, perhaps as a sign of solidarity, older people had joined, even grannies, cutting the driver down with a look. So, he bided his time, knowing there was no sense in getting himself into a lather over these people. He had bigger fish to fry.

'Look at that,' Palweni, seated in the middle, said. He was pointing at the concrete sculptures fronting Isibonelo High School. Illuminated by the high-pressure, bright yellow sodium street lights, the figures looked curiously lifelike, a shadowy impi crouching in ambush. Stander shivered and closed his eyes to dispel a blasphemous image that had just flashed into his mind. He was slightly irritated with Palweni, for whom every new feature was a marvel. Boy, these exiles and their childlike fascination with progress. They never paused to think that all this, the skyscrapers, bridges, tarred roads, for heaven's sake, the whole enchilada, was built by the white man. Okay, let's give the devil his due. The white man came with the know-how and resources and the black man the muscle, okay? He smiled, remembering a cartoon depicting one of those moronic platteland types, complete with safari shorts, floppy hat and velskoene, sitting in the shade and supervising a workforce on a construction site. 'Just give me forty kaffirs,' he says proudly, 'and I'll build this town single-handed.'

'What's tickling your funny bone, Jan?' asked Bobo Jones, seated in the back, next to Angelo de Matos. Taking up the rear was a handcuffed Strella, still unconscious and bleeding.

Jan? Stander couldn't quite get used to the American's pronunciation of his name, which rhymed with 'can'. Where's the can, Jan?

He waved a hand airily instead of an answer, knowing that Bobo Jones was, like Palweni, starry-eyed about going into a township. Can you beat that, a white man chaperoning two black people, leading them into Darkest Africa. Look at those rows and rows of box-like houses, almost all of them with an added dwelling of corrugated iron, pumpkins and rubber tyres and boulders holding the roof down, children running around the yard – at this hour, where are the fucking parents? Probably in some meeting somewhere, hatching up strategies to commit mayhem against white people, devising plans to turn this beautiful land into another African disaster. Congo? Zambia? Take your pick. And the dogs milling about, upending dustbins: mostly scrawny mongrels of all shapes and sizes that dash out of nowhere, forcing drivers to apply their brakes. Who owns these mangy dogs? Palweni, an ancient AK-47 rifle held between his legs, seeming to notice the dogs, muttered under his breath. 'Jesus.'

Like the dogs Jan Stander realised that all of them in Angelo de Matos's red Toyota 4Runner were scroungers of sorts, survivors, perhaps, all looking for something. Palweni standing – or, better still – sitting on his dignity in the moving car, pretending that he had actually held to his side of the bargain. His responsibility was to ensure that the operation was kept supplied with men and material. He wanted the box of goodies they were supposed to have long liquidated – the dollars, diamonds, drugs, whatever was of value. Jan Stander was at the same time ambivalent of the trunk's contents, especially the intelligence documents, which could implicate some highly placed officials of the ruling party as well as senior members of the liberation movement. He'd brought Angelo along to assess the stuff, evaluate and cost it, the Budget Man. And then Angelo would have the satisfaction of putting a bullet into Strella's head. Stander suspected that this had absolutely nothing to do with the killing of Luis Bernado Muchave or the depriving of Mariela, Angelo's niece, of a future husband. He suspected it had lots to do with Angelo's own bloodlust, anger against South Africans for cosying up to Samora Machel, the late Mozambican president, former military commander and revolutionary leader who had died in October 1986. Stander remembered teasing Angelo de Matos over the *não vamos* – we are not moving – slogan of the Portuguese hordes that had streamed into South Africa, fleeing Machel's Frelimo. 'That's not funny,' Angelo de Matos had said, bristling. He had then gone on to lecture Stander on the Portuguese contribution to Africa. No one, Angelo had said, seemed to appreciate that the Portuguese had developed the colonies and put so much into the infrastructure that the negros took for granted. And he had lamented that most of his countrymen had been reduced to clichés, famous for making babies and fish and chips, in no particular order of importance. Stander had had to stop Angelo de

Matos from executing Strella there and then on the streets of Yeoville, in full view of everyone. So, yes, Strella was going to get it. It made no difference that, during the beating before he was bundled into the car, Strella had admitted that it was Doctor who had actually slaughtered Luis Bernado Muchave. He would, though, wouldn't he? That was the routine reaction of a cornered criminal – blame it all on the dead man. Doctor was dead, and could not be punished. Strella was alive.

Then there was Bobo Jones, a travelling correspondent of sorts, a revolutionary. Hah, that nearly had Stander in hysterics. Apart from the nation builders and frontiersmen, warriors who risked life and limb to fight against greater odds, Stander knew only a few men he could call revolutionaries, namely Holden Roberto and Jonas Savimbi. Throw into the mix a Lech Walesa, Reagan and Thatcher, admirable figures thumbing their noses at world communism. The rest, including his own General Magnus Malan and P W Botha, were just uniformed, powerful cowards who used …

'I digress,' he said, half to himself.

'What?' Palweni asked. Stander suspected he might have started to doze off. 'Where are we?'

'Getting close,' Stander said. 'Angelo? How's our VIP back there?'

Angelo turned and, none-too-gently, examined Strella's bonds. 'Still okay. Out like a light.' Then, plaintively: 'We should have put a plastic sheet on the floor; he's bleeding all over my car.'

'Just keep a watch on him,' Stander said. '*Hy's 'n groot skelm.*'

'What's gonna happen with him?' Bobo Jones wished to know. He was obviously anxious over Strella in the back, now and then craning his neck like a paramedic with victim of a bomb blast.

'When it's all said and done,' Stander said, 'we'll hand him over to the authorities.'

'But I thought you guys were the authorities,' Bobo Jones said.

'Exactly.'

They were discussing him as if he didn't exist. As if he were nothing more than a side of beef being transported from the abattoir, bleeding all over their precious carpet. He'd make them bleed.

He'd woken up to the harsh orange light of a toll plaza, not too far from Durban. This he had deduced from the hearty exchange between Colonel Stander and one of the attendants. Possibly spurred on by a generous tip or expecting a handout, the flunky was notifying Stander that he'd enjoy the warmth of Natal women.

'Do you think they'd even send a glance in my direction,' Stander asked, 'old and shrivelled *madala* like me?'

'Ah,' the attendant replied. 'Women don't notice the age of a white man.'

At first Strella had thought the beam piercing his brain was part of a cloudburst of lights first experienced when the Portuguese man whacked him across the head with a hard object. He remembered the moment he fell, his knees filling with water. Countless feet lashed at him. Someone restrained a knifeman from slashing his throat. Wait, Joe; we'll give him a necklace. A crowd's throaty roar as more blows landed. Strella repeatedly told himself that he should protect his face. Don't let them touch my teeth. Then he felt it would be impossible to stay upright, the river in his knees now roaring in his head. He fell and this seemed to annoy people. Get up, fucking scum, preto, kaffir, black shit, maybe he's not even from here. This, another bloody *kwerekwere*, let's fucking burn him. His hand locked into Doctor's still-warm fingers, the final gift before darkness.

Waking up in the moving car, he took his bearings, his body stiff from lying in one position, the teeth of the handcuffs biting into his wrists. The Portuguese had started it, cursing him verbally and stunning him with a blow from a cudgel. Even as this was happening, Strella had taken in the man's appearance, casual jeans and trainers, a tan sports jacket over a red sweatshirt, a paunch, a man in his forties with a thatch of black hair, a sallow, shaven face, a handsome man bizarrely sporting an unkempt moustache, lips opening and closing like a valve.

It was the man's eyes, however, that made him memorable. Cold, cold eyes: the hatred behind them totally over the top in relation to the wrong he imagined Strella had committed against him or his family. Of this Strella was sure, just as he was sure that, at that juncture, he was dead meat. No one would come forward and disclose that it was actually Doctor who had killed the Mozambican that morning. Boy, this was ironic, being punished for a murder he didn't commit, against a foreigner, getting beaten up by a foreigner and being mistaken for a *kwerekwere*, how fucked up was that?

But not as fucked up as Jan Stander's about-turn. Talk about betrayal. The man had literally thrown him to the wolves. Whose idea was the mission to Sanza Pombo in the first place? It was Stander's, even though he might have acted on the orders from the Old Man, if Barak the Greek was to be believed. Stander was instrumental in the acquisition of the trunk. It was under his direction that all those People's Army men were snuffed out in the caves in the Western Transvaal. But, on a more personal level, it was Stander who had entrapped Strella and made him into what he was today. He was conflicted. He had learnt so much from the man. He had learnt how to survive, to be resourceful. He had hoped to extend the service to Doctor, smooth out the rough edges. And now Doctor was dead. And Stander was out to kill Strella. That trumped any good the old policeman might have done in the past. Even if it's your own father; if he tries to kill you, it's time to send him to the cemetery. He experienced a pang of regret, something important having flown past. The old crew was truly dispersed. A spasm of pain went through him, scrambling his viscera, leading him to wonder if he hadn't ruptured some of the vital organs. He now had to go deep into himself and face this setback. Go back to the training; that was the way to go.

He shifted, careful to keep his movements quiet. He felt a different type of pain, a sharp pinprick in his thigh. Working slowly, he inched his manacled hands over the fabric of his jeans, probing for the opening of his side pocket until, finally, he managed to slide his fingers inside. He immediately snatched back his hand, suppressing a cry of pain, as something sharp jabbed the tip of his forefinger. More carefully, he worked his fingers around the object in his pocket. His fingers closing in on the lapel pin badge, which he knew was imprinted with the picture of Eduardo Mondlane, he remembered Mabitla and his toothed contraption to thwart pickpockets. Fingers stiffened into tweezers, he fished out the badge. Then: oops! The badge slipped off his fingers and rolled on the floor, lodging directly beneath him. Strella gritted his teeth, bracing himself against the noise. Jan Stander hated surprises.

'*Como é o nosso* VIP?' Stander asked.

Lying dead still, breathing shallowly, Strella was aware of the Portuguese man's hands fiddling with his handcuffs, running over his body, fondling his genitals. Probably wishing to ascertain that what he'd heard about black boys was true.

He heard him murmuring words of reassurance. '*Tudo está bem.*' Everything's all right.

On the evening of 2 January 1990, Nerissa agreed with the rest of the people assembled in Ngobese's house – Django, Mchinda, Rex, Muzi and Ngobese himself – that it was time to open the trunk and do an inventory of its contents. The guerrillas were a little uncomfortable with the decorousness of the moment, the fact that Nerissa seemed to want to make a ceremony of it. In fact, supported by Muzi Thabethe, Nerissa suggested – and it was agreed – that they should all wait for the rest of the Committee members. Nerissa might have had her views, but she believed in the structures. And so, they had to wait for Johannes Sibisi, Zephaniah Zondi and Nomasonto Sokhela. Democracy was necessary but, boy, it could surely slow things down!

'Is Laura coming?' she asked Muzi Thabethe, wondering what Laura's status was in the Committee. Nerissa had a sense she was some kind of a spare wheel, an adjunct that provided support to the collective. Was she happy to be Ngobese's mistress?

She felt herself flush at the idea and wondered if Muzi Thabethe was an observant man. If he'd been observant, she thought unkindly, he'd have long put an end to this nonsense.

'Laura's probably coming in later,' Muzi Thabethe said.

Nerissa still wrestled with the implications of Laura Mdunge's betrayal of her husband. Knowing that she'd never finally understand what went on in Muzi Thabethe's household, she opted to let sleeping dogs lie. Making a cuckold of a comrade was unconscionable and comrades must play nice, but, as Georgina would say, it be's that way sometimes, children.

Even though all the people assembled in the room appeared nonchalant towards the trunk that was now placed on the coffee table, Nerissa surmised that they were all having a hard time containing their excitement. She was amazed at how unprepossessing it looked, just a chest with a big padlock and hasps and handles, the corners fortified with steel plates against scuffing. It was a traveller's bag, the one featuring in films in which people went on voyages aboard steamers or ancient ocean liners.

She marvelled at the discipline of the comrades from the People's Army. Wondering whether, under similar circumstances she would have trekked hundreds of miles with a chest containing treasure without succumbing to the temptation of at least peeking inside, she concluded that she might not have passed that test. Who were these men? Boys when they left home, they became men in the bushes of foreign countries, where they fought wars that had nothing to do with the freedom of their land. Nerissa corrected herself. There wasn't a single war, skirmish or engagement, there wasn't a single act of hostility or outrage that took place in any one part of Africa that had no relevance to the rest of the continent. The headache experienced in Ras ben Sakka, Tunisia, reflected itself as some form of trauma in Cape Agulhas, the southernmost point of Africa.

'Any idea when the others are coming?' Nerissa asked. Once the contents of the trunk had been inspected and logged, it would be up to the higher structures to effect the disbursement. She'd also take part in evaluating the material, whatever it would turn out to be, as she knew just the right people for the job. Hopefully. It all depended on what was inside.

'Bra Zeph, Johannes and Sonto should be on their way,' Ngobese said. 'You know how it is with transport.'

'I know,' Nerissa said. She was unsympathetic even though she wouldn't admit it to anyone. She was of the old school that held that punctuality was the politeness of kings, even if she didn't think much of the king credited with the saying: Louis XVIII of France, who suffered from obesity, gout and gangrene. When South Africa is free, she wondered, which of our leaders will also die from leadership diseases?

'I see a car,' said Rex Mabena, who'd been monitoring the approach to the house from the window. 'It's stopped.'

'That should be Bra Zeph and Johannes,' Ngobese said. 'They're always together, those two.'

'Maybe there's more honesty in that type of comradeship,' Muzi Thabethe said. 'Instead of people who pretend to be friends.'

'Amen to that,' Nerissa Rodrigues said. Even though she was aware it was Muzi's desperate barb, for her it was an apt observation that connected her with Georgina. She missed her friend.

There was an expectant silence.

The silence was shattered by the sound of gunfire. The guerrillas rushed to put out the lights. They got the civilians to take cover and then man defensive positions in the dark. It was as if this were the moment they'd been waiting for, *la hora de la verdad*, as the Cuban instructors would say back in the camps. The hour of truth.

Wearing a new wristwatch, courtesy of one Bra Gab, Spider stood at his usual corner – at his post, according to Bra G – and checked the time: 7:15 p.m. There was the usual edgy traffic in the neighbourhood. Spider noticed a dark-brown Nissan Skyline parked at the other end with four or five fellows in it wearing Sporties, hats that lent menace to any wearer's features. Even a choirboy ended up looking like Ngqavini the Axeman in the headgear. The Skyline moved slowly, even slower abreast of Spider, before picking up speed. It cruised down to the corner and wound its way up the hill and disappeared. Spider had a feeling whoever it was had killed the lights.

He wondered if Bra Gab was also in the vicinity. It was difficult to know with him; sometimes he'd say he was going to be gone awhile and then turn up at the shopping centre, always alone, even though Spider knew from the information he was able to pump out of Tikka Joe that Bra Gab was like this with Sis' Sonto. They didn't know that he knew. He had a sense that Sis' Sonto disapproved of him, avoiding eye contact with him as if she harboured a secret that cast Spider in a negative light. It was worse since Tikka Joe's disappearance, little twerp just split from the scene like exhaled smoke. He supposed that even if Sis' Sonto and Bra Gab knew that he knew they were diddling each other, he was so low in their estimation – a seventeen-year-old tsotsi, no less – it didn't really matter. Like Tikka Joe, Spider was also tall and gangly with a bad reputation and that made him seem older, but he knew Bra Gab was aware of his real age. Bra Gab knew everything. Except that Spider had had a serious fallout with his uncle, which had coincided with his mother getting in touch after a long time, all the way from Clermont Township – and she wanted him back there. She'd heard about his scrapes with the law and had promised to fetch him and frogmarch him back to Clermont. If there was one person Spider feared more than anything on this planet, it was his mother. When he was full of nonsense in the past, she just had to give him a look and he'd stop. At school, before he jumped out of the window of the principal's office when he'd been brought in for punishment, the teachers had known how to get him to behave. 'Steven Hlongwa,' they'd say, calling him by his given name, not this Spider nonsense, 'we're going to bring your mother here and she'll sort you out.' The threat. It was much later in KwaMashu that he understood the power of a threat. But now, he worked for Bra Gab after threatening Tikka Joe with physical harm; just shows you.

He checked himself out: black chinos, Converse All-Star sneakers, a Pringle jersey over a Viyella button-down shirt and of course his own signature Sportie. Slung over his shoulder was an imitation-leather jacket, some stupid brand name, from the Indians on West Street, but, hey, when his boat came to shore he'd get the real McCoy. Even though fashionable, he felt he was still wearing second-hands, hand-me-downs and stuff from the black market. Bra G promised him more, but he'd have to prove himself and take more risks, although the nature of the risks had never been clarified. His uncle, a schoolteacher, saw him casting off his usual clothes for more respectable threads and that increased his suspicion.

Already suspicious by nature, like most schoolteachers in the township, he kept on going blah-de-blah about crime. Recently, Spider had to pull a knife on him, since his gun had been confiscated and that led to one unholy row. 'I'll fuck you up,' he told his uncle, 'cut you long, deep and wide.' He'd heard that in a movie featuring West Indian gangsters, the Yardies. *Come on, mon, an' I'll cot you lon' deep an' wide.* They talked funny like the Ghanaians who'd started coming into the township, selling stuff; but they weren't rough and tumble like the Yardies. It was the Yardies that gave Spider the idea to form the Nabobs; you need a gang to survive, although the Nabobs still had a lot to learn about organisation. They had a debate, the young members, whether they needed something that would distinguish them from, say, Lucky and Khehla, who had formed the self-defence units and who were known as the Young Lions. They wore red, black and green armbands of the Movement and they carried big guns. People whispered that Bra Zeph had given them weapons. Everyone had a crew; the political parties were just a crew on a larger scale. Come to think of it, the government was an organisation of gangsters with crews like the army and the police in uniform. When he grew up, Spider told himself, he'd get to London and see if it were possible to hook up with the Yardies.

He laughed at the memory of the confrontation with the uncle, how the sad sack had called him a vile boy with a dirty mouth. 'Someone ought to wash your mouth with soap,' he said. Ja? Let them try. But now his real ma wanted him back, got a good school and a vac job lined up for him, keep him off the street. He couldn't say no to his ma. For one thing she'd just kill him, no messing about. She'd almost killed his father, but that was another story. Right now he had to figure how to end this thing with Bra G and still get something. You didn't just rock up in Clermont Township empty-handed. He'd have to score something – something big – before retiring. He laughed at his own wit. Retired at seventeen. Then the taxi pulled to a stop at the corner and Sis' Sonto got off, carrying a nice yellow bag that seemed chock-full of goodies.

It was surprisingly light around 7:16 p.m. on 2 January 1990 when Nomasonto Sokhela stepped from the minibus taxi, holding carefully onto the handle of the sliding door, lest it snagged on her clothes or her bag. The bag, more capacious than the ones she normally carried, was both a source of torment and pride. She knew that her life had taken an irrevocable turn for the worse. In the morning, she tried to send word to Aunt Maisie to make sure little Thembani was kept safe, out of sight, perhaps – much better – taken to the her uncle in Ntuzuma Township, near KwaMashu. To her dismay, there was no word from Aunt Maisie. All her attempts had come to naught. In her mind, Sonto could already imagine what must have happened. He'd either snatched them or facilitated their abduction. Remembering the ease with which he'd shot the kneeling kid, she knew that both her aunt and her sister didn't have a chance against him. What have I done?

His messages at daybreak that she should take a parcel to Ngobese's, with the directions where to place it, told her she was beyond the pale. It was not so much that she'd been put in this position, where she had to go against her convictions; it was the fact that there must have been something about her, in the first instance, which had convinced someone that she was ripe for the picking. So, here she was with a time bomb in her bag. Listening intently, she thought she could even hear it ticking. 'Those people,' he said, 'have something that belongs to me. It was stolen from me.' Of course he meant the bloody trunk that had got everyone in a tizzy. 'I hear my old friend Chaplain Nerissa will be there,' he said. 'This is a welcome home present for her.' Sonto wasn't able to make a case against what she saw as lunacy. She just asked: 'If this goes off, what's going to happen to your precious trunk?'

'Don't worry your sweet head about it,' he said. 'Leave it to me.'

Your sweet head, the little insults aimed at inflicting damage. Life with him, brief as it was, had been an eye-opener. It was a rollercoaster hurtling towards an inferno. It was a waking nightmare in which she could see how her fiery end would come. And now, she was in the belly of a huge paradox because she was going to die. On this day of wonders, in a New Year when, come hell or high water, black people were going to seize freedom, she would be reduced to ashes. Unaccountably, everywhere she looked, people were either burning things or jumping into the air, exulting in expectant joy. People were delirious, like the newsreel she once saw of the end of the Second World War, citizens thronging the squares, vestal virgins kissing soldiers. There was no one to kiss, not her, whose sins weighed heavier than the trunk that had led to so much malevolence. She couldn't bring herself to think what might be happening to Thembani; with Auntie Maisie, it was different, she was an old trooper, but a child ...

'Hey ... Sonto!' And then: 'Miss Sokhela?'

For a dislocated moment she thought he had caught up with her, although he never called her by her given name. The thought surprised her because she hadn't put it in her head that she was actually running away from him. Whirling round, she saw Bra Zephaniah Zondi in a passenger seat of a small, red Honda Ballade, with Johannes Sibisi at the wheel. Bra Zeph waved at her, shouting: 'Sonto?'

Wondering if they had been following the minibus taxi – for what reason, though? – she headed to the car. She examined the writing on the men's faces, relieved and agitated at the same time. Of course, she remembered, the meeting, with the guerrillas and Aunt Nerissa. She couldn't see Nerissa as a comrade; aunt would do. Bra Zeph leaned across and opened the back door for her. He was unable to hide the happiness he was feeling. 'I feel lousy you had to use a taxi here,' he said. 'We should have picked you up from your home.' Sonto got a whiff of alcohol on his breath.

'Have you been celebrating without me?' Sonto asked, disappointed because she'd heard that Bra Zeph had kicked the habit. She eased herself into the car and placed the bag on the floor. My legs will go first.

'So you heard the good news?' Johannes Sibisi asked, seeking her eyes in the rearview mirror. When he saw her face wrinkling in anxiety, he explained: 'Comrade MT and Nerissa have called the Committee to Ngobese's place. The guerrillas from the People's Army will give back the trunk. The Movement will be able to work again.'

But the Movement has been working well without the fucking trunk, she thought. She wondered if it was just pure exuberance on Bra Zeph's part, this talkativeness, or was it the effects of alcohol. She felt suddenly even more depressed than she'd been earlier, if that was at all possible. She wondered what death from a bomb explosion was like. Do you even hear it?

'Hear what?' Johannes asked from the front. 'Hear what, Sonto?'

It's bad, I'm even thinking aloud like an old woman. 'The people?' she said. 'The noise? The sound of celebration?'

'People know that freedom is at hand,' Johannes Sibisi said, his cheeriness grating on the young woman. 'We'll be getting our allocations so that we can set up more cells in the township.'

'And Comrade Nerissa will make the allocation?'

'Exactly,' Bra Zeph chipped in. 'That's one of the reasons we're going to Ngobese's,' Bra Zeph said. 'To meet Comrade Nerissa and Bra MT. They'll have all the details.'

'The other reason?'

'To have a party.'

Nothing like a reformed abstainer, Sonto thought. Somewhat embarrassed over Bra Zeph's uncharacteristic peppiness, Johannes chose to engage Sonto in conversation.

'So how have you been?' he asked.

'Oh,' she said, 'it's been a bit uphill. But that's life.'

'Uphill is good,' he said. 'One you've reached the top, you're able to get a clear perspective on things.'

'Ah,' she teased, 'so now you're Johannes Sibisi the Philosopher.' She was aware of Bra Zeph who seemed to be struggling to focus, an expression alternating between vacuity and clear-eyed soberness flashing across his face. Having seen Aunt Maisie's customers in the shebeen, she knew when a man was on the verge of a massive blackout. What bothered her, though, was a suspicion that Bra Zeph's inebriation could have come from mixing alcohol with other substances.

'Is he okay?' Sonto asked.

'He'll be fine,' Johannes said. He drove for a short stretch towards Ngobese's, glancing at his older comrade and then concentrating again on the road. 'He's had a hard life.'

'I suppose that explains everything,' Sonto said. She was amused at how carefully Johannes handled the car, the hands gripping the steering wheel in the regulation quarter-to-three position.

'Are you always like this? Sonto asked.

'Like how?' Eyes still kept on the road.

'Careful …' Sonto wanted to say 'ponderous' but stopped as she had offended too many men already. 'Yes, careful and … guided.'

'Guided? That's a new one.' He gave a small laugh.

'You know what I mean.' She hoped she wasn't being too forward. In any event she might not live long enough to regret an indiscretion.

'I got that from my aunt. She helped me get to where I am.'

'And where are you, Johannes?' Sonto asked. Then, without explanation, she burst into tears.

Bra Zeph had dropped off to sleep and was snoring quietly.

In the back of the Toyota 4Runner, Strella could literally feel his own blood vessels opening and his fingers getting all the more slippery. Determined to unlock his shackles, he kept his eyes closed. He wanted perfect sight when he next opened them in the dark. Click! The release of the handcuffs brought a relief flavoured with pain, a bite into a cold apple reactivating a toothache. Pain was all he felt, remembering the days and nights in the Libyan desert camp. Right now, though, he was also a little thankful, thankful to the gods that looked after scoundrels. He imagined himself sitting on a street corner, a begging bowl in front of him. A few more hours lying in the same position with his arm taking all that pressure could have resulted in a loss of a limb.

He couldn't tell how deep the cut was on the wrist, which had taken the brunt of the tearing of the skin. Covered by the sleeve of the jacket, the point of Doctor's trusty knife was trapped flat under his watch-strap, the hilt cradled in the hollow between the upper arm and the forearm. This was the major source of the sticky wetness of his fingers apart from the punctures from the pin with which he had unlocked the handcuffs. Having disarmed him after conducting a cursory search of his person, his captors had been in such a hurry to hustle him from the scene that they had missed the knife. It was enough for them to bundle him in the car like a sack of potatoes.

They were in KwaMashu. You didn't need a road map to know you were in a township. The buzz of energy, the voices electrifying the atmosphere. The rumble of traffic, a train trundling along and the ground shaking became invaluable markers for a man in the dark, in the vale of shadows.

The voices in the car belonged to people who had no business in the township – turkeys. Except, of course, Colonel Stander; having been an architect of township strife, setting up bases in Ondangwa and Angola, Stander knew all there was to know about the pulse of a settlement. The rest knew bugger-all, especially that Portuguese guy, De Matos, who had taken the lead in assaulting him, or the fellow with a funny accent – and, of course, General Palweni. They knew nothing. Palweni had spent all his years in exile; what he knew of townships wouldn't fill a thimble; he was as much of a turkey as the rest of them, never mind that he was black. Blackness in Africa wasn't a guarantee that you knew things African. Black visibility didn't automatically mean black power. Where had he heard that? Was it from the professor with the fuckable wife, perhaps? He couldn't tell now. He knew just one thing: he had to get out of here. He heard Palweni complaining: 'When are we getting there?' Just like a carsick kid on a long outing with the mama and papa.

'We're almost there,' Col Stander said, sure as shit. That's one thing about white people – they were brought into this world totally in control of things. Even a white kid asking directions didn't ask where such-and-such a place was but simply ordered you to give him the fucking directions. Show me the way to the bus stop. Or Woolworths. And if you didn't know, well, shame on you for being such an ignorant, woolly-headed, limp-minded good-for-nothing. That's just how the world was configured. But Strella had configured his own world differently, taking chances, doing something daring, never stopping. As someone who'd been incarcerated, he knew that anything, anywhere, a piece of string, a nail on the ground – anything – could come in handy at some crucial moment. For Strella, even time could be honed into a weapon. Make time work for you, someone had said in Libya, one of those fellows from the Popular Front for the Liberation of Palestine, the PFLP. Funny he remembered that, a Japanese volunteer training to fight alongside Palestinians. Make time do your bidding. The car slowed down and pulled to a stop. No other moment, Strella thought. It's time. Then he jumped.

'Hey –?'

Angelo de Matos had been in his own world, wondering what the hell he was doing there hundreds of miles from Joburg. Okay, he had told Stander that he was going to wreak some serious retribution – the likes not seen since maiming some Frelimo sympathiser in 1974 – on the killer of Bernado, Mariela's betrothed. But now after pummelling the man, seeing the other one dead with his brains oozing out on the road in Yeoville, he wasn't so sure he had the stomach for more. Besides, he was nursing a rising resentment towards Stander. First off, Stander hadn't kept his side of the bargain. The whole deal with recovery of effects from Portuguese families in Angola and Mozambique … Stander was supposed to see that people got recompensed. He would intercede on behalf of the families with Savimbi and Roberto. There'd be no negotiations with fucking communists in MPLA. Stander had boasted that where there would be no negotiations, he had the muscle – his word, *músculo* – to get some of it back. He had achieved nothing. And he'd been paid *muito dinheiro* for his efforts. And now, there he was driving the Toyota 4Runner like he owned it, hitting these stupid potholes and probably ruining the suspension on uneven ground like he was out to win some off-road rally. He could do that in his own car, for God's sake. What's more, Angelo de Matos didn't for one single minute buy the suggestion that his inclusion in this little jaunt was for him to help assess the contents of the box that the *filho da puta* Strella had found in Uige. It was just too far-fetched. And Mariela, sweet Mariela, pity … then the rustling behind …

'Hey –?'

The blade pierced Angelo de Matos's throat and the fibreglass handle quivered in Strella's hand, a knife with a life of its own. Disoriented, De Matos stiffened and then coughed as the blade sliced the carotid vein open, warm blood gushing forth and splashing all over Bobo Jones. Panicked and horrified, Jones jumped up and screamed. He was shaking, trying to tear off his clothes, his flailing around managing to frustrate Stander's intention to shoot Strella, a pistol having suddenly appeared in his hand.

In that split second of confusion as Palweni also scrabbled for his AK-47, Strella elbowed the back door open while snatching De Matos's Remington 700 bolt-action rifle off the seat. Landing hard on the road, he felt something cracking in the region of his shoulder. He knew that if he paused to indulge the pain for even one second, he would never get up. It would be curtains and he wasn't done, not just yet.

Calling upon all his reserves, even the gods he hadn't prayed to in years, he sprinted towards a cluster of garbage cans along the pavement on the street corner. Half-bent, he raced on, expecting a bullet to slap into the space between his shoulder blades, where the dizzying pain was throbbing. Ahead, a street lamp cast a sallow tone on a group of men shooting dice. They turned at the sound of his footfalls. The sight of a blood-spattered apparition armed with a rifle and a bloody knife must have seemed like a scene from a horror movie.

One of them yelled out: 'Space, *madoda*!' Then the players scattered into all directions. They were in no doubt that the approaching spectre simply meant that more men with bigger guns and a deeper lust for blood were about to come into sight.

LOG #7

At 6:30 p.m. he dresses in his choice military uniform, the pale-green Cuban battledress together with a peaked cap. He straps his Makarov 9 mm to his waist, the belt webbing and holster buffed, the shining metal buckles bouncing off the mirror affixed to the wardrobe. His father, the old man, the doddering old man neutered by the rules and regulations of playing fair and forgiving the enemy and turning the other cheek, appears at the door, eyes expectant and brows arched in a quizzical and sardonic fashion.

Nice boots, the old man says, pointing with his snake-headed stick at his son's feet, at the leather laced halfway up the leg, the moulded soles, combat boots in which his son tore across Cacuso and all over the bloodied terrain of the Eastern Front, boots with which he once stomped to death an enemy agent.

I like them, he tells his father.

Going to war? His father asks the question, taking in the spruce uniform, the trunk on the floor, the room tidied for departure and the AK-47 leaning against the bed.

The time has come.

For what, Gabriel? Japhet Makhunga asks. To kill your people?

I'm not Gabriel. My name is uNozishada.

Is that the name they gave you? In the camp?

It's the name I chose, he tells his father. I chose it because uNozishada was a warrior to the end.

But do you know why he chose to die during the battle with Mpande's army?

Because he was tired? He didn't want to be captured alive and turned into a slave?

It was because he could see that that battle was futile and marked the final defeat of amaZulu as a fighting force. Japhet Makhunga sounds tired but he speaks on, patiently. The brothers, Dingane and Mpande were fighting each other. That's why uNozishada, the son of Maqhoboza, the son of Nzuza, threw away his assegai and told Nongalaza to kill him. Did you know that?

Not to that detail.

You patterned your life on a man whose history you know in brief, tasty bits ...

It's enough for me that he was a warrior.

That's the problem with us, isn't it? Japhet Makhunga asks. We've got all these young men whose scrotums are full of the seed of war. We don't read the situation we are in today, the fact that we need to learn the skills of leadership. We will take these warriors and put them on our shoulders and thrust their heads into the clouds and then ask them to lead us. And we will again wallow in ignorance, poverty and disease and some of us, in the not-too-distant future, will be crying for the white man to return, like Children of Israel asking to be returned to Egypt.

What you're saying doesn't make sense, Nozishada says.

Okay, Makhunga says. In prison, we represented the best that this country could offer. But even there, we could see that people had gone into the struggle for diverse reasons. And where there is no political clarity, the hyenas take over. We are heading for a new country; soon enough, and some of us will regard the past with fondness.

Nozishada says: What do you propose then?

The leaders have to be straight with the people. They have to admit where we are weak so that we can all pull together. We must have honesty and share in the resources as equally as possible. We must create a world that will discourage greed. He pauses, looking at his son with tired eyes. To me, the hand of greed and blood has already touched you.

Don't worry about me. I'm set to reclaim all that belongs to me.

There's no 'me' in the struggle, Gabriel ...

I'm not Gabriel ...

Gabriel ... That's the name your mother and I gave you ...

Yes, Nozishada says, bristling with bitterness. My mother ... what happened to her by the way? You returned from prison and sought to cage her into your own prison cell ...

You cannot say things like that ...

I can. She's my mother. Dissatisfied with words that seem ill-equipped to wound his father, Nozishada continues. She left you for the same reason your comrades deserted you. You might have been part of the Movement but deep down you hate people. You despise them. That causes people to await your downfall with bated breath. And when it came, with you falling sick, your wife gone with another man, they took the first train out of your town. I'm the one who helped you pick up the pieces.

Unhesitatingly, Makhunga strikes Nozishada with his stick, the feeble blow catching the younger man on the shoulder. Raising the stick again, Makhunga says: You have to reckon with me as your father. To which Nozishada responds: I might be an issue of your loins as they say, but you're not my father. You were never my father. When you were arrested, like a lot of your buddies who ended up in prison, it was for pure stupidity. You underestimated the enemy and planned like idiots.

Quick as a flash, Makhunga demonstrates agility that belies his age and state of health. In one coordinated action he grabs the AK-47 and is swivelling to aim at his son when Nozishada, with effortless fluency, the pistol seemingly an extension of his outstretched hand, shoots his father, once, in the neck. Falling, Makhunga snatches at his throat as if to staunch the flow of blood. He drops to the floor. The stick adorned with a snake's head slides tiredly into the pool of blood.

Without looking at his father, Nozishada collects his AK-47 and closes the door behind him.

Outside, the afternoon spreads ignorantly like a cloud of normality. He gets into the car and drives out of KwaDambuza, something telling him that he won't be coming back. When he returns, it will be with an army of men resolute about change.

The old men at the helm of the struggle do nothing but run off at the mouth and make compromises. He will build a force that will make real the cry of Amandla Ngawethu, *all power to the people. The masses will rise and take power. They will wrest power from the fast-talking so-called revolutionaries that believe in theory.*

He stops at the corner where he has a vantage view of the house where Ngobese is holed up with the men. He tries to imagine what this part of the world must have looked like in the days of Shaka or Dingane, sons of Senzangakhona. Did the villagers in that idyllic past know that their dwellings, adobe huts topped with thatch, would transmute into shacks and lean-tos spread higgledy-piggledy along dongas and patches of terrain scarred by erosion, where water either flows into houses or stagnates in pools spawning pestilence and torment? This shit has got to stop and the old fogeys aren't up to the task.

He raises his eyes just in time to see another old fogey, Zephaniah Zondi, a little unsteady on his feet, followed by Johannes Sibisi and – what do we have here? Sonto – all getting out of the small red car. Distantly, he hopes Sonto won't lose her nerve; if she does then her people will lose their lives, simple. The three are proceeding to the gate. Then, wearing Converse All-Star sneakers, a streak of lightning makes a dash for Sonto's yellow bag.

11

AMANDLA NGAWETHU

'Down!' Mchinda shouted. Someone, Django, put out the lights and peered at the road, from where the sound of gunfire had come. Rex Mabena passed the weapons out to the men. There was a little, whispered conversation about grenades. Mchinda shook his head. Nerissa, Ngobese and Muzi kept their heads down.

Nose pressed to the floor, Ngobese had a vision of Refiloe's murder. The scene appeared to him. A young man who was knowledgeable about weapons and their handiwork came face-to-face with a superior adversary. This was someone who he had known from a previous existence. In that moment of recognition, he had died, imprinting the killer's image on his brain, an undying brain that became the surviving witness. This was part of the lore, passed down exclusively to generations of healers; when a killing happened where the perpetrator's face registered in the mind of the victim, that image hovered in the arena of death until released through a ritual. The ritual had taken place, if incompletely during the funeral rites for the young guerrilla. Sometimes the ritual didn't have to be elaborate and mere tears and remembrance of the grace of the departed sufficed. The smell of dust assailed Ngobese's nostrils exactly at the moment that the killer's face flashed through his mind, a man with a strong face who was well versed in the art of killing. He reasoned that the killer must have got inside help, perhaps from someone in the unit. There was no way he could have known of this house if it weren't for someone, one of their own, pointing out the location. Silently, Ngobese did an inventory, conjuring up the images of the members of the Committee. Bra Zephaniah Zondi – does he have an axe to grind for being passed over in the leadership stakes? Johannes Sibisi, there was a candidate. He was young, ambitious, wouldn't he be the type to augment his earnings with a little extra untraceable cash from the enemy? What about Nomasonto Sokhela? Sonto tended to disappear into her own private world. She was beautiful, desirable, committed, more committed than many people her age, but could she be the one selling them out? It was always easy in a group to pick on a woman as the one likely to be the source of weakness, but could it be true? The Movement derived its strength from solid women. They were the steady rock. Was Sonto made of sterner stuff or was she the quicksand – mire – into which everything the Movement had worked for would one day subside and disappear?

Someone breathed deeply beside him. Ngobese had been aware of Comrade MT's hostility this past twenty-four hours, the snide remarks reflecting his disaffection with some aspects of the unit's operation. Or was it something deeper, perhaps connected to Muzi's insecurity, a suspicion that someone in the unit was doing the dirty with Laura? Could MT be so spiteful as to betray comrades, a mission that had taken such a long time to put together? Despite his antipathy to the man, Ngobese couldn't quite accept this as possible. It was not true.

But wasn't the struggle the most rigorous test of individual integrity?

He knew that there were other elements that changed the programme when introduced into a group of lifelong comrades. Many a stalwart fell prey to the lure of money, power and prestige – an unlimited access to the sweet thigh. Was this what finally brought General Palweni into what his old man, also an inyanga but given to quoting holy writ, called a descent into wickedness? Ngobese could see his wizened face, hand aloft as he cited a passage from Proverbs. *The righteousness of the perfect shall direct his way: but the wicked shall fall by his own wickedness.* Perhaps it was Palweni mounting an attack on the house.

Ngobese had another vision, of people trapped inside their houses burning to death, the emergency personnel trawling through the charcoal for smouldering flesh. The idea of dying chilled him. What would happen to his children? Vezi, where are you when I need you?

'Ngobese?' Muzi Thabethe called in a whisper.

'Yes, Comrade MT?'

'What happened when Laura came to live in Stanger?'

'It was a long time ago.'

'I know. It matters.'

'What matters now,' Ngobese said, 'is that we get out alive.'

At 8:00 p.m., there was another burst of gunfire outside, closer this time.

Laura Mdunge also heard it and felt her heart lurching and wondered if she was going to faint. She'd been feeling out of sorts lately and a visit to the clinic had confirmed that she was pregnant. The father was either Thulasizwe Ngobese or her husband, Muzi Thabethe. In a curious, detached way, as if all this were happening to someone else, it gave her a sense of guilty freedom. For the first time in her life, she could say that she didn't actually care.

Of late, she had been thinking of Vukani Majozi; to a large extent, her whole life had gone full cycle. She had loved Vukani or, to be more exact, had been infatuated with him, possibly because she was aware that he was unattainable. Then there was Muzi Thabethe, her husband, who could well be the father of her unborn baby and whom, she knew, had merely served as a crutch for her. As for Ngobese, he was charming and fun to be with but she suspected he could be as empty as a banana peel. Maybe he was as slippery.

The walls were closing in on her. It was time to face the music or, at least, come to terms with her demons.

At 7:15 p.m. Laura Mdunge locked up the house she had shared with Muzi Thabethe since his release from prison some six years ago and made her way to the taxi stop. Although a little concerned that, as it was Friday night, she might have to deal with unwelcome elements, she pressed on. She walked down the cobbled path and out of the gate. She heard the gate latching to, something final and satisfying about the click, like tumblers falling in a combination safe.

She smiled at the notion of everything falling into place, for that was exactly how she wanted to run her life from this point onwards. She wanted to do things in an orderly fashion. This need has asserted itself the morning after the party with the guerrillas.

Muzi Thabethe was more uncommunicative that morning than usual. She was aware of a heaviness in him, his eyes following her every move. 'I also want to be there when you open the trunk,' she told him.

He peered at her from above a steaming mug of coffee. 'Why?'

'Why?' Laura asked. 'I'm also part of the structures.'

'I see. You've become quite the social butterfly since the men came into our lives.'

'I've always been active. I've always interacted with people. Long before you came out of prison, I was doing the work of the Movement.'

She paused, letting her words sink in. 'Or did you hear otherwise?'

'It's just that since …' He stopped.

'Since what?' She could see stubbornness putting up a shutter across his eyes. 'Since what?'

'Since the men arrived ...'

'There's an accusation there somewhere, an ugly thought. Who are you afraid of, Thabethe?' She never addressed him by his first name. *And we've known each other for all these years*! The thought depressed her.

'You're nervous when there's more than one man around me,' she went on. 'I saw how you'd cast accusing looks every time we were with Vukani or Zweli.'

She was struck by how lonely he looked since emerging from prison. It must have been hard. Had he missed her? Had he spent nights thinking about her? She didn't want to imagine what the men had to do to confront their loneliness inside prison cells. Laura accepted for the first time that, perhaps, they had got together for the wrong reason. I will no longer allow myself to be a victim, a martyr to loneliness.

'I watched you dancing with Django,' he said. 'You seemed very happy.'

'Ah,' she said. That was all she could say. She was afraid of the words that tingled inside her throat like the beginnings of a cold. Once out in the open, she knew, those words would never be called back. She was aware of something odd happening to her, but under the circumstances, it would have been a futile exercise, a waste of time.

'That's all you can say?' Muzi Thabethe's tone was low.

'There's nothing more to say.'

'Suit yourself.'

'One thing, though,' she said. 'I'm coming with you to see the opening of the box.'

And so, here she was, keeping a promise she had made to herself. She was owed that little courtesy to be among the select few who would witness the act of the trunk being opened. Maybe – just maybe – she'd be able to disclose her own secrets. The hour of truth had arrived.

In the taxi, she was wedged between two women who engaged her in a long chat about Mandela. 'The Boers will never free Mandela,' said the first woman, clicking her tongue to underscore her scepticism. The second woman, younger and simultaneously ageless under the diffuse interior light, laughed and voiced her own hope. 'He's such a handsome man,' she said.

'How would you know? He's been in prison all these years?'

'From the pictures when he was young. If you're a pretty man in your youth, you'll be a handsome man in your adult years.'

'Too bad about Winnie – she's so pretty.'

'She's pretty but will cut your heart out if you try some monkey-shines with Mandela.'

Laura half listened to the continuing exchange. One of the women sighed. It was the younger woman, suddenly irredeemably old. 'Jehovah, King of Kings,' she said, 'I so do wish my Sipho had also gone to exile like the other children; maybe he'd have come back a better man and not this *mfukumfuku* of a drunkard he's become.'

The other woman agreed. These were sisters united by the trouble they'd seen. They looked at Laura, as she got ready to get off at the nearest corner to Ngobese's house. 'And what about you, sister?' One of them asked.

'Things are going to be all right,' Laura said. She climbed out and closed the door.

Then a man covered in blood grabbed her by the throat and dragged her into the small bush overlooking Ngobese's house. 'You scream,' he said, 'and I'll fucking cut your throat.'

Earlier that evening in KwaDambuza, Mrs Leticia Sigodo had just come back from the day shift at the poly-clinic and, tired and weary of the smell of despair, wished for a cup of tea, tea that cured all, much more potent than all the medicines in the dispensary. She also wanted to shut out the sounds of people groaning, babies wailing, nurses' heels going clickety-clack on the tiled corridors. She wanted to forget the sibilant whispering of wheelchairs being pushed by men and women whose ears were closed to the telltale and distant whine signifying the failure of machines to keep a heart pumping.

It had been bad since the state of emergency, a time that required that people hear and listen. Hearing only, without actively listening, meant missing the nuance, the unstated, the little flutter in the voice that could make the difference between life and death. It was this thing about most township women; they might listen to the radio, take in all that information while actively sifting the airwaves for the sound of a baby, of a child in crisis, a woman in peril. It was exactly this sensibility that drove a woman to spring up in the middle of a sermon and rush out and save a neighbour trapped in a burning shack.

Leticia Sigodo would relate the story later, that it was a cough that spurred her into action. 'I've been in the church choir for over forty years,' she said, 'and I can tell you without having to look if so-and-so is present or absent, from the voices. Sometimes it's not so much what you hear as what you don't hear – the absence – that matters. On this day, this afternoon, I heard a cough, a thump followed by a great silence.'

It was this silence that told her something was amiss. And then she remembered seeing the strange, unloved though admired Captain Mkhukhu doing his rounds, tapping on the pebbles with his terrible walking stick, like someone already practising for a sightless future. She recalled hearing him entering the door of his even more peculiar son's room. Then raised voices, a car backfiring, a cough, a thump and a tremendous silence. Without knowing why, she started screaming, alerting the neighbourhood.

She was still screaming when they found Japhet Makhunga lying on the floor in a pool of blood. Someone slapped her across the face and told her what she had known all along: that Mkhukhu had been shot and was dying; she'd better do something. They said it in words that handed her the responsibility of life and death, the way people address those suspected of practising witchcraft when someone has been struck by lightning. And so, kneeling above the old man no one loved, she ordered that all the children be shooed out and she scrutinised the wound to see if the windpipe had been severed and nodded her satisfaction that the bullet had punctured the fleshy part of the neck. It had missed the trachea by a fraction of an inch. Its path had avoided both blood vessels, coming out below the ear. There was blood everywhere. Sister Leticia, as she was called in circles where people needed miracles performed, listened to the gurgling of the blood in the man's mouth, relieved yet horrified, knowing that it was a sign of life, of a struggle to breathe. But it could also mean the approach of the end. Aware of the eyes around her, she became not an aghast neighbour but a nursing sister striving to save a life.

'Why did the boy do this?' she asked, aware that no one could answer.

It took a while before the Toyota station wagon came and the many extended arms and hands carried the man who should have died into the back. Sister Leticia got into the back with him like a relative who'd have to explain what had happened, something she didn't know but which she would in any event try to explain. There was nothing knowable about the lives of the people of KwaDambuza.

'Do you have any other children?' she asked the man, having heard that he actually had a daughter, and a wife somewhere, a wife who had run away. Unlike men, women tended to admire other women who could summon the courage to flee the marital home. In their quiet way they cheered and ululated, the same way people cheer and ululate at the news of a successful escape from prison. They knew, however, that some of the escapees hitched up with other men in the belief that a new man would be different from the warder who held the keys to the last prison. And the cycle would start all over again. Wise women, Sister Leticia concluded, were the ones who never got ensnared in the first place.

News of Nelson Mandela came across on the car radio. She wondered if the dying man, whom she had heard, had also spent time in prison, had ever met him. She wanted to ask him but thought it would be impertinent. It would be cruel for him to die thinking how stupid it was to survive prison only to be slaughtered by the fruits of freedom. As Sister Leticia pondered the absurdity of it all, the skies opened and a hard rain fell and she reckoned that, perhaps, her patient would live to tell the tale.

At Kwam'shayazafe, a few kilometres due north, the news of the death of Bhekisisa Luthuli set off a flicker of anger. Hoping that the flicker would not grow into a bush fire, Warrant Officer Brian Khumalo deliberately downplayed the gorier details of Luthuli's death, reporting laconically that the deceased had met his death in police custody. But the small assembly of men and women, Bhekisisa Luthuli's relatives and extended family and age-mates and friends, wanted it called for what it was. They were not strangers to death. They had all been scarred by the violence that had raged through the length and breadth of Natal, especially the township and the hostel.

Bhekisisa Luthuli's cousin, known simply as Bhekimpi, was smaller in stature, shorter and wirier, and struck Brian Khumalo as being as mean as a mamba. He spoke without looking up at Khumalo and Booi, asking after Ngobese and Neliswa who had been under the protection of hostel dwellers when the Special Branch officers came to Kwam'shayazafe. Khumalo told them that there was no doubt that

Ngobese and his family were also in trouble. So was Neliswa, whom Warrant Officer Khumalo immediately understood to mean Nerissa. The group had already lost a young man called Refiloe Mokoena, most likely murdered by the Special Branch. It wasn't clear, but there was suspicion that in all these things, the Third Force, a state security organ known as hand of the baboon, was implicated.

'Does Ngobese need our help?' Bhekimpi asked. The divisive hand of the baboon, the campaign of disinformation by the regime, had already caused untold suffering among the people of Natal. It meant war. People aligning themselves with the hand of the baboon were fit for one thing, a necklace. 'Can we bring our men until the threat blows over?'

'It's likely that the hand of the baboon is involved,' Warrant Officer Brian Khumalo said. 'But you'll have to be discreet. Else you put us in jeopardy.'

'*Siyabonga,* Mntungwa,' Bhekimpi said, looking up for the first time. 'We thank you because even if you work with these people, you keep an eye and ear for the benefit of your people. We were one before they came and put a knife that divided us as people. It is time for us to remove that knife from our communities.'

When Khumalo and Booi had left, Bhekimpi addressed the community. It was quiet outside of the hostel. The cars whooshing up and down to KwaMashu and other areas were the only sign of life.

'We shall go in small groups to my cousin's place,' Bhekimpi said. 'I want us to take with us our weapons, the weapons we use when facing the enemy. Bhekisisa was more than a brother. He was our pillar.'

Outside, as the platoon-strength group piled into two taxis, Bhekimpi chanted the praise songs – *izithakazelo* – of the Luthuli people.

Mshibe, Madlanduna, abadl'insikazi belambile,
Ngoze ngikwenze owangenza khona …
Zingwazi ezidl' inyama abanye bedl'inyamazane …
Mshibe kaMakhiph'inj'efukwini kuzalele yena,
Donda …

12

A SENSE OF JUDGEMENT

Col Jan Stander had a good mind simply to shoot dead both the African American called Bobo Jones and the equally stupid excuse for a general, Absalom Palweni. Jesus Christ, have you ever seen such foolishness?

When Strella jumped out of the car, his reaction quicker than any other warrior Stander had trained, it took everyone by surprise. This, of course, is what Stander had drilled into his men back in Ondangwa, the importance of surprising your enemy and striking with deadly accuracy. Shock and awe was the catchphrase; the boy was like greased lightning, springing from the back where he must have lain doggo for miles on end, slashing Angelo de Matos's neck, the blood splashing out and spooking both the spook and the fake general. And, how do these jokers react? They start firing, no sense of weapons handling in a moving vehicle, spraying lead, almost killing everyone in the area. Strella is not the kind of person you kill from a distance – that's *his* speciality. You have to get up close and stick the knife into the ribcage and twist it and see the light going out of his eyes.

Following the wild scramble to pursue Strella on foot, everyone leaving the car and the dead man unsecured, Stander felt that he needed to take overall control. This was at a crossroads. To the right was the rough track leading to the house harbouring the four men who had escaped from Zeerust: Hickory, Sassafras, Stinkwood and Pomegranate. *Hickory, dickory dock, wait till you swallow my Glock.* Normally a serious, no-nonsense person, Stander was surprised by this little lapse into levity. Yep. Life is all about rhyme and reason. The box in the house contained its own poetry, a revelation that would knock the jumped-up general off his perch.

Returning to the car after Strella had simply dematerialised like smoke, Stander remembered that their primary objective wasn't to spend the night looking for Strella. Taking the road to Ngobese's place, he noticed a small, red Honda Ballade pulling to a stop in front of the target house from the opposite direction. Fearing that someone might see Angelo de Matos's dead body in the back seat, especially since the overhead cluster lamps illuminated a wide perimeter, Stander drove on, searching for a suitably secluded spot. Some twenty-five metres on, Stander turned the wheel of the Toyota 4Runner, edged the 4x4 onto the side of the road and killed the engine. It was dark here, off the beaten track.

The interior of the vehicle carried the metallic odour of blood and cordite. Jones had shifted as far away from the dead body as possible. Stander cleared his throat. Let them sweat a little.

'Why have we stopped?' Bobo Jones asked.

'Yes,' General Palweni said. 'Why here?'

'Bobo?' Not Mr Jones, just Bobo …

'Yes, Jan?'

'Pop the body into the back,' Stander said. 'Where Strella was.'

'What?'

'I said, please be a good fella and stick our dead friend in the back,' Col Stander said. 'Can't treat our comrades with disrespect, hey?'

'I'm not doing it,' Bobo Jones said, sounding like a twelve-year-old.

'What?'

'I said I'm not touching him. You can't make me.'

'Sure I can,' Stander said. Turning around, he raised his fist holding a Glock 19 and shoved it into Bobo Jones's face. 'Here's what's going to happen, Bobo. You're going to pick up Mr de Matos and do it like they do it in the mortuary, easy, steady, making sure he doesn't spill more blood than he's done already. You'll then place him nicely in the back like I asked you and cover him with tarp, so the *goggas* and *miggies* don't get to him. You understand me, or do you want me to shoot you in the face?'

'What are you doing, Stander?' General Palweni asked.

'Instituting some discipline here, General,' Stander said. 'Do you want to say something?'

'No,' Palweni said. 'I'm all for discipline.'

'That's what I thought.'

'Aren't you worried about Strella?'

'I think I know where he'll be before the night is over.'

'Where?'

'In a body bag.'

Minutes passed. The two military men listened to Bobo Jones retching and gagging as he laboured with the dead body. When done, Bobo Jones sat glumly in the half-dark, making strangling sounds.

'We'll find a washroom at a garage,' Stander said. 'You can freshen up there and join the human race.' Turning to Palweni next to him, he said: 'We've seen the location of our target. Strella, we'll get in due course. No hurry in South Africa ...'

He started the car and let it proceed along the road for a while with the lights off until they were on the road again. 'Think that's right, General?'

'That's about it.'

'Good man.'

Good man. I will not be patronised by this rotten son-of-a-bitch, General Absalom Palweni thought. He's the one responsible for the mess we're in. First of all, Strella is his creation, even though he was seconded to our covert unit. The boy's had excellent training, an impala on two feet. However, he's the enemy, out to kill anyone who stands in his way. But he's also Stander's responsibility. Like De Matos. Or Bobo Jones, the whimpering American fool whose sphincters must have loosened for the car was now as funky as the inside of a pit latrine. What's he want here, anyway?

'What's he want here, anyway?' General Palweni asked.

'Who?' Colonel Stander asked. 'Strella?'

'Him,' Palweni said, jerking his head in the direction of the back seat. 'He's a basket of nerves. No use to anyone now.'

'We need him,' Col Stander said. 'He's got some expertise in decryption that will come in handy.' He bugged his eyes out, in an exaggerated, non-verbal query: *You remember*?

Palweni was a little uncomfortable about talking about a subject, a person, who might be within earshot. They had made the same mistake with Strella with dire consequences – but he was too upset to care. 'What do you mean?'

'The future of this enterprise,' Stander explained with devastating patience, 'depends on us taking possession of certain sensitive documents. My understanding is that there were files that hadn't been processed in your camp in Sector 37. Some came from your intelligence people, some from other services operating in Angola at the time. It's information that can compromise a lot of people in the coming dispensation. It's my understanding that a person who's familiar with the workings of both the liberation movements and our own government can help us make sense of the encrypted gobbledegook. Bobo Jones has expertise in decryption and analysis. I could do that myself, but it will take time.'

'That's all in the trunk?'

'Yep … Names, places, minutes. Secret stuff.'

'Whose secret stuff?'

'Ours. We're brothers in arms, aren't we?'

'I don't get it,' Palweni said. He actually wanted to say, *I don't like it*. He had a feeling that Stander just might have too many tricks up his sleeve. 'I thought I had supervised the material that was added to the boxes.'

'Ja,' Stander said. 'That might be the case. But the contents of the trunk originated with us, stuff from Roberto and Mobutu. Then it went to your people. But some of them were working for us.'

'In the People's Army?'

'Yep. An agent. He loaded files with biographies of our agents in the PA. Some of them were being handled by very senior people in the Movement.' Stander paused. 'I think some of the names are going to be very surprising.'

'Meaning?'

'Some of the higher-ups in the Movement might just turn out to have been working for us, who knows?'

'Is my name appearing anywhere, Stander?' General Palweni asked, quietly. Even though it was dark, small neon beads of sweat had formed on his upper lip.

'I wouldn't know.' Stander's tone could not quite carry off the lie.

'You'd better start knowing, Stander. Ignorance can be quite expensive. I wouldn't like to be embarrassed at the negotiations.'

'Ah,' Stander said, feigning amazement. 'So there'll be negotiations?'

'Don't fuck with me, Stander. Of course there'll be negotiations. Why do you think your people have been traipsing all over the African continent, wanting meetings with our people?'

'Hunting, maybe?' Stander said, nonchalantly. 'I hear the big game in some of these Frontline States is something to die for.'

'Stander, you've got to start taking things seriously.'

'Look, General,' Stander said. 'We've carved a very sweet spot for ourselves with this operation, if you'll pardon my mixed metaphors. We've got a boxful of goodies to sell. We've got information that will ensure we retire happily and never have to carry a weapon unless it's a golf club or a hunting rifle. So, please wipe the gloom off your face, it spoils the good looks you're famous for.'

'Gentlemen?' It was a timid, hesitant voice in the back. Bobo Jones.

'Yes, Bobo?' Stander's bullying instinct was instantly rekindled.

'Look over there.' Bobo Jones pointed at the street behind them.

A series of images, shadow and light flickering like a dance under the street lamp. Two men and a woman got out of the car. A boy sprang out of nowhere and snatched the women's bag. Immediately, out of the gloom, another man emerged and gave chase, something steadfast about his loping sprint. A shot rang out. The front door of Ngobese's house burst open and two shadows tumbled out with guns at the ready and took up defensive positions.

'Shit,' Stander said and made a U-turn.

Spider had once heard someone sing a tune about certain boots being made for walking. Well, even if he'd thought the song stupid because, really, what are boots made for if not for walking, he could still admire these Converse All-Star sneakers encasing his feet – which were made for walking, gliding and running! Calculating the distance between his outstretched fingers and the bag, deciding it would take him less than thirty seconds, no, not even that, a heartbeat, to get what he wanted.

It had got dark very quickly and a slight drizzle was coming down.

He didn't appreciate the rain, which had a tendency to dampen things, spoil people's sense of style. However, he was sure that whatever setback the rain might bring, it was going to be generously compensated for by the contents of the madam's bag. He'd come to think of her as a madam, as she was accustomed to swanking, putting on airs and carrying on like someone from the suburbs – these political princesses. Pity about Bra Gab; if he got to hear about the kind of score Spider had hit, well he was sure to take a dim view of that. Hopefully by then he, Spider, the boy who knew when to leave a party, would be well and truly gone.

As he tensed to get into gear, Spider noticed Sonto turning and peeking over Johannes Sibisi's shoulder as if sensing a presence in the dark. It was after all a Friday night and muggers were still abroad. Then she stepped purposefully on, her gait causing both men to step up. Even in the gloom, Spider thought he could see Johannes ogling her, clearly sweet on her. The unsteady old guy was in his cups, no doubt about it and nothing to worry about there. Johannes Sibisi seemed fit, though, like he kept himself in shape. But let him try.

One ... two ... three ...

Although he wasn't actually conscious of himself running, he had a curious sensation of witnessing a performance by someone else, another smoker perhaps, making an escape while toting an unexpectedly heavy bag. Behind was an old guy in hot pursuit. That was a surprise. Johannes and Sonto had just taken a few half-hearted steps and then stopped, leaving the chase to the old geezer, Bra Zeph, who seemed to gain vigour with every step he took. And he was gaining on him.

And then Spider heard it, Bra Zeph going 'Argh,' like someone getting a stitch in his side – and then the report of a gun going off – and he knew that his pursuer has been shot. Part of him wanted to stop and lend a hand but he had a feeling that it would be suicidal; the shooter was probably a thoroughly evil bastard. So he scuttled on, doing a zigzag manoeuvre like MacGyver, now and then leaping into the air at the sound of a bullet chewing up the ground and sending out sparks. Bloody hell, the bastard was now shooting at him!

When the latest burst of gunfire echoed into Ngobese's house, there was no longer any discussion about what action to take. Mchinda, on the floor like everyone else, shielded Nerissa's body with his while manoeuvring them across the floor and down the corridor, past the kitchen and out the kitchen door. He remembered the training in VIP protection, the concept of the least important person in a group. This was where, for instance, if a lobbed grenade or missile threatened a principal, the bodyguard could use the least important person around as a shield, something to absorb the shock. Since knowing her, Mchinda had no qualms about becoming the person to safeguard her life. He knew – it had been drilled in him – that there was nothing more shameful than a bodyguard outliving his principal.

Glancing at her, Mchinda was happy that she'd had the presence of mind to drape her shoulders with a shawl, which was on the sofa in the lounge. Crouched, his AK-47 rifle pointed into the sky, his forefinger in the trigger housing, he studied the terrain between the back of the house and the fowl-run, the only structure that could offer cover. He was aware, however, that whatever offered itself as sanctuary could provide a hiding place for an enemy lying in ambush. Ears pricked, he let the sounds of the night wash over him, editing out ambient sounds, like the raindrops on the roof and the corrugated sheeting that formed part of the hedge between the main house and the cottage. Punctuating these sounds was Nerissa's laboured breathing. From the road, another burst of fire, distant crackers.

Ever since Sector 37, when he was Thabo Stone and then Sassafras and then Mchinda, he'd always regarded Nerissa as his principal. She was a leader. Like many of the men and women who had spent time in combat situations, who had trained militarily and who understood the essence of leadership, he could be exacting in expecting the highest standards from those who had to be saluted. But Nerissa was one of those leaders who didn't expect to be saluted or treated with deference. She could stand next to a president or potentate of any country and people would defer to her more than the leader. His respect for her was derived from her conduct during that difficult time in Angola. Mchinda knew that the measure of a real leader was how he or she acted in times of trouble. It had nothing to do with a smooth tongue or the capacity to dispense alms and meretricious goods. He thought back to Palweni and was overcome by a great sadness.

'You have integrity, Chaplain,' he said, apropos of nothing.

His voice caught her off guard while also calming her down. 'Why,' she said, 'that's very generous of you, Mchinda.'

'What will happen?'

'You mean about the future of everything? I don't know. We might have a happy circumstance of evil being punished and good rewarded, but I wouldn't bank on it. The world is much too complicated for that.'

She sensed that Mchinda was struggling with questions.

'Does it surprise you that we're at war with ourselves?' he asked.

'In the camps, I know the commissars wrestled with the issue of black people preying on each other. Truth is, we have to clean up our house first before we can dictate to the neighbour.'

'And Palweni? Is he a neighbour?'

'Palweni is a feature of our struggle.' She sounded reluctant to continue, but went on, nevertheless. 'There's no doubt that in the future some of our trusted sons and daughters will betray the revolution. It's human nature. Some of them will do that under the mistaken notion that they are doing it for the good of the people. They will be driven by lust, which, in their heads, will register as love. The looters raiding the national treasury will convince themselves that they are saving up for everyone's rainy day.'

'Which is why we have to get you out of here,' he said.

'We have to get the trunk,' she said.

'Yes, Komandir.'

In the ugliness of the grip around Laura's throat and the stark reality of the knife, the long blade that seemed, even under the street lamp, to have been used not long ago, she could still marvel at the deadly symmetry of structures. Everything minimised escape and maximised capture. The road, though uneven and potholed, adjusted the eye to the straightness of the fences, the verticality of stanchions and the unerring angles of the four-roomed houses. It drew attention to the square openings for windows, the rectangular doors, lines and lines of human industry that faded into the folds of the night. Even the arm around her neck, now and then letting go, the owner knowing she could not escape, was lined, muscular, a beauty complete in its ability to create the finality of death.

'Are you going to kill me?' Laura asked. She knew that there existed two possibilities: survival or death; there was no in-between. If she died, her baby would also die and that was unacceptable. There were now knots of Friday night people hurrying, scurrying, all afraid of the man or woman coming towards them, their expressions of horror convincing her that, even if they would have wanted to help, the knifeman must have looked as scary as a figure out of a nightmare.

'Depends on what you do,' he said. 'There's only one person I still have to kill. Maybe you know him.'

'Who's that?'

'Mabitla.'

'I don't know any Mabitla.' Then she realised that, perhaps her life depended on whether he accepted or rejected her own relationship or otherwise with Mabitla, whoever he was. 'What's he done?'

'He wants to turn my head around,' Strella said. 'I thought we'd reached an agreement that he should leave me alone. But he's come back.'

'How old were you when you met him?'

'I was seventeen or eighteen. In Botswana.'

'And how old is he?'

'I never asked him when I killed him. Sixty, maybe even seventy. He smelled of old age.'

'Your parents ... did they know him?'

'I never had parents,' Strella said, suddenly angry and pressing the knife deeper into the neck hollow below the jaw line. 'They drank. I left.'

'You're hurting me,' she said, beginning to get dizzy. She could feel the blood trickling down her neck into the collar of her blouse. 'Can we sit down?'

'If I sit down now, I'll never get up.' He swallowed, something more viscous than mere saliva: blood. 'They shot me.'

'Who?'

'Them,' he said. With the free hand he guided hers around and pressed it flat against his back, in the region of the small of his back. She felt him flinching against her back as her fingers encountered an indentation. Her hand was wholly covered in blood. 'I was running.'

They shuffled like the walking wounded bound for the casualty department. Life around them bustled on: cars, people, the nervous giggle of the shadows. 'Where are they, now?'

'They were my parents,' he said. 'They grew us up and taught us everything. Barak and me and Jolene and Macaco and others. We learnt how to create victims.' And then, distressed: 'I lost my gun.'

They approached Ngobese's house from the back. 'The people here will help you,' she said.

'Who are they?'

'There's a medicine man. He saves lives.'

'No one can save my life. It's not worth it.' He reeled. She still couldn't tell with any certainty what was more crushing for him, a worthless life or a futile struggle. It could have been one and the same thing. He was slurring his words, saliva or blood dripping into a vulnerable spot on her neck. She suspected he was about to pass out, but was surprised when he twirled her around to look at her and she imagined that his expression reflected more triumphant malice than pain. She wondered how badly hurt he really was. It was like worrying over the fate of a snake that had been run over by a car. As it writhed, it would be unclear whether its lethalness lay in its fangs or in the ruined and exposed body.

'Come with me,' she said, the knife still menacing her. Now leading him, she pressed down the fence so that he could climb into the yard. When he stumbled, she steadied him, careful not to touch the knife hand. She had a feeling that the knife was at once inanimate and possessed of a life force and could slice her up into nice little pieces even without its handler's prompting. 'I'm pregnant.'

Laura didn't know why she volunteered this piece of intimate information. But there was something about the man, possibly the imminence of his death, which made her throw caution to the winds.

'That's very good,' he said. He mumbled something, perhaps his own version of congratulations.

And then the two of them were staring into the muzzle of Mchinda's AK-47. Standing a half-step behind Mchinda, Nerissa looked small, her eyes bright.

When she saw Laura emerging out of nowhere with the injured man in tow, Nerissa blinked, thinking that she must be seeing things. For, there he was, Strella. In that split second of mutual recognition, she experienced a welter of emotions: joy at seeing a familiar face and then an abiding anger. Even in that moment, she knew – her spiritual training, her calling – she would forever wrestle with the defensibility of hate; she hated this lithe frame, this contoured face with lifeless eyes. She had had scruples, a mistake committed in that long-ago moment when she had life and death power over the patient from Sanza Pombo. She should have inveigled the Angolan medical staff into simply snuffing out this useless life. Such a specimen should have long been consigned into an incinerator.

'Ah, the chaplain, the conscience of an army.' Strella lowered his gaze to take in the weapon trained on him, the hands and then the soldier behind the gun. 'Ah,' he continued wearily, 'Thabo … Thabo Stone. We're far from the land of the giant kudu. Is that a gun for me, my brother?'

'I'm not your brother, Strella,' Mchinda said. 'Keep still.'

'You are not only my brother,' Strella said, swaying as if whatever were holding him together were about to let go. 'You're what I am.'

And so saying, he shoved Laura hard towards Mchinda, a motion that introduced a different element, a subtlety and a shift of stance. As Nerissa instinctively stepped forward to protect Laura, Strella lunged with lightning speed and buried the knife in Mchinda's chest. Doctor would be proud of the move, he thought absently. The two men were locked in an embrace, Strella holding on and gazing into Mchinda's eyes with an expression close to affection. Stepping back, he snatched the AK-47 from Mchinda, executing a sequence of movements worthy of an arms drill. With the wet knife in one hand and the other on the handgrip with the forefinger curled around the trigger, Strella watched Mchinda fall while the two women howled in horror. A strange, conflicted expression flashed across Strella's face as he regarded Mchinda. Sighing, he motioned the women to get onto their knees.

Her hands examining Mchinda for signs of life, Nerissa raised her head to look at Strella. 'Did you have to kill him?'

'He was going to kill me,' Strella said.

'But isn't that something that you've been wanting, all the time?'

'Yes. But on my terms.'

Thulasizwe Ngobese and Muzi Thabethe realised that all the military men had left – and so had Nerissa Rodrigues – leaving the two of them in the dark. An ex-political prisoner and an inyanga; their combined set of skills counted for naught in a state of siege. If the sounds of war heard earlier pointed to a serious attack on the house, it wouldn't do the men much good; several raids on dwellings followed a pattern. First a sustained barrage with automatic weapons followed by petrol bombs. Anything emerging out of the flames was mowed down. Moreover, in their case, the front door was ajar and they could both hear the raindrops dripping on the stoep. The sound increased their sense of isolation. Ngobese peered into the gloom, hearing Thabethe's measured breathing.

'I thought I heard Johannes and Bra Zeph stopping in front of the house,' he said. 'What's keeping them so long?'

'Why?' Muzi Thabethe asked. 'You suddenly have a craving for your comrades?'

'Well, they should be here.' Ngobese ignored the barb. That Thabethe was responding to him – however caustic the remark – was a promising sign.

Then two screams, hair-raising in their desperation, split the night.

'No!'

'No!'

As one, Thabethe and Ngobese jumped up from their prone positions, almost knocking into each other in their rush across the kitchen to the back. Muzi was the first to come out. He stopped short, Ngobese bumping into him.

Hearing footsteps coming from the direction of the house, Strella swivelled round, the rifle covering the approach. The two men, Ngobese and Thabethe, emerged from the house. 'Gentlemen? Come and join the ladies.'

They edged forward, the two men in Laura's life, Thulasizwe and Muzi. Strella covered them with the gun. 'Which one is the medicine man you told me about?'

'I'm the medicine man,' Ngobese said. Thabethe gave Laura one of his strange looks.

'And the other kalkoen?'

'That's my husband,' Laura said. Then, unnecessarily: 'Muzi.'

'Ah,' Strella said. 'A happy family.' Then he took out the knife, which he'd stuck into his waistband, and handed it to Laura. 'I want you to choose. There are two people here. You are going to kill them; you choose which one goes first, the husband or the medicine man.'

'I can't do that,' Laura said, accepting the knife, fingers closing around the handle, feeling its heft, the power.

'Well,' Strella said conversationally, 'it's really up to you. As a pregnant woman, I'll let you live ...'

'You're pregnant?' asked Muzi Thabethe.

'You're pregnant?' asked Thulasizwe Ngobese.

'Yes,' Strella said. 'That's what happens when you stick it into a woman. She gets pregnant. So, she's carrying a child. A baby.'

While the two men looked at each other, trying to digest this latest piece of information, Nerissa was still on her haunches. Her hands continued probing. 'Are you proud, Strella, of holding a big gun on unarmed people?'

'I was ready to die a minute ago. But now all I want is the trunk.'

'But the trunk's got nothing of yours.'

'Everything in there is mine.'

'Well,' Nerissa said, straightening up, the movement taking an inordinately long time. 'Here's something that belongs to you.' In her hand was a 9 mm Makarov pistol retrieved from Mchinda's waistband. 'God be with you.' And she fired ...

As Strella's face registered surprise, he managed to bring up the gun, set on single-fire and squeezed off a few rounds. Ngobese gave a yell of pain and fell to the ground. Still holding the bloody knife, Laura rushed to him, her face wreathed in concern. The bullet had smashed into Ngobese's thigh, splintering the bone. Strella tottered but regained his balance. Hobbling still, he vaulted over the low fence and fell in a heap on the side of the cottage. Muzi Thabethe rushed to check and immediately ducked as a bullet zipped past his head. When he next raised himself, he found that Strella had bolted.

'No,' said Nerissa.

'No,' said Laura.

A jagged bolt of lightning streaked across the sky and was followed by a thunderclap. It sounded as if it had found a target.

Colonel Jan Stander recalled a short anecdote about how an adrenalin rush could endow some people with superhuman qualities.

'Some five clicks from the main training camp in Ondangwa, this must have been around August 1975, the old man, Holden Roberto organised another property, a compound, really, where we kept the rest of our stuff, extra ordnance, stockpiles of fuel and ammunition – and food, grain, cooking oil, dried stuff we got from our friends in Europe. The people around were starving, *jislaaik*; you've never seen such starvation. Forget Biafra and the stick legs and pot-bellied pickaninnies. Those people, the villagers, were the underdogs, in fact worse than the underdog, if you can imagine that. The terrorists also raided them and took their food, fucked their wives and took able-bodied men, usually boys, the *umfaans*, forcefully to fight their stupid war. And what do hungry people do? They steal, fucking right. We put up a high breeze-block fence and topped it with all sorts of spikes and broken bottles and some sharp razor wire. Strella had to work with one of the laziest *munts* I've ever seen, a night-watchman who just sat there, growing fat on the supplies and doing bugger-all, armed with a knobkierie and a spear. We thought we should give them their cultural weapons; maybe there'd be some production. Night after night these *skelms* came in from outside and stole stuff; one time we caught them in the village with a whole water pump, still in its plastic wrapping. Anyway we sent Strella and he was armed with a pistol. The thieves came on this night; Strella and the useless guy were guarding. When sure that all of them were inside, Strella locked the only gate. Then he fired, just above the heads of these fools. They sprang and scampered and actually scaled the eight-foot wall with all the spikes and stuff, leaving pieces of themselves in the razor wire and bottles. In one minute flat the compound was empty. That was the last time there was any raid or theft. What's funny, however, is that the night-watchman dispensed with any pretence of taking responsibility for guarding the facility. Very often he would fall asleep and wake up in fright, sometimes woken up by the sound of his spear or *kierie* clattering to the ground and he'd yell, "*Shoot, Mr Strella, shoot*!" There was a burst of gunfire, one-two … one-two … in quick succession.

'Now the shit begins,' Stander said, changing gears and accelerating along the road. 'Something's really up. Are you excited, General?'

'I'm thrilled,' Palweni said dryly. He squeezed his legs together and stroked the barrel of the AK-47. 'Just like old times.'

It was old times, also, for Lucky and the SDUs. He liked the ring of that, being a former pantsula dancer. He could see it clearly, *lucky and the sdu's*, written in lower-case letters on the cover of a demo-tape. But now was not the time to reminisce or dream dreams; man had to be alert, especially since the posse of Young Lions in the car looked up to him to provide leadership. That's another thing he'd internalised, the political language from Lusaka, which he got from the clandestine radio broadcasts, where people spoke of the seizure of power and rendering the country ungovernable.

From the hill, which stood perhaps some six metres above the row of houses marking Ngobese's section, they had a vantage view of the goings-on down below. At 7:45 p.m. it was dark in patches. The illumination provided by the overhead cluster lights, a pain in the ass if you were up to no good, gave the scene a surreal effect, with people seeming unreal like shadows. The headlights of the few cars moving along, foreshortened and squat, lit up the road, now and then slowing down for passengers recently alighted from taxis at the corner.

Khehla, apart from being the shortest member of the group, was also cursed with the weakest bladder. He got out of the tawny Nissan Skyline to take a pee. Lucky watched him aiming his stream at a bush, later doing a quick and quirky shake as he zipped himself up. Then he froze, turned around and ambled over to the window. He was so short he hardly had to bend.

'What's up, K?' Lucky asked.

'Come see … there.'

Lucky got out, the inside roof light momentarily exposing the three members of the group in the back seat. Their eyes spoke louder than words: *shut the fucking door.*

'What is it?'

'You see what I see down there?' Khehla asked. 'Look. That double-cab across Bra Thulasizwe's house has been standing there for a while. There's someone inside.'

'And so?' Lucky was impatient to get back into the car. A light rain had started falling. Lucky was a city boy, born and bred, and he hated getting wet. Besides, Khehla had a tendency to see things.

'Check who's hanging around at the corner of the road.'

'Who?'

'That jiver, Spider.'

'Why concern yourself with Spider? I hear he's useless; Bra Zeph's people did one thing with the Nabobs.'

They snorted derisively at the ridiculousness of the name, *Nabobs, what the fuck*? Then, face clouded, Khehla asked a question. 'You remember we passed him hanging around a few minutes ago? It's just come back to me. I was told by Big-Boy that Spider took over from Tikka Joe, digging holes on behalf of some big mamba, Captain Mkhukhu's son.'

'Captain Mkhukhu has a kid?' Lucky asked. 'I thought he just specialised in boys ...?'

'Yep. I haven't seen him,' Khehla said. 'But he's around. I reckon that's his car there. Think they're watching Bra Thulasizwe's house?'

'I don't know what to think.'

Just then a red Honda Ballade pulled up and parked on the side of the road, directly in front of the house. Two men and a woman came out, one man a little unsteady on his feet.

'That's Bra Zeph, isn't it?' Lucky asked, not really expecting an answer, for he would have recognised that spare frame, rigid posture and the trademark brogue shoes any time of the day, even if the subject weren't properly sober. Beside him, Khehla caught his breath.

As in a movie, the kid, Spider, dashed across and grabbed the woman's bag. Then he sprinted as if pursued by the Devil himself.

Immediately, Bra Zeph gave chase, the big shoes hitting the ground with such rapidity that the road surface could have been red-hot. Gone was the earlier unsteadiness; the old guy was flying. The younger man and the woman both made half-hearted attempts at a chase and gave up.

Lucky's gaze was drawn to a flicker of light as the door of the parked double-cab pickup opened and a man, lankier and wirier than Bra Zeph, also joined in the chase. As opposed to Bra Zeph, whose arms were free, the new entrant in the race was carrying what seemed to be a stick. It was a rifle. Two, three yards on, he slowed down and brought the rifle up to his shoulder. There was first a flash of the muzzle and then a shot rang out.

Lucky didn't know exactly when he got behind the wheel, but, in a minute, the Nissan Skyline was bouncing over the uneven road, racing downhill towards Ngobese's house. Now and then the undercarriage scraped the ground, loosening soft stone, clay and shrubs. Behind and beside him, people in the car were cocking their guns and Lucky prayed that they would take good care and not shoot each other – or him – especially with the car jouncing up and down.

Django and Rex Mabena moved purposefully across the yard, keeping their heads down as they stepped out of the gate onto the road.

The night air was fresh, purged of pollution by the storm. Soft voices of Friday people wafted from the nearby houses. Curious onlookers alerted to the gunfire, most of them bulked up by big overcoats and blankets, huddled in small groups on their stoeps. They also kept their heads down for fear of stopping stray bullets.

'All that firing,' Django said. 'What do you think happened?'

Before Rex Mabena could respond, more shots rang out, an unmistakable *pop-pop! pop-pop!* of an AK-47 set on semi-automatic fire. Both men knew that the rifle was at its most accurate in this mode, where the recoil that could misalign the weapon on automatic was somewhat reduced. They concluded without voicing it that a pro was at the working end of the gun. They pitied whoever had got himself in Mchinda's gun sights.

Suddenly, Sonto and Johannes appeared, both highly agitated. 'You must help Bra Zeph,' Johannes said, barely able to keep himself in check.

'What happened?' Django asked, having to shake the younger man. 'We heard gunshots.' He turned to Sonto, whose distress was of a different quality.

'Sonto? What's going on?'

'They took the bag,' she said, blubbering. 'The boy.'

'What bag? What's in the bag?'

'I don't know.'

'What do you mean, you don't know?' Rex Mabena asked. 'What's in the bag?' He was about to strike her. Django restrained his hand.

'He gave me the bag ...'

'Who gave you the bag?'

'Gabriel ... Captain Mkhukhu's son ...' Sonto could hardly speak.

'What's in the bag?' Convinced that all this blubbering was a smoke-screen for something more serious, the name of Gabriel triggering a red light in his head, Django immediately changed tack. 'Sonto,' he said softly, 'Rex is simply going to shoot you like a dog if you don't answer truthfully. What did Gabriel put in the bag?'

'A bomb.'

Strella sprinted out of his hiding place and tried to flag down the Nissan Skyline rolling along the road. Its occupants opened fire, the bullets pinging on the road. Here we go again, Strella thought ... on the road again. Up ahead and across the road was a low wall, perhaps a structure that was part of a culvert, which could form a suitable parapet. He turned to get a measure of the Skyline, which had slowed down behind him, obviously the better for its trigger-happy occupants to aim and shoot at him. But he decided to go for broke, accelerating as he dashed diagonally across, knowing how hard it was for a person in a moving car to hit a moving target. Gripping Mchinda's AK-47 in one hand as he would a pistol, he fired off a few rounds and heard them clanging off the bodywork. Hoping the burst would at least stall the exuberant kids inside, he made it across to the other side. Winded, his body having taken a beating that had started on the streets of Yeoville, he collapsed in the bush. Looking up at the leaden sky, Strella knew he had to regroup.

Running and still concerned that someone behind might be gaining on him, Spider surged ahead, gunning the engine of his body as he would a stolen car. Questioning the wisdom of stealing the bag, he became aware of the Skyline approaching from the opposite direction, a good hundred metres away. Before his eyes could take in the full meaning of the vehicle, he noticed a figure racing towards him, also periodically alternating between springing and crouching, executing a military tactic of evasion much more refined than Spider's own movie-inspired antics. The man fleeing towards Spider slipped in and out of the harsh gaze of the headlights, creating in an instant a silhouette and its after-image. Coming from the vehicle were rapid and uncoordinated muzzle-flashes that accompanied a crackle of gunfire.

As a hard light blinded him. Spider experienced a moment of righteous anger before a fist slammed into his side, ripping through the fashionable fabric of his jacket, exiting through the back and biting off a chunk of his flesh. He halted in mid-step, sighed and dropped to the moist road.

❂

As the Toyota 4Runner rolled past Ngobese's house, the evening's excitement was proving to be beyond General Palweni's expectations. This was what a soldier lived for, riding beside a driver, a favourite rifle in hand and watching everything unfolding before him. In a remote corner of his brain a warning light flashed. It was long past the hour for his blood pressure and cholesterol medication. Instead of alarm, he felt a surge of pride. A thrill coursed through his body at the very thought that he'd been in perpetual combat with both man and nature and would most likely die in his sleep. Why bother about a few tablets? Who sets those deadlines anyway? Doctors, pah! He lived for these moments of exhilaration. And today was proving to be the one for the books.

He was already composing the first line of his memoirs, *I rode shotgun even though I was in command.* Anyone reading that would never, for one moment, imagine it coming from the mind of a man who'd just thumbed his nose at tablets for hypertension and cholesterol, so-called silent killers. He was *the* silent killer, ask those blighters feeding the worms in the caves of the Western Transvaal. Maybe, he thought, revising the text in his head as his creative juices continued flowing, that would be a much more dramatic opening scene. *I was a silent killer who put paid to apartheid.*

Even though he knew it might be stretching the truth, apartheid being a system that had taken decades to perfect and would call upon the effort of battalions to vanquish, no one, in the euphoria of the future, would be wasting time splitting hairs. By the time Mandela got released, he would have carved a name for himself, as someone who had turned the tables on one of apartheid's most vicious agents. He laughed inwardly, thinking how stupid Stander must think he, Palweni, was. That was one thing great about paternalistic white people. They made the job of thwarting them so easy, because their prejudices paved the way for their downfall. The Standers of this world operated from a superior understanding of things; they had all the answers. By the time they became aware, it was all too late.

Palweni didn't realise that he had nodded off until the car hit a pothole and he thought they'd had a blowout as he awakened to the reality of screeching tyres. All around him were pinpoints of watching eyes in the dark and hundreds of running feet beating a tattoo on the tarmac. It was as if the whole of KwaMashu township was either welcoming returning heroes or driving off an invading force. Aware of a flicker behind, a movement perceived through peripheral vision, the general turned halfway around and saw the subject earlier identified as Zephaniah Zondi coming up from behind and racing down the track behind a fleeing boy. As in the slow motion favoured by nightmare sequences, Zondi, who was gaining on the boy a moment earlier, slackened and was immediately overtaken by a vaguely familiar figure. As the Toyota

4Runner slowed down as if in deference to the party of the pursuers and their quarry, Palweni became aware that the man leading the pursuit was none other than Nozishada, in full combat gear. Bending, with his upper body almost parallel to the ground, Nozishada decelerated to walking speed, the AK-47 held at the low ready position. Zephaniah Zondi, seeming to have recharged his batteries, resumed his sprint, this time approaching the boy fleeing with the yellow bag from the right side of the car. That bag, Palweni surmised, must hold a lot of exciting things. For a moment, Zondi ran level with and then past the moving Toyota 4Runner as if his brogue shoes were fitted with wheels. Inside the car, without seeming to make an effort, Colonel Stander brought up his Glock and fired, hitting Zephaniah Zondi in the back. Hearing the blast, Nozishada veered off into the bushes while continuing with his running crouch alongside the car. Slowing to a crawl, Stander signalled for Palweni to direct his own shots into the bushes. Happily obliging, the general fired a salvo that shaved the tops off the shrubbery and sent up a cloud of dust. There was silence for a moment, the echo of the explosions filling the air. And then Nozishada responded, sending a burst that took off the wing mirror. Colonel Stander floored the accelerator and the Toyota 4Runner peeled out, the wheels spitting out gravel. 'Shit.'

All the things for which Django had been trained – each moment in which he had borne hardship without a whimper, each skirmish, each experience of loss or utter helplessness during a combatant's funeral – congealed into a confusing roar akin to the whoosh of water bursting through an encumbering wall. He recalled the images in the cave, the dead flesh still oozing blood and loud with an invitation to insects both airborne and earthbound, animals whose engorgement would usher in the process of putrefaction. The sightless eyes and tongues stilled forever – friends, brothers, comrades. And then this woman admitting her complicity in the carnage that was supposed to finish the job.

As someone who'd never laid a finger on a woman, the impulse to strike out at Sonto filled him with revulsion and told him that he was losing control.

'What made you do it?' he asked.

She tried to explain, a narrative that came out garbled and disjointed, mainly because Rex Mabena kept on interrupting, pressing her when he thought she was not forthcoming with the truth. But, eventually, it came out. It was the story of Gabriel, Bra G, who preferred the name of Nozishada: the story of Captain Mkhukhu, the young boy – Tikka Joe – the execution in the sand dunes, and about some of Gabriel's men, his connections in H Section. It all came out, hot and rancid, like vomit, Sonto bent double, almost about to topple forward.

'Why did you do it?' Django asked again.

'I don't know,' Sonto said, sniffing. 'I thought it was love.'

Both Rex Mabena and Django suddenly noticed that Johannes Sibisi was still standing, mouth agape as if totally stumped by Sonto's confession.

'How could you?' he asked.

Sonto looked at her one-time comrade and secret admirer with an expression stammering between malevolence and pity.

'Gabriel was a man,' she said.

Django found it interesting that she referred to her lover in the past tense. Sporadic gunfire split the night. It sounded close by.

'Tell you what,' he said to Johannes, 'let's escort her into the house and you'll wait there. You and Muzi and Ngobese will have to man the fort. We'll get Mchinda and see about Gabriel's crew in H Section. As for you, Sonto, for your sake, you'll have to account to the chaplain. She'll decide your fate.'

They hurried back to the house. For both Rex and Django, the rush of adrenalin was like a narcotic in their veins.

Clear now that his hiding place might not be ideal, after all, knowing that someone might toss a grenade and he, Strella, would be history, he broke cover and resumed his running. Now, going at a good clip up along the road, the gunfire ringing in his head, Strella felt the heat sapping his energy. It seemed to him that he was fated to run until the end of his days, which could be any time now. Running offered him time to reflect that his life had always been marked by two realities – pursuit and flight. Today he was not pursuing anything except the possibility of survival. He was not even chasing down the trunk; the trunk had actually led to this flight. He was a fugitive from everything. Normally people were fugitives from the law. He was running, at large, fleeing from people who had broken the law ten times over. How fucked up was that?

Part of his mind told him that, since he was running in township terrain, a mix of built-up areas and open fields – and his pursuers were driving – he should use the topography to his advantage. Get off the road, fool! But then, jumping into someone's yard had its downside. People could take you for a common thief, a criminal. Nowadays, people didn't wait for the cops. They simply slung a tyre around your neck and set you alight. He knew of a few cases of people fleeing for genuine reasons, ending up barbecued. By the time someone said, 'Oops!' they were already sizzling like burnt pork chops.

He had no doubt that all sorts of people were out to get him. And kill him. There was Palweni. And there was Stander. This was the big brass with big guns. Well, they had tried and Strella had no intention of falling into their clutches. There was Chaplain Nerissa, who shot at him, braver than Muzi Thabethe. There was Ngobese with a bullet wound somewhere in his body, of that Strella was sure.

Then there was Laura. He found himself softening, warming to her. She was feminine, like the professor's wife, only smarter, and yet, he knew, the deadliest of them all. She was as deadly as the chaplain. That one was like those religious guys at the camp in Libya, the jihadists, who'd slit your throat and watch you bleed without batting an eyelid; that was how focused she was. Laura could grow to be like that, too, under different conditions. He recalled how she held the knife, the small fingers curling around the shaft, something a bit sexy there, and those fingers. She couldn't – he couldn't really accept that it was Muzi Thabethe who'd made her pregnant, no way. There was something too proper, political and polite about Muzi, someone who must have learnt his behaviour from older people, another generation. Had he grown up with his age-mates, Muzi wouldn't have allowed Ngobese to say anything about his wife's pregnancy. What business of his was it? He'd have gone forward and snatched the knife from his wife's delicious fingers and slashed the motherfucker's jugular.

But right now, he had to get out of this place. He had to forget the trunk for a moment – nobody knew what it held – and just keep on running. Lack of motion meant death. Just run! And as he ran on, he saw another figure framed in the lights – a kindred spirit, also hell-bent on surviving. The yoyos behind him were firing, small arms fire, popguns, really. As the runner came towards him there was a crack of a gun, something loud and large, and he fell. Another man dropped to the ground. Hell, Strella thought, I'm in the middle of a firefight, here. He took in the hulking Toyota 4Runner, in which he had been transported, coming up. He noticed that the fallen man, a boy, really, had dropped a yellow bag. Being Strella, the picker-up of things, he reached over the inert figure and snatched up the bag in one fluid motion as he ran. He heard the bullets whipping the ground ahead and the ping and crash of a ruined headlight, the intensity of light dimming momentarily. Then

Strella threw the bag into the air as he dashed back into the bush at the edge of the road. Unseeing, because something had hurled him into the air, he heard the deafening crunch of metal against metal. And, as the air got sucked out of everything, something exploded in his head.

A few seconds before the two cars collided in a clash of metal, as the bag containing the bomb drew a slow, parabolic arc above the vehicles, Palweni experienced a vision. His whole life did a circuit from his birth in the northern Cape to this moment in KwaMashu, thirty-odd kilometres north of Durban. There was something satisfying about the circle being closed. Somewhere in the distance, the sea throbbed and crashed against rocks; it was a sea, a vast, stammering ocean – an infinity, really – that was located somewhere in his body, a body that had endured everything. He'd been through arrest and torture. He had known the taste of an enemy's spittle against his face. He knew pleasure, the texture of every type of hair in his fingers, from the burred kink of Nubia, past the rough Asian cascade to the cornsilk of the Caucasus, the thighs of all shapes and sizes and shades harbouring depthless pudenda that purred in the universal language of joy. He'd had it all, and he'd seen it all.

His inner eye apprised him of the immediate predicament, the instinct of a soldier on a battlefield, where there was alertness to the whine of a mortar shell before it even started its ascent. He remembered the Marxian principle of self-criticism and wondered if he'd ever be eligible for forgiveness. I don't qualify for mercy. I have blasphemed my Movement. I have squandered money meant for the struggle. He had an image of a pitiless glass eye staring at him, before the face disappeared in the dark.

Everything ceased to matter for General Palweni, one-time son of the soil and former hero of the revolution, long before the two cars collided and the bomb blast welded steel to flesh.

Lucky woke up to the crackle of flames, the cars and the bush ablaze. He wondered where his crew, Khehla and the rest, were. Getting to his knees, being pulled up and examined by what suddenly seemed like hundreds of hands. 'You're very lucky, sonny,' said a man who was small and wiry like something fashioned out of copper wire, with a face that struggled between laughing and crying. 'I brought my people from Kwam'shayazafe, and we're going to do one thing with those dogs.'

Lucky followed the direction of the finger that was pointing at three bloodied men, two black and one white. He thought he could recognise the youngest of the wounded men, who was half-naked, his pale-green trousers shredded, presumably, by the explosion. It was Captain Mkhukhu's son, last seen running at full speed behind Bra Zeph, who was chasing Spider, the fleet-footed bag-snatcher. But he had to ask: 'Who are those people?' he asked. 'The dogs.'

'General Palweni,' said the copper-coloured man. 'And he's with Colonel Stander, a dog if there ever was one. They killed my cousin.'

'Who's your cousin?'

'Bhekisisa. Bhekisisa Luthuli.'

Just then some women started to ululate, a sound that sent a shiver down Lucky's spine. He got to his feet and looked for Khehla. When he found his short friend famous for his weak bladder lying in the bush with a broken neck, he went back to Bhekisisa Luthuli's cousin. 'We have the tyres,' he said.

'And,' said the coppery man, his skin illuminated by the flames, 'we have the petrol.'

13

ATONEMENT

In the morning following the night of fire, ashes denoted the arena where, very recently, life had pulsed with the quickening of flesh. Here, where previously voices rang out as the women ululated and men sang praise songs, silence was loud. Even the dogs normally given to approaching their masters with their eternal craving to be stroked, avoided the hands that only hours ago had wielded cudgels and edged weapons – and later scattered the ashes over the guilty patches where blood had congealed.

Chaplain Nerissa made her phone call to Georgina Smith and told her about the events of the second day of January 1990, a day that would stay etched in her mind for the rest of her life.

'Many people died,' she said. 'For me, the most personal loss was Thulasizwe Ngobese. We mistakenly concentrated on the bullet wound in the thigh. He bled a lot. But we missed a quiet bullet that had punctured his lung, until it was too late.'

'You sound as if you're taking responsibility for that,' Georgina said, 'but there's nothing you could have done. You're not a doctor.'

'They believed in me,' Nerissa said. 'In a way, I was some kind of doctor. A mother, a commander, a saviour.'

'You're not a stranger to those roles,' Georgina insisted. 'Now you need to come back and become a lover.' She paused. 'And Strella?'

'You don't want to know.'

'Tell me.'

'He disappeared. I have no idea where.' After a beat, she said: 'I don't think Strella is a human being.'

'Meaning?'

'I don't mean he is a ghost or a zombie. I just think he's a creation that was sent here to teach us something about evil.'

'Why? Because he is totally inhuman?'

'I don't know,' Nerissa said. 'Enigmas are never human. He is a shadow.'

'Forget the shadows,' Georgina said. 'Yusuf says you're due for another appointment with him.'

As she hung up, she knew that Georgina would never fully understand. The only people to whom Strella would start making sense would be those who'd borne witness to the goings-on of the night. The police would come; she was sure that Khumalo and Booi must have been around, possibly watching everything from a distance. They would give a report, omitting certain facts, possibly stressing those that spoke to the strangeness of everything. She was sure no one would mention the kombis that had trundled in from the hostel, or that it was the bomb that had flushed out the other killer skulking in the bushes. She had experienced great sadness – and, in the same vein, vindication – when she witnessed his fiery transition.

In a sense, she started to accept, understand even, her role in this whole enterprise – this journey – as that of a witness, a beholder and not an interpreter. Because, she knew, she should be dead. All of them should be dead. Last night was straight out of Hell. It was a night of eternal torment.

When the explosion came, it was louder than the thunderclap that had preceded it. Then there was a light that turned night into day. It was in that light that she saw that Ngobese was dying. He had been struggling but still able to talk, even joke that Muzi and Laura's unborn baby would be coming into a wholly changed world, where apartheid would be a thing of the past. Laura argued that apartheid would be with us for many decades to come. Its obliteration would only happen once all the generations that had been touched by its evil hand had passed on. By the time Muzi unexpectedly voiced his doubts that he was responsible for the baby, they were all talking to a dead man.

When Django and Rex returned, there was a brief conference about Sonto, mainly because both Rex and Johannes had debated the merits of Sonto's summary execution. 'She's responsible for so much,' Rex had said, his eyes red. 'Yes,' Johannes put in, 'but she's the only one who knows where the rest of the men are.'

Nerissa realised during those moments that Johannes was leadership material, for he had managed to speak quietly to both Rex and Django, preparing them for the news about Mchinda's death. When the two men saw their dead comrade, they went still as if immobilised by some unknown force. Nerissa was grateful that Johannes was around because, without him, the two guerrillas would have wanted to mount an offensive against the remainder of Gabriel's group in H Section. And it was likely that they would never have come back.

Now, having to pay respects to their own dead, they formed a small, informal congregation that looked up to Nerissa – *you're after all the chaplain* – to say something. On her part, she intoned a half-remembered verse about sinners excommunicated from God's grace. According to 2 Thessalonians 1:9, *these shall be punished with everlasting destruction from the presence of the Lord, and from the glory of his power.* On a roll, feeling the others' eyes on her, she recited from the Book of Common Prayer:

> *I am the resurrection and the life, saith the Lord. He that believeth in me, though he were dead, yet shall he live: and whosoever liveth and believeth in me shall never die.*

It was at that moment that Muzi Thabethe looked set to crumble; perhaps the reality of death was beginning to sink in. Muzi began to weep, saying that he was sorry he had misjudged Ngobese; Ngobese had been a real comrade, and so on. Sonto, who was beginning to show signs of delayed shock, presumably from having been duped by Nozishada, joined in, crying, '*I'm so sorry*,' until Johannes Sibisi told her to stop it:'*Cut the crap*.'

Laura, whose eyes could deliver judgement, gave Sonto one look and then took charge, growing in Nerissa's estimation. She organised everyone, including her husband, to help carry the bodies inside the house.

'We can't leave them here,' she said, 'staring at the non-existent stars. If the police come, we'll tell them we were attacked, which is true, but we felt that the bodies could not be left to the elements.'

It fell on both Muzi Thabethe and Johannes Sibisi, however, to deal with the actual carting of the dead men into the bedroom, where they were laid side by side on one bed. Rex and Django felt they had had their fill of death to last them several lifetimes.

Leaving Muzi, Johannes and Sonto in charge of the house, Django and Rex Mabena joined Nerissa and Laura in the car as they set out in the direction of the explosions. Nerissa rolled down the window. The car had been to hell and back but the smell of alcohol still lingered. 'I wonder how Bra Zeph fared,' she said when they were on the road.

'I'm afraid we're soon going to find out.' Laura wasn't big on small talk. She also had a feeling that something bad had happened to Bra Zeph. She liked him for the simple reason that he had made public his struggles with alcohol addiction. It was sad that he had now fallen off the wagon.

The foretaste of what they were going to see, even before they heard the clamour of voices, was the figure of a man laid out on the side of the road. Although covered with a blanket, with two young men standing over him, Nerissa saw from the exposed shoes that the body belonged to Bra Zeph. He was the only person she knew who had a fetish for the tan brogues handmade by Crockett and Jones. Absently she wondered if Bra Zeph would be fitted with these shoes in his coffin.

Some twenty metres ahead, totally blocking the road, were hundreds of people, their voices raised to the level of spectators exulting over a goal scored by their side in a football match. Beyond the throng, in the centre, a fire raged; it was a different fire from the one consuming two cars, a 4x4 and a Nissan Skyline, standing in an eternal kiss on the side of the road. It was characterised by black smoke and carried the acrid smell of burning rubber.

'I wouldn't go in there,' Rex Mabena said to Nerissa and Laura.

They parked the car and got out. Drawn by an unknown force, Nerissa signalled for Laura to remain with Rex and the two young men keeping vigil over the body. In a way that was in keeping with Laura's new status as a guarantor of propriety around the dead.

Wending her way through the crowd, Nerissa was struck by how everyone's eyes were focused on the centre of a circle that had been formed in the middle of the road. It was much like a clearing in a forest where three men, all showing signs of having been severely beaten, squatted on the ground, their hands tied behind their backs with wires. There was something eerily familiar about the scenario. The chants and songs, which had a hypnotic cadence, started to infect her senses and she feared she would soon be swaying to an unknown rhythm. At the core of the songs was the refrain about the need to burn the sell-outs, *shis'impimpi*, set fire to the traitor. Although it would come as no surprise to recognise the three men being prepared for death, it took her a good while to admit to herself that, indeed, she knew Nozishada, Colonel Stander and General Palweni. The distance, the unwillingness to acknowledge them was from a reluctance to concede that she, too, lusted after their violent end. There was no trespass – she had heard it repeated at the seminary – which necessitated a death sentence, even though prophets in the Old Testament justified retribution, an eye for an eye and a death for a death. In given cases, the very fact that a transgressor would be forced to spend the rest of his life contemplating the baseness of his actions would be a fitting sentence in itself. She held on to this, holding on to a humanity that was seriously being tested.

Someone, a young man Nerissa had never seen before, also bare-chested and sporting prison tattoos on his body, all the way up to the neck, held a pistol to Nozishada's head with one hand while offering him a drink of petrol from a bottle held in the other. 'Drink, fucking spy,' he was saying, trying to force Nozishada's lips apart with the muzzle.

'No!'

It took Nerissa by surprise to realise that the shriek of protest was actually from her lips, as was the fact that she was striding across to the menaced trio. For a moment the singing seemed to stop before resuming, now with renewed strength. Someone, a man dressed in a loud dashiki suit, a dead ringer for Luis Bernado Muchave, who spoke with an accent, pulled her aside, gently, *Best haul ass, Sister, they're gonna kill you …*

Haul ass, what a quaint notion. Then she watched without it actually registering the tyre being jammed over Nozishada, the liquid splashing over his head and trickling like sweat down his muscled body, the match being struck, the tiny flame hesitating in the gentle drizzle. And then the little light surrendered itself to the wind with a whoosh, becoming elusive and ferocious and gifted with a voracious appetite as it licked skin basted in its own juices, warping and crackling elatedly at aqueous eyes and melting soft tissue.

'Don't look,' said the foreigner, attempting to cover her face with his hand. But she still could see and hear the progress of fire, the stink that filled the air. Soon, she was almost outside the crowd, seeing images in snatches, a film tripping over the sprockets of a faulty projector.

And then, in the quiet and reflective moment, a lull marking Nozishada's death, the tattooed incinerator stood over Colonel Stander, aiming to repeat the ritual of the gun and the petrol bottle. Much smarter, perhaps and certainly more attuned to the psychology of torturers – having been an accomplished one in his heyday – Stander averted his face, ignoring the threat of the gun pressed against his head. Somehow, with a herculean effort, he got to his feet, towering over the young man – whom Nerissa learnt was named Lucky – and continued dodging the bottle aimed at his mouth, bringing to mind a big kid reluctant to take his medicine. People were shouting, voicing their displeasure at Stander for being such a bad sport. 'Get down,' someone shrieked.

'I see your little plan.' Lucky was now pistol-whipping Stander. 'You think I'll shoot you and you'll escape the treatment …'

'I don't care for your necklace,' Stander said. 'You go ahead and do what you want. We gave you the idea for this …'

Then he looked straight into the crowd, his fevered gaze locking on into Nerissa's. He smiled, someone harbouring a secret he wouldn't divulge on pain of death. 'The liberation struggle,' he said, blood frothing at his lips, 'is not only about black people fighting for freedom. It's also about white people protecting blacks from themselves. You think that's being paternalistic? You'll see. Before long, your people …' His syllables were getting more and more clipped and guttural, refinement escaping with the blood, *yorr pippel.* 'Your people will thank me …'

Something exploded inside Nerissa. She felt that this bona-fide mediocrity, this man who had ridden roughshod over people for all his adult years, this washed-out racist, should not go to his grave unanswered. 'Fuck you, Stander,' she shrieked, losing it. 'You will rot in Hell!' Someone tapped her on the shoulder. She whirled round.

Django was looking at her, studying her face like a doctor examining a patient for an elusive disorder. 'Who's the boyfriend?' he asked, pointing at the tall black stranger in the dashiki.

'I don't know.' Nerissa turned to address the man. 'Who are you?'

'Bobo Jones at your service, sister,' he said, nodding. 'What a show.'

And then Palweni, who had all along been bent staring at the ground, someone already doing penance, looked up as if wanting to put a name to a voice. Perhaps it struck a chord with him, a voice he might have heard at a time when everything was harmonious and the liberation struggle was an ideal for which people were ready to die. Perhaps he heard and was spurred on by the woman's curse, because he also tried to get to his feet. He must have imagined, then, the futility of aligning himself with a lost cause. He must have asked himself if it was all worth it. What had he hankered after? Money? Glory? Comfort? Women? Perhaps in that moment, all the words of people in struggle, the young people full of hope, dreaming dreams, striving in the camps and dying in prisons, came back to him. Perhaps. Perhaps nothing.

Palweni managed to rise three-quarters of the way before a high-powered slug smashed into the side of his head, spraying Lucky and Stander with blood, bone fragments and brain tissue. There followed the sound of a shot. Before anyone could react, another bullet slammed into Stander's brow, straight between the eyes, the small entry hole belying the chunk of gore that exited through the back of the head.

'Let's get out of here before all hell breaks loose,' Django said to Laura and Rex Mabena where they stood outside the red Honda Ballade.

'And Bra Zeph?' Laura asked.

'These guys will watch over him until the cops come,' Rex said.

'And the brother-in-law here?' Nerissa indicated Bobo Jones with a jerk of the head. 'Is he coming with us, too?'

'I suppose he might as well,' Django said. 'He looks like someone with a story to tell.'

After a short while, Nerissa said, 'I wonder what's in the trunk.'

'We shall see,' Laura Mdunge said.

Above them, the night sky shimmered in deference to the fire.

POSTSCRIPT

I'd have liked to tell you everything ended well, that Strella was captured and handed over. It would have given me immense pleasure to stand witness and testify against him. But then, of course, I am ashamed to admit that I did heave a sigh of relief when we couldn't find him, when the cops, despite a countrywide search, couldn't locate him. His handiwork remains – all those corpses. Perhaps he helped us by dispatching the highly placed vermin that had plagued us in the first instance.

With Madiba released, the fanfare will continue and everyone will have been on the side of the angels. Stander and Palweni will become a faint memory of a past we'd all rather forget and you'll be hard-pressed to find anyone who actively supported the regime; the children of marauders, beneficiaries of today's preoccupation with forgiveness, will evolve a new language of arrogance and self-absolution. We will have to live with that.

We're therefore fated to discover that when the struggle loses its currency, we'll be forced to face each other, our mirror images, and we'll probably not like what we'll see. However, we have to overcome a difficult hurdle. If we accept the role thrust upon us, of midwives overseeing an exceedingly complex birth, we have to face the unaddressed impulses throbbing within our own ranks. In no time we'll have to nurture the toddler. Before we know, we'll be wondering whatever happened to the adolescent that no longer bears any resemblance to its parents.

I hope that we'll have time for the people who went to the bush to learn how to bring peace by taking up arms – a paradox, I know.

We've cobbled together a somewhat respectable list of the living and the dead. We still have to scour the terrain of Angola and Mozambique and Botswana and Lesotho – just to name a few arenas where our young people fell – and collect all those bones and bring them home.

There are bones inside the country, some of them pulverised into this earth. We have to make peace with them too. We have to find a way to embrace the women who, despite having lost so much, have helped us gather most of what has been scattered into the four winds.

The guerrillas of the People's Army are home. They've emerged from the shadows. They want to start living and taste life. Perhaps, like us, they will also learn to make mistakes on their own terms.

THE END

ACKNOWLEDGEMENTS

Thank you to the following individuals without whose contributions and support this book would not have been written:

Carina Gomes and Antonio Muchave for their help with Portuguese;

Comrades 'Mfazwe' and a few unnamed others who shared their experiences in Angola: *a trincheira firme da revolução*;

My sister, Queen Mirriam Langa, holding the fort in KwaMashu Township;

My wife, June, who stood by me in moments of doubt and despondency;

Our daughters, Ntsiki, Linda, Lerato and Asante, whom we're trying to dissuade from becoming future novelists.

The string of patronymics accompanying the praise poem of the Luthuli people on page 330 is sourced with permission from zuluringblogspot.com. The originator is Mandlana Zulu.